PRAISE FOR

Fall

"Clark's second Detective Harriet Foster title (after *Hide*) provides a compelling plot as well as significant character growth . . . The lead detectives are new to each other and building trust, and readers will become invested in the fragile bond they currently have, as well as the mystery surrounding Foster and her former partner."

—*Library Journal* (starred review)

"Another worm's-eye view of the city . . . marinated in savory civic misdeeds."

—*Kirkus Reviews*

Hide

"A Chicago cop still mourning her late partner transfers to a new precinct just in time to catch a truly creepy case. Solid . . . work from a writer who knows the dark side of the Windy City."

—*Kirkus Reviews*

"[Detective Harriet] Foster's dogged approach to catching killers will resonate with Michael Connelly fans. May the wait for the second Harriet Foster police procedural be brief."

—*Publishers Weekly*

"*Hide* is an astonishing crime novel that broke my heart and then sewed it back together again, stronger than before. It hits all the right notes—a captivating protagonist up against a nightmarish serial killer, their hunt played out across a Chicago so immersive, so flawlessly rendered, that you can hear your own footsteps slapping the streets—while managing to create something completely unique. One of the best books I've read in years."

—Jess Lourey, Amazon Charts bestselling author

"Tracy Clark's not-so-hidden talent is for conjuring characters who are engaging and achingly real. Detective Harri Foster is a stellar recruit to her new team and to our crime fiction shelves. *Hide* is a page-turner with heart."

—Lori Rader-Day, Agatha Award–winning author of *Death at Greenway*

Runner

"You know those books that are wonderful, but that envy, the worm in the bud, makes you shy away from praising because you wish you'd created that prose or those insights? *Runner* by Tracy Clark. She understands the streets, kids, the way a PI and a cop really work. Kudos."

—Sara Paretsky, *New York Times* bestselling author of the V.I. Warshawski series and cofounder of Sisters in Crime

"Clark writes with purpose, her sense of social justice never venturing into dogma but remaining fully rooted in Raines's actions and personality. She saves, but is no savior, because she operates in a world where survival is the benchmark, and pain remains in the aftermath."

—*New York Times*

"Clark has a unique voice in the PI genre, one that is articulate, daring, and ultimately hopeful."

—S.A. Cosby, Anthony and ITW award winner, *Washington Post*

Broken Places

"Engrossing and superbly written—I can't say enough good things about *Broken Places*!"

—Lisa Black, *New York Times* bestselling author of
That Darkness and *Unpunished*

"Unforgettable . . . Distinctive, vividly written characters lift this promising debut. Readers will be eager for the sequel."

—*Publishers Weekly* (starred review)

"Clark's compelling, suspenseful, and action-packed debut introduces a dogged, tough African American woman investigator who is complex and courageous and surrounded by a family of fascinating misfits. Fans of Sue Grafton's Kinsey Millhone or Sara Paretsky's V.I. Warshawski will welcome Cass Raines to their ranks."

—*Library Journal* (starred review)

"This street-smart first mystery boasts great characterization and a terrific new protagonist. Get this writer on your radar now."

—*Booklist*

ECHO

ECHO

A DETECTIVE HARRIET FOSTER THRILLER

TRACY CLARK

THOMAS & MERCER

Text copyright © 2024 by Tracy Clark
All rights reserved.

Published by Thomas & Mercer, Seattle

www.apub.com

Amazon, the Amazon logo, and Thomas & Mercer are trademarks of Amazon.com, Inc., or its affiliates.

ISBN-13: 9781662517327 (paperback)
ISBN-13: 9781662517334 (digital)

Cover design by Damon Freeman
Cover image: © Alexx60, © fgwim, © Ievgenii Meyer, © fontein76 / Shutterstock

Printed in the United States of America

The gods visit the sins of the fathers upon the children.

—Euripides

CHAPTER 1

Justice isn't blind. It always peeks from beneath the blindfold. How else to smite with the sword those whose thumbs weigh the scales? Justice must see to hold evil to account. It must see as evil sees, to exact retribution.

We are Justice.

They stood together in silence, their jury of four outside Hardwicke House, every light inside the gothic mansion ablaze, the boom and blare of harsh music an affront to the night air.

The strangers, clad in black hooded robes, watched through open curtains as lustful young men made plays for coy coeds. How many were already high on cheap beer, skunk weed, and rainbow-colored pills of unknown provenance?

This was how it began, Justice knew. With shortsighted decisions made on a night like this, with one bad choice, one step too far. All it took was one snap for the world to tilt, for a life to end, and for the lives left behind to change and hurtle toward ruin. Someone had to pay. There had to be a reckoning. Some recompense.

Four watchers. All Justice. Here to take what was owed. An eye for an eye. A life for a life. Not in a vengeful, heated way, not in an act of passion. Tonight, Justice's blood was cold. Justice's heads were clear.

They stood in forbidding shadow, trees with barren branches black against a watchful moon, the winter night eerily still, except for the raucous house on the edge of the elite campus.

The house was owned by the Collier family, who'd made their fortune in railroads back when barons ruled them, and later, when their stake grew to billions, in banks and textiles and stocks. On campus, there was the Collier School of Science and Technology, the Collier Library, and the Collier School of Business. And somewhere inside Hardwicke House, as the party raged, there was Brice Collier, the family's prince, who had been raised having every blow softened, every hurdle lowered. Brice, who wore the family name like a suit of armor, confident the steel would always hold.

That was why Justice was here.

One spoke for the four. "Keep to the path." Justice eyed the narrow trail that led around the side. "Stay out of the light."

There would be no footprints left behind, no path when they were done. No one would ever know that Justice had been here. They would enter through the basement and make their way up the back stairs to the roof. All planned. Justice knew the way. And that was where Brice Collier would meet them, willingly, and where justice would be served, while the foolish below rolled the dice and gambled that one beer, one drag, one risky pill wouldn't end with the ER or the grave.

The old bell in the craggy tower of Collier Chapel struck 10:00 p.m., though Justice knew that no one inside would pay the resonant gong any mind.

"It's time." They moved slowly as one, two by two, heads lowered, hoods up, blindfolds in their pockets, keeping to the way. Tonight, judge, jury, and executioner.

The charge? Murder. The condemned? Sebastian Collier, the father, but he was out of Justice's reach. Brice would serve as his proxy. If Justice could not take the one they wanted, they would take his blood, his son, his name.

It was an old debt. Thirty years. Sebastian Collier and his pampered clique had gleefully plied a scholarship boy with alcohol, left him for dead, and then tossed him into a field to choke on his own vomit. So long ago, more years than the boy had been alive, and yet like yesterday. Justice stopped, for a moment, to whisper the boy's name.

Michael James Paget.

It was a chant, a mantra, one Justice had uttered a million times before tonight, only this night the biting wind snatched the name and carried it away.

An accident, they'd said. Afterward there'd been a vigil, and prayers, and then *Michael Paget* had been forgotten. Ten drinks or more too many. Too much pressure to fit in. The magical thinking held by the young that nothing bad could ever happen no matter how reckless the act. The four knew that was a lie. Death didn't care who it took or when.

They stood in funereal gloom, their faces hidden, their resolve set. Together in one purpose. To stand for those who couldn't. To avenge. Three gone, three to pay. That was the plan. Finally, another said, "We still agree? All of us? It has to be this?" The voice was low, clear, as pensive as a verdict.

Three nodded. Together. All of one mind.

"We all know what they did, what they took," said the one who spoke for them. The sharp look that followed silenced further dissent. "We go. *Now.* We do *this.*" They waited for Collier on the roof. Four folding chairs positioned north, south, east, and west, with one chair in the middle. They'd arranged for the note to be left for him, the one supposedly from the girl he liked, the one promising a good time on the private roof deck. The one telling him to bring two beers and the note along, and to tell no one.

Justice could feel the party below vibrate under their feet but knew there would be no police called to quiet the disruption. Even campus security knew not to intervene. For an institution with the name Collier so prominently displayed, the tacit agreement was that Hardwicke House and whatever happened inside it were of no one's concern.

3

Justice sat waiting in the dark, their eyes peeking through small holes cut into their blindfolds because Justice was never truly blind, because Justice had to see to take.

"Judge, jury, and *executioner*."

They whispered the words over and over again, together. They had decided that this was not revenge, it was a righting of a wrong, a clearing of the board so that the clock could start again.

They didn't have to wait long. At the appointed time, the door to the roof opened and Brice Collier, the golden boy, the heir apparent, walked through holding two bottles of beer and their note, a rakish smile on his face. He looked around wide eyed, impatient, for the girl he'd been promised.

Justice waited. As still as monuments and just as unyielding. Justice knew the door would lock behind the boy. Justice knew no one below would hear a sound coming from the roof. Justice also knew not a soul would see them leave with Brice.

"Sit." The command came in unison.

Brice, his eyes glassy, his face flushed, an insipid grin on his entitled face, scanned the rooftop, confused. His obvious disappointment borne of expectation, of security, of believing the world would always bend its knee to him. Though Justice had grown cold, the look on the boy's face alone threatened to heat the blood again.

"What the hell?" Brice took in the four. "Way too late for Halloween, guys."

He was drunk already. They knew he would be. And Justice also knew his drunkenness would make him careless, rash. Impaired, Brice had taken the note at face value and had asked no questions. Of course the girl would want him. He was a Collier.

One took the lead. "Sit," he said.

"Screw you clowns." Brice held up the note. "Where's Hailie?"

For a moment there was only a ghostly hush, then the One broke the silence.

"Sit. *Down*. Collier *filth*," he said.

The smile left the boy's face. This wasn't the deference he was used to. "Hey, what is this?"

There was no need to hurry. It would be hours yet before the party petered out and the stoned revelers stumbled back to their holes to crash. Would anyone even realize or care that Collier had slipped away? Brice was the big man on campus because of his name, but respect and affection were not the same.

It quickly became clear to Brice that there was no girl, and he grew angry. His face flushed. He wasn't used to being denied.

"This your idea of a joke? You're fucking idiots! I'm out of here."

He walked to the door and turned the knob. Locked. And it would remain so until Justice was done.

Brice reeled, stormed back to the chairs, his attention suddenly diverted by the sight of two lit candles sitting in front of the middle one, the chair meant for him. The candles sat beside a keg of beer, just like the ones downstairs.

"What are you freaks playing at? Open that door. It's cold as hell up here, and I'm missing out." He walked around them, still holding the beers and the note, still checking for the girl, hopeful even now. "How'd you even get up here, anyway? And what's with the dumb robes and the blindfolds? You look like rejects from some Greek tragedy. Who the hell are you?"

Justice studied the boy but said nothing. There was time enough to savor the experience.

Brice patted his pockets for his phone. "Whatever. You're all dead. I'm calling the police. This is private property, and I didn't invite you freaks, so *that's* trespassing."

One hooded hangman rose and grabbed Collier by the back of his shirt, pushed him down into the middle chair, then snatched the phone and beers from him.

5

"Hey. That's theft, my friend, and also kidnapping. I want to leave. You're preventing me. *That's* a crime. You do know who I am, right? And where you are? I *own* this whole place."

Brice tried to stand, but rough hands pressed down on his shoulders. Then Justice watched as the gravity of Collier's situation slowly dawned on him. This wasn't a prank. Justice wasn't here to frighten *this* Collier.

"Open that door right now, or all of you are fucked!" Brice yelled. "You hear me?"

Justice ignored the empty words and instead stood to pronounce their sentence.

"Brice Collier. You're condemned to pay for the sins of your father. The charge is murder. The sentence is death."

One leaned over and took the note from Brice's hand, then calmly held it over the candle flame, watching as the paper caught fire and flew off into the world as ash. It had all been neatly planned—the chairs, the fire, the pronouncement. Weeks it had taken, slow and deliberate. Justice had been patient.

Justice stared down at the condemned. "*We* are Justice."

Brice's eyes darted around the rooftop looking for escape, but there was none.

"You're serious. Look, this isn't funny anymore, all right? What are you even *talking* about? Sins? What murder? Who?"

"Michael James Paget."

They said the name as one as they'd agreed to.

Collier's face blanched, his eyes ricocheted from blindfold to blindfold, wild, trapped, powerless.

"You know the name," One said. "We can see it on your face. Guilt. You know *exactly* what he did."

"That was like fifty years ago, or something. An accident. My father said—"

One held up a hand to quiet the boy, then leaned in close, years of barely contained rage visible in a clenched jaw. "It's death. *You* pay because he didn't then. *You* pay because he's a coward and a killer." One leaned back with a smile the boy couldn't see beneath the mask. "He pays next. It will be slow and painful. There will be time for him to think about who and why."

Collier fought the hold, tried to escape the chair but couldn't. "You're all crazy as *fuck*. Let me out of here *now*. You can't do this. Get your hands off me, you idiots. Help!" Brice yelled. "Get *off* me. It was an *accident*."

One slowly turned to the candles and blew the first one out, then lowered to whisper in the boy's ear. "Well, Brice Collier, son of Sebastian Collier, *this* will not be."

CHAPTER 2

Detective Harriet Foster moved fast through the CPD cop lot at Eighteenth and State, her eyes shielded by a squint against a light sleet, focused on the door of the station. Cold, wet ice pellets pinged against her face in a mildly unpleasant way, like a barrage of tiny needles. Late February was holding on with a tight grip, winter refusing to even think about ceding an inch to the coming spring. The lucky ones were asleep in their beds on this cold winter's morning, the devout, up and preparing for church, but Harri was here ahead of her shift, and it didn't matter to her overmuch whether it was Sunday or Tuesday, midnight or noon, Christmas or Groundhog Day.

Cold day. Gray. Chicago. Maybe nobody would kill anyone today, she thought. It was a common wish, not a prayer, one rarely granted.

A car horn sounded aggressively. Startled, Harri reeled, lowering her bag to the slush, her right hand going for the zipper on her jacket, ready to open her coat to get to the gun at her hip.

Her eyes scanned the cars in the lot, looking for the threat, then landing on an idling black Subaru Outback with its headlights on. Recognizing the car, she breathed a sigh of relief, and her hand moved away from the zipper, and she picked up her bag.

The car belonged to her boss, Sergeant Sharon Griffin. Through the side window, she could see her sitting in the driver's seat. Harri waved to the blond enforcer, expecting a simple wave of acknowledgment back.

Instead, the passenger window rolled down and Griffin beckoned her over with the come-hither of a manicured index finger.

"The heat out in your office?" Harri asked when she met the Outback. There was strange music coming out of Griffin's speakers, like the sound of cats drowning in a whirlpool and then somebody beating their dead carcasses against a drum. The chords were loud, discordant, discombobulating.

Griffin clicked the door locks free. "Get in."

Harri stared at the radio. "What is *that*?"

"It's a radio."

She slid Griffin a look. "*On* the radio."

"Are you serious? That's 'Drowsy Maggie,'" Griffin replied, as if that was all she needed to say. "You're telling me you don't know the *Chieftains*?"

Harri shook her head, lost. She figured it was some Irish thing, since *nobody* was more Irish than Griffin. The boss's office was filled with kelly green hats and banners and shamrock decals. Even the knobby shillelagh leaning against the wall behind her desk had green ribbons tied to it. Sergeant Sharon Griffin lived Saint Patrick's Day all three hundred and sixty-five.

Harri shook her head. "Must have missed them. Is there news from Internal Affairs?"

Harri had been waiting weeks to hear if the department would investigate the calls and photos she'd received from the anonymous voice that appeared to implicate her former partner, Detective Glynnis Thompson, in wrongdoing, and explain her putting a gun to her head and pulling the trigger.

The images were seared into Harri's brain—G accepting an envelope from an unknown man in an unknown place—but Harri would never believe that G had been dirty. She was good police, family, and Harri would go to her grave fighting to prove it.

Griffin punched the radio off, and then turned in her seat to face Harri, fixing her with those icy-blue eyes. All cop now, the Chieftains and "Drowsy Maggie" put away for another time.

"I wanted to catch you before you went in. We need to talk." Even her voice was different—lower in tone, as far from casual and easygoing as either could get. Griffin reached into her console and drew out folded pages, then handed them to Harri. "Internal Affairs' report."

Harri's eyes widened. "Report? You're kidding. It's only been a couple weeks. They couldn't possibly have done a full investigation that fast."

Harri took the report. There were only two pages stapled together at the top left. She read every word, greedy eyes moving left to right. Griffin sat quietly, watching her do it.

"They didn't do a damned thing." She flipped over to page two. "My meeting with Sutton isn't even on here. I told them *everything*." Harri turned the page back over, hoping she'd missed something, anything, on page one, though she knew full well she hadn't. She fixed angry eyes on Griffin.

"You had me hold off for IAD. The right channels, you said." She held up the report. "This is time wasted. Explain this to me."

Before Griffin could respond, Harri began again. "He delivered those photos to her *house*, to her husband. Her kids could have seen them. I turned over burner numbers. Times, dates of the calls. He came to *my* house. None of that's even in here. Those photos could have been faked. They could have picked up a trail from one of those numbers. I told them I thought he was one of us. That would make *him* the dirty cop, not G."

"I know you're angry," Griffin said. "You want answers. To do right by your partner. They're not thinking about that. You read it. You read between the lines too." She slid Harri a look, her gaze steady, softening as her voice shifted from official to unofficial. "And just between you and me, coming straight from Riven, whose eyebrows I likely singed off when he delivered that crock of shit to me late yesterday—because Detective Thompson took her own life, which reflects badly on the department, it's in the department's best interest to not stir up any dirt. Half the people in this city think every cop's on the take, so IAD's not going to give the press any red meat on a possible dirty cop who killed herself. That's the plain truth."

Harri glared at her. "I knew her, you didn't. There's more to this. G was good police."

Griffin nodded. "I believe you. But they've decided to let her rest." She glanced down at the report in Harri's hand. "And there'll be nothing more than that for the record."

Harri sat stunned for a moment, then hurriedly stuffed the report in her pocket, disgusted by what was in it and livid about what wasn't.

"And about him asking me to lose evidence on an Elan Dreyer?"

The voice thought he'd locked her into an arrangement, one he claimed he'd had with G. She'd be a cop on the inside, feeding him information, dishonoring her badge, putting lives at risk. He would be the puppet master pulling her strings, running her. The thought of it made Harri sick.

"Dreyer's a low-level dealer," Griffin said. "You found that out your-self. He's a small fish not worth the DA's time. My feeling? This guy threw out Dreyer as a test. To see if you'd bite. We both know that was never going to happen. Which proves that he doesn't know you, only knows *of* you."

They sat in silence for a moment.

"Any new contact?" Griffin asked.

"Nothing."

"And it's been weeks. Maybe he's moved on."

Harri sat back in the seat. "He hasn't. I can feel it. And he knows what happened with G."

She stared out the window at the gray and the sleet, her mood matching.

"Speaking for the department, you're to drop this, let it go," Griffin said. "Unless he makes a more overt threat or action."

"Because she's dead, she gets swept under the rug. For politics."

"You're to stand down, Detective Foster. Is that understood?"

The official tone was back in Griffin's voice. The boss had just given her an order, duly sanctioned by the department, an order that drew an imaginary line separating her life on the job and one she would be forced to live off it.

For a moment Harri considered what letting the voice go would mean, how it would feel to just do nothing because it was expedient, easiest. She would never know what led to G's death. Harri would never know what she'd missed or failed to do. And the voice would get away with causing pain to G's family, to her, for sport. Griffin's order felt like a razor blade raking across her skin. How could she stand down?

Harri reached for the door.

"Harri?"

Her fingers gripped the handle. She couldn't look at Griffin. "Her kids shouldn't have to live with the question mark."

"Her kids. Or you? At least allow for the possibility that you could be wrong. That knowing might be worse than *not* knowing."

"Believe me, nothing's worse than *not* knowing."

Griffin stared out of the foggy windshield and let out a defeated sigh. "That's it then. One word of advice? Don't go so far that you tie my hands."

Harri pushed open the passenger door and got out, holding on to it for a moment.

"Nothing wrong with finding yourself some peace," Griffin said.

"Is that what you'd do?"

Griffin nodded. "I'd sure as hell try. I really would." She let a moment go, then added another on to it. "But, no, that probably wouldn't be what I'd do."

"See you inside, boss."

Harri slammed the door and turned for the building. Glynnis had given her all to the job, and the department wasn't going to lift a finger for her now. Dead and gone. Out of sight, out of mind. Cop suicides made the department look bad, and the attention was unwanted at the top. Easier to let the losses quietly slip away, mark them as personal failures, as though the job's human toll was something shameful and catching.

She stopped midway through the lot, needing to get herself centered before she went in. "I know I'm right."

Harri leaned into the sleet and raced the last few yards, feeling as though with every step her body was turning from muscle, tendon, and bone to steel and bolts and wire—heavy, hard, invulnerable—for G, for Mike, for their kids, and for her.

She'd missed something with G. A signal. A cry for help. A chance to intervene. It was the guilt she fought with now. That was what she buried deep, along with the loss. She wanted G back, whole, and alive. She wanted whatever forced her into despair to pay for what it did. She wanted justice. If she could get it for others, and she did every day she clipped her star to her belt, why couldn't she have it for herself?

Steel, not bone, she pushed inside the building of cops to find blue shirts, white shirts, and plainclothes compatriots moving about inside. Orderly chaos. Despite the highly charged atmosphere, the guns, the badges, the law, the politics, the often soul-searing waste that kept it all going, she couldn't imagine what she'd do if she couldn't do this. But Glynnis had been her partner, her friend. She felt an obligation to stand for her.

"Find some peace," she muttered as she wove her way through the lobby. Who had *peace*? Nobody, really. She didn't need peace, she decided; she needed the *truth*.

CHAPTER 3

"Stop. Don't take your coat off," Symansky said just as Harri reached her desk. She watched as he worked himself into his parka, and waited for an explanation. "We got a body at something called Hardwicke House. Sixty-three hundred north. Off Sheridan."

"Belverton College?"

"Adjacent." He looked her over. "You all right? You look like you got sideswiped by a snowplow comin' in. I can grab somebody else. Kelley and Bigelow are on that liquor store shootin', but they should be poppin' back soon. Lonergan's gonna be late, but he can head up there, if you need to take a pass."

She glanced over at Li's empty desk. She knew her partner was taking a personal day, but Li's absence, even for a shift, left her feeling as though she was working without an arm. How quickly she'd come to rely on Li, though she wasn't at all sure that was a good thing.

"I'm all right." She rebuttoned her coat and turned around to head back out, convinced she could feel the IAD report in her pocket, sitting there like a bad omen. "Let's go."

She and Symansky met Griffin coming up as they rushed down.

"We got a body," Symansky told the boss. "Keep you posted."

Griffin looked Harri over. "You don't want to take a minute?"

Harri stood defiant. "What would a minute do for me?"

She wasn't angry at Griffin, not exactly. She had only been the messenger, but the department's callousness still stung. Her anger had to go somewhere.

Griffin gave a thumbs-up and then moved past them without another word.

"What was that about?" Symansky asked. "You two got a beef goin' on?"

"It's nothing."

"And since when does the boss give thumbs-up to people? She's more the middle finger type, which she'll probably cap off with a kick to the family jewels and a Taser blast."

Harri said, "You want to drive?"

"In this weather? Hell no." He tossed her the keys. "I'll ride shotgun and count the potholes."

———

It didn't seem possible that it could have gotten colder and grayer and drearier in the twenty-five minutes it took to get from the district to Hardwicke House, but Harri felt that it had, though she had to admit the feeling had more to do with her mood.

It couldn't be the drive. Twenty-five minutes was good time on Lake Shore Drive in winter, considering she'd driven most of the way on thick black ice in the wake of a dented city salt spreader. By the time she and Symansky squeezed onto the exit ramp at Sheridan to follow the bend north toward the Evanston border, the unmarked car's windshield was caked with salt. Harri gave the window a spritz of fluid and hit the wipers, which gave her two streaky half circles to squint through.

There were squad cars and emergency vehicles pulled up outside the house when they arrived, lights flashing, though Harri could see that calling the structure a "house" wasn't exactly accurate. It was a Gilded

15

Age mansion, a statement piece, with glimmers of its old glory in the stonework around the eaves . . . fleurs-de-lis, coronets, mythical faces, that sort of thing. A showplace built to impress back when impressions meant everything.

Harri stared up at the roof; it was flat, like a battlement, with gaps and indentations along the top in case somebody in a tuxedo needed to shoot a defensive arrow out at marauding passersby. But there were also turrets. An odd mix, she thought. A case of too much money with too many fanciful whims? The mansion would have been home to a wealthy family who was assisted by footmen, valets, cooks, and nannies. Maybe it still was.

A uniformed cop waved them not toward the house but toward an empty field next to it, where Harri could already see what she had expected to—crime scene tape, the crime scene van, the ME's car, and off to the side, an idling ambulance and a fire truck, ominous reminders that death, especially the kind she and Symansky were here to see about, never took a holiday. So much for her earlier wish for a death-free day.

She pulled the car up a few feet from the tape and stared both at the huddle of city personnel and the cluster of reporters with news cameras who'd been pushed back across the street. Symansky growled when he saw them too.

"Worse thing they did was give those vampires police scanners," he said. "They beat *us* here."

Harri sighed. "They're highly motivated."

"They're a pain in the ass. You'd think they'd a burned themselves out blowin' up that alderman mess we just wrapped. But, no, here they are again. Standin' in the cold, gawkin', yappin', pickin' at every little thing, stickin' their big honkers in. And nothin' brings 'em out faster than somebody dead up *here*." He stared out the window at the large, well-maintained houses on the street, their porch lights still blazing.

"Our salary wouldn't even cover the upkeep on one of these. Or the lawn guy."

Harri smiled cynically. "But look at all the perks we get."

Symansky snorted. "High blood pressure, flat feet, the city nickel-and-dimin' us on our contract? And don't get me started on the bosses. Heads up asses, most cases."

Harri scanned the field, unable to disagree with any of what Symansky had just said. "Ready?"

"Nah, you go. I hit my dead-body quota for this month."

She turned to look at him, saw the mischievous smile. He was joking.

"Quotas would be nice, wouldn't they?"

Symansky let a breath go. "We can dream that little dream, Harri. Ain't never gonna happen."

The campus of Belverton College stood less than a half mile away to the south. The lights from its dormitories and academic buildings were on and cut through the dewy curtain of the early morning. A block or two north were the tony homes of Evanston. Along the campus's east side stood Lake Michigan, locked in by ice, the wind racing off the surface like an unmanned freight train hurtling along greased tracks.

Belverton was private and selective in its enrollment and didn't have a reputation for being a party school. They didn't get many calls up here besides the occasional stickup or stolen car. She and her ex-husband, RJ, had eyed it as a possible spot for their son, Reg, but that was before things happened.

Staid, Harri would label it, if forced to. Kids came to Belverton to become movers and shakers in their chosen fields, not to get trashed, though she suspected they did it anyway on the down-low.

She squinted through the windshield at the campus in the distance. "What do you think, Al? About a ten-minute walk from here to the school?"

"For you, maybe. Me? More like twenty. For a kid? They could run it in five. The little shits wouldn't even be winded." He referred to his phone. "I did the google while we were slip-sliding up here." He flashed her a smile. "I see I impressed ya there. Old dog, new trick. The house is owned by Sebastian Collier."

"The billionaire?"

Symansky frowned. "Yep, and I hope to hell it's not him we're here about. Those honkers over there would wet themselves."

"We passed signs for the Collier Library and the Collier science building."

He rolled his eyes. "Why do rich people have to put their names on every friggin' thing? They're like cats markin' off territory. Piss, piss, piss. Mine, mine, mine."

"The call didn't give any details?"

"Nah. Just that a body'd been found." He squinted out the side window. "I guess it's over there in the field where all the hoopla is."

Harri grabbed her radio and bag. "Let's go, then."

Symansky pushed the passenger door open and stepped out into the cold like he'd done a million times on a million mornings like this. Harri did the same on her side, only to be met by the sting of cold air hitting her lungs as if she'd swallowed a thousand needles. She looked over the field, knowing there was a person dead in it, someone somebody loved and would miss.

They trudged toward the field, a light dusting of snow beneath their feet made crunchy from the icy sleet that had stopped for the moment. They flashed their stars for the PO guarding the perimeter before ducking under the tape to see what they were up against. All Harri could see of the body on the ground as she approached were the soles of a pair of running shoes. *Not a kid,* she prayed. *Not today. Not out here.*

But it was a kid. A young white man who looked to be in his early twenties, half-clothed, gone. And, strangely, it wasn't Rosales, their

18

usual ME assistant, kneeling over the boy; it was the ME herself, Dr. Olivia Grant, wearing her usual green scrubs under a red Canada Goose parka that looked like it could get her to the North Pole and back without even a hint of frostbite.

"Dr. Grant?" Harri asked, a bit taken aback by the substitution.

Grant didn't come out in the field, preferring instead to hold sway from her autopsy room. In fact, Harri didn't think she'd ever seen Grant outside the ME's office. Certainly not at one of their crime scenes taking body temps. She and Symansky shared a look that acknowledged the unusual replacement, but they made no comment. Grant was extremely direct and easily confrontational in the best of times, and this situation was far less than that.

Grant peered up at them, her brow furrowed, her dark face solemn in the murky light.

"Yeah, it's me. Get over it," she said.

Her keen eyes peeked over the top of a serious pair of horn-rimmed glasses attached to a chain around her neck, her pointy chin nearly touching her chest.

"Detectives Foster and Symansky. So, you're the lucky two called out on this cold, brittle morning?" Her full lips curled into a half smile–half scowl. She looked around. "Where's that pain in the ass Li?"

"Ouch," Symansky muttered under his breath.

"Off today. Back tomorrow," Harri said. "Rosales?"

"Same. And we're shorthanded, so you got me. Joy, joy. I just got started. Not much to tell you yet. Dead white male. Twenty, or just over. No visible signs of violence. No shots. No stabs. No slices. If you're thinking about pestering me for more than that right from the jump, like you do with Rosales, one word of advice—*don't*. You'll get it when I get it. And I won't be rushed. *Capiche?*"

"You're a real charmer, doc," Symansky said.

"You should see me at a cocktail party, Detective."

Symansky squinted, angled his big head. "That's a party of *livin'* people, right?"

Grant stared up at him, not a hint of humor in the look. "I don't discriminate."

Harri moved closer to get a better look at their victim. His thin lips were blue, his light hair frozen solid, flecks of ice in it. He was wearing jeans and running shoes, but no shirt. On his right upper arm there was a tattoo of a mythical creature holding a double-edged axe.

"That the only tattoo?" she asked, bending down to study it closely. "A minotaur?"

"Only one I see so far," Grant said.

"Looks like somethin' from a video game," Symansky said. "Kids are into that crap."

Harri turned to him. "Enough to put a character on their body, *permanently*?"

Symansky burrowed into his collar. "What's permanent these days?" He stared down at the body. "Except *that*."

The body had been out here in the cold for hours, it appeared, which meant the young man had stumbled here or was dumped here at night, when the temperature would have been far more brutal than it was now. *So, why no shirt?* Harri wondered. In February, like this was Miami Beach and not Chicago, where the wind blew in off the lake like an evil fist that punched you in the chest, then grabbed you by the throat and closed off your airway.

This unexplained detail, along with all the other preliminary ones Harri managed to glean with her own eyes, was overpowered by the strong rank stink of alcohol and vomit.

"I'm not the only one to smell the alcohol, right?" she asked.

"Or the vomit? Nah, we all got noses," Symansky said.

"I saw no reason to state the obvious," Grant answered. "Blood alcohol levels will come later too."

Harri's mind began to click. Kid. Alcohol. Campus nearby. Maybe a party got out of hand, and he staggered into the field and collapsed? Those were the assumptions, which she quickly pushed away. Cases ran on facts, not theories.

She straightened. "Right. Okay. When you have something, then."

Harri backed away, scanned the ground around the body. There were no drag marks, no clear footprints in the patches of snow, no significant cracking in the ice. She bent over again and checked the bottoms of the boy's shoes. No mud, no dirt, just some ice and snow packed into the grooves of his running shoes, and the toes were a little scuffed. She studied his hands, keeping out of Grant's way. No broken nails. Nothing obvious she could see embedded underneath, like blood or skin. No defensive wounds.

"Maybe he got out here on his own," she said.

Symansky was facing the field. "Looks like the field's a shortcut. There's a path cuttin' right through over there. Faster this way then goin' all the way around. Somebody *could* have carried him in. Dumped him there." He bounced on his feet. "Ground's pretty solid. There'd be no way for us to tell."

"Half-naked? It's twenty degrees out here," Harri said, appalled by such a cruel act.

Symansky turned to face her. "I'm thinkin', him bein' drunk, being a guy, some kind of hazin'. I can see you're thinkin' it too."

"We don't know he's drunk," Grant said.

Symansky frowned. "Look, doc, all due respect, I don't need a test tube to tell me what drunk looks like. Plus, you can smell it on him. He probably had more than he could hold, and some of his frat buddies carried him out here to sober up, and instead he froze to death chokin' on his own spit."

Harri stared over at the house. "Out of the house, or he never made it in?"

"Either way. Out of sight, not their problem," Symansky said. "It's how kids think."

"Both of you, stop thinking *anything*," Grant said. "At least until I know how he died."

Harri sighed, resigned, knowing what came next. Some unfortunate parents were about to get the worst call of their lives. A call she knew from experience they would never recover from.

Symansky peeled off his winter gloves and plucked his cell phone out of his pocket to check for messages. "For a second there, doc, I was thinkin' you fired Rosales."

Grant growled. "Are we back on that?"

Symansky carried on as if she hadn't spoken. "Because if that was the case, that woulda been a real cock-up on your part. Rosales is all right. Not too talky, always gets us what we need toot sweet. You? Jury's still out." He watched to see if the playful needling was landing. "I mean, you coulda gone soft all those years inside that cushy autopsy room of yours."

Grant looked Symansky up and down, unimpressed by the sixtyish white guy in the wool overcoat with decades of late-night bags under his droopy eyes, a heat pit in his stomach borne of years of departmental bullshit, and a perpetual clenched jaw from standing at scenes like this on mornings like this.

Grant's eyes flicked to his feet and the dusty oxfords inside his rubber overshoes. "You can expect what my grandmama used to call an old-fashioned kitchenette whippin' if you don't back up and get your big cop feet out of my field."

Harri smiled surreptitiously at Grant's use of the old saying, one her grandmother had used frequently, and not always in jest. The look of confusion on Symansky's face was priceless.

Poor guy. Grant was no shrinking violet. She was perceptive and off-putting, both to the nth degree, an unshakable force of intelligence and self-assuredness—her confidence in her abilities off the chain, and her unmasked disdain for most people legendary.

"Huh?" It was all Symansky said as he backed up a couple of steps. Grant turned back to the young man. "No worries, Al, it's like falling off a log, only it's a log you wish you didn't have to fall off of." She released a woeful sigh, then began examining the victim's eyes more closely. "All the bodies I've worked on, I never forget their faces."

Harri stiffened, knowing that one of those bodies had been her son's, who'd been taken by a thug's bullet five years ago at age fourteen. The pang of hurt Harri quickly banished and reburied for now. This field was not the place to fall to pieces. She and Symansky had work to do. Job. Procedure. Both a blessing and a shield.

"Did we find a wallet? ID? Phone?" Harri asked.

Grant turned her head halfway. "Not on him. But I hear the ones who found him knew who he was."

Harri turned toward the nearest PO and waved her over, reading her name patch. "Officer Paulsen. We have an ID on the deceased?"

"Our caller ID'd him as Brice Collier," Paulsen said. "He lived there in the big house." She pointed at the mansion. "And he's a student at Belverton. A junior. Or was."

"*Collier?*" Symansky's eyes went wide. "*Noooo.*"

Paulsen looked confused. "Detective?"

"This is goin' to be another A-class shit show," he said. "Startin' now." His thumbs worked his phone's keypad a mile a minute. "Yep. Here he is." He held his phone up so Harri could see it. "That's him. That's his kid, all right. *Goddamn it.*"

Harri stared at the boy's photo—he was vibrant, happy in life, a stark contrast to how he looked now. "Brice Ferguson Collier, twenty. Student at the business school named after his family, no less."

Symansky shoved the phone back in his pocket. "And heir to the whole friggin' shebang. Press is gonna be all over this."

Harri glanced down at what was left of Brice F. Collier. Twenty. Not her son, but someone's. Who his father was made no difference to her.

"We don't know anything yet, Al." She looked over at him. "Till we do, it's by the numbers. Like always."

Symansky grumbled something under his breath and shoved his hands into his pockets, ill humor pulsing off him like waves of toxic radiation. "Fuck it all to hell and back."

"Well, that's how I'm going to work it," Grant said. "All we can do, really. Just off the top, though? No blood. No petechiae. But, of course, we all smell the alcohol, and the emesis. I won't know about any other substances, of course, until I run the tox."

Symansky glowered at Grant. "Emesis?"

She shook her head, sighed. "Vomit, Al."

"Then why didn't you just *say* vomit?"

"Because my mama worked three jobs so I could go to medical school, that's why."

"Then what do you call a pain in my ass?"

Without missing a beat and without cracking a smile, she answered, "Al Symansky."

His eyes narrowed. "Walked right into that one." He turned to Paulsen, who was standing by. "Where's the one who found him?"

"More than one," Paulsen said. "There were two girls waiting when we rolled up."

Paulsen, petite, slim, dark hair tucked under a CPD beanie, her pale cheeks colored by cold, pointed toward a squad car parked on the far end of the tape. "Shelby Ritter made the 911 call." Paulsen consulted her notes. "Hailie Kenton was with her when we rolled up. Both eighteen, nineteen. Students at the college. They say they were cutting through the field."

"And they ID'd him," Harri said.

Paulsen nodded. "They knew who he was straight away."

Symansky exhaled deeply. "Probably on account of him bein' a Collier."

Paulsen shook her head. "We got as much as we could, then put them in the car to warm up and calm down."

Grant checked Collier's neck again, turning his head slightly right, then left, then sat back on her heels. "Okay. Let's get this done. I want to get this poor boy off the ground as quickly as I can."

The cops backed up while the techs moved around Grant and the body, taking photographs, measuring distances, documenting the corpse as it lay there. Every angle. Numerous shots of the same thing. The work would take a while, a macabre dance played out under a dull sky in sight of barren trees. A necessary evil when death appeared to be unnatural. Harri turned to Paulsen.

"Let's search the field. Maybe he dropped his phone and his shirt."

"Like he drunk stripped?" Symansky said, incredulity in his gruff voice.

"There's science to that," Grant said. "It's called vasodilation. Alcohol speeds up your heart rate and widens the blood vessels, which makes you feel hot. The wider the vessels, the more blood flows through. Your skin feels warm, you feel flushed. That's *if* he was impaired. We don't know that yet."

"I'd be willin' to bet," Symansky muttered.

Harri turned to Paulsen. "Quick run-through again about the girls, please."

"Walking through around six. They spotted something on the ground. They got closer, saw Collier. Ritter says she just managed to get the call to 911 in before they both freaked out. When we rolled up seven minutes later, we found them huddled together under that tree over there, looking like they'd seen a ghost."

Harri flicked a look toward Hardwicke House. "Did they say why they didn't go to the house for help?"

"No, but we couldn't get much more out of them; they were like zombies. They did say Collier lived there."

"Anybody from the house come out?" Symansky asked. "All this activity, the lights and all."

Paulsen shook her head. "We rang the bell. Lights were on inside. No one answered. We circled the house and found fresh tracks, lots of them, running from the back door heading toward the campus. Looked like something broke up one helluva party. Red cups were dropped everywhere."

"Big house," Harri said. "He couldn't have lived there alone?"

"He didn't. The girls said he has housemates. Guys. Again, all students. It sounds like an *Animal House* deal. Off campus. Not a lot of supervision. The front door's locked. We checked."

Harri looked down at Grant. "Dr. Grant—"

Grant interrupted the question. "No keys in his pocket."

Harri slid her notepad out of her bag and jotted down the detail, along with all the others Paulsen had relayed.

Symansky popped a stick of Juicy Fruit in his mouth, started working it. "Did they say why they were out walkin' that early on a Sunday mornin'? Too early for church."

"Just walking, they said."

"Yeah, right. No kid I know walks when they can ride, especially at the crack of friggin' dawn when it's cold as a witch's tit. They were at that party." He motioned toward the field, sweeping his arm from it to the house. "They were comin' from the house and saw him. They weren't comin' from the other way. They look drunk to you, Paulsen?"

Paulsen shook her head, stared down at the body. "No. But if they were, I think the sight of *that* would have sobered them up long before we got here."

Harri glanced up at the sky, the color of metal, the sun peeking through thick clouds. "It was still dark at six."

"Another reason this don't smell right," Symansky said. "College girls walkin' in the dark?"

"Anything else?" Harri asked Paulsen.

"That's all we have."

Harri snapped the cover of her notepad closed, the short pen, black ink, nestled between the pages. "Okay. Thanks. We'll talk to them in a minute." She turned back to Grant.

"Don't let me stop you," Grant said. "Go. I don't need you two breathing down my neck."

Symansky rolled his eyes. "Then I guess we'll be heading over there *now*." He looked over at Harri. "I'll get that field search started. Meet you over there."

"You didn't mention time of death," Harri said to Grant.

"Because I don't know it. It's cold. He's been lying here awhile. That affects everything."

"A range would work for now."

Grant peered over her glasses. "Only an estimate. Likely between ten, maybe, and midnight?"

"Thanks."

Harri gave Collier a final look, then headed toward the squad car with their witnesses sitting in it. As she walked, her eyes swept along the ground, looking for anything that might be connected to the boy, but there was nothing beneath her boots but dead grass under ice and patches of hard-packed snow. Maybe they'd find something useful when they searched the entire field. Maybe Collier's death would end up being just a horrible tragedy, self-imposed and not anything they had to pursue.

For now, all she had were questions. Why wasn't Collier wearing a shirt or a coat? If he lived in Hardwicke House, why was he in the field? A party. The smell of alcohol. Had he been confused, disoriented? Drunk, did he stumble out into the cold, collapse, and die? Where were his friends, his housemates? Why no activity from the house? Was Symansky right? Trouble. Panic. Kid thinking.

She heard Grant call for a body bag and turned in time to see the ME rise, stretch out her back, and then stand over Brice Collier, prepared to escort him to a safe, warm place. She never forgot their faces, Grant had said. Harri wasn't quite sure if that could be considered a burden or blessing.

She slid her hand into her pocket to rub the paper clip she'd secreted there. It was a way she centered herself and beat back dark thoughts. The feel of the tiny tangible thing, the smoothness of the thin metal as it warmed between her fingers, settled her. She knew it was because of Reg. She hadn't needed these things before she lost him. But she needed them now to remind herself to breathe, to move, to stay anchored in the here and now, to choose, sometimes minute by minute, between the difficult and gone.

The clips, the small little things she pressed in her hand and worked with her fingers, were a reminder that life was real and so was she.

Harri stopped at the edge of the field, just for a moment, to note where she was, and why, knowing she was standing at present not for herself but for Collier. That made it easier. Her eyes settled over the scene as she let everything around her seep into her bones. She inhaled the field, listened to it, became a part of it. This was the side of her life that made sense. One paper clip. One breath. Fifty clips. Fifty inhales. Life, one beat at a time.

"Ready?"

She jumped when Symansky eased in beside her. She let go of the paper clip and pulled her hand out of her pocket. She'd only needed the one minute, that moment's touch, before she could move forward again. "Always ready, Al."

He looked back at the body being gently lifted into the bag. "The calm before the storm."

They made their way toward Ritter and Kenton, Harri sliding a glance toward the group of reporters hovering on the sidewalk, all competing for the same sound bite. As the pair passed them on the way to the car, a few of them shouted out questions from across the street to her and Symansky, bullet fast and insistent, each pressing for information they didn't yet have. "We can't stop the storm," Harri said woefully. "All we can do is dress for it."

Ice crunched beneath their feet, a comfortable silence between them, until Symansky said, "The stats on alcohol-related deaths on college campuses are enough to curl your hair. You send your kids to school so they can turn out to be somethin', you spend all that money, hockin' practically everythin' you own, and half of them spend their time chuggin' rotgut they shouldn't, thinkin' nothin's ever gonna happen to 'em as a result."

"Weren't we the same?"

He chuckled. "Maybe *you* were. I came outta the womb just like you see me now."

"A jaded curmudgeon?"

He chuckled. "I'm alive, ain't I?"

"Good point."

CHAPTER 4

Harri opened the back door of the idling squad car to find two trembling white girls holding on to each other in the back seat. She introduced herself and Symansky and was met with two sets of wide, shell-shocked eyes, like those of frightened fawns caught in a snare. She searched their faces, looking for the one who appeared most capable of answering questions. There was no clear winner, so she dove in, starting with the one who'd placed the 911 call.

"Ms. Ritter?" she asked gently. "Shelby?"

A young woman with big green eyes raised her hand. "Yes?" Her voice quivered. "When can we go home?"

Harri stepped back so as not to crowd them. It was a lot finding a body. It was a lot more being hemmed in by police officers with guns and hard faces. Nodding first to Symansky to signal her intent, she opened the front passenger door on the squad and eased into the front seat, then turned around to face the back, the seat acting as buffer, which the young women appeared to appreciate. Symansky and Paulsen stood outside the car, close.

Harri offered a smile to put them at ease. "Soon. Can we get you anything? Coffee? Hot tea? It's pretty cold out here, and police cars aren't really built for comfort."

They both shook their heads.

"Is he really dead?" Ritter's eyes searched hers, hope still in them. "Brice?"

"Yes. I'm sorry. Did you know him well? Was he a friend?"

The girls tensed at the same time. Harri watched as each girl slid a look toward the other, then shook her head.

Ritter stared unblinking at something only she could see. "Oh my God."

"I'm sorry you had to start your morning this way."

Kenton looked at Harri bewildered. "How do you do this? See dead bodies all the time."

"She's probably used to it by now," Ritter answered for her. "They don't scare her, do they?"

Harri let a beat go, her smile faded. "You never get used to it. You just do it."

"So, you knew him?" Symansky asked.

"Everybody on campus does," Ritter said. "He's . . . *was* very popular."

Ritter was dressed in a jacket, too light for February, Harri thought. No boots. Like Collier, running shoes, leather. Jeans. No hat, no gloves, and only a T-shirt underneath the jacket. Typical for the age. Only later, when the bones began to creak and a winter wind wreaked havoc on temperamental sinuses, would this flippant way of dressing for the cold cease and the gloves and hats and boots come out. She knew this from experience. Kenton was similarly underdressed, but with her jeans fancifully appliquéd with large sunflowers and her tight shirt a vibrant blast of purple-and-pink swoops and swirls.

"Can you tell us again how you found him?" Harri asked.

"But we already told the other cops," Kenton said as she pushed back a tousled tangle of brunette hair.

"Unfortunately, you'll have to tell it a few more times." Harri turned to Paulsen. "Knock at the house again, please. Maybe we can move them inside, where it's warmer."

Paulsen turned to leave but stopped when Ritter spoke out.

"No. I want to stay here. I mean, we do."

Kenton nodded. "It's not so cold. Really."

Harri nodded at Paulsen, who stayed put, and then studied the girls, finding their responses odd. She flicked a look at Symansky to see if their reaction had hit him the same way. His narrowed eyes, his suspicious look, told her it had. Why choose the back of an idling police car in the cold when they could be inside, where it was warm?

"You're sure? You'd be a lot more comfortable inside."

They each burrowed down in their flimsy jackets and shook their heads.

"I'm sure, at least," Ritter said.

"I'm sure," Kenton added.

"Who lives here besides Collier?" Symansky asked. "You know somethin' about housemates, you said?"

Ritter looked over at him. "Not much. A few guys live here. Mostly upperclassmen. I don't know them. I'm only a sophomore."

"You walk past here a lot?" Harri asked.

Ritter shrugged. "I guess. Campus is right over there. The field's a shortcut."

"So, you found Brice, you called 911, and you waited out here until the police arrived. Did you see anyone else around or hear anything?"

The girls shook their heads, their chins to their chests.

"Why were you out walking so early by yourselves?"

Ritter answered. "I couldn't sleep. I thought if I got some air . . ."

Harri looked at Kenton, but the girl wouldn't look back at her.

"And Hailie decided to join you?"

Ritter nodded. "Yeah."

"No," Harri said. "You want to try again?"

"We *were* just walking," Kenton said. "That's not illegal."

"Lying to the police can be," Harri said.

The girls exchanged a cautious look. Harri wondered what they were transmitting between them and why they were lying.

"So, you're walkin' and you see somethin'," Symansky said. "Then what?"

"We didn't know what it was at first," Kenton said. "When we saw it, *him* . . . we lost it, I guess."

"What do you mean you lost it?" Harri asked. "Did you scream? Yell for help? Run? Knock on doors?"

"We ran away from him, then Shelby called 911."

"And nobody else was around, you said. Just you two."

"Not really."

"Not really, or no?" Harri pushed.

"No," Kenton said.

"And you didn't knock at the house. Why?"

"Somebody had to show the police where he was, didn't they?"

Harri noticed how Ritter wrung her hands, how her eyes never seemed to land on anything for very long, how her legs bounced nervously.

"Yes. Thank you for doing that."

"And you thought he was dead right off?" Symansky asked. "Not passed out or anythin'?"

Ritter looked confused by the question. "He was blue, and his chest wasn't moving up and down."

"We could tell he was dead," Kenton said, her hands knit together in her lap. "We never touched anything. We know you're not supposed to."

Harri gripped her notepad but didn't open it, more interested in watching the body language. "You were coming from campus, not from the house, is that right?"

The girls nodded.

"And neither of you were friends with Brice?"

They shook their heads.

"He was a junior," Ritter said as though that explained everything.

Harri glanced over at the half-dozen cars parked in front of the house. "Which one of those is his?"

Kenton pointed to a black Tesla. "That one."

Harri looked up at the windows of Hardwicke House. "And his bedroom is in the front or the back?"

Ritter opened her mouth to answer, then appeared to catch herself. "We don't know. How could we? I really want to go home now. I need to feel safe."

"Me too," Kenton said.

Harri could see in the wasted faces that she and Symansky had gotten all they were going to get for now.

"One last question. Do you two live on campus?"

"Hailie and me live in Devlin Hall," Ritter said, pointing to a building in the distance. "That one with the green roof."

Harri gave them one last look, then eased out of the front seat and turned to Paulsen.

"Let's get these young women home." To the girls she said, "Thanks for the information. We'll be in touch if we need anything more. Unless there's something else we should know about now?"

They conferred again with a look, and then Kenton answered, "We told you everything you need to know."

Harri's eyes swept over them. She very much doubted that she'd been told everything she *needed* to know, but she let it go for now. "All right. Then let's see you home."

She closed the front door and stepped away from the car, watching as a PO got into the driver's seat and pulled away. Harri and Symansky stood watching the car head toward Devlin Hall.

"Poor kids," Symansky said. "Bet they'll never forget this day."

Harri said nothing.

"What?" Symansky said.

"They weren't telling the whole truth. Shades of it, maybe. They weren't Brice's friends, but they know which car is his and which part of the house his bedroom is in."

He scowled. "Car's not a stretch. He probably revved that little black commie car up and down the place like he was Richie Rich showin' off. As for the room, I miss somethin'? They never answered."

Harri's eyes narrowed. "Ritter almost did. I bet you she could have."

"Huh. I musta missed that."

Harri eyed Hardwicke House.

"Nuh-uh. What now?" Symansky asked.

Harri slid him a sly look. "I didn't say anything."

"Yeah, but you think stuff louder than anybody I ever met."

She glanced over at the uniformed cops searching the field. "Shock of their lives," she muttered under her breath.

CHAPTER 5

Harri and Symansky stepped inside the house and were immediately smacked in the face with a strong smell of lemon-scented cleaner with bleach undertones. Odd for a Sunday morning. Odder still in a house inhabited by college upperclassmen, one of whom had just been found dead half-naked in the field outside.

"Alarm bells," Symansky muttered as he scanned the tidy living room. "They cleaned up."

Harri did her own scan. "Question is, cleaned up *what*?"

He frowned, sniffed. "We both know what. Bet this place looked like hell on wheels before they hauled out the bleach."

She turned to the officer at the door. McAfee, a rotund white guy with red hair and a deep, jagged scar on his square chin. "Who've we got? What do we know?"

"Three guys. Hungover. We put them in the dining room with a pot of coffee. Officer Azariah is in there with them."

"Residents?" Symansky asked.

McAfee nodded. "Three others, too, but they're not in the house. One of the guys, a Todd Renfro, said they're off at some debate tournament. These three say they were in bed when we knocked earlier and didn't know anything was going on before then."

"But you don't believe that's true," Harri said, noticing the tiny shift in McAfee's facial expression, one that hinted at more than a little skepticism.

"I went to Southern. I lived off campus too. I cleaned up in a hurry a lot of times half in the bag. I know the signs. Plus Azariah says the kitchen floor was still wet when he escorted one of them in there to put that pot of coffee on. My experience? No frat rat's mopping a floor this early on a Sunday . . . or anytime, if you want to get real."

"They say what prompted the hasty cleanup?" Harri asked.

McAfee shook his head. "But I think all the squad cars pulling up out front might have had something to do with it. We got signs of a lot of feet hustling out of here by the back door."

The three moved toward the dining room and stopped at the doorway. Harri peered in to see three hungover white boys sitting at a long dining room table, nursing mugs of coffee, a nearly empty carafe sitting in the center on a folded Belverton hand towel.

"Any of them legal?"

McAfee scoffed. "Nope. And not a parent or guardian in sight."

"Good thing none of 'em are *my* kid," Symansky muttered. "They'd never see the light of day again."

Harri took a step back, drawing the other two with her, then lowered her voice. "Nobody missed Collier?"

"When we got them all up, one of them knocked on his door and seemed real surprised when he wasn't in there."

"Which one?"

McAfee pointed to a dark-haired boy with bloodshot eyes, his nose plastered to the rim of a coffee mug. "Renfro. He's the least hungover, and it looks like he's used to speaking for the other ones. Big man in the house, I guess."

"They didn't cop to the party?" she asked.

He shook his head. "They're acting like we're stupid and we can't smell Pine-Sol. They tidied up the place, but didn't have time, I guess, to clean themselves up too. They reek."

She turned to Symansky. "Nothing illegal about throwing a party. Why cover it up?"

"The party mighta been legal," he said, "but chances are good some of the party favors weren't."

Harri turned back to McAfee. "Were there any noise complaints called in last night?" She needed to pin the level of disruption somewhere between a quiet little gathering and a full-out bacchanal.

McAfee shook his head. "Nothing. The houses up here are not that close together. This size? The windows are going to be pretty thick too. You could probably hold a rave in here and nobody across the street would hear it."

Harri leaned in to confer with Symansky. "No cause of death yet. No signs of physical injury."

"In other words, we're flyin' blind here," he said.

"Renfro first," she said. "Then the others?"

Symansky nodded. "Why not take 'em together like we did those girls? See how they play off each other? Body language alone's bound to tell us somethin'."

She thought it through but was unsure. Hungover with coffee was still hungover, and these were kids.

"We flip a coin." Symansky, having picked up on Harri's apprehension, reached into his pocket and dug out a quarter. She had worked with the man now for almost five months, and it still mystified her why he got dressed in the morning and dumped pocket change into his pants as though he needed to feed a million tollbooths between his house and work. But she'd never asked; wasn't her business.

Symansky caught McAfee looking, the officer's mouth slightly agape, his brows knit together.

"You never bought a cup of coffee, PO?"

"Yeah," McAfee offered flatly. "And Venmo's a lot easier."

Symansky held up his quarter. "Easier than *this*?"

McAfee stood firm. At least thirty years Symansky's junior, he looked from the quarter in the old cop's hand to the saggy pocket where the quarter came from. "Yeah."

"We're not flipping coins," Harri said, slipping out of her coat, then tossing it onto a nearby chair, leaving the zip-up light jacket beneath it on. "We'll take them all at once. Out here."

McAfee smiled at Symansky and his quarter. "We'll rustle them up for you, then."

Harri crossed over to the couch, sat, and flipped open the cover of her notepad. Symansky took his coat off and sat beside her, glancing around the slightly shabby room.

"Don't look like much, even from the outside. Big is all it is. Wonder how much it costs to heat this thing."

Harri took in the grand woodwork, which leaned heavily toward cherubs and grapes and Grecian urns, as well as the delicate light fixtures fashioned to look like flowers, accented in gold filigree. The grandness ended when her eyes shifted back to ground level, where the furnishings looked well worn. The scarred end tables sported cup rings, and there were stains on the carpet. The askew lampshades smelled of dust. Nothing she could see, aside from the golden fixtures, looked like it was antique or worth a great deal. Like the good stuff had been carted away long ago and replaced with cheaper versions just good enough for a home filled with college boys left to their own devices. Still, the furniture and decor, which had obviously seen better days, felt like too much. It was a stark contrast to her own place, Harri having taken minimalism to an unhealthy level, no remedy in sight.

Symansky pulled back his blazer so that the star clipped to his belt showed. "Johnny Law has come to call," he announced boldly.

"Do not scare these children, Al."

"I'm not gonna scare them straight, just a little crooked. Collier reeked like a barroom crapper at closin'. We both know he loaded up right here, and those party fools know it. Besides, their parents will probably thank me later. You can be good cop if you want."

"Thanks. I will. And so will you, right?"

Symansky scoffed, covered up his badge. "Killjoy. I had a feelin' that's how you and Li rolled. Couple a Goody Two-shoes."

Harri said nothing as she underlined the names she'd just written down. *Shelby Ritter. Hailie Kenton.* And then the sentence *Why wouldn't they come into the house?*

CHAPTER 6

The three young men McAfee and Azariah escorted into the living room looked like they were being marched in from an orgy that hadn't gone well. They were bedraggled, spent, green around the gills. The trio sat in a line on the lumpy couch facing the detectives and stared at them blankly, their baby faces sporting spotty stubble and wispy hairs above dry lips. Boys to men, but not quite yet.

Sober enough just about pegged it, Harri thought as she stared at the droopy bloodshot eyes, the hastily combed hair, the pallid faces, sure signs that they'd each done their best to down a distillery's entire output in one wild evening.

Not only had the house been quickly put right, but their jeans and T-shirts looked clean. Yet as McAfee had said, they each smelled high, reeking of sweat, weed, and Listerine.

Symansky didn't say anything, but she could just imagine what he was thinking and fully expected to have that affirmed once they got back in the car.

She searched for the soberest face. Found it in a boy who looked about twenty. Dark hair. Gray eyes squinted half-shut as though he were a vampire lured into the sunlight, as though even the sound of the heat oozing out of the floor vents hurt him down to his core, as though it wasn't heat but spikes being driven into his brain.

She stared at the vampire. "Todd Renfro?"

His eyes widened, then focused on hers. There was life in them. He was sober enough.

"I'm Detective Foster. This is Detective Symansky." She glanced down the line at the two zombies sitting next to him. "Do you know where you are? Why we're here?" Her eyes held his. "What day it is?"

"Yeah," he answered feebly. "Is Brice really dead? You're sure? What happened to him?"

"That's what we're hopin' you can tell us," Symansky said, not bothering to keep his booming voice low. He knew what effect it would have and seemed to relish it. Not bad cop so much as dad cop. "Tell us about the party."

Harri could tell Renfro was about to lie. It was in his eyes, that glint of indecision as he fought with the choice to tell the truth or completely mislead them.

"There *was* a party here," she said. "Alcohol and drugs. We're not here for that. Tell us about Brice. When did you see him last?"

"Somebody really found him in the field? That's messed up."

Harri angled her head. "Yeah, it is. Any idea how he got there?"

Renfro shook his head. "No idea. Was he robbed or something? Was he shot? I didn't hear a shot, or anything like that." He looked over at his friends on the couch. "You guys?"

The boys shook their heads. No one did.

"Why ask if he was shot?" Symansky's eyes lasered in. "Not that any of you woulda heard a gun go off in your state."

Renfro glared up at him. "This isn't the safest city anymore, is it? Kids get robbed right on campus in broad daylight now. You can hardly walk anywhere without somebody coming up to you with a gun or a knife or a tire iron. It happens practically every day. You police barely even show up."

"Numbers say different, kid."

Renfro scoffed. "Right. Numbers. We all know how *that* works."

Symansky opened his mouth to respond, but Harri jumped in first.

"Let's focus on last night. Anything happen out of the ordinary at the party? Did Brice get into it with somebody? Could he have gotten hold of something he shouldn't have?"

They were questions asked as delicately as she could. The last thing they needed was for Renfro and the others to shut down and refuse to answer anything.

"By accident," she added. "Or by mistake."

Renfro leaned forward, his elbows on his thighs, his head in his hands. "There was nothing like that, okay? It was just a party. Beers. Some . . . other things. Recreational stuff. It was cool. Everybody was cool. He was here, having a good time last time I saw him."

"What time was it you saw him?"

"A little before nine, maybe? Things were just getting really started." A pained expression crossed his face. "He's really dead? Like *dead* dead? This isn't a joke?"

Symansky sighed. "Son, when's the last time you saw cops show up for a laugh?"

Harri checked the other boys. "Any of *you* remember seeing Brice around nine?"

On the end, a skinny boy with old acne scars raised his hand. "I saw him in the kitchen. He was grabbing beers out of the cooler. I figured he'd found somebody to hang out with in record time."

"He say anything to you?"

"Nah, he just walked right past me, so I went back out front where the action was."

"Walked right past you headed *where* if he wasn't going where the action was?" Harri asked.

"I figured the roof to hook up. Because of the two beers?"

"What's on the roof?" Symansky asked.

Renfro glowered at him. Symansky's voice was still too loud. "There's a deck up there. A firepit. Chairs."

"It's February," Symansky shot back. "You're sayin' he'd go up there just to meet up with a girl?"

The boys stared at him like he had just stumbled out of a Neanderthal's cave, spear dragging, completely ignorant of the realities of campus life. Harri made it a point *not* to look at him.

"Any particular girl?" she asked.

The boys didn't answer. Harri waited, listening as Symansky grumbled beside her.

"We're not doin' this, fellas," Symansky said. "Your friend's dead. What girl?"

Renfro answered. "Her name's Hailie."

Harri's eyes widened. "Hailie? Hailie *Kenton*? She was here last night?"

Renfro nodded. "There were a lot of girls here, but yeah, she was one of them."

"And you think Brice was going up to the roof to meet *her*?"

"Yeah. He had his eye on her."

"What broke the party up?" Symansky asked. "And at what time?"

None of the boys answered.

"Approximately," Harri said. "If you had to guess."

Renfro shrugged, keeping his eyes away from hers. "Two, maybe? Three?"

"Two or three?" Symansky's eyes narrowed. "Not at six, when the cop cars pulled up and everybody hightailed it outta here?"

"And when you thought it'd be a good idea to clean up and then pretend you'd all been sleeping when the officers rang the bell?" Harri said.

"And none of you realized Brice wasn't even in the house," Symansky added. "Too drunk. Too high."

Harri watched Renfro grow more and more uncomfortable. "I don't know. Okay? I can't think straight. He was my bud, you know? A good guy. This is just so messed up."

"You got security cameras around the place?" Symansky asked. "Seein' as how the city's such a snake pit?"

Renfro shook his head. "Too Big Brother, Brice always said. He didn't want his privacy invaded."

"Do you know when Hailie Kenton left the party?"

"No idea. It was packed. No one checks who comes and goes."

"And to be clear, you never saw Brice again after about nine? And that didn't worry you."

"We're not his mother," Renfro snapped. "We figured he got lucky. It's his house. He can do what he wants in it."

Harri let that sit for a moment.

"Anything else?" she asked. "Maybe there was somebody here Brice didn't get along with?"

Renfro and the others shook their heads. "Like we said, it was all cool."

"Until it wasn't," Symansky added snidely. "You got an invite list for who was here?"

Renfro stared at Symansky, unblinking. "A what? No. People just come. There must have been a hundred people. And you *still* haven't told us how Brice died."

"We don't know yet." Harri closed her notepad. "But when we do, we'll let you know." She flicked a look toward the stairs. "Which room is Brice's?"

"The big one at the end of the hall."

She stood. "Mind if we take a look? You come with us. You can tell us if something's not how it should be."

Symansky stood too. "These hundred kids. Were they all from Belverton?"

"Most," Renfro said. "There were a few crashers, and then people always bring people."

"Are you friends with Hailie?" Harri asked.

"Nah. I've never said two words to her."

Symansky took in the other young men. "What about you guys? Either of you say more than two words? Maybe she mentioned meeting up with Brice?"

They each shook their heads, but then the skinny kid said, "But she was looking for him at one point. I saw her coming down the stairs. I don't know if she found him, or he found her."

"Okay," Harri said. "Todd, you come with us. You two stay here." She motioned to McAfee. "They stay put until we're through." She checked with Symansky and got a nod.

On their way up the stairs behind Renfro, Symansky's pocket change jingled and jangled.

"How much do you pay for coffee?" Harri asked, curious.

"A buck twenty-five."

She stopped. "Where?"

"Little place on my way to work. Millie's. And she don't do Venmo, or those robot things they got you orderin' burgers from now. It's all people at Millie's. You one of them Starbucks groupies, Foster?"

She smiled. "The coffee at the district suits me fine."

Symansky stopped abruptly. "You're shittin' me, right? That mud?"

"You can get used to anything."

He turned, took her in, an earnest look in his eye. "Gettin' used to messed up crap isn't livin', Harri. Take it from an old guy who knows."

Something in the way he said it told her they weren't talking about coffee anymore.

CHAPTER 7

Renfro walked them down a long carpeted hall to a door at the end. Then turned the knob and stepped aside to let them through first.

"Nobody was in here last night," he said with great conviction. "The rooms are off-limits." He had the good sense to look sheepish when Harri gave him a skeptical look. "Or they're supposed to be."

Symansky sneered. "Right. *Supposed* to be. Neither one of us was born yesterday, kid. One of your drunk buddies already said he saw Kenton comin' down the stairs last night. Let's skip the gloss over, huh? What kinda mood was Collier in last night?"

Renfro took a moment to think. "Same as usual. Pumped up. Saturday night, you know. I can't see him going out in that field."

Harri turned. "Why not?"

"He just wouldn't, that's all. None of us would either."

He slid his hands into his pockets, stared down at the tops of his shoes, shifted his body weight from right to left. Symansky caught the little dance; so did she.

"You got a thing about open spaces, kid?" Symansky asked.

Renfro glanced around the room at his friend's belongings now left behind and meaningless. "The cold, I mean. Who'd want to go outside in the cold?"

Harri looked around the room at clutter and confusion that only a twentysomething college kid could accumulate. Clothes tossed on chairs, beer cans, a rumpled bed, a messy desk. The smell of funk and cologne. Running shoes kicked off into a corner. Posters of half-naked fantasy women and hip-hop stars taped to the walls. The room of a kid who, though he was twenty, hadn't completely made the turn toward adulthood, and now, sadly, never would.

"Does all of this look normal to you?" she asked Renfro, who'd taken a few steps in but looked uncomfortable having done it.

He nodded. "This is how he kept it."

"Who else had access to the house besides those who live here? Seven of you, right? You, Brice, the two downstairs, and the three who're away?"

"Nobody. No. Wait. Anna. The cleaning lady. She comes once a week. Fridays. And there's the maintenance guy—Freddie. Sometimes there's a guy who helps him."

"You have last names?" she asked.

Renfro shrugged. "I don't. Brice . . . did."

Symansky walked over to the bedside table and began opening drawers. "So, just Anna and Freddie and the other guy you don't know, who sometimes helps out the first guy you don't have a last name for?"

"Yeah."

Symansky scowled. "Helpful. Thanks."

Harri approached Brice's desk. His laptop was there, along with an iPad and a tangle of chargers and cords, a couple of textbooks, cans of Red Bull. A lamp. But more importantly, his wallet was sitting there, along with a small ring of keys, and an iPhone. She picked up a pen and flipped the wallet open with it, finding the key card to Brice's Tesla tucked securely inside, along with credit cards and a fair amount of ready cash.

"All this his? Nothing here that shouldn't be?" She looked at Renfro out of the corner of her eye. "Nothing missing that should be here?"

He craned to see. "Everything looks normal."

So, Brice hadn't been robbed, and he hadn't planned on leaving the house, she assumed, or else he'd have taken his wallet and his phone with him. She slid her phone out of her pocket and took a photo of the items as they sat. "Al, you have evidence bags on you?"

"Fresh out."

She didn't want to touch any of the items, needing to leave all that to tech. Instead, she took one last look around, then moved out of the room, followed by Symansky and Renfro, closing the door behind them. "All right. Let's see the roof."

A cautious Renfro led them through the large dated kitchen, through a back door, and pointed them toward a flight of wooden stairs that had likely been used by staff back in the day to move around with silver trays and such, out of sight of the house's well-heeled inhabitants. Not seen or heard, like skittering mice, all but indentured to a life of hard work, attached to the house and the family in it.

The light on the stairs was dim, so Harri pulled a small flashlight out of her bag and shone it up toward the top. "Looks like this also accesses the second floor bedrooms." She turned around to Renfro for confirmation. "Does it?"

"Yeah, the door at the end of the hall leads to these back stairs. It's good for if we want to get to the kitchen for a snack without having to go all the way around front, especially if someone's in there."

"So, Brice might not have been goin' to the roof at all," Symansky said. "He coulda been goin' back to his room."

"I guess. But why would he? The party was down here, and he was hyped for it, like I told you."

Symansky stared him down. "No chance he was sneakin' to his room with two beers and the girl he was makin' a play for, right?"

Renfro just shrugged.

Harri started up the stairs, stopping at the second floor, then turning the knob on the door that separated the back stairs from the bedrooms. The door was unlocked. The stairs led up another flight, so she, Symansky, and Renfro kept going until they reached the roof. Again, this door, like the one below, was unlocked.

Frigid air, crisp and unforgiving, hit them in the face the second they stepped out onto the deck. There was a little sun shining now, but not enough to give off any warmth. It was still February. The trees were still barren. And the gray wasn't so far off that it couldn't return in the snap of a finger.

"Not much up here," Symansky said after he took a good look around. "What do you guys use this for?"

"It's cool most of the year. We sit up here all night sometimes. Talking. Looking at everything below."

"Drinkin'," Symansky muttered. "Smokin'."

Renfro frowned. "Whatever."

Harri noticed a stack of folding chairs flattened and leaning against the side of the house. The surface beneath their feet icy, a thin dusting of fresh snow on top. No footprint tracks, except for theirs. Last night it snowed off and on.

She eased over to the side to look down into the now empty field. The grid search was done. They'd found nothing of Brice's, or else she'd have heard about it. In the distance, maybe a half mile away, was Belverton College. She stepped back. Glanced around. There was nothing more to see up here. If anyone had been on the roof last night, they didn't leave anything behind she or Symansky would be able to see without the benefit of a magnifying glass.

She turned to Renfro. "The music would have been loud. No one downstairs would have heard anything going on up here. And they likely would have missed somebody slipping up those back stairs. Unless they were unfamiliar, right? But you mentioned crashers."

"There are always a few, but it's no big deal. Brice figured the more the merrier."

"So, Brice ran the show is what you're sayin'?" Symansky asked.

Renfro nodded. "The Colliers always *do, don't they?*"

Harri studied the hungover boy for a moment. "What's in this for you and the others?"

Renfro went pensive. A moment passed. Then he smiled. "The sky's the limit."

She watched as the young man's energy began to flag. His eyes narrowed as though he were finding it difficult to take the daylight, despite the fact that it was mostly gray and winter flat. Renfro slumped back against the side of the house, she suspected to keep from falling over.

"I can't see Brice coming up here," Renfro said. "He wasn't one for roughing it."

She looked out over the campus, the field. She didn't know Brice, but she couldn't see any young woman willing to sign up for freezing to death on a roof for a beer and the pleasure of his company.

"What do you think, Al?"

"I say we get off this roof. There's nothin' to break the wind up here."

McAfee met them in the kitchen.

"We got a couple of guys up front wanting to talk to the detectives in charge," he said. "One says he's the president of the college, the other works for the Collier family."

"All right. We'll talk to them," Harri said. "Take Todd through to the others. Put them in the dining room. We'll swing back and talk to them again. Oh, and get tech up to the big room upstairs to grab Collier's personal effects—phone, wallet, keys, his computer."

McAfee nodded, then escorted Renfro out to rejoin his housemates. Harri and Symansky stood for a moment—the calm before what came next. Then they strode out into the living room to find two white men standing by the couch. The first, a thin, bespectacled man who looked to be about fifty, who'd obviously dressed in a hurry in a pullover sweater and brown corduroys; the second, a nattily dressed man who could have been anywhere between forty and sixty, dressed in a black suit, tie, and overcoat.

The first man Harri pegged as the academic, though he seemed a little young for the job. Weren't university presidents usually at least a hundred? The flustered man appeared to be a man in crisis. His jumpy eyes darted around the room as if he expected something to pounce on him. The worry lines on his face were those of a man used to struggling with problems, but not this kind, not problems that ended in death. Every movement he made looked awkward, like he didn't know what to do with his hands or legs, like he was a strange man in a foreign land far away from the place he felt most comfortable—a quiet office in an ivory tower, perhaps, or a tucked-away library carrel filled with dusty books.

She could almost hear his frantic mind wrestle with his current reality. He had a dead student. There would be factions to deal with—alumni, the student body, faculty, media, her and Symansky. This was a PR nightmare for Belverton, potentially, and the weight of it showed through in his pained expression, in the tightness in his bony shoulders.

The other man was different. Calmer, almost serene in his composure, she noticed, like a tranquil lake—still and placid. The black suit looked tailored and expensive, the coat too. Everything fit him just so.

He wasn't tall or short, not large or small. His eyes were dark and deep set, and it appeared they didn't miss a single thing in the room. He worked for the Collier family, he had told the PO. Lawyer, maybe? Harri took a breath, noting again the contrast between the two—one frazzled administrator and the enigma in a suit.

The anxious man spoke first. "I'm William Younger, president of Belverton. Who's in charge here, please?"

Harri imagined that in his office under normal circumstances, William Younger's deep voice would have carried an air of authority and erudition. Here, now, with Brice Collier on his way to the medical examiner's office, he just sounded desperate.

"That'd be us," Symansky offered indelicately. "Seein' as we're the ones standin' here with badges on. I'm Detective Symansky. This is Detective Foster."

She heard the exchange but was far more interested in the man in the suit.

"And you are?" she asked him, her eyes steady, unblinking.

"Lange. I'm here for Sebastian Collier."

"*Here for.* Are you his lawyer?"

The corners of the man's mouth turned up, but nothing changed in his eyes. It wasn't a smile. Not even close. Harri wasn't quite sure what it was, besides odd.

"I'm no lawyer."

She waited, but he did not elaborate. For a moment there was only silence.

"How did this happen? He was found outside? Was he assaulted? Another robbery?" Younger ran a hand through his graying hair, then turned around in a slow circle, taking the room in as though they might have scrawled the answers to his questions on the walls. "This neighborhood has—"

Symansky stopped him there. "Yeah, yeah, crime's out of control. We already heard about it from the drunk kid in the other room. Look, before we start pointin' fingers, how's about you let us at least *start* to do our jobs, huh?"

"Right now, it's a death investigation," Harri said. "We'll know more once the autopsy's complete." She turned back to Lange. "Will Mr. Collier be available to ID the body?"

"I'm afraid not. Mr. Collier is in Geneva. He has asked that I handle any arrangements for Master Brice."

Master Brice. "Is Brice's mother also in Geneva?"

The nonsmile was back.

"There's no mother in the picture."

"What's that mean?" Symansky asked.

Lange's head made the slightest of shifts, his bottomless eyes landing on Symansky. "She is, unfortunately, deceased. I will need to speak with Master Brice's roommates."

"Why?" Harri asked.

"Mr. Collier expects it."

Symansky scoffed. "Not gonna happen. You're no lawyer. You said so yourself. More important, not *their* lawyer. We get 'em first." He turned to Younger. "You know about the party here last night?"

"This is private property. Off campus. I have no authority to—"

Symansky held a hand up. "Stop. We're not the ones who're gonna hold your feet to the fire on that. And it might not be your property, but they're *your* students. Somebody's kids." He cocked a thumb toward Lange. "Collier's for one. That's why *he's* here."

"I will need positive identification," Lange said. "Not just visual."

"And Brice's father doesn't want to do that himself?" Harri asked.

"I've been authorized—"

"Yeah, you said," Symansky interrupted.

Harri studied the man in black, unsure what to make of him. "Sebastian Collier must be a very busy man."

"He's a very *important* man."

"But his son has died," she said pointedly.

Lange said nothing. She wondered why.

"Did you know the kid?" Symansky asked Lange.

"I've worked for the Collier family for many years. I'm well acquainted with Master Brice."

There was a finality to the statement that told her Lange would not offer more. She turned to look at Younger.

"Did Brice have any issues at school? Disciplinary problems?"

"Not at all."

"No psychological stuff? Depression?" Symansky asked. "Bad grades he was dealin' with?"

Younger shook his head, adamant. "Never. Brice Collier was one of our best and brightest."

Harri looked over at Lange again, still trying to get a sense of him, and still failing. And the family dynamic troubled her. Deceased mother. Distant father? Wealthy heir left on his own in a mansion at the edge of a college his family held sway over. She could see how excess and privilege might have played out, but that didn't mean it had. And the entire thing felt more than a little incestuous.

"So, Mr. Collier will *not* be returning from Geneva to mourn his son?"

She was unable to let it go. This simply didn't make sense. What parent wouldn't drop anything and everything for this?

Lange paused. "I will deliver his son to him. Meanwhile, I am to keep him apprised of all developments. Every detail will be relayed."

"That's how billionaires do it, is it?" Symansky asked.

The half smile was back, but nothing more was given. Harri took another full sweep of the careful man. "Who called you, Mr. Lange? To tell you about Brice?"

"I did," Younger offered forcefully. "He's on Brice's contact list."

Symansky asked, "And who called *you*?"

"The president's residence is just across the way. I got a call from campus security that Brice had been found dead."

"What time was that?" Harri asked.

"Just before seven. I notified Lange right away. We set up a virtual meeting with Sebastian. He's devastated."

Harri checked her watch. "It's almost eleven. You're just now coming over?"

"There was a lot to discuss. Arrangements to be made. I also needed to inform our support staff. There will be inquiries. Statements have to be distributed. Parents notified. Belverton has a reputation to uphold."

Symansky scoffed. "And you had to make sure the guy with his name on half your buildings was taken care of first, right?"

Harri looked over at Lange and found him watching her. "Do you have a business card, Mr. Lange? So we can reach you when it's time to ID Brice and make those arrangements."

He reached into his tailored pocket and pulled out a white card with bold black writing on it and handed it to her. All that was on it was the name Lange and a local telephone number. The paper was heavy and expensive.

"And it's just Lange," he said, "no Mr."

She handed him one of her city-issued cards in exchange, much lighter in comparison, then slipped his between the pages of her notepad. "We'll be in touch."

Younger balked. "Wait. I need information. I have to know what's going on. Can I at least call this a random attack that had nothing to do with Belverton?"

"I wouldn't," she said. "We don't know what this is yet."

"So, that's what you tell whoever you have to tell," Symansky said gruffly. "You don't know squat. Period."

Younger's spine stiffened. "You don't appreciate the complexity of this situation, obviously."

"When we have more, we'll share it." Harri turned to look for McAfee, then motioned him over. "This officer will show you out."

"I'm staying," Lange said. "I'm Mr. Collier's eyes and ears."

"Mr. Collier's eyes and ears are in Geneva," Symansky said. "Yours we don't need."

Harri held her arm out, gestured toward the door. "When we have something to report, we'll make sure you're informed. Until then—"

Younger bristled but followed McAfee. Lange lingered a second longer, then slowly buttoned his coat. "You have my number. I have yours. But know that Sebastian Collier isn't a patient man."

Lange followed Younger out, leaving her and Symansky standing there.

"Well?" she said finally.

"Younger's scared out of his boots. Dead kid on his campus? They'll be clawin' at his skivvies like nobody's business. And John Wick there needs to work on his people skills. What'd *you* get?"

"The two of them seemed kind of chummy, didn't they? He calls Lange before he even comes over to check anything out? Then they both call Sebastian Collier to arrange things, and all that takes four hours? Ritter calls the body in a little after six. The first squad pulls up minutes later. The four-hour gap tells me Brice isn't the priority here."

"Paulsen didn't mention runnin' into campus security," Symansky said. "Neither did those girls."

"I didn't see them outside when we pulled up either," she said. "Seems odd they wouldn't be all over this."

She glanced over at the door to the dining room, where Renfro and the others were sobering up. "Let's take another pass at them, then we figure that out."

Symansky sighed. "All right, but this time, I'm scarin' *somebody* straight."

CHAPTER 8

Harri sat in her idling car in the police lot, eyes shut, her breath visible as warm exhalation met the winter nip. The day had been long, filled with interviews at Hardwicke House, reports to complete, and a possible media onslaught to prepare for . . . again. It'd been less than a month since three aldermen had been murdered, a case that had whipped the city into a frenzy. Now a billionaire's son had been found dead. She could just imagine the headlines and the public interest that would kick up.

She stared out the windshield, past the melting ice as cops came and went . . . off shift, on shift. Tough job. Tough people doing it. Most the right way and for the right reasons. The unease she felt had an origin. She couldn't imagine ever not feeling uneasy sitting in an idling car here, or anywhere, since G's death. The flashes of disjointed memory it evoked were just too painful to endure.

How long had Glynnis idled in the lot before she raised her gun to her head and pulled the trigger? Had she wrestled with her decision? Had she thought about reaching out to Harri, to anyone? If so, what had stopped her? None of it sounded like G. Something wasn't right. She couldn't have. She wouldn't have.

Harri pulled the crumpled IAD report out of her bag and held it in her hand. It was useless, nothing, final. Up to her, she thought. She'd have to be G's backup one last time.

Harri stuffed the report in her pocket and grabbed the notepad she'd zipped into a side compartment of her bag, the one she'd started for him.

After flipping the cover open, she read through her notes, the times and dates she'd had contact with the voice, what he'd said, how long the calls lasted. She'd scribbled down the various numbers he'd called her from, numbers she couldn't trace. It was everything IAD had thrown back in her face.

There wasn't enough information yet. That's why she'd gone to IAD, why she'd counted on their help. He knew her. He knew G. How?

The dread that sat in the hollows of her gut whispered *cop*. He was one of them, maybe. He knew too much not to be at least familiar with the job, with how it all went.

So now what? She had an envelope of photos, a threat, a list of random numbers, a voice, and the name of a small-time drug dealer nobody cared about.

Harri squeezed her eyes shut. Just for a moment. Sitting silently in the cold car, firmly in the in-between that separated now and what she would do next.

"I don't know what to do," she whispered finally, sliding a look toward the passenger seat as though Glynnis might be sitting there with the answer. "G? I don't know what to do."

Of course, there was no answer. There was no one in the passenger seat. There wasn't even that otherworldly feeling that she wasn't alone. She felt alone. The cold and quiet hammered the feeling home. It was her, or no one. It was now, or never.

"Right," she muttered finally. "Through it."

It's what G had always said. *The only way to it is through it.*

She picked up her phone, scrolled for the familiar number, her thumb hovering over the screen when she came to it. She had absolutely no right to make the call. He would have every right to hang up or not answer, and she couldn't blame him. But she wasn't doing this for her. She drew in a breath and tapped the green button, her heart beating wildly.

"Hey," she said when he answered. "I need your help."

———

It would have been better to meet at a coffee shop, a diner, or even a car pulled to the side of the road, but she was the one who needed the help and the time she didn't deserve, so she rang the bell and waited for Detective Colman Sylvester to open the door to his North Side brownstone. A part of her dreaded the door opening, while another part couldn't wait. The door opened after only one tentative press of the bell. And there he stood, dark, clean shaven, fit, brown inquisitive eyes taking a survey of her on the stoop.

He was a cop who'd known G. He'd worked with them both at the same district for a time before transferring out to a better spot, one with promotion prospects. And then there'd been the other thing between them that G's death cut short. Harri had walked away with little explanation, not that she could have given a good one, then or now. All she knew then was that she couldn't do it. She couldn't open herself up to losing another person out of her life. It was cowardice, self-protection, she knew it. Yet here she was, hat in hand at the door she'd run out of months ago.

"Sly," she said. "Thanks for seeing me."

For a moment they stood staring at each other, then he stepped aside to let her in. "I made chili, if you're hungry."

The offer of dinner felt like a kick to her chest. She wasn't sure what to say. She couldn't get her feet to move.

"You going to stand out there in the cold, or come in? I'm letting the heat out."

She glanced down at the envelope in her hand, the one with G's photos inside. Despite the cold, it seemed to burn through her gloves and singe her fingertips. She wasn't even sure what she was doing here; it was only that this was the first place she thought to come when she didn't know what else to do. She stepped inside. Sly locked the door behind her. The house smelled of chili powder and cumin, spicy and warm.

"Get out of that wet coat. Want a drink?"

"No, thank you. I'm fine."

He looked her over. "Just got off?"

She nodded. "Long day."

She took her coat off, and Sly hung it in the closet. He'd done away with the beard and moustache. His hair was a little grayer, but his smile and his eyes were the same as she remembered. She wasn't quite sure how to start. There was a flood of things she could say, and needed to say, if she allowed herself to let it all go. But she couldn't. There was just too much of it. A deluge would surely break her.

He smiled. "Hot chocolate?"

She smiled back. He remembered she liked it. "That'd be nice. Thank you."

His eyes dropped from her face to the envelope in her hand. She'd given him just the basics over the phone. "That it?"

She handed it to him. "This started it. He slipped it into G's mail-box for her family to find."

"Follow me back. We'll run through it."

They headed back down a long carpeted hallway toward the kitchen. She followed solemnly past his barely lit living room and dining room, both decorated artfully with African paintings of beautiful Black people and wall tapestries full of color. She remembered his collection of djembes, the small West African drums he collected. Underneath the aroma of the simmering chili, there were subtle notes of African wood, iroko and bubinga. Sly's was a home that was lived in. It was full, alive, a sheltering place. The familiar kitchen gleamed in stainless steel and color just as she recalled it. Almost instantly, she could feel herself become calm and settled.

This was the room where Sly had once told her he found the most peace after a long day of sifting through death and blood. A quiet place was necessary, he had told her, when each act of depravity, each violent theft of life, chipped away at your armor and threatened to leave you exposed and battered, with very little faith in humanity. Sly's kitchen, his home were his protection.

What did it mean, then, that her own house was little more than a shell? And what did it mean that Glynnis had the home, the husband, the kids, and that still hadn't been enough?

"Can I help with anything?"

"I'm good. Sit. Hot cocoa coming up."

He went about getting the kettle on, then pulling the chocolate tin out of the cupboard. Sly didn't do instant anything. He took the time to get things right.

"How've you been, otherwise?"

Harri eyed his table. The last time she'd sat at it, she and Sly had a painful conversation. The memory of it still saddened her.

She managed a wan smile. "How've I been." She repeated it slowly, not knowing how to answer.

"Should be an easy answer, Harri."

"Should it?"

When he joined her at the table minutes later, the mug of hot chocolate he placed in front of her had whipped cream, chocolate sprinkles, and a cherry on top. It was almost too pretty to drink. She looked up to find him watching her.

"Yeah," he said, "it should."

She curled off a bit of whipped cream on the tip of her finger and slipped it into her mouth. "I'm okay, Sly."

He looked skeptical but left it there, replacing the worried look with a smile. "Don't know how all that's going to mix with chili, but we'll see."

He reached for the envelope he'd tossed on the table and opened it, sliding two photographs out. She could tell he immediately registered their implication and watched as his entire face changed.

"Now I know these have *got* to be a lie. Thompson didn't even jaywalk." He turned the photos over and back again, but there was no secret explanation to be found. "And IAD tossed these back?"

She dug into her pocket for the report and handed it to him in a ball. "I thought G might have said something to you? Or maybe there was a slight chance you recognized the guy she's with? Or maybe Stern or Oglesby might know something? I can ask them next. I'm clutching at straws I've already clutched at."

"A million times, you know that," he said. "Who saw what, who knew what. If G seemed off or stressed about something. We didn't miss anything because there was nothing there for us to miss."

"Things don't just come out of nowhere, definitely not something like this."

"Yeah, they do. You've seen it. You're living your life and shit flies in and hits you in the face all the time. There's nothing you can plan for to help you avoid it either. Out of nowhere and you're fucked until you find a way to get unfucked." He studied the photos. Held them up close to his face for a better look. "I've never seen this guy, but he looks like a goon. Not a boss. Somebody the boss sends."

"Sends for *what* is the question," she said.

She took a sip from her mug and paused while the warm chocolate trickled down her throat.

"That's in back of the Oval," she said. "It took me a while to recognize it. It's closed now. Has been for years. The back of the place is all weeds and garbage and empty lot. I walked it. You couldn't pick a better place to meet without anyone seeing. I didn't spot any security cameras, but there were plenty of places to lay in wait. *Somebody* took those photos."

"The Oval? That old skating rink?"

She nodded. "The rink was on the ground floor, offices and storage areas were above it. Everything's boarded up now, sort of, and the building's crumbling in on itself. Prime candidate for demolition if the city ever gets around to it."

Sly scoffed. "They won't get to it until we pull a body out of there. Anything significant about the spot?"

She shook her head. "G never mentioned it."

"Now whoever's calling you thinks he can squeeze you?" He chuckled. "I don't know who *he* is, but he sure as *hell* don't know who *you* are."

"He called me Harri. He knew G's husband would come to me. He knows where I live. He knows enough."

"But your hands are tied," he said, "unless he makes a move you can't ignore."

"Every move I make going forward will be off book," she said. "Doing nothing is not an option."

Sly put the photos down, pushed them toward the center of the table. He'd seen enough. "You've already decided."

"I don't have much of a choice, do I?"

"This guy could be a CI."

She shook her head. "G didn't have one."

"As far as you know."

She shot him a look, defensive, but he was right. There was, maybe, a lot she didn't know about her former partner.

"Look, I know a guy who's into photographs and digital stuff. I trust him. I can show him these if you want. Maybe he can tell us if they're real or fake."

Harri reached out and turned the photos over, not wanting to see them anymore. "G wasn't *this*, Sly."

Sly got up for the chili. "I know. We're not seeing what we think we're seeing."

He brought two bowls of chili back along with two Cokes and a pan of jalapeño corn bread. He pushed a warm bowl of chili in front of her. "It's spicy."

"I like spicy."

He dug a spoon into his bowl and paused a moment with the spoon to his mouth. "I know."

She looked down at her spoon but didn't pick it up. "I'm sorry for how I left things. It wasn't you. It was . . . everything else."

"You took another hit. I got it. I'm a big boy. I knew what it was. I know what you need to do. I'm choosing to play the long game."

She wasn't sure she understood what he meant and was still parsing it out when he smiled and spoke again.

"Breathe, Harri."

She closed her eyes for a moment, the aroma of the chili and the chocolate banishing temporarily the weight of the tasks ahead of her. Sly's long game, Collier's autopsy in the morning. The voice. It had startled her when he'd called her Harri instead of Harriet or Detective Foster. He was too familiar, too close. That made things worse somehow. When she opened her eyes again, Sly was still watching. She spooned chili into her mouth.

"How is it?" he asked.

"It could use some salt."

He chuckled. "Woman, you lie."

She stared at him, grateful for the safe space, conceding that she missed having it even though she was still not in a place that would allow her to live in it.

She grinned. "It's perfect. Thanks."

There was a moment of silence between them, not awkward, safe, like the kitchen, like the house.

"Door's always open," he said.

"Thanks for that too."

CHAPTER 9

Harri was at her desk at eight as the team trickled in, everyone with bakery bags and paper cups of real coffee to get their motors running, smelling of cold and wind and ice. She nodded her morning greeting to Kelley, Bigelow, Symansky. No Lonergan yet, for whom lately clock-in time was merely a suggestion. There were also times when he slipped away in the middle of a shift without a heads-up. Curious, but not really her business.

She gave the struggling plant on her desk a quick look. She'd rescued the half-dead thing from the trash bin, and it pleased her now to see more green leaves sprouting.

She pressed a finger to the soil and found it a little dry, so she poured in some water from a Styrofoam cup, then turned the small pot around so Polly faced the grimy windows from a fresh side.

A white bag dropped onto her desk. Harri jumped. *"Jesus."*

Detective Vera Li stood there in a beanie and a damp navy peacoat. Ready for the day, her dark, keen eyes having no doubt scanned the room and everybody in it.

"Crullers from Mason's," she announced.

Vera dropped her battered backpack on her desk, then plopped down in her squeaky chair, dropping a similar bag in front of her.

"The line was halfway out the door, but they're worth it."

"What's the occasion? It's not my birthday."

Harri eyed the bag in front of her, then the one in front of Vera, grease splotching the sides of both. "Or yours."

Vera's brow furrowed, skeptical. "You know my birthday?"

"March second. You want the year?"

Vera lifted her pack, opened her bottom drawer, shoved it in. "Should I be afraid?"

Harri shrugged, offered a small smile. "I can't tell you what to be."

They reached into their bags at the same time, Harri pulling out two crullers, Vera two raspberry Danish; both licked sticky icing from their respective fingers.

"Heard I missed some action yesterday," Vera said. "A Collier. Accident, or something we have to suit up for?"

"Autopsy's underway. We'll know soon."

"Not soon enough for the reporters downstairs. I passed four of them on my way up. The Collier name has them all stoked up. What do we have so far?"

Harri filled Vera in on the details. The girls who'd stumbled onto the body, the drunken boys, the search of Brice's room, the roof, Younger and Lange.

"Four hours?" Vera said. "Wow."

"That's the most interesting bit," Harri said. "But Younger didn't lie about campus security. Officer Robinson clocked them on scene at ten to seven. The guard, Dillard Stone, said he saw the police lights while he was doing his last sweep through. He nearly lost his dinner, Robinson said, when he found out there was a body lying out in that field. Robinson watched as he called Younger to break the news that the girls had ID'd Brice Collier. When Stone hung up, he left. Never came back."

"You can see why, right? Campus *security*, and a kid dies right under your nose? There's going to be a lot of finger-pointing."

Harri sighed. "And so it begins."

Vera stared across the desk at her. "And the other thing? Where are we with that?"

Harri told her about the report and the copies of the photos she shared with Sly. The underlying complexity of their history, she held back, not ready to open herself up quite that much. She'd gone home after the chili to go through it all again, not getting a lot of sleep. She'd even pulled out her old notes to go over the cases she and G had worked before her death, thinking there could be something in them that explained what happened, but she discovered no correlation. Harri copped to the extracurricular work, but not the loss of rest. "Griffin thinks he's done, played out."

Vera shook her head. "No. He's having too much fun twisting you."

Harri pushed the bag away from her. "Sure feels that way."

"IAD," Vera groused. "There when you don't want them, never there when you do. Doesn't matter. We find out who he is. We stop him." She bit into her Danish, squishing raspberry jam. "You and Al, though, huh? Did he do bad cop?"

Harri looked over at Symansky leaning back in his chair with a paper coffee cup in his hand, the morning paper in his lap.

"No comment."

Vera grinned. "That's a yes."

The door to Griffin's office opened, and the blond woodchipper walked out, a somber look on her face. Harri didn't have to be a detective to know bad news was coming.

"A minute of your time," Griffin said, her hands on her hips, her face grim. "Lonergan's taking some personal time. His daughter was just diagnosed with stage-two cancer."

The room went quiet.

"Naturally, he's needed there, not here, so we'll work around him until he's back." Griffin appeared to pull herself in, keep it unemotional. "No further details. Cancer flippin' *sucks*. Back to work."

She turned and went back into her office, slamming the door behind her.

The team sat stunned for a moment.

"Damn it," Bigelow muttered. "*Cancer.* Lonergan's not my cup of tea, but even I wouldn't wish a sick kid on him."

"I think we can all agree on that," Vera said.

Harri stared at her half-eaten cruller. "Stage two."

Harri didn't care for Lonergan on a personal level. He was gruff and regressive and felt a certain way about working with women and specifically women of color—that meant her and Vera—and it made for often uncomfortable encounters. But Bigelow was right, she thought, none of them would wish a sick child on him or anyone.

Vera ran her hands through her hair. "Jesus, when does life ever stop kicking you in the teeth, huh?"

Harri assumed the question was rhetorical and her answer obvious, but she gave it all the same. "Never."

CHAPTER 10

Harri and Vera walked into the medical examiner's office at Harrison and Leavitt a little after noon. The building always felt cold to Harri, even though in reality it was likely no colder or warmer than any other county building. Still, voices always seemed to lower here, and conversations, at least those in the public areas, were often spoken in hushed tones. The dead, those taken violently, naturally, or from unknown causes, old and young, Black or white or brown, were just halls and floors away, property of the county until Grant and her staff released them to those they'd left behind.

Harri hated the place. She hated the cold. She hated walking in to view yet another body on a table, to witness someone else's tragedy, to see what was left after the worst had happened. No one should see their child on an ME's table as she had done. That's when her hate for the place started.

There had been little talk in the car on the ride over. What was there to say? Lonergan's Katie was just sixteen. She thought of Lonergan and how powerless he must feel. He could catch a killer, solve a case, but he couldn't arrest leukemia, couldn't lock it up. She knew firsthand that there was nothing more frightening than being powerless to protect the ones you loved. She couldn't speak for Vera, but for Harri, the heavy world now felt even heavier than it had before.

The first face they saw when they entered the building was that of Dr. Grant's new assistant, Tybo Sawyer, a Black woman in her late thirties, who was as short and stout as the proverbial teapot, but with an encyclopedic brain and the efficiency of a mainframe computer. Grant's assistants came and went as regularly as CTA trains on the Blue Line. Harri suspected it had a lot to do with Grant's acerbic personality and exacting standards, but Grant hadn't yet bounced Tybo, who appeared to be the only one in a long line of predecessors who could keep up with Grant's grueling schedule and often caustic idiosyncrasies.

In previous encounters, Tybo hadn't proven herself to be a woman of great humor. She was efficient, capable, highly organized, and focused, polite, direct, not chatty. Like Grant, only more compact.

Tybo didn't appear to require friendly words or positive affirmation, two things no one rational should ever expect to get from Dr. Olivia Grant.

But they were used to seeing Tybo inside the autopsy room preparing instruments, taking notes, assisting, not out here in the lobby, apparently waiting for them.

"Good afternoon, Detectives. You're here about the Collier autopsy. Dr. Grant would like to see you in her office instead of the autopsy suite. Follow me, please."

There was no use asking questions Tybo wouldn't answer, and so they followed her to the elevator and got deposited at Grant's door like a couple of FedEx packages. Harri watched as Tybo, her task complete, power walked down the hall to a destination unknown.

"She went to recharge her batteries," Vera whispered. "There's probably a little Tybo closet around the corner where she plugs in her circuits."

"Nothing wrong with being all business," Harri said.

Vera sighed. "The fact that you just said that tells me I've got a lot of work to do."

Harri raised her fist to knock at the door but didn't get the chance. "I hear you two whispering out there. Get in here," Grant called out.

They stepped inside a small, cramped county office to find Dr. Grant in her scrubs and lab coat, sitting behind a cluttered desk, her palms flat against two short stacks of file folders. It was an odd way to sit, Harri thought, Grant with her back straight, left hand on a stack, right one on a stack.

"Li. You're back. Good. Both of you. Sit."

They sat in two cheap office chairs crafted of molded plastic, each facing Grant's desk. The desk was neat, just the stacks, a short lineup of ballpoint pens, a full inbox, and a framed photo of Grant and a woman about her age. It wasn't the apparent closeness that struck Harri, but the smile on Grant's face. A real smile, not the faking it kind, she noted. It took her a moment to process it, the smile, not the other woman. Harri realized then that she didn't know a thing about Grant outside her job and efficiency. It hadn't even occurred to her to ask. Vera's eyes had apparently taken the same sweep.

"Sister?" Vera asked smiling.

Grant stared at her.

"Girlfriend, then," Vera said. "Pretty."

Grant's eyes narrowed. "Wife. *Beautiful.* Can we move on now, Nancy Drew?"

Vera smiled. "Ready when you are, Dr. Grant."

They waited for an explanation about the change in venue. Nothing on Grant's face gave anything away. There was no stress there, no sign of agitation, only the woman with her hands on the files. Harri felt as though she'd been called into the principal's office for some egregious offense, the secret to which could be found in one of the folders. Would she be asked to pick one, she wondered?

"The autopsy's complete." Grant raised her right hand, then dropped it down again. "Collier's."

Harri raised her hand, confused. "Excuse me. Sorry. What are we doing?"

Vera cocked a thumb toward her partner. "What she said."

Harri looked around and found the room wanting. It was no bigger than a walk-in wardrobe, with two narrow windows that didn't open and a bright institutional light recessed into drop-down ceiling tiles stained from an old water leak.

Vera grinned. "Not that this isn't lovely."

"Cut the cute, Li," Grant said. "You know as well as I do I work for the county, and we're here because I just had to bounce a hit man out of the building. I've locked the autopsy room to keep him away from Collier's body."

Harri stared at Grant. "What did you just say?"

Vera's mouth hung open. "Hit man? What hit—"

"Lange," Harri interrupted.

"Ding. Ding. Ding. Foster gets it in one. A heads-up would have been nice."

"He came to identify Brice Collier," Harri said.

"Which he did. He even brought in a copy of the boy's fingerprints to match the ones we'd taken. ID's been confirmed."

"He had his prints on file?" Harri asked.

"In the event of kidnapping," Grant said. "I suppose rich people have to worry about that sort of thing."

"Yeah, can we get back to the hit man?" Vera said. "Is he really?"

"If he isn't, he'll do until one comes along," Grant said, expression deadpan. "He's got eyes like a snake. I don't trust him. He insisted, forcefully, on having the body released today. Something about flying it to Switzerland for the family. The insistence got him tossed out. The snake eyes compelled me to lock the room and the body." Grant looked from one cop to the other. "I release the body on *my* schedule, not his. When I'm sure there's nothing more it can tell us, and that *you* won't need it."

Neither detective responded, knowing nothing good could come of it.

Grant leaned back, then raised her left palm off the files. "I'll get to these in a minute." She picked up the top folder on her right. "Collier first."

Harri slid her notepad out of her bag, poised the small pen over a fresh page, and waited for Grant.

"Simplifying the science, Brice Collier died of fatal ethanol intoxication, meaning he consumed far more alcohol than his body could tolerate. Otherwise, he was a healthy young man in peak condition. Everything new and shiny. No underlying illnesses. Nothing he would have needed to worry about for quite a while."

"Accidental, then?" Harri said. "He partied, wandered outside, and then collapsed in the snow."

Grant stared at her. "Maybe, maybe not."

Vera leaned forward. "Why maybe not?"

Grant pulled an autopsy photo out of the folder and handed it across the desk to Harri. "Two fresh bruises at the back of his neck along both scapulae. They look like pressure marks from thumbs, as though someone held him down. Bruises in front along the collarbones to correspond. I didn't see them out in the field. Conditions weren't good." She handed over another image. "And this. Found in his throat. Nylon fibers. Not many. It's possible he inhaled them. It doesn't appear he was punched, kicked, or otherwise manhandled."

Harri stared down at the bruises, then handed the photo along to Vera before taking up the photo of the fibers.

"Someone forced alcohol down his throat, then held his mouth shut so he couldn't evacuate it." Harri placed her hand over her mouth, then pulled it away. "The fibers could be from a glove, maybe?"

Grant nodded. "Perhaps. All I can say for sure is that someone left bruises consistent with constraint."

Vera frowned, then handed the photo back to Grant. "Which, with the fibers, would indicate *force*."

Grant said, "The bruises were hours old, not days old. Safe bet."

"You haven't mentioned prints," Harri said, realizing the futility of getting Grant to form an opinion. "That means there weren't any."

"Not a one."

"*None*," Vera said. "As in *zero* prints? How's that even possible?"

"That's a *you* question," Grant offered, "not a *me* question."

"Drunk. No shirt. No prints. Bruises. Party in the house." Harri ticked off the details.

Vera picked up where she left off. "College kid. Stupid. Keg challenge? A dare? Some kind of initiation?"

"He was a junior. Too old to be initiated into anything, or am I wrong? And Hardwicke's not a frat," Harri said.

"Who says he staggered from the *house*?" Vera said. "He was at a party. Doesn't mean he stayed there. He could have left, gotten into something, and was on his way back when he got as far as the field."

"Or somebody dumped him there and left him," Harri said.

Vera looked over at her partner. "Leaving a clean crime scene? We're not talking kids, then, are we?"

"The wrong kind of kids, maybe. Either way, it would be a deliberate act. Planned, not random. It would mean—"

Vera jumped in. "Murder."

"Which brings me to this," Grant said, plucking the top folder off the stack on her left.

Again, she handed over autopsy photos, this time of a young man about Collier's age, only thinner, with dark hair instead of light, brown eyes instead of blue, and a deep cleft in his chin.

"This has happened before. Thirty years ago. Same field. Same cause of death. Minus the bruises. Michael James Paget."

"Thirty?" Vera said, shocked.

They stared at the new photographs, handing them back and forth between them.

"When I entered Collier's findings, Paget's similar details popped up. Hardwicke House. Field. Intoxication. His death was classified as accidental. Nothing to turn over to your people."

"So, wait," Vera said. "Two kids. Same field. *Thirty* years apart. Same cause of death. One ruled an accident, the other you think might not be?"

"Yes. But I'd be an idiot not to see a connection."

"No bruises. Fully clothed?" Harri asked. "Intoxicated."

Grant nodded. "Paget was found in his shirt, which he'd vomited all over."

"Was the type of alcohol consistent in both cases?" Harri asked.

"No, actually. Whiskey for Paget. And cigar particles in the lungs."

"Whiskey and cigars? How old was he?" Vera asked.

"Eighteen."

Harri's eyes bore into Grant's. "Paget was a student at Belverton College, wasn't he?"

"He was a freshman."

"We came about one body," Vera said, "and you've given us *two*?"

Grant stood. "I've given you a place to start, and I've given you context. Don't shoot the messenger. You two will want to see Collier for yourselves, I take it?"

They stood too. Harri nodded, then slipped her notepad into her pocket; she was ready to view the body. It was always better to see for yourself, she reasoned, even if the moment was difficult and unpleasant.

"You know most cops I deal with don't step a foot in my autopsy suite. They wait for my final report and work from that. They claim it's because they're pressed for time, busy with other things. BS. They're scared. Big, tough guys and gals scared of the blood and the steel and the bone saw. One actually came in, took one look at the body, and ran out the room. I had another faint dead away on my floor."

Vera grimaced. "That's embarrassing. Who was it?"

Grant turned to Vera, a glint in her eye. "My lips are sealed." She shifted a more sober gaze at Harri. "Thorough by nature, or something else? I haven't decided."

Vera said nothing. Harri said nothing, but she could feel the small room get smaller, closer, warmer, though none of it showed on her face. The room was silent, except for the sound of street traffic outside and activity down the hall.

"We'll need the reports on Collier and Paget sent right away," Vera said sternly, hoping to cut the tension and divert Grant's attention away from her uncomfortable partner. "In addition to us seeing the bruises close up. Since we're grown women cops, not chickenshits."

"Of course," Grant said. "Whatever you need."

Harri's jaw clenched while she counted to ten in her head. "I promise I won't faint on your floor."

Their eyes held for a time. Grant had seen Harri at her lowest point, standing gutted at her son's body, and she feared the ME knew more about her than she wanted her to. Vulnerable, unmasked, is how she felt, the impulse to push Grant away and retreat nearly uncontrollable. But she stood there, emotionless, determined not to give Grant a single thing more than her badge required.

"No, you won't," Grant replied. "But there are other ways to fall."

CHAPTER 11

When they got back to the car an hour later, neither Harri nor Vera said a word. They just sat watching the lot, the cars, and the mounds of dirty snow a plow had piled up along the fringes.

"February's an ugly month," Vera said finally.

Harri sighed. "Always is."

It felt to Harri like spring would never come. Everything was covered in rock salt and city soot. The mounds of snow everywhere were covered in black grime spit up from car and bus tires and threads of dog pee. Even the people who raced from here to there—to buses, to trains, to cars, to work, to church, to the store—were gray and colorless. Like mole people tunneling through a bombed-out hellscape, having forgotten how the sun felt or what fresh air smelled like.

"Definitely bruises," Harri said. "And we don't know enough to say who put them there."

"Back to Hardwicke House?"

Harri started the car. "Yep. Call Al. Maybe we can double up, interview everybody again. Whoever's free, ask them if they can help?"

Vera shot Harri a look out of the corner of her eye. "You good?"

After a moment's hesitation, she answered, "Yeah. Fine."

Kelley and Bigelow met them in front of Hardwicke House. Four stern-looking detectives huddled on the quiet street. It was a sight Harri imagined the neighborhood wasn't used to.

The cop cars were gone, the police tape, too, but reporters were still swarming around the house, a few standing at the edge of the field in front of news cameras shouldered by rumpled operators who looked as though they'd been in the game for decades. Brice Collier and his billionaire father were a hot story, at least until the next big thing overtook it.

"They see us," Vera said.

Harri squinted over at the reporters, making brief eye contact with a couple she recognized. "Part of the job."

"Doesn't mean I have to like it. No *comment*." Vera cleared her throat, repeated it, this time in a deeper voice. "*No* comment."

Harri looked over at her quizzically.

"I'm practicing."

Harri glanced over at Kelley and Bigelow. The two made an odd duo standing next to each other, she thought. Kelley, runner slim, tall, bespectacled, light; Bigelow, broad, football-tackle solid, dark. Maybe were it not for the job, the two would never have met, never traveled in the same circles, she thought, but here they were not the same, yet the same, like she and Vera, like every cop in a department of thousands.

"You guys were here before us. How'd they leave you two alone?" Vera asked, cocking her head toward the reporters, who looked antsy to cross the street to bombard them with questions, but stayed put on the sidewalk.

Kelley grinned. "They're scared of Bigs."

Bigelow smiled. "I've been told I can be intimidating."

Vera considered him for a moment. "Not to me."

Bigelow snorted. "That's because *you're* scary as fuck in a situation, Li."

Kelley nodded in agreement. "Truth."

Vera appeared to melt. "Aww, you guys. Thank you."

Harri ignored the banter. "No Al?"

Bigelow shrugged. "He's on something. You got me and the bard of Avondale."

Vera rubbed her hands together to warm them, looked sideways at Kelley, who was known for breaking into Shakespeare at the drop of an Elizabethan hat just to piss off Symansky. "I just call him Hamlet."

Kelley shrugged. "I like them both." He flicked a chin at the house. "How many are we looking at?"

"Three," Harri said. "They should be sober by now. But there's also a housekeeper, Anna, a couple of handymen. We need last names and to talk to everybody."

She looked around, her eyes landing on the college in the distance. "And then we have to double back with the girls who found Collier. Vera and I will take them."

Renfro answered the door, looking showered, sober, and suspicious. The house's odor of bleach and weed had dissipated a bit.

They split the boys up and talked to them individually. Bigelow took John Miller, Kelley took Trevor Finch, and she and Vera took Renfro.

Bigelow in the den, Kelley in the dining room, she and Vera in the living room. Divide and conquer, efficiency itself.

Renfro still looked nervous. It was midday on Monday, and Harri wondered why he and the others were still here and not in class. She looked at the nervous boy sitting on the couch in his Belverton T-shirt and sweats, his feet bare, and wondered if his parents knew what he was getting up to.

"Did you find out what happened to Brice yet?" he asked.

"Tell us about the drinking that went on here Saturday night," Harri said.

Renfro's eyes widened. "What?"

"Your friend died of alcohol poisoning," Vera said, watching Renfro for a reaction.

81

Renfro leaned forward. "No way. There was nothing like that. We had kegs, sure, and maybe some people got into them more than they should have, but *nobody* got that wasted."

"Then how do you explain Brice?" Harri asked.

"I can't. Nobody was watching him the whole night. We told you. He was here, then he wasn't."

"There were no drinking games?" Vera said. "No flip cups, Kings, Pong?"

Harri slid Vera a curious look.

"It was just a party, all right? Seriously. Music. Girls. Beer. It was just normal."

"Okay, let's go over it again, then," Harri said, giving no indication that the retelling was optional.

Renfro repeated himself, reluctantly, and as he did, Harri watched his eyes and his hands and his body language, the way his body closed in on itself, how he folded his arms across his chest, his fingers toying with the sleeves of his shirt. Nervous movement. He was uncomfortable. Harri had no way of knowing if it was because he was sitting in front of two cops or if he was lying.

"You've all had a chance to talk about this," she said. "Among yourselves. Are you still sure that none of you saw Brice after he walked through the kitchen Saturday night?"

Renfro ran his hands through his hair, a look of utter cluelessness on his face. "Nobody saw him. That's the truth. We weren't his babysitters. You don't know how this works."

Harri and Vera leaned in.

"No? Then explain it to us," Vera said.

Harri nodded. "Tell us how it all works."

Renfro blanched, swallowed hard, feeling the heat, knowing it was more than he could handle.

He sat back, lowered his head. "Just a party, man."

"Tell us about who was here," Harri said. "Students from campus, but you mentioned crashers. Anybody you knew?"

"Mostly kids from campus, but we don't card anybody. People hear there's a party, and they show up. It's cool. No problem."

"So, there were people in the house who could have come from anywhere?" Vera asked.

"I guess."

"Photos," Harri said. "Everybody's got a camera on their phone. Have you got party pictures?"

"Maybe."

"Wrong answer," Vera said.

"You have party pictures," Harri said. "Mind if we see them?"

"I don't know if I feel comfortable with that."

Vera's brows rose. "Oh, no? I get it. You want to go put something warmer on? It's kind of cold out."

Renfro's eyes narrowed. "Why would I care?"

"Because we'll be taking you in for further questioning. You might want to call your parents. They can arrange to have a lawyer meet you there." Vera stood. "You might want to also grab a snack or something before you go. We don't know how long you'll be with us. Our snack choices aren't the best." She shrugged. "And our coffee sucks, but we'll try to make you as comfortable as possible until we can get a court order to gain access to your photos."

"You can't do that."

"You and your friends, and somebody at your party, were the last ones to see Brice Collier alive," Harri said. "That makes you persons of interest in a homicide investigation. Yeah, we can." She stood. "Maybe a sweater, or a fleece? And warm socks. Our interview rooms are drafty."

Vera shrugged. "That's the city for you. Iffy on the heat."

Renfro dug in his pocket and pulled his iPhone out. "*Fine.* Jesus." He scrolled through his gallery, then handed the phone to Harri. She eased back down on the couch to take a look, while Vera continued with the questioning.

Harri swiped through Renfro's gallery, taking in all the photos of hyped-up, drugged-up, and lit up college kids crowding around a row of kegs set up in the same room they were sitting in now. There were dozens of pictures, more than twenty, more than thirty, as though Renfro had documented every second of the party from every angle. She spotted a few of Brice. He looked younger in life than he had in death. The photos were probably for social media posts. Not many kids today didn't have an online presence. She made a mental note to check Renfro's posts and Brice's too. Maybe there was something there that might help them figure out what Brice might have been into. Harri went through as many photos as she could on the fly but needed to study them all when they were back at the office. She handed the phone back to Renfro.

"Mind sending those to me?" She dug her CPD card out of her bag, handed it to him. "There's a city email on there." She saw the pained expression on his face. "We're not singling you out. We'll ask your friends to do the same."

"We're particularly interested in photos of Brice."

"*All* of them?"

"Everything you have from the party, yes," Harri said. "That going to be a problem?"

Renfro looked from Harri to Vera, then gave in. He read the card, then his thumbs went to work. "Feels like I'm being robbed," he groused.

Harri heard her cell phone ding in her pocket and lifted it out to confirm that the photos were coming in. They could move on.

"There were bruises on Brice's body," she said. "Like someone held him down. Any idea how he got them?"

Renfro shook his head. "Nobody here would dare touch Brice. He was the top guy. Whatever happened to him has nothing to do with us."

Renfro rubbed his arms as though he had suddenly caught a chill, and Harri noticed when his sleeves were disturbed that there was a tattoo on his right upper arm, one she'd seen before.

"Interesting tattoo," she said. "A minotaur, isn't it?"

Renfro tugged his sleeves down. "I don't know. It's just a tat."

"You have any others?"

"Now you're going to strip-search me?"

Vera pulled her phone out, and her thumbs got busy. Harri knew she was googling. One tattoo was one tattoo. The same tattoo on two residents of the same house was more than a coincidence. The same tattoo on two residents of the same house and one of the residents was now dead under unexplained circumstances was a lead.

Harri pointed to the tat. "Any significance to that one?"

"It's just from some rando place in Uptown. A night out. Too many beers. Seemed like a good idea at the time."

"You go out drinking with your friends from the house? To bars?" Harri asked. "Which ones?"

Renfro paused on the precipice of a jam. "I didn't mean out."

"Seeing as the legal drinking age in this city is twenty-one," Vera said without looking up.

"You ever hear the name Michael James Paget?" Harri asked him.

She could see from Renfro's blank expression that the name didn't register. No reason it should have, seeing as Paget died before he was born, but his connection to the house and to the college made it necessary to ask.

"No," he said. "Who is he?"

"We'll come back to that. How many beers did you see Brice drink the night of the party?"

"I didn't. Like I said. I wasn't his babysitter. The stuff was there. Everybody was at it. No limits. But Bry wasn't one of those party drunks, if that's what you're trying to say. He was all right, and so were we . . . sort of."

"So, how would you explain his bruises? They weren't old enough for him to have gotten them earlier than Saturday night," Harri said.

Renfro bristled. "Nobody here *touched* him."

"Why'd everybody run when the police arrived?" Vera asked.

Renfro thought for a moment. "Past curfew, obviously."

"How'd they expect to get back in the dorms without getting busted?" Harri asked.

Renfro smiled. "You serious? You figure that out freshman year."

Harri closed her notepad. "We'll get back to you. Thanks for the photos."

"Yeah, right," he offered sourly.

"One last question," she said. "Was Brice drunk when you saw him last? At about nine, you all said."

"He was *fine*."

"And you never saw him again after that?" Harri asked. "In here. At the party with everyone else."

Renfro shook his head. "That's right."

Vera watched him. "Was it just kegs?"

Renfro hesitated. Harri could almost see him formulating the lie in his head. "Yeah. Just beer. It was just a *party*."

"How many kegs?" Harri asked. She had counted at least a half dozen in the photos she'd just looked at, but wondered if there were more.

Renfro squirmed a little on the couch. "Six."

"Were all six accounted for at the end of the night?"

Renfro looked confused. "Sure. Why?"

"You're sure," Vera said. "You had all six."

"Six kegs, yeah. The guy we buy from gives us our deposit back when we return the empty kegs. We brought back all six."

Harri turned to Vera. "That's all I've got for now. Detective Li?"

Vera stood. "I'm good. We'll be in touch if we need to talk to you again, Mr. Renfro."

Renfro walked them to the door in silence, locking it when he closed it behind them. Harri and Vera stood on the steps outside for a moment.

"Not drunk at nine," Harri began.

"But good and drunk and dead an hour later," Vera said, "but no kegs missing."

They exchanged a look.

"So, two questions," Harri said. "Where and how?"

Vera started down the front steps. "Only two? Piece of cake."

CHAPTER 12

Vera and Harri met up with Kelley and Bigelow outside. This time, the reporters wanted a statement, despite Bigelow's uninviting presence, and crowded them on the street, throwing out questions. A campus-security officer stood leaning against his car, arms crossed, watching, not intervening. Not his job, apparently, Harri decided. Vera pulled out her practiced "no comment" more than a dozen times, but the questions kept coming. Reporters weren't easily turned back.

"Was this a murder? What happened? What aren't you telling us?"

They all turned at the questions, surprised to see that they came from a gangly twentysomething in horn-rimmed glasses, a light jacket, and no hat. He stood there, unflinching, his phone up, videotaping them.

"Tim Clausen. Investigative reporter. Belverton *Coronet*," he announced proudly.

Bigelow's brows raised. "The school paper?"

"That's right. So, what happened to Brice Collier? Was this a hit? A kidnapping gone wrong?"

Vera was ready. "No comment."

Bigelow glared at the reporters. "And that goes for the rest of you. We won't be making any statements today."

Harri watched as the seasoned journalists retreated. They knew the drill. Clausen didn't. He stayed. A contemporary of the boys they'd just interviewed, he held his ground, wide eyed, eager, green, but determined.

"We don't make statements to the press unless authorized to," Harri said as way of instruction. "Though they always try." She nodded toward the other reporters. "Did you know Brice?"

"Yeah, maybe you were at the party here Saturday night," Bigelow said.

Clausen looked increasingly uncomfortable. He lowered the phone. "I'm the one who gets to ask the questions." He looked at the four detectives. "The public has a right to know what happened here. I won't be intimidated."

"Would you rather be arrested for trespassing and impeding a police investigation?" Kelley asked.

The phone came back up. "You can't do that."

Kelley smiled, then reached around for the cuffs on his belt. "Want to bet?"

"Freedom of the press."

Bigelow snorted. "You can explain that to Mommy and Daddy when you call them to come get you down at the station."

Clausen began backing away, phone still up. "Threats. Big Brother in action."

Bigelow grinned. "The *biggest*. Go away."

"I'm free to stand here," Clausen said, his chin jutting out, defiant. "City sidewalk."

They stared at him, full cop faces, Bigelow the fiercest one among them.

"Ask another question," Bigelow said. "Go on."

Clausen took a step back, then turned and rejoined the others. "Big Brother lives!"

"Little shit," Bigelow muttered as they all watched the boy reporter try to mingle with the working journalists with deadlines to meet.

Kelley shook his head. "The Belverton *Coronet.*"

"We could be looking at the next Woodward or Bernstein," Vera said.

Bigelow slid her a look. "No *comment.*"

"Can we get back to work now?" Harri asked. "What'd you two get?"

"I don't think my guy was lying," Kelley said. "He was all into the party and wasn't thinking about anything else. I did get one thing, though. Finch says he, Miller, Renfro, and Collier are all legacies. Grandfathered into the school because of their fathers or grandfathers. Hardwicke's where they all land. I get the feeling the house is like some kind of private club you have to be special to get into."

Through the windows, Harri could see bodies move back and forth behind the curtains. She and Vera hadn't gotten all that much from Renfro, but she relayed to Bigelow and Kelley the similar tattoo and the information on the kegs. And they now had photos to look through.

"Well, Finch didn't say if the clubbers took it as far as matching tattoos," Kelley said. "He was wearing long sleeves, so I couldn't have checked."

"You got more than me, then," Bigelow groused. "My kid, Miller? Says he didn't see a damned thing all night. He got wasted right out of the gate. He remembers having a couple beers, then cruising around the party, and then lights out, Marie. Next thing he knows, he's laying across his bed out cold, and the next thing after *that*, he's getting roused up by Renfro with police at the door."

"I asked mine about crashers," Kelley said. "He noticed a few, but they didn't cause a problem. Also, no unusual activity around the house before the party started. Earlier in the day, the handyman was by fixing a window in one of the bedrooms. In and out."

"Who cleaned up the place in a hurry?" Vera asked. "You can still smell the bleach in there."

Bigelow chuckled. "My guy had that bit. When the kids saw the squads pull up, the call went out, like you'd expect. Everybody scrambled around the place grabbing cups and kegs and . . . whatnot. Then they booked it out the back with all of it. Miller helped bleach the place and get rid of the kegs." He nodded at Harri and Vera. "Your guy and a few others hosed the place down."

"They sure went to a lot of trouble," Kelley said.

"And it was all business as usual?" Vera asked.

"Who's going to step up to piss off Sebastian Collier?" Bigelow asked. "His kid could have used this field as a runway, and nobody would have called him on it."

"You'd think Younger would have shown some interest, if only to look out for Collier," Vera said. "I can practically spit on his house from here. Why would he need to wait for security to alert him that something was up? There were cops crawling all over this place."

"He was quick to tell us he has nothing to do with Hardwicke," Harri said. "It's private property."

"Covering his ass," Bigelow said, "for when Collier comes breathing down his neck."

"So, what's the plan?" Kelley toggled from one foot to the other, his shoulders hunched against the cold. "And can we talk about it *in* the car, where it's warm?"

"Anybody get the housekeeper's info?"

"Anna Bauer," Bigelow said. "Miller said her number was on the fridge. It was. Want us to call her, have her come in, or you want to do it?"

Harri looked over at Vera. "I'd like to talk to her. After we take Ritter and the others again. Could you and Kelley check on Collier's phone and computers? See if there's anything weird there? Then we'll meet back and see what we've got. What about Freddie and his friend?"

"Nothing," Bigelow said. "My kid seemed to think they came as a package deal with Bauer. They needed something fixed, and Anna knew some guys, that sort of thing. When you talk to her, hopefully, she can tell us more."

Kelley was already moving. "Yep. Works for me. Electronics. Us. Bauer. You two. See you back at the shop."

He slid into the passenger side of the car and honked the horn for Bigelow.

"Kelley doesn't like being cold," Bigelow said. "Or hot. None of the extremes, matter of fact. He's like Goldilocks with a badge."

He eased into the driver's side, rolled the window down a crack. "We'll be in touch."

Harri and Vera watched them pull away.

"I don't mind the cold," Vera said. "I don't particularly care for the heat, though."

"Neither do I," Harri said.

She got in the car behind the wheel, leaving Vera standing on the sidewalk for just a second longer.

"Don't tell me all your secrets, Harri," she quipped. "How would I handle the flood?"

Harri slid the passenger window down. "You going to stand there all day?"

Vera got in, buckled up. "God forbid."

—

The reception they got at Devlin Hall couldn't have been chillier if they'd actually been greeted by ice people in an ice village on an ice planet. The rolled eyes, the sneers, the signs of distrust were unmistakable. Harri knew that here they were the enemy to some, the oppressor. The badge, the guns stood for everything they claimed to despise. She got it. Vera got it. But it didn't mean it was true. In the end, though, they were here to do a job, not compete for Miss Congeniality.

They asked the RA for Ritter and Kenton and waited for them on the ground floor in a seating area for visitors right inside the front door. Brightly lit, the small communal space offered a blue sectional couch and a few chairs arranged for open conversation. Large windows faced the frozen lawn outside. Both remained standing, their backs to the wall, heads on a swivel. Harri watched as students, hunching against the cold, raced past them in hoodies and running shoes. She shook her head, worried about frostbitten fingers and toes.

Vera shook hers too. "Not even a scarf."

Everyone who passed them in the lobby stared. It was impossible for either of them to look unobtrusive, nonthreatening, normal. They stood tall and ready, keen, hard eyes assessing every face for threat levels, watching out for sudden movements, ever on alert, never complacent.

"Seriously, *nobody* here likes us?" Vera whispered as they watched distrustful students give them the widest of berths.

"Try not to take it personally."

"Too late."

A young woman sporting a ponytail and carrying a pink tote passed them. "Oh, *somebody's* getting arrested today," she teased.

A few girls in the lobby heard and chuckled. "Maybe *you*, Trisha," another joked, giving her friend a poke to the ribs with a playful elbow.

Harri stared at the ponytailed girl. "No one's getting arrested."

The chuckling stopped, and the girls moved along quickly.

"Have a nice day," Vera called after them. She then turned to Harri. "Someone *could* get arrested. Trisha could have had anything in that tote bag."

"We're dealing with kids here," Harri said. "A little less cop?"

Vera paused, thought about it. "I have no idea how that would even play out."

Harri stared out the window to look at the scurrying half-dressed kids slipping their way to class. The dorm building wasn't much to write home about. Just a brick box erected cheap and fast to house a lot of students being charged top dollar for the privilege of cramming their stuff into it. But it wasn't supposed to be fancy, just functional.

Behind them, the bell on the elevator dinged, and Harri turned to see Shelby Ritter and Hailie Kenton step off into the lobby, looking guilty, holding on to each other for support.

Ritter looked just as wired as she had the day before, not at all rested or calmed by a night's sleep. Kenton's eyes were wide, fearful, as though Harri and Vera might bite.

Harri would have thought the shock of stumbling on Collier's body would have worn off at least some in the ensuing hours. But both girls appeared just as keyed up, just as pale and unsettled as they had before. Ritter's baggy clothes looked like they'd been tossed on without thought of coordination. Kenton was dressed in layers—shirt, sweater, fleece. Young women in distress.

Harri noted their grasp on each other, as though they were about to face some trial by fire and were hanging on to each other for support.

"Which one's Kenton?" Vera whispered.

Harri studied the girls. "The one in the fleece."

A moment passed as the girls stood like cornered fawns.

"Um," Vera said.

"I see it," Harri said.

They both saw it at the same time, the very second Ritter and Kenton decided to run. Like a shot, the girls bolted for the door.

"And there they go," Vera muttered.

"Uh-huh."

The girls barreled through the door and sprinted out across the lawn. Through the window, Harri and Vera watched them slip and slide across the icy ground, headed in the direction of the student parking lot as though the hounds of hell were chasing them. Seconds later, a white Honda Civic spitting exhaust peeled out and sped north with the girls inside.

A round of applause went up behind them, and they turned to face the students giving the runaway girls support for evading the big bad cops and striking a blow for . . . what? Harri wondered.

Every eye was on them to see what they'd do next. Every hand had a cell phone with a camera trained on them. Harri glanced over at Vera.

"Smile," Vera said.

They were prohibited from giving chase, not that the situation warranted it. Department policy. No chase. No foot pursuit. It was controversial, especially with the rank and file, but some bureaucrat somewhere had decided that the nonaction ensured the safety of suspect, cop, and civilian, no matter the circumstance. It was just one of the policies that tied their hands and made their jobs more difficult.

Harri dug the car keys out of her bag and handed them to Vera. "Your turn. We'll try again later when they've had a chance to calm down. Meanwhile, we go back in, lay out what we've got? See where we need to go next?"

"May as well." Vera turned to Kenton and Ritter's hype squad. "Have a nice day, ladies. Stay safe."

They walked out of the building and made it back to the car, Vera taking the wheel, Harri engaging her seat belt.

Vera smiled. "This is going to look good on your whiteboard. You should draw little running feet under their names."

"You're mocking the whiteboard?"

"Me? Mock the whiteboard? Never."

Harri nodded, then stared back at Devlin Hall as the car warmed up.

"So, they lied about something."

Vera backed the car out of the spot. "Can't wait to see what Anna Bauer lies to us about."

———

Bauer's apartment was on Sheridan Road, not far from the bend off Lake Shore Drive or Belverton. As they pulled up in front, Harri wondered if that had been a selling point for the woman.

"Nice building," Vera said as they walked in. "Condo, maybe." She glanced over at Harri. "And she's cleaning up after Brice Collier and his pals? Nuh-uh."

They rode up in the quiet elevator to the third floor. "I pass no judgments," Harri said.

"You pass quiet judgments," Vera countered. "It's all in your eyes."

Harri looked over at her, bemused. "What are my eyes saying now?"

Vera chuckled. "Too late. I've figured you out. I have no fear."

They knocked on Bauer's door, and a dull-looking woman soon opened it, staring at them in the doorway, like she was seeing ghosts.

"Anna Bauer?" Harri asked.

"Yes?"

She was a woman maybe in her late fifties. Lean, dark hair flecked with gray. Flat eyes, a tired expression. Harri noted there was nothing that seemed lively about her as she stood watching them, seemingly with little interest.

"Chicago Police," Vera said. "We'd like to ask you a few questions about Brice Collier."

As Vera spoke, Harri studied Bauer, wondering if her dullness was due to medication or drugs or something else.

Behind them a door opened across the hall. An old woman peeked out of the crack.

"And your job at Hardwicke," Harri added.

Bauer glanced over at her neighbor and in a tired voice said, "There's nothing to see, Mrs. MacCallum. There's *never* anything to see."

The old woman's door eased closed, and Bauer stepped back to let them into her small, tidy apartment that appeared as bland as she did. Livable, not ostentatious, Harri noticed, as far removed from the faded lavishness of Hardwicke as any place could get.

Bauer rubbed her forehead as though she had a massive headache. "I heard the news. It's been on all the channels. Sorry. Can I get you something? Coffee? Tea? Not sure what the protocol is here. I've never had police officers in my home."

"Nothing. Thanks," Harri said.

Bauer pointed to a two-cushioned couch. "Sit, please."

The couch was barely wide enough for the two of them, but they made it work and sat watching a sunken Bauer eyeing them from an overstuffed chair, a low coffee table topped by an empty candy bowl separating them.

"What can you tell us about Brice?" Harri asked.

Bauer shrugged. "He was a kid. I didn't know him. I cleaned. He paid me."

"Do you work for a service?" Vera asked.

Bauer shook her head. "I find my own jobs."

Vera nodded. "Do you advertise?"

Bauer stared down at her lap. "It's word of mouth, mostly."

"So, you have other clients?"

"I'm sorry. What does any of that have to do with what happened to the Collier boy?"

Bauer appeared uncomfortable, which was likely Vera's intent, Harri decided. To push and see what spilled out.

"Then let's talk about Brice," Harri said. "Did you notice anything out of the ordinary with him or the house when you were there Friday?"

"Like what?"

Vera scooted forward and angled her long legs to the left of the table to get a little more room. Harri had already angled hers to the right.

"Anything. I assume you saw Brice?"

"He opened the door. We exchanged a few pleasantries, then I got to work. I didn't see him when I left."

"How were you paid?" Vera asked.

"Digitally. It's easier."

"You knew there was going to be a party," Vera said.

"I saw the kegs. There are always parties there. I'm often called in afterward to clean up. That cleaning, I charge more."

"Any tension in the house?" Harri asked. "Conflict? Someone Brice didn't get along with?"

Bauer shook her head. "Everyone seemed to get along just fine. They were all very close."

Harri watched Bauer, noticing the drop of her shoulders, the washed-out face. "Big house. Too big for one person to stay on top of."

"I only cleaned the occupied bedrooms, the bathrooms, the kitchen, the dining room, and the great room. The others, including Mr. Collier's private office, are locked and off-limits." Bauer bowed her head. "I would have been called in to clean today, but . . . so many tragedies in the world, aren't there?"

"Was Brice well liked?" Vera asked. "Was he a nice guy?"

"I don't know. I just cleaned. He seemed . . . sure of himself."

"Where were you Saturday night, Ms. Bauer?" Harri asked.

The woman didn't seem taken aback by the question. "Here. I try not to go out after dark." She looked around her apartment as if suddenly finding it lacking. "This is what I have."

"One of the boys told us the bedrooms are off-limits during their parties," Harri said. "Is that true? You clean the rooms, you'd know."

Bauer hesitated. "I don't believe they were off-limits."

Vera glanced around. "You live alone?"

"Unless you count Mrs. MacCallum, who is very invested in what goes on in my apartment. I'm divorced. We never had kids. It always felt too risky." Bauer rose. "What with the world as it is. The things that go on. The people in it." She turned to them. "Evil. You must see it. You deal with the evil things people do to each other every day. How? I've always wondered."

The question, Harri knew, had no easy answer, and it was one she'd been asked many times before. How, not why. How she took day by day, senseless act by senseless act. The why she knew was different for her than it would be for Vera or any other cop. *Why* was personal. *How* was function, vocation. Either question, however she answered it, was too long a discussion to have here, with a body on Grant's table waiting for resolution.

"It's our job," Harri said curtly. "So, just to sum up. You cleaned on Friday, and there was nothing unusual happening. Brice seemed fine when he let you in. You noticed no tensions, conflicts, or upsets in the house. The boys got along fine."

Bauer nodded. "All fine. All of them going in the same direction for the same reasons. All confident they'll succeed. I almost feel sorry for them."

"Sorry? Why?" Vera asked.

"Because they'll never be what they could have been. They'll always be just replicas of their fathers. That has to be a lot of pressure. But you still can't allow yourself to forget what it means to be a *person*. To be in the world. To care about people. Part of it's the age, I know. They're young. Still learning who to be. That's what makes it all the more tragic when something like this happens. We'll never know what they could have been."

"Does the name Michael James Paget mean anything to you, Ms. Bauer?" Harri asked.

Bauer frowned. "Is he one of the boys in the house?"

"What about the handyman, Freddie?" Vera asked. "What do you know about him?"

"When I was hired at Hardwicke, they also needed a fix-it person to do small jobs and maintenance things—cutting the grass, raking leaves, replacing loose shingles, shoveling snow. I asked around. I found Freddie. He brought on a friend he knew."

"Freddie have a last name?" Harri asked. "And his friend?"

Bauer shrugged. "I don't think I ever asked. He mostly worked outside; I worked inside. Brice seemed satisfied with his work."

"Where'd you find Freddie?"

"At church. There was a postcard on the community board."

"You still have his number?" Vera's eyes held Bauer's. "From the board?"

"I threw it away when he got the job. Why would *I* need it? I don't know what more I can tell you."

"Which church?" Harri asked.

They waited for her to answer.

"Maybe not church. I think I saw his posting on the board at the grocery store. The one a block over. Brice mentioned needing someone; I saw the post, and brought it to him. I don't think he'd ever hired a fix-it man before. I don't know anything else. Sorry."

Harri and Vera stood. Vera handed Bauer one of her cards. "If you think of anything else you feel we might need to know, give us a call?"

Harri gave the woman one final study. "And thanks for your time."

The door across the hall opened up a smidge the second they stepped out into the hallway. Mrs. MacCallum.

"Hello," Vera said. "Mind if we ask—"

The door shut abruptly.

"Invested but not helpful," Harri muttered.

Vera slid one of her cards under MacCallum's door. "In case she changes her mind. I'm betting *invested* runs deep."

"Strange woman," Vera said as they pushed out of the building into February.

"Which one?" Harri asked.

"I meant Bauer, but MacCallum's special, too, at least the parts we saw of her through the crack."

"Hurt woman," Harri said.

Vera let a beat pass. "I noticed. Also, a liar."

"Definitely about Freddie," Harri said. "Shades of the truth about the other things, I think. Doesn't mean she killed Collier, though."

"Why would she want to? And in the way it was done?"

"Good questions. No answers."

The moment they got in the car, Harri's cell phone buzzed. Unknown number. She just knew.

"Unknown number," Harri said.

"It might not be him," Vera said.

"It's him."

For a moment Harri thought about letting the call go, just cutting him off. Instead, she tapped the green button and put the call on speaker.

"Foster."

"I'm baaaack. Did you miss me, Detective Foster?"

His tone was slow and low, playful. She could almost hear the smile in it, but there was an edge of menace mixed in too. Enjoying himself, running a game only he knew the rules to, a game only he wanted to play. It had been two weeks since she'd heard from him. There'd been false hope, though she hadn't held it firmly, that like Griffin said, he'd moved on. But here he was again; only this time she was tired of playing along, tired of bracing at unknown calls.

"I know you're there," he said. "I can hear you breathing. And since I'm on speaker, I know that Detective Vera Li is with you?"

Vera looked over at Harri but said nothing. They both understood what was at stake.

He chuckled. "This is good. Two hero detectives for the price of one. I gave you a task, and you didn't come through."

"I never intended to," she said.

"Hmm. I didn't really expect you to do it. It was a test of sorts. Dreyer isn't even important. A name I pulled out of my ass. He's dead now, anyway. It was just me having fun."

"You call this fun?"

"For me? Yes. And now that I have your attention . . . I am owed, Detective Harriet Foster. I was wronged. And you have a debt to pay. Not your fault, I can admit that, but someone has to be held accountable, right? I can't get satisfaction from the grave, can I?"

Harri looked over at Vera, confused. "What the hell are you talking about?"

"You've stepped into a dead man's shoes, Harri. I haven't decided yet how you'll pay the debt, but when I do, you'll know it."

"So, this is about *me*, not Thompson?" she asked, aware that Vera was monitoring her every breath, studying her every move.

"It always was," he said. "Why not tell you, right? It's about *you*. *You're* the get. Where the road ends."

Harri had no idea what he was talking about. He was talking in riddles, in circles. Nothing made sense. What dead man? What debt? What road?

"Don't call me again," she said, prepared to push the end button. "You've wasted enough of my time."

"That's how you treat an old friend?"

Harri stopped. For a moment there was only silence on both ends of the line.

"You death cops always think you're better, smarter," he said, a sudden hardness to his voice. "You're not. By the book, though, right? Never a wrong foot put forward. Crusaders. Are you a crusader, Harri? I think you are. Fighting the good fight. That's the garbage you would have been fed.

"You really should be thanking me. I could have let you see, but I didn't. I spared you. I *can* do good things when I want to. And I'm sorry it's you who'll have to pay. But . . . oh well. I'll be in touch."

"Don't bother."

He chuckled. "It's no bother."

She listened to his breathing.

"Do you ever visit the dead, Harri?"

"What?"

"Just to say hello. I do."

The line went dead. Harri reached down and hit the red button.

"What the hell was *that*?" Vera asked.

Harri replayed the cryptic conversation over in her head. *Old friend,* he'd said. *A debt.*

"Mind if I drive?" she asked.

They switched seats. Harri put the car in gear.

"That part about visiting the dead." Harri pulled away from Bauer's building, headed south. "I need to make a couple of stops before we go back. That okay?"

Vera settled back. "Go."

CHAPTER 13

She didn't visit Reg's grave often. There was no need, as far as she saw it. She could stand at his grave until her legs fell off, and it wouldn't bring him back. Besides, he wasn't there. The hole only held what got left behind.

As she and Vera approached his gravesite, their feet crunching across the frozen ground in the quiet cemetery, she could feel her pulse quicken. Aware that this blurred the lines between her private and professional lives, lines she's tried hard not to cross. With every step, she felt more and more vulnerable, more and more exposed. She cursed the voice for putting her in this position. There was no emotional cover here for her to burrow beneath.

Vera had offered to stay in the car, but Harri had declined it. They'd come too far for that. Some of the walls had already fallen; the others would too.

They reached Reg's grave. Despite the bite of the air, Harri's hands began to sweat inside her gloves as she stared down at the rose-colored headstone with the details of her child's short life etched into the marble. BELOVED SON AND GRANDSON. The date of his glorious birth, and then the date he was stolen from her. Fourteen years. Not enough time.

Harri looked out over the cemetery grounds. There was just her and Vera and headstones as far as her eye could see. He'd asked if she visited the dead.

"I don't know what I expected," she said. "That he'd be hiding behind a tree, holding a sign?"

Vera stood a few inches behind her. Harri knew she was trying not to crowd her.

"He's playing with us," Vera said.

Harri nodded, then took in the headstone again, her eyes landing on the single penny sitting on top of it. *Just to say hello,* he'd said. *I do.* He'd put the penny there.

"He stood right here," she said to Vera through gritted teeth, her anger so intense, so raw, she could hardly bear it. Here. With Reg. She picked up the penny and hurled it as far as she could. She didn't want the dirty thing on Reg's headstone. He had no right . . .

There was no possibility he'd left prints on the coin. He was far too careful for that.

"I don't see any surveillance cameras," Vera said.

Harri heard her but didn't respond. She couldn't be a cop here. Instead, she brushed her hand across the top of the headstone, then rested it there for a time. It was all she could do.

Harri turned and made her way back to the car. "One more stop."

They eased up to Glynnis Thompson's grave miles away in the Catholic cemetery. Harri hadn't been here, either, since the day of her partner's interment. She didn't even want to think about what lay six feet underground.

She and Vera encountered the same grim rows of stony graves, bedraggled flowers frozen in ice in overturned planters. Death in winter when everything lay dormant was twice as cruel a thing. The trees and grass and birds and all would return in spring, she knew, but now, the lifelessness felt like the end of the world, a hollow thing, a cold spike embedded in the heart.

"There's a quarter on the headstone," Vera said.

"I see it."

Vera stepped closer, took it in. "What am I missing? I've heard of people leaving coins and stones on headstones out of respect."

Harri scanned the grounds, then turned to watch traffic race by on Kedzie Avenue. People rushing, struggling, likely trying not to think about how it all would end in a place like this. Reg's and G's plots were miles apart, yet the same.

Harri picked up the quarter, clenched it in her fist. "My father was in the army. Way before I was born, or my brother. He joined the department but never wanted to be a detective. He liked wearing the uniform and preferred being out on the street where the people were and where he thought he could do the most good."

"He sounds like a special guy."

She smiled. "Yeah."

Harri opened her fist and stared at the quarter. "He told me about coins on a soldier's grave. That the whole thing went back as far as the Roman Empire, when soldiers would put coins in a fallen comrade's mouth to pay their way across the River Styx into the afterlife.

"A penny means you visited the grave. A nickel means you and the dead soldier trained together. A dime means you served together." She held the quarter up between thumb and index finger so Vera could see it. "And this."

For a moment she couldn't say the words. Her brain, her mind, her body were too full of anger. The heat of it almost consumed any rational thought she could hope to have. All she wanted was to tear something down, destroy something. All this time, the years, the months, the days, the lid she'd put on all her pain and grief and hurt had stayed firmly on the pot, but now she could feel the lid lift; she could sense the steam build, and it didn't feel as though she could stop it.

The voice. He'd visited her son. He'd been here with G. Both times he'd left the one thing that ensured that she would never let him go.

"A quarter means that you were there when the soldier died."

Vera fell silent, and so did Harri as the enormity of what she'd said hit them both.

"You had a feeling he might be a cop," Vera said.

"'Old friends,' he said." Harri placed a hand on the headstone. "About *me*. 'Dead man's shoes.'"

They stood over the grave for a time, neither of them speaking.

"If you're thinking about saying something stupid like 'stay out of it, Vera,' or 'this isn't your fight, Vera,' or 'piss off, Vera . . .'"

"I was thinking all those things."

"Then I saved you saying it." She turned for the car. "Let's find the son of a—" She stopped herself, aware she was in a cemetery on hallowed ground. *"Biscuit."*

Harri brushed past her. "If this looks like it's going sideways, you're out."

"I don't think so."

Harri glared at Vera. "You're so fucking stubborn."

"As a mule, so there's no use arguing about it. I don't like sick freaks," Vera said. "And you can't do this alone."

"I *can* do it alone."

"The fact that you think you *can* do it alone is why I won't *let* you do it alone."

Harri turned to face her. *"Let* me? This has nothing to do with *you*. This is a mess I brought with me. Not your fight. I'm not losing another—" She stopped herself.

Vera paused for a moment. "Partner. I'll say it, even if you won't. But let's stick a pin in that for now. First, we deal with this guy. He's getting on my nerves with all the games."

Harri grabbed her head in frustration. "Sometimes you make my head hurt."

Vera wouldn't give an inch. "I've got aspirin in my bag. Need one?"

The graveyard silence felt eerie and ominous.

Walking on, they were careful to step around the plots. Harri didn't know what to say.

"I think I'll go mausoleum," Vera said. "Tidier. What about you?"

Harri was still thinking about what Vera had said earlier but welcomed the shift, knowing Vera had made it purposefully. "I don't have a preference. Gone is gone. I won't know where I am."

"No heaven? No hell?"

They reached the car, and Harri yanked open the driver's door.

"There's heaven and hell right here on earth every day, isn't there?"

CHAPTER 14

Detective Matt Kelley leaned a haunch on the side of his desk, his arms crossed. "They just ran?"

Vera leaned back in her chair with her legs crossed at the knee, watching Harri at the whiteboard. She'd been observing her closely since their cemetery visits earlier, knowing she'd put away the feelings they'd stirred up, and knowing that would cost her in the end.

"Like the wind," she said.

Bigelow skimmed through his phone. "Guilty of something."

Kelley made a face. "Or just afraid of police. You know we get that."

Bigelow looked up, an expression of mild amusement on his face. "A couple of white girls afraid of the police? Nah. They're guilty of something." He pointed to Harri at the board. "Write it down with that marker, Foster. Ritter. Kenton. Guilty of *something*." He then pointed at Kelley. "I want fifty when that turns out to be true."

Kelley smiled. "We'll see."

Bigelow scoffed. "I better *see* fifty."

Despite the fact that the office was noisy with the turnover from second watch to third, as tired cops clocked out and fresher ones came on to face whatever jumped off for the night, the team still remained behind. There were details to share, a path ahead to plan. The bruises on Collier's body, the fibers in his throat, said force. Force meant murder, and murder meant there was someone out there walking their streets who shouldn't be.

Bigelow looked over at Harri and Vera. "Mayor had one of his little press conferences. You missed it. Press ate him *alive*. All he had was hems and haws and nonsense. I thought the guy was going to shit his pants, the sweat was so heavy on his forehead. I refuse to state the obvious. We all know how this goes. Rich kid. Front of the line. All kinds of shine." He eyed Griffin's door. "That's why she's not in there. Down at city hall with the brass, dancing on a string. They want us all to snap to on all this. Get it locked up ASAP. More pressure on us, as always. No extra bodies, of course. No overtime approved. We got to get it all done in close to forty. Priority. Because he was a *Collier*. Never mind the other kids whose parents aren't anybody special. Gotta wait. Meanwhile, the suits hide in their little holes, covering their asses, pointing fingers *our* way." He took in the jaded faces around him. "You all know I'm right." He straightened his tie, having appeared to get the worst of it off his chest. "Clausen, boy reporter, and the rest of them thinking they run us because they got pens and cameras. All in with the questions and the accusations. Nowhere to be found when the bullets start flying in our direction. Don't even get me started on the mayor." He took in a breath, let it out. "No more bitching for now."

For a moment everyone was silent, then Harri turned around, looked over at Kelley and Bigelow, and got back to it. "Anna Bauer. Housekeeper. Says she didn't have much personal interaction with the boys in Hardwicke. She came in, did her job, left them to it. She knew about the parties, of course, because she had to clean the mess up afterward. According to her, the bedrooms were *not* off-limits."

"She'd have the lay of the land," Bigelow said.

Kelley shifted his weight. "But nobody says they saw her Saturday night."

"I think they'd have noticed if their sixty-year-old housekeeper crashed," Bigelow offered.

Harri jotted down the name Freddie and then a question mark after it for the "helper" they hadn't yet identified. She then relayed the rest of what they'd learned at Bauer's.

"Her not knowing anything about the fix-it man sounded like a lie," Vera said.

Harri underlined Bauer's name. "She claimed she saw his name on a card at church, then corrected and said it was at the grocery store in her neighborhood. I don't think either is true."

"We have any ideas on a motive?" Kelley asked. "Because nothing we've got is pointing in that direction."

"You're right," Harri said. "All we've got is people, no physical evidence. There's something there with Bauer, though."

"Have any idea why she might've lied about the fix-it man?" Bigelow asked.

"No, not yet."

Vera reached around for the legal pad on her desk. "Well, since we got back, I did a little digging on Mrs. MacCallum."

"You ran an old lady?" Kelley asked.

"We run old ladies all the time. Why are you getting your knickers in a knot all of a sudden?"

"Seems rude," he said. "I mean, who could she be? Mata Hari?"

Vera scowled. "I was just about to tell you. She's Rose MacCallum. Retired schoolteacher. Eighty-six. Mother of three, grandmother of five. No driver's license. Owns a cat. Volunteers at the local food bank. Knows everybody's business in the building. Considers keeping on top of everything her civic duty."

"How'd you get all that from a data run?" Bigelow asked.

"I also made some calls to some of the other neighbors. Nobody had a good sense of Bauer. She's friendly enough in passing, they say, but doesn't spend a lot of time conversing or hanging out. Keeps to herself. MacCallum's the opposite. She's all up in the business."

"Helps with safety," Kelley said. "Somebody keeping an eye out."

Vera snorted. "Mrs. MacCallum keeps *both* eyes and two ears out at all times."

Harri watched a quiet Symansky sitting at his desk, his mind obviously somewhere else. He hadn't reacted to Bigelow's grousing, or anything else. She suspected his distractedness had to do with Lonergan's bad news. The two had worked together the longest. They had kids around the same age. They butted heads all the time, but she knew there was a real bond between them.

"Al?" she asked. "You okay?" He didn't answer. *"Al?"*

"What's that?"

"I asked if you were okay."

He had to think about it before he got up and faced the team. "I'm still on Katie. I'm gonna clock out, if that's okay. Hit it again in the mornin'. I can't think of anythin' else right now. Sorry, guys."

They watched him leave, the reminder of Lonergan's misery reemerging and darkening everyone's mood.

"Symansky knows when to call it," Kelley said. "I'll give him that."

Harri concentrated on the board, her fingers gripped tightly around the black marker as though it were something her frustration could kill. She didn't know when to call it. All she knew how to do was keep moving, keep working. Maybe, she reasoned, if she moved fast enough, long enough, she wouldn't have to face the other things.

She drew a question mark next to Anna Bauer's name, then circled it. "More to come on her. Same for Kenton, Ritter, and this Freddie."

"Are we thinking Collier and this old Paget case are connected?" Bigelow asked, glancing around at the others. "Or are we thinking unlucky coincidence?"

"I think the location connects them, obviously," Vera said. "But Paget looks like a straight-up accidental death. ME at the time ruled it that way. The file on it makes no reference to him finding a single bruise on the body. And Renfro didn't appear to recognize the name, or if he did, I didn't catch it."

As the others worked it through, Harri scribbled the details on the board, making sure all the people they'd talked to were up there. She also made a note about the party kegs. If Brice didn't get drunk at the party, where did he? When she was finished, she capped the marker.

"This is our start," she said. "Wait."

She hurried back to her desk to grab the stack of photos she'd printed out from her phone, the ones Renfro had reluctantly given them. She tacked them up on the board and pointed to the ones she'd found of Collier, Kenton, and Ritter.

"The first lie," she said. "Kenton and Ritter *were* at that party. So, that early-morning-walk story is bogus."

Harri pointed to Kenton's photograph. "Hailie's the one Brice was reportedly circling that night." She pointed to another image. "Here's one of Brice talking to both of them. Neither of the girls look happy. There isn't a photo of Brice and Hailie alone together."

Kelley said, "But they could have met up alone at some point."

Vera's brows lifted. "And if something went wrong . . ."

"Either on the roof, where they think he was headed," Kelley said, "or in his room. Nobody was keeping track."

"Something made them run," Bigelow said.

"We'll look through everybody's socials," Vera said. "These kids don't blow their noses without posting about it. We might find something else."

Harri wrote down the word *HAZING* all in caps, then followed it with an equally bold question mark. Next to it she scribbled *HARDWICKE HOUSE. TATTOOS. PAGET.*

"Everything okay over there, Foster?" Bigelow asked. "You seem to be working that marker real hard."

Kelley squinted at the board. "I was about to mention that. It sounds like a bunch of angry mice over there."

Harri turned from the board. "Fine. Long day."

She put down the marker and stepped away from the board. "Brice Collier and Michael Paget. No. Scratch that. Let's take them one at a time. Collier. What do we know? No."

Harri took another step back, slid her hands into her pockets, and felt around in the right one for the quarter she'd taken from G's headstone. "What *don't* we know?"

She pressed the quarter in her palm, and her thoughts flew off in a million directions. Collier. Paget. Hardwicke. The voice. He'd gotten too close. He'd visited her son. He'd stood at G's grave. It felt like an assault, a punch to the stomach.

Photographs. Coins. Lange. IAD. Old friend? Cemeteries. It took her a moment to realize that no one had responded.

"*Nobody?* There is *nothing* but open space on this board, and there are *four* of us standing here. A boy is dead. No ideas? No theories? What kind of cops are we, huh?"

Her tone was harsh, and her voice shook and was higher than normal, but she couldn't seem to control it.

"Whoa." Kelley lifted off his desk. "What's happening right now?"

Vera stood. "Little break."

She grabbed Harri by the arm and pulled her toward the locker room down the hall.

Harri snatched her arm free once the door closed behind them. "What are you doing? We have work to do."

Vera faced her, hands on her hips, ready for it. "Let's talk."

"*Are you serious?* There's a dead boy on a slab right now—"

Vera shook her head. "Not about that." She flicked her chin. "Let's go. Let's have it."

Harri put distance between them, knowing full well what Vera meant and not wanting to go there. "I don't need more mothering, Vera."

"Good, because you're not getting any. You're getting partnering. And I can see you're not handling it." She checked her watch. "It's after four. We've got no leads. Nothing on that board's going to get done tonight. We have a solid place to start in the morning. Hailie Kenton and Shelby Ritter being number one and two on the list. We call it for today. Hit it fresh then."

"Four? Since when do we keep bankers' hours?"

"You've stood at one crime scene and two graves today, Harri. It's enough, don't you think?"

Harri opened her mouth to protest, but Vera stopped her.

"It's enough," she repeated. After a beat passed, she added, "Let the day be over. You're burning it at both ends."

"I know what I'm doing." Her right hand lunged for the quarter in her pocket and squeezed it tight. "I can find him. If he keeps talking, I can figure it out."

"In your free time? When's that? You're drowning. He's hit you where you live, and it's taken pieces out of you. On top of that, we're on this case. But there's always going to be another case. It's day in and day out. Body after body. It's what we do. And all of it's hard. You can't keep going the way you're going. You have to drop something before it drops you. Today it's markers, tomorrow, the next day, who knows what it'll be. Or do you want to end up like Thompson? *Talk*, damn it. For once, just *talk*."

Harri flared. "Why do you do this? At the cemetery, here. Why are you always on my *ass*?"

"Because your ass is tied to my ass, that's why. We're not sitting at desks shuffling papers for a living, Harri. We're out there with targets on our backs. You and I both need to know the other's solid, completely there, in it to win it. Are *you*?" Vera ran a hand through her hair. "Look, you've had a lot happen. Stuff that would have buried most people. Stuff I don't even want to imagine . . . you need to talk about it. If not to me, then with somebody else. *Anybody* else."

Harri backed up to get away from the words she didn't want to hear or acknowledge. Truth, she knew, but not a truth she was ready to embrace or accept. "So, no more jokes, then?" she said. "No more snarky remarks? We're beyond all that, are we? You're my shrink *and* my partner now? Nice."

"Anger's good. Keep going."

Harri's eyes narrowed. She could feel heat rising in her gut. "Screw you, Vera. You want me to pull out all my childhood traumas? Tell you my greatest fear?" She looked around the locker room. "I don't see a therapist's couch in here. Maybe you'd like me to just stretch out on the floor instead?"

Their eyes held. No jokes from Vera, no snark. This was real talk, long delayed. "If you're comfortable sharing it."

Harri could feel her chest burn, her heart race. It felt like a heavy weight was pressed against her rib cage, and she couldn't get a good breath in or out. She shook her head, fighting to keep it all in. "Yours first, *Dr.* Li." She meant it facetiously, as a way to push Vera back and away and give herself some emotional space.

Vera took a step forward. "Okay. My greatest fear is dying in the street and leaving my son without a mother. That became my greatest fear the second they put him in my arms after he was born. I looked down at that little face, knowing he was mine, knowing that I'd do anything and everything for him no matter what it took. Then I remembered what I did for a living. I could walk out of my house tomorrow and never come back. We all could. I could put my son to bed on an ordinary night, kiss him good night, and that could be the last kiss I ever give him. *That's* my fear, Harri. So, my ass is tied to your ass. And *your* ass is drowning. Who stands by and watches somebody drown? Could *you* do it?"

Vera's truth struck her like a lightning bolt. It pierced through the wall she had put up to protect herself from getting too close. It was a frightening place to be. For a moment, neither of them spoke. The only sounds in the room were the traffic from outside and the office noise down the hall.

"He's taking pieces away," Harri said finally. "My fear is that I don't have many left to take."

Vera smiled, appeared to relax. "That's a start. Want to—"

Harri crossed to the door. "No. I'm going home."

Vera followed. "We'll find this guy, Harri. We'll end it."

"We will. And there's no way in hell I'm letting you die in the street."

Vera smiled. "Thanks."

Harri opened the door but stopped for a moment with her hand on the knob. "I'm not saying anything out there."

"They should know what's going on," Vera said. "They might be able to help."

"Not yet. Okay? Not right now."

Vera's brows lifted. "I wouldn't worry about it just now. Think it through. You're having a moment. No way do they want to get cornered by that kind of drama. They're guys."

They walked back into the office to find Bigelow and Kelley gone, their computers shut down, their coats missing from the backs of their chairs. Vera threw her hands up.

"What'd I tell you?" Vera said.

"You could be wrong just once."

"Honestly, I don't think I can."

———

Harri did go home, or what passed for it. It was an old house, an empty box on a run-down street. A place to sit and sleep but not to live, not to flourish. She told herself it didn't matter that there were no paintings on her walls, no treasured things displayed on shelves. She had made no attempt at all to make the box a home. She'd had that once and lost it. The importance of the box was not what she'd failed to put in it but that the box sat facing the tree where her son died. Alone. Without her. It was the tree she needed to be near for now.

Walking in the front door, she dropped her bag on the one chair facing the front window, then approached a large vase sitting on the one side table she owned. A bowl of colorful marbles sat next to it, and she plucked a marble up, intending to drop it into the almost full vase as she always did at the end of a day, as she'd done at the end of every day since Reg's death. The marble marked a victory, a survival of another day. But as she rolled the marble around in her hand, as she stared at the vase with so many marbles already in it, she paused, no longer seeing the need to drop another in. Was that progress? Healing? It didn't feel like that profound a thing. It just felt unnecessary.

Dropping the marble back into the bowl, she turned away from the vase. Maybe she didn't need it, either, anymore? She slid the quarter out of her pocket and held it up to the light. No secrets. It was just a quarter. Its importance was in the who and why.

She set the quarter on her one table, grabbed an apple from her nearly empty refrigerator, and sat down in her chair to think.

That's how you treat an old friend? he'd said.

She took a bite of the apple, not really wanting it, lost in thought as hours slipped away. *Old* friends.

Harri was halfway up the stairs to her bedroom when it finally hit her. Shoes. *Dead man's* shoe. She flicked a look at her watch—8:00 p.m.—hesitated for a moment, and then rushed down the stairs to stand in the darkened room.

"No. *No.*"

She grabbed her bag and her coat and raced out of the house.

CHAPTER 15

Harri drove up to the gates of the cemetery to find them closed. She got out of the car and walked up to the sign displaying the hours. The cemetery had closed at 4:30 p.m.

She peered through the gaps in the wrought iron gate. There had to be security on the premises. In the office, maybe? There was a call box at the entrance with a button to push. She did, then waited for what felt like an interminable amount of time, her hands shoved in her pockets for warmth, her ears flirting with frostbite.

"Yeah? Who's there?" the female voice came back.

Harri drew closer to the box. "This is Detective Harriet Foster, Chicago Police Department. I need to get inside."

"What for? This some kind of raid?" The woman sounded slightly amused. Like a raid on a graveyard was the most preposterous thing she'd ever heard of.

"Not a raid," Harri said. "I need to check a gravesite. I won't be long. But I need to do it *tonight*."

There was a big sigh over the intercom that sounded like a cruel gust of tired wind. "You better have some kind of ID."

"I do."

"All right. Hold on."

The line went dead. Harri stepped back from the box and turned around to face the street and her car, ever aware of her surroundings, ever cautious.

When she heard a motor drawing close from inside the gate, she turned to see a golf cart approaching with a rotund woman driving it. The cart stopped at the gate, and the woman got out and walked toward it, her put-out expression unmistakable even in the dark.

Harri held up her star, close, to the wrought iron, so the woman could clearly see it.

"You're free to call and verify," she said. "I can wait."

The woman studied her for a moment, her mouth twisted into a surly scowl. "Won't need all that. You got po-po written all over your face." She dug in her pocket and produced a ring of keys.

The woman was dressed in a security uniform. Forest green with the patch of Allied Forces Security on the breast of the bomber jacket. Her wool cap, which was pulled down past her ears, sported the same patch. Harri watched impatiently as she flipped through her ring of keys, looking for the one to the gate.

"Ya'll taking up arresting dead folk now?" the woman asked, her generous lips twisted in snark. "Because I can tell you, if you think anybody in here committed a crime, you're barking up the wrong tree."

It was taking too much time, Harri thought. She needed to get in and see, but rudeness here at the gate wasn't going to gain her access. "Nothing like that. I just need to check one gravesite."

The woman worked the key in the lock. "Hmm. Your business. But I'll have to fill out a report. I didn't memorize that badge, so I'm gonna need your details. Name. Numbers, all that."

"Sure. No problem."

Lock on the gate disengaged, the loud click and slide sounded ten times as final and funereal at night as it would have at noon.

The woman eyed her, her hands on the gate. "You got a gun on you? Cuz guns aren't allowed inside. You'll have to leave it in the office."

"I'm not leaving my gun in the office," Harri said, the tone in her voice broaching no discussion and no negotiation.

"Hmm. I'll have to put that in the report."

Harri pulled her city card out of her pocket and handed it to the security guard. "Name. District. Phone number and email address. It's all on there."

The woman took it, pulled the gate open wider to admit Harri's car, and then went back to the cart. "I'll follow you," she said. "Can't have you wandering around doing lord knows what."

She had no problem finding her father's grave, even at night. She navigated the windy pathways from one area of the cemetery to the next, the puttering golf cart following behind her, its flickering headlights casting ominous shadows over the gravestones.

Harri didn't fear the dead; they couldn't hurt you. It was the living, the broken ones, the evil ones, who hurt and ruined lives and took things that didn't belong to them.

The cemetery was peaceful, though driving past the headstones in the dark felt a little otherworldly. She and the security guard were not alone. There was a whole other world beneath their feet.

Finding the grave she wanted, she got out of the car and slowly made her way across the icy earth to the right row, aware the guard was watching every move she made. The woman had turned her walkie on, and Harri could hear the crackle of broken-up communication between her and whoever she'd left behind in the security office.

Harri stopped right before she got to the headstone, having a good idea what she'd find but not wanting to find it all the same. One deep breath taken, she started again, counting the headstones from the start of the row. Six graves in, she remembered. Right in the center. There it was.

She stopped, her heart beating wildly and aching at the same time. Her headlights yards away cast some light, but she drew a small flashlight out of her pocket and flicked it on, training the orb of light on the words etched in stone. CHARLES MILLAR FOSTER. LOVING HUSBAND, FATHER, GRANDFATHER. 1944–2014.

There was a moment's trepidation before she lifted the light to the top of the headstone, but she found what she'd expected to find. A coin. A dime, specifically, which glinted in the faint glow her flashlight provided.

"Damn it."

A penny on Reg's grave, a quarter on G's, and now a dime on her father's.

"Who is it, Daddy? What does he want?"

She kept her voice low so the guard wouldn't hear. This was just between her father and her.

She could feel the guard squirming in her golf cart. Nobody in their right mind wanted to spend a frigid night driving around a graveyard.

Her father had been a police sergeant with CPD until he retired. The dime left behind meant that whoever she was seeking, whoever was targeting her, had served with him, worked alongside him. Harri gripped the dime, hard, like it was possible to squeeze life out of it.

"One of us," she whispered to her father, through gritted teeth. She shook but not from the cold anymore. It was fury, rage. She stepped back from the headstone, flicked her light off, took a moment.

"I'm done," she called to the guard. "Let's fill out that report quick. I'm in a hurry."

———

Annemarie Foster stood waiting at her front door when Harri pulled up in the driveway.

"Harriet, what on earth?" she asked as she let her daughter in. "What's going on? You sounded strange on the phone."

Harri gave her mother a peck on the cheek, then moved past her into the front room.

"I needed to ask you some questions," she said, taking in the customary aroma of lemon Pledge and the remnants of the evening's dinner. Red beans and rice and corn bread?

"You were on the phone," her mother said. "My ears were working."

Annemarie's brown hair, graying slowly for a woman of seventy-two, was perfectly combed even at this late hour, and she stood there in a robe, matching pajamas, and slippers, expectantly, but not agitated. Her mother's superpower was her calmness, her ability to wait and patiently assess a situation, and then act in absolutely the right way.

"I know it's late," Harri said. "This couldn't hold until the morning."

It was after nine, past her mother's usual bedtime. She would be up at 4:00 a.m. for her morning coffee and first crossword of the day if her habit held, and Harri knew it did.

Her mother searched her face and saw what only a mother could see. She then turned for the kitchen. "I'll make us some tea."

While Annemarie readied the teapot, the water, the tea bags, Harri told her about her visit to the cemetery and about the other visits to Reg's and G's graves. She downplayed the calls from the voice, telling her mother only that she had heard from someone who appeared to hold a grudge against her, only to suspect the grudge might have originated somewhere else, somewhere closer to home, which had led her to her father's headstone.

"Did Daddy have any enemies?" she asked gently once tea was in front of her, beginning to smooth some of her rough edges. "Somebody who might have had something against him? I can't imagine he would. Everybody liked him. He was a good man, a good police officer. I've been racking my brain trying to remember if I ever heard anything that might have been off, and I can't. Commendations all over the place. Daddy was the best."

She was talking too fast, her brain cycling quickly through her childhood, looking for anything that might explain the situation.

Annemarie nodded. "He *was* the best, and he was so proud you followed him. He told you all the time how proud he was."

Harri took a sip from her cup to keep her eyes from flooding with tears. "But do you remember *anything*? *Anyone?* Maybe an arrest that went wrong?" She paused for a second, not wanting to say the last part. "A bad cop?"

She searched her mother's face and saw a flicker of remembrance. There was something there. "Mama?"

"You said you heard from somebody," Annemarie said. "What does that mean?"

"Phone calls. Standing outside my house. Talking in riddles about things that make no sense to me. Said he was an old friend. He mentioned something about a dead man's shoes. He keeps teasing that he's got some inside information on what happened to G. He left a quarter on her grave. I don't know if you remember when Daddy told me and Felix about the significance of coins on military graves?"

"I remember." Annemarie ignored her tea. "What have you been doing about the calls, Harriet?"

"They've been cryptic. Teasing. Then nothing for a while. I'd gone to IAD by then."

Her mother's keen eyes looked into hers. "I asked what *you* were doing about the calls."

"I'm looking for him since IA won't."

"You're taking risks," Annemarie said. "Putting yourself in danger. Walking through cemeteries at night. By yourself. Not caring what happens. File a report. Let the police handle it."

"I *am* the police."

"You know what I mean."

"Ma, if you know something, I need to hear it, please."

Her mother let a beat pass, then slowly rose from the table. She stared down at her daughter, knowing silence wouldn't work, knowing that whatever she didn't say wouldn't stop her child from pursuing a single thing. "Come with me."

Harri followed her mother into her father's office, now converted into a TV room and filled with books, folded-over newspapers turned to the crossword puzzle page, of course, and baskets of colorful yarn used to knit scarves and sweaters and socks for everybody in the family and booties for every new baby at her church.

"Sit," her mother said as she crossed over to her father's desk, still in the room, the one article of furniture in the entire house she knew no one in the family would ever part with.

"Remember when you came home from school for a couple months? Because your father was sick? Sophomore year."

"Of course. It was his heart. I thought he was going to die. Felix came home too."

Her mother returned to the chair with a wooden box she'd taken from a drawer. She set it on the table between them. "Your father was fine. He just needed you both where he could see you, to protect you."

"Protect us from what?"

Annemarie slid the box toward Harri. "Your father and a few others he worked with testified against a detective who worked in the gang unit. This person was shaking down businesses. He dealt drugs and robbed dealers who also sold women. Not even women, girls. It was a whole mess. You know the department. On some levels it was an open secret, but nothing made it up the chain. That code of silence you all have? How you stick together?"

Harri bristled at the implication. "We stick together for protection. It doesn't mean we turn our backs on what's right."

"*Some* turn their backs," Annemarie said. "Some even take part. Your father wasn't one of them. Neither are you, I'm proud to say. But he couldn't abide the bad ones."

"Mostly bad cops don't last long," Harri said, still defending. "Good cops don't trust them and won't work with them."

Annemarie smiled. "That was your father."

Harri reached for the box, opened it to reveal layers of yellowed newspaper clippings. She started reading but couldn't read fast enough to satisfy her insatiable need to know.

"Daddy's all over this," she said. "He testified in court and everything." She read on. "How did I not know about any of this?"

"You were a busy college student away from home, living your life. No good reason to worry you about police mess. Well, except for that short time when your father didn't think it was a good idea for you or Felix to be so far away that he couldn't get to you quickly. You know how he was. He couldn't stand anything that wasn't right. Police who didn't behave like they should. Like—"

Harri scanned the clipping and found the name of the gangster cop. "Detective Edward Noble."

"Fast Eddie," her mother scoffed. "A lot of them knew what he was doing but didn't say a word. They'd arrest some of the gangbangers, and they'd actually tell them what Noble was up to, but nobody listened, nothing changed."

"How'd Daddy get involved?"

"There was a shooting. A young girl was killed by one of the animals Noble worked with. Noble tried to bury the whole thing. Your father and a couple others caught him at it and spoke up. It took your father, Bert Easton, and Mario Degas to bring him down. You remember them, don't you?"

Harri thought back more than twenty years. "Vaguely, I think."

"Noble got something like twenty years. He's still down in Dixon Correctional, as far as I know."

"I don't think he is. Unless Daddy took some other cop down too. I think he's out."

"It wasn't just him. Noble's partner got dragged down with him. Noble even testified against him trying to save himself. Fast Eddie told everybody he was just as guilty as he was and that half the money they made went to him. The jury believed it."

"You remember the partner's name?"

Annemarie offered a look. "Harriet, I remember everything about that case. I'm convinced it's what drove your daddy to an early grave. Leonard Krieg. When he got sent to prison, he had a five-year-old and his wife was eight months pregnant." She shook her head. "Oh, how that woman wailed when that verdict came in. It cut right to my heart. Noble ruined lives. Krieg got half as much time as he did. I haven't heard anything about him since."

She made a mental note to track down Krieg. "Noble came out looking for Daddy and found me." She didn't mention G, what she suspected. That would be for later. "What happened to Easton and Degas?"

"Retired. Moved away. I heard that Mario passed not long after your father. Heart attack from all the stress, I would guess. Bert? I don't know. He and his wife moved south. Arizona or Texas. They wanted nothing else to do with this city or CPD, and nobody could blame them."

Harri gathered up the box, excited that there was finally something concrete she could do. "I can check to see if Noble is still locked up. If he is, I'm dealing with somebody else. If he isn't, I have a name I can put a face to."

"I don't want you *dealing* with him, Harriet. Noble's a twisted person."

"I'll be careful."

"Harriet." Her mother's voice took on a commanding tone. "This is not something you can do on your own. Your father knew he couldn't. Noble is corrupt, ungodly."

Harri looked over at her mother. "Is he the kind of person who would do something to G just to get to me?"

Her mother's eyes softened, but the concern and the unspoken message they conveyed came through. Harri had her answer. She held the box like a prized thing full of treasure.

"If I can prove it, I'll make him pay." She rose. "Don't worry."

"Too late for that," her mother said. "Be careful, Harriet. Remember, I'm old. Act accordingly."

"Maybe you should go visit Aunt Ceecee for a few days?"

Harri gently proposed the idea even though she knew it wasn't going to fly. Her mother was as stubborn as she was.

Annemarie shook her head. "I'm not letting Eddie Noble run me out of my own house. I'm staying right here. I've got the alarm. Your daddy's gun is upstairs. I still know how to shoot it. And I have a feeling you and Felix won't be giving me a moment's peace, am I right?"

Harri smiled. "You're right." She kissed her mother on the cheek again. "I'll stay close."

Her mother smiled back. "Well, that right there is the best news ever."

"If you see Noble around here, you call 911 first, and then you call me. I'll call Felix and let him know what's going on. He'll probably make you come stay with him and Tamara."

Her mother's brows rose. "*Make* me? Huh. I'd like to see *that*."

"Safety in numbers, Ma," Harri said, turning serious. "I don't know what he'll do."

"They're hoverers, Harriet. You get to be my age, you don't want all that. I'll be fine right here."

"All I'm saying is, if—"

Annemarie got that look. "Harriet? Hush now. I'll be just fine sleeping in my own bed. Eddie Noble knows better than to bring himself around here." Their eyes held. "So, it's settled?"

"Yes, ma'am."

There was no use arguing with her, Harri knew, and so she didn't. Outside on the stoop, she waited to hear the front door locks engage and the alarm beep into action before she hurried down the front steps, jumped in her car, and drove away.

"Fast Eddie Noble," she muttered, her eyes burning holes through the windshield. "Damn you."

CHAPTER 16

The president's house stood dark on the quiet street as the large bell in the campus's tower tolled ten times, announcing the hour.

The Four sat in the car, robed, waiting.

Anna Bauer sat in the back seat with two others, her head lowered, her mind uneasy, guilt sitting in her chest like a giant rock of shame. Brice Collier had been retribution. A necessary thing. Fair. She had been able to convince herself of that. How easy it had been to do it too. After all this time, the emptiness, the blame, had eaten away everything that had been good in her. The Colliers had loomed large in her mind. She loathed them, wished them dead, and so when a plan was decided, when justice needed to be handed out, she agreed.

She stared down at the black robe she wore, suddenly feeling ridiculous. What was she trying to prove? The robe was nothing but cloth and thread. Who did she think she was? They called themselves Justice, but nobody could really be so lofty. They'd killed that boy. That was evil. It was bloodlust, madness. And solved nothing in the end.

"This is as far as I go," she said. "We need to stop."

Outside the car, Anna listened to the wind howl. She flicked a look at Younger's house, dreading the plan. She turned to look at Hardwicke House a distance away. Lights blazed there. Down the street many houses had their lights still on. It didn't matter that Brice Collier was dead. The world still turned. No one had come back. Nothing had been reversed. There was just one less person in the world, a person they took out to cause pain. Every second someone else was born, someone else died. That's how the world worked, Anna reasoned solemnly.

"It all keeps turning," she whispered. "No matter what we do. No more, Ethan."

"We agreed," he said from behind the wheel. "We pledged. One life sacrificed. Two lost as a result. They took three, we take three. They have to suffer, slowly, like they did. They died a little bit more every day, and you know it. You saw it. Somebody has to answer for that."

Anna looked up, met his eyes in the rearview. "It's no good. We killed his son, but what did we get? Tell me, what's changed for us?"

"We hurt him. That's a start," Ethan said. "Now, he knows we're coming. We take care of Younger, then he'll know we're coming *fast*. Payback. Slow. Steady. Cold. We blow up his world like he blew up ours."

"Did we hurt him?" Freddie asked from the back seat. "He didn't even bother to show up for his dead kid. He sent his butler guy instead. And Younger? I can't see Collier losing sleep over him." He turned to his brother next to him. "Am I right, Jesse?"

Jesse, a rail-thin rake, smiled back, his crooked teeth of no concern to him. "I'm with Ethan. We take 'em all. You know yourself, Freddie, the Pagets gave us a shot when nobody else would. Right out of the joint like we were. And that rich guy wrecked 'em. What he did? He might as well have put a gun to their heads and pulled the trigger. I say we go. We do it." He grinned. "Besides, Ethan's paying good."

"Money," Anna muttered. "That's all it takes for you?"

"It helps," Jesse said. "And we'd better get it. Clowning around in these dumb robes. What's the point if we don't get paid and they're not dead in the end?"

"And loyalty," Freddie added. "Don't forget that. I'm okay with Collier getting what's coming, only I don't see nothing wrong with just doing it. Why all this fooling around?" He pulled a gun from his pocket. "One shot. He's gone. We're out. Clean as anything. He's still dead. That's what we want, right?"

Ethan turned, his look deadly. "Put that away. We're not some common thugs. This is accountability. It's what's fair. My parents died a little more every day. We all saw it. Slow death. Agonizing death. That's what Younger and Collier deserve, and that's what they're going to get."

Anna stared at Ethan. "See? This is what we've become. We dishonor them. We've dishonored ourselves."

"He was my brother," Ethan said. "They were my parents. My *family*. I lost *everything*. It would be a dishonor *not* to avenge them. Collier and his friends don't just get to go on with their lives. Collier gets to make more and more money? No accountability at all? He's a billionaire, for Christ's sake. What do *we* have? No. He ruined the Pagets, now we ruin him. Younger's next. He's the one who swore he didn't see or hear anything the night Mikey died. But he lied." His eyes met Anna's in the mirror. "You know he did. He helped dump Mikey. Like a dog. Younger pays, and then Collier."

Anna studied the eyes and saw the pain in them. "I failed you. I failed myself. We should have been able to carry on and make lives for ourselves."

"How could we? Collier left us *nothing*."

"Mikey's death broke them. It didn't have to break us too. We let it. I should have been able to help you."

Ethan bristled. "They didn't break, they were *murdered*. By Collier, by the lawyers, the courts. There's no justice for people like us when we're up against all that money. Sweetheart deals, backroom negotiations. They stick together. The little guy always loses. The business was the last straw, the last thing. That's what killed them."

His eyes fired in the mirror. "You can't make me feel bad about this. To feel sympathy for them. They don't deserve to live when my family is dead. I'm going to finish this. Whatever it takes."

Anna buried her head in her hands. "We've already damned our souls to hell."

"*This* is hell," he shot back. "*This*. The first one's the hardest. The others will be easier."

"What about the police? They've already been snooping," Freddie said, his voice unsure as he jutted his chin at Anna. "It's like they know something."

"They don't," Ethan said. "Collier's not going to want to admit what he did. Besides, it'll all be done before they even get close. Just two more. The ones responsible. And we're done."

"Will we suffer less, then?" Anna asked.

"The plan is set. Slow deaths. I want them to feel every second as they're dying," Ethan proclaimed defiantly.

"That's fair." Anna sighed. "We're killers. The same as them." She slid her hood off. "I won't do it. I'll answer for my sins soon enough, but I won't do this."

She glanced over at Freddie and Jesse. "I would suggest you put the robes away and get out of here."

No one moved. It was the money, she knew. Ethan had promised them each $5,000 to be Justice. It was all the money he had left from the family, and all he'd been able to save on his own. But it was Anna who had reeled them in, playing on old loyalties. As she stared at them now, Freddie, beady eyed and avaricious, and his brother, Jesse, whose five thousand would most likely go in his arm or up his nose, she could clearly see what she'd become. A predator, a manipulator. Worse than Collier and Younger, far worse.

It hadn't been until Brice Collier breathed his last breath that she truly understood that. She was a killer. Not by accident or mistake. She had killed deliberately. It had been her hand over the boy's mouth. That made her contemptible. Lower than low. It made her a monster.

"So much death," she muttered. "So much darkness. I'm so far from heaven."

"You can't turn your back on family," Ethan said.

She could see her sister in his eyes. Her funny, loving, gifted sister who had shattered like a china cup right before her eyes at the death of her firstborn. Hannah had failed to save her second.

"I'm sorry," she whispered.

His eyes blazed. And in a flash, her sister's eyes were gone, and she didn't recognize Ethan anymore. She gave him one last look, seeing the boy he'd once been, knowing how much his parents loved him, and feeling the weight of her failure. She had had an opportunity to guide him, heal him, and instead she'd let her own weakness consume her. She offered up a silent prayer of forgiveness, then worked her way out of her robe and set it on the seat between her and Freddie.

"Goodbye, Ethan."

She opened the back door a crack, then held it there for a moment, searching for something to say that might turn her sister's son away from his purpose, but there was nothing she could think of that he would listen to. It was too late for both of them.

Without another word, she got out, closed the door behind her, and walked away.

"God forgive me," she whispered to the wind.

She turned to give the car one final look, then melted into the night.

CHAPTER 17

Harri sat at her desk, the clippings in front of her, her eyes blurry from strain and stress and lack of sleep. She hadn't gone home after her mother's house. How could she? She had a name at last. Eddie Noble. She even had a why. It made sense. It fit. Nothing she'd learned yet connected Noble to G, except the quarter and what it meant, but she had a feeling she was getting close. How could he have been in the lot when she died? He would have been just two months out of prison, no longer a cop. Wouldn't someone have noticed him there? *Harri* must have. Why couldn't she remember?

Noble likely still had friends on the job. It wouldn't have been hard for him to find out where Harri worked or lived. It wouldn't have taken much to find out where Reg or her father were buried, or even G. The cop network of interconnectedness was vast and deep. Someone always knew a cop who worked with a cop they knew.

She'd track down everybody Noble touched—family, friends, his gang contacts, if they hadn't dried up years ago. Noble had been in prison for nineteen years. Gangbangers had a limited shelf life. How many of them could still be active or alive?

She had uncovered Noble's last known address, but the house had been sold and bought by someone new. She also found a divorce on record, the date of which coincided with his conviction. He had two kids, teenagers then, young adults now. Neither kid had any run-ins with the police, no arrests on record. Noble's ex-partner, Krieg, served his ten years, and then fell off the face of the earth. Nobody she found had heard or seen him since his trial. She also had the names of a couple of the thugs Noble betrayed his badge for: one was in prison for murder, the other was still on the streets causing havoc.

Looking down at the quarter on her desk, she was sure she had a plan, a way forward. Picking up the newspaper clipping, she studied Noble's grainy photo again, then turned to his official departmental headshot, which showed him facing forward in his dress uniform, a tough, self-assured expression on his narrow face. Tough cop. Dirty cop. It turned her stomach to think he had threatened her father and caused him even a moment's worry for himself and for them.

"Why can't I remember his *face*?"

"Whose face?"

Harri turned to see Vera standing behind her with a paper cup of coffee and two bags that smelled of sugar and yeast. Doughnuts.

"You're in the same clothes you had on yesterday. So, you *didn't* go home?"

Harri looked down at herself. Up until then she hadn't given a single thought to what she was wearing or how tired she was. But Vera had somehow broken whatever spell she'd been in. She suddenly felt grungy and stressed.

"I did. I came back. Thanks for noticing and pointing it out. More doughnuts?"

Vera dropped a bag on Harri's desk. "You like doughnuts."

The tension between them from the day before was gone. Secrets revealed, confidences shared tended to wipe things like that away. For sure, Harri knew Vera a little better today than she had yesterday, and she felt certain Vera could say the same held true for her. But they didn't need to talk about it. The doughnuts said so.

Vera walked over to her desk and put her cup and bag down. "All right, then. What's new since last night? These clothes can't be because of your friend Sly; you're avoiding him like the plague. And it can't be anyone else because there are far too many paper clips on your desk. So, I deduce you *worked* through the night. Not ideal for a lot of reasons, but you insist on pushing yourself. The Collier case or the bastard on the phone?"

Harri gathered up her notes and the clippings, shoving them all back into the box her mother had given her, then slid a look toward Griffin's door. The door was closed, Griffin not in yet.

"I have a name. And reason."

She pushed the box over to Vera and waited while she read through the clippings, watching as her partner's face went through a series of astounding changes—brows lifting, eyes widening, mouth agape, then a scowl, narrowed eyes, followed in the end by a sharp clench of her jaw and a dangerous glower.

"What. The. Fuck."

"This takes away his advantage," Harri said. "I know who he is. I can deal with him straight on now."

Vera shook her head, a frown on her face. "No wonder they don't trust us. Dirty cops make us all look bad. So, we pass this on to Griffin. We snatch him up. He's on parole. He's in violation. We find out who his parole officer is, and he's back inside before he knows what hit him."

Harri's eyes met hers. "That's one way."

"That's the *only* way."

Harri stood. "You're forgetting the quarter. You're forgetting G. It's not just the calls. He was there. He knows what happened. I need to know. I turn him in, he goes back, he tells me nothing."

Harri walked away.

"Where're you going?" Vera followed after her.

"Locker room. Shower. Change of clothes. Then we're back on Collier. Meanwhile, I have a line on Noble's parole officer."

"So double duty? For how long?" Vera asked.

"Until it's done," Harri said.

The women's locker room was a gritty, dark room with peeling paint, a short row of metal lockers in it, and a wooden bench facing them. Off in the back was the restroom and a narrow shower stall, which was little more than a rusty nozzle, a drain, and squeaky spigots. It wasn't luxury, just functional, and all the city was going to pay for.

Harri worked the combination on her locker. "I find him. He talks. I know what happened to G. I end this."

Li's eyes narrowed. "End it? What does that mean, *exactly*."

Harri turned to face her. "Sending him back where he belongs. What did you think I meant?"

"I'm not sure. I can't tell where your head is right now."

Harri grabbed fresh clothes out of her locker and slammed the door shut. "It's where it's always been." She let a moment go. "My mother says Noble's a nasty piece of business. We'll have to keep our heads on the swivel, protect our families. I'm giving you another chance to step away. I hope you'll take it."

Vera's eyes narrowed, then she turned and strolled to the door. "Hurry up. You might want to cut that three-minute shower in half. We have double work to do. And doughnuts to eat."

Vera closed the door behind her, and Harri glared at it, frustration taking over. "Gawd, she's as stubborn as a *mule*."

"I heard that," Vera called from the other side of the door. "And don't you forget it."

CHAPTER 18

At eleven, Vera eased the car into a slot at Belverton, right across the row from Shelby Ritter's white Civic. Harri matched the plate to the information they had.

"That's it," she said. "You want to do the flush, or you want me to?"

Vera considered it for a moment. "Which one of us can look the most intimidating?"

"You," Harri answered without hesitation.

Vera grinned. "Aw. Thanks, partner." She left the car running, tapping her knuckles on the hood as she strode toward the front door of Devlin Hall. They were counting on a repeat performance of the day before. This time, though, the finale would be a bit different.

Harri got out and slid into the driver's seat and waited, her eyes on the door, her foot on the brake. It didn't take long, less than five minutes, actually, before Shelby Ritter came running out the door, alone this time, headed straight for the Civic. She dipped her head down but needn't have bothered. Ritter appeared singularly focused on a quick escape. Harri flicked a look toward the door to see Vera emerge from the building and head her way, unhurried. When the Civic started up, Harri shot the unmarked car out of its slot and blocked Ritter in at her back bumper.

Ritter rolled her window down. "Get out of the way, you idiot. *Move.*"

Harri put the car in park, then got out to stand at Ritter's driver's side window. Ritter's face fell when she recognized who she was.

Her hands gripped the wheel, her head slumped against them. Ritter groaned in defeat.

Vera joined Harri at the window. "She called you an idiot."

"I'm choosing to believe that's before she knew it was me."

Vera opened the driver's side door, and a dejected Ritter turned off the ignition and got out, her eyes downcast.

"Step this way to the idiot-mobile, please," Vera said with a smile, pointing Ritter toward their car. "No charge for the ride."

They were on the Drive headed toward the station when Ritter spoke. "I have class in an hour."

Vera glanced out the window at the Drake Hotel as they turned into the bend toward the lake. "Yeah, you're going to miss that."

The rest of the ride was silent, with Ritter sitting morosely in the back. When they arrived, they put her in the nicest interview room, the one where the heat worked, then gave her a few minutes alone to compose herself before walking in to find her not sitting at the table but standing at the window overlooking State Street, her arms wrapped around her body, the hood of her Belverton sweatshirt over her head.

Before they even had a chance to open their mouths, Ritter asked, "Why'd you arrest me?"

"You're not under arrest," Harri said. "That would be a whole different procedure. We just have a few questions we'd like you to answer for us."

Ritter looked suspicious. "Shouldn't I have a lawyer, or something?"

"We can get you a lawyer," Harri said. "That's your right."

"We'll let you call your parents," Vera said, "and they can arrange for a lawyer. And we'll wait until your lawyer gets here before we talk to you."

Ritter looked from one to the other, nervously. It didn't appear to Harri that she was too keen on spending a second longer here than she absolutely had to. "How long does *that* take?"

Vera shrugged. "Depends on your parents and the lawyer. One hour. Six. Ten. We'll try to make you as comfortable as possible while you wait."

"My parents," she muttered, eyeing the chair like it was a death trap. "I don't want to get them involved. I told the truth. We found him like that. I don't know what else you need me to say."

"So, to be clear, you *don't* want a lawyer?" Harri asked.

"I just want to get out of here," Ritter said. "I didn't do anything. Ask your stupid questions."

Harri and Vera took their seats at the table and watched as Ritter plopped down in the empty chair on the other side of the table. Then she scooted the chair back several inches to put more distance between her and them.

"I don't feel safe here," she muttered.

Harri focused on her. Young. Skittish. Hiding something. She wondered what.

"I'm curious," Vera said. "*Why* don't you feel safe here? Our job is literally to serve and *protect*. It's even on the side of our cars."

Ritter scanned the small room, the room hundreds of suspects and witnesses had sweat in, cried in, fought in, pissed in, vomited in. It wasn't the Ritz. Wasn't even the Motel 6. It was a box with a table and chairs. A portal in for some, a way out for others, nothing to write home about.

Ritter said nothing.

Harri checked her phone sitting on the table in front of her. She had feelers out on Noble and was waiting for something to come through, but the two missed calls and the texts were from her brother. Fearing an emergency, she checked, but it was just Felix wanting an update. It would have to wait.

"Why'd you run?" Harri asked Ritter. "I got the impression when I spoke to you the other day that you feel some kind of way about

Hardwicke House. Did something happen there, maybe at the party, that upset you?"

"I never said I was at the party."

Vera smiled. "You didn't, but you were. Your friend Hailie was too. We have photos of the two of you, so let's start there. You and she also posted about it on your social media pages."

Shelby looked shocked. "You checked that?"

Vera shook her head. "Yeah, we checked that."

"You were both at the party, and then . . . what?" Harri asked.

Ritter burrowed into her hoodie; her mouth clenched shut. Harri reached over to the folder on the table and slid out a photograph of Ritter and Kenton at Hardwicke House. Ritter swallowed hard when she saw it.

"You were at the party from when to when?" Harri asked. Ritter stared at the photos on the table as if mesmerized by the images. She appeared to be a million miles away from the chair she sat in. Harri wondered what was distressing her. What was it that had her foot bouncing under the table?

"Shelby?" she asked gently. "Why are the photos upsetting you?"

Ritter glared at her defiantly. "I'm not upset. What was the question?"

For a moment Harri's eyes locked on to Ritter's and bore in deep to find the fear the girl was trying hard to mask. "When were you at the party?"

"We got there about nine. Maybe it was two or so when we left."

Vera leaned forward. "Two? And *that's* when you found Brice? Not at *six*?"

Ritter nodded, and her chin fell to her chest. "That's the only thing we lied about. I *swear*."

Harri's brow furrowed. "Four hours passed before you called 911? Why?"

"We were figuring out what to do. We didn't know he was dead at first. We thought he'd passed out. That he'd wake up and stumble back into the house at some point. So, we left him. But we kept thinking about it. How he might, like, actually freeze to death? So, we went back to check. We were sure he was dead then. That's when we called 911." Ritter paused and looked down at the hands she had now clasped in front of her. "We ran because . . . we thought we left him to freeze to death. But that's not murder, right?"

"He didn't freeze to death," Harri said. "He was already dead when you passed him at two."

"He was? For sure?" She squeezed her eyes closed for a moment— relief, it appeared to Harri.

"You *do* know that leaving a person in distress is not what you *should* do?" Harri said.

Ritter bowed her head. "Yeah."

"Then why leave him lying there, even if you thought he was just passed-out drunk?"

"It was stupid. We weren't thinking straight. We shouldn't have gone to that party in the first place. We just wanted to see what it was like. We thought we could handle ourselves if we stuck together. We blamed Brice for . . . things, so we weren't in a hurry to help him."

Harri thought she knew what was coming next and shifted uncomfortably in her seat. Beside her, she heard Vera take a deep breath and hold it. College party. Alcohol. A house full of guys. Young girls out of their depth. "Safety in numbers. It's a good strategy, usually," Harri offered. "Why was that necessary Saturday night? What *things* were you mad about?"

"They told us the parties there could get wild. They're all-nighters, which is kind of cool. But all those guys, used to getting what they want? The stories had gotten around. Spiked drinks. Closets. The roof. Girls waking up without remembering what happened. Brice always seemed to be in the middle of it. That's why we made a pact to stick together. We wouldn't go anywhere alone, not even to the bathroom. Nothing really happened, but it could have, easily. It *would* have if—"

Harri stared at Ritter, small in the chair, scared. "That's why you didn't want to go back into the house to talk to me?"

Ritter nodded. "I'll never go back in there."

Harri could feel Vera tense. For a moment, they let Ritter sit, not wanting to push or add more stress than they already had. It wasn't something that either needed to discuss.

"It's a party house," Ritter said finally. "Full of rich party boys. They call themselves the Minotaur Society. It all sounds like bullshit, but they take it seriously. It's been around for decades, apparently. All hush-hush, elite. They only take one or two regular kids, but if you get in, you're made. The networking potential, the contacts, everything is just ultra."

"*If* you get in?" Vera asked.

"You can't pledge. They don't recruit. I don't know how they choose. No one ever talks about it. So, the guys go to the parties hoping to get picked, and the girls, some of them, go looking for a boyfriend who's going places." Ritter searched their faces. "Not everybody. A lot of kids don't care one way or the other, but enough do, believe me. It's all they talk about."

"The school knows about this Minotaur Society?" Harri asked. "And it lets the parties go on?"

Ritter scoffed. "Everybody knows, but the Colliers can do whatever they want. We all know nothing's going to happen."

Harri let a moment go, thinking about Younger and his obvious capitulation to Sebastian Collier and his entitled son at the expense of his students. "So, what happened Saturday night?"

"Hailie and me went, and we watched out for each other, like we said we were going to do. We never put our drinks down and left them.

We only drank out of cans we opened ourselves. If anybody looked weird or sketch, we beat them back."

Harri thought of Renfro's statement of seeing Hailie coming from the second floor, and the other boy's claim that he'd seen Collier head to the roof with two beers in hand. She offered Ritter a small smile of encouragement. "But something happened."

"Brice was on Hailie like a heat-seeking missile. It was like he had picked her for the night, or something. He kept trying to get her alone, but we hung tight. Eventually, he gave up. We still had a good time, I guess? The place was packed. Kids we knew from school but a lot of kids we didn't. A few nice guys. Brice and the others—Todd something, and a couple of their friends—were circling, really loud, obnoxious. And then Brice was gone. We didn't know where, and Hailie sure didn't care. She could finally breathe."

"And you stayed together the entire time?" Harri asked.

Ritter nodded.

"What time did you lose sight of Brice?" Vera asked.

Ritter shrugged. "I don't know. We were . . . there was a lot of beer and stuff."

"An approximation would help," Harri said, trying not to dwell on the "and stuff."

"We hadn't been there that long."

"Where did you think he went?" Vera asked.

"Honestly, I figured he found somebody else to hang on, and settled for her. Then—"

Ritter stopped suddenly and stared again at the photos, her eyes transfixed, as though they were bringing back bad memories.

"Then?" Vera coaxed.

"At midnight they turned the lights out, and everyone got scattered around. They obviously planned it when they saw that we were sticking together and were going to stay that way. I got pulled by somebody.

Hailie too. I fought. The lights came back on after a couple minutes, and everybody thought it was a big joke. They acted like it was a game. Everybody was laughing, even some of the girls."

"Do you know who grabbed you?" Vera asked.

"No idea. All I felt was hands. And when the lights came back on, no one was near me. I felt sick."

Harri thought back to Grant's report. By midnight Brice Collier had likely been dead for two hours.

"But you and Hailie stayed until two?" Harri asked.

"Didn't want to miss the fun, did we?" Ritter answered sourly. "It's all about being there. It was stupid to go, stupider to stay. I've learned my lesson. I don't want my parents to know anything about this, though. They're . . . they'd blame me."

"They'd be glad to hear that you're safe," Harri said.

Ritter's mouth twisted into a scowl. "No, they'd blame me for going, for drinking, for not being in the library studying on a Saturday night . . . for having a life."

Harri pulled back, reminding herself that it wasn't her job to parent here, that in fact she knew nothing about Ritter's home life, which could indeed be tough. Instead she scribbled a few notes and waited for Vera to jump in. She didn't have to wait long.

"How long were the lights out? Two minutes? Five?" she asked.

Ritter sneered. "Long enough for them to cop a feel and try to push us upstairs toward the bedrooms."

Vera shook her head. "You got no help from the administration, but did anyone ever think to contact campus security or us?"

"Campus security *is* the administration. No one touches Hardwicke or the Minotaurs. They treat the house like it's an embassy. It's literally like another country. The parties keep going because they're the invite to beat all invites. There's even breakfast in the morning. *Catered.* As long as you're careful, as long as you stick together . . ." Her voice trailed off.

"But you were assaulted," Vera said. "Groping is *assault*."

Ritter blinked innocently back at them. "It could have been worse."

It was bad enough, Harri thought, as she looked up from her notepad and fixed stern eyes on the young woman who would learn at some point that her autonomy was valid and that "could have been worse" was not a compromise she needed to make. It was difficult to get that at nineteen for some, but it would be imperative to get if Shelby Ritter was going to navigate through the world safely as an adult woman.

Harri put her pen down. "Were the same girls there when the lights came back on as when they went off?"

Ritter thought for a moment. "I think so. I was kinda . . . we'd been drinking. And I was shaking so hard, I was so angry at what they did. After that, we didn't dance or anything, we just sort of huddled together and tried to act like it was all okay. Until we just had to get out of there. That's when it all happened. We could have screamed, but no one in the house would have heard us over the music, and we weren't going back inside, that's for sure."

"So, the lie is why you and Hailie ran from us?" Vera asked.

"We thought you were coming to arrest us for leaving Brice. For killing him."

"And just to be clear," Harri said, "neither of you were out of each other's sight the whole night?"

Ritter thought about it for a moment. "We were together, and we left together. That's all I know."

Ritter looked over at them, exhaustion playing across her bleached-out face. "Can I go now, *please*."

"One more question," Harri said, feeling obligated to get through to Ritter. "Why would you and Hailie put yourselves in such danger like that?"

"You guys don't understand how it works. It's *Hardwicke House*. The money? The prestige? The connections you could get access to if you were in any way close to the Minotaurs? Brice's father is a freaking billionaire. He knows everybody, and they know him. One phone call, one recommendation, and your future's all but set." Ritter looked from Vera to Harri. "I can see you don't get it. The student loans alone are enough to bury you for like thirty years. I'm a scholarship kid. Hailie too. A shot at a six-figure job in the corporate world? Sebastian Collier recommending you for it? Who's not going to go for the hookup if you can get it, right? It's how you play the game." Ritter picked at her nails. "It shouldn't matter where you start out, but it always does."

"Where'd you and Hailie go when you ran from us yesterday?" Vera asked.

Ritter stared down at her fingers. "Nowhere. We just drove around until we thought you two had left." She met their eyes. "But you came back today."

"And we would have come back tomorrow," Vera said.

"For future reference," Harri said, "running from the police is not something you want to get in the habit of doing. Anything else you think we should know?"

Ritter shook her head. Harri and Vera stood up, ending the interview.

"We'll need to talk to Hailie," Harri said. "You know her schedule?"

Ritter nodded. Harri slid a legal pad toward the girl and gave her a pen. "Write it down for us. Times, location. Her cell phone number."

"But she didn't do anything," Ritter said. "I told you."

"We still need to talk to her. Write. Then we'll see about getting you out of here. Meanwhile, sit tight."

Vera rapped her knuckles on the table. "Want anything to drink? We have Coke, Sprite?"

Ritter allowed herself the tiniest of smiles. "A Diet Coke?"

"Coming right up."

They walked out of the room, closing the door behind them, then stood in the hallway, keeping their voices low. "Hailie Kenton," Harri said.

Vera scowled. "Collier was a heat-seeking missile."

"Who maybe found his target?"

"Doesn't explain the bruises. Kenton couldn't have done that on her own."

"With a friend she could have," Harri said.

Vera frowned. "Stop. You're giving me a headache."

Harri's phone pinged. Another text from her brother but also an email from one of the feelers. She smiled.

"I have the name of Noble's parole officer and the address of his sister where he's supposed to be staying."

"Game on," Vera said.

"I have a quick call to make, then we'll take Kenton."

They walked back to their desks.

"God, those girls, huh? Were we ever that naive?" Vera asked.

"Sure we were," Harri said. "But they'll grow up, understand how tough the world can be, how to find the right people. We all have to."

CHAPTER 19

Lange straightened his tie before the Zoom call went live. He'd left his suit jacket off, choosing to present only in his silk button-down shirt with his monogram on the left breast pocket. Tailored, of course. He always wanted to look his best, especially when speaking to Sebastian Collier.

When his boss's face popped up on the screen, Lange was all business and relayed the latest information he had concerning his son's death.

"That's it? That's all they have?"

"They're not sharing much more than that. I will, of course, follow up. I know you want the body released as soon as possible. The fact that they're holding Master Brice indicates strongly that they've found something of interest."

"We know what this is. It's Paget's family."

"His parents are dead."

"There was a brother. Where's he? That field is no coincidence, and you know it."

"The location didn't escape me," Lange said.

"I thought you had somebody on him?"

"For a while I did, but he never made a move. He was just some guy working a shift in a plant. No life. No wife. No threat. Why pay for the eyes?"

"Where is he now?"

Lange shrugged. "It's been years."

"Find him. You do it, Lange. *Personally.*"

"Of course. But if it's Paget, you aren't the only one he's coming after. There's Younger."

"He's not my problem. He's always been the weakest link. Paget can have him. We sacrifice the pawn to save the king, Lange. Understood?"

Lange nodded. "And?"

Collier smiled. "You know me well. A price *must* be paid. He doesn't walk away clean. Am I clear?"

"Completely," Lange said.

"Then get it done. Send me updates."

Collier clicked off, and Lange powered down the laptop and rose from his chair. He closed his eyes and breathed in and out, slowly, deeply. He wasn't bothered by the order. He'd expected it. Lange knew it wasn't the boy Sebastian Collier lamented the loss of so much as the hit to the family name. Master Brice hadn't exactly set the world on fire, in his opinion. He was a rich kid who had been swaddled in privilege, and he'd taken full advantage of his circumstances. Sebastian Collier had wanted a young lion, an emerging titan, to mold into his own image. Instead, he had produced a lazy lothario for whom he displayed not an ounce of affection or pride. In all the years Lange had witnessed their relationship, there had been not a hug, not a smile, not a moment of encouragement between them. Brice was an heir, the only one. As such, he was a resource, an extension of the old man, nothing more, and Lange knew the moment he heard of Brice's death that Sebastian would take it as a personal affront more than a profound loss. He'd often wondered why there'd been no more children, no more chips off Collier's block. He'd finally decided after observing Sebastian for years that it was simple greed and avarice. Sebastian Collier was a grasping, closefisted, niggardly man who didn't like to share anything, not even his name. It was likely why he hadn't named his son Sebastian Collier Jr. It was all interesting to observe, but nothing he felt he needed to get invested in. Lange stepped up to the mirror in his room and studied his expensive shirt, the handmade tie. He was a far cry from where he started so many years ago.

Poor, trapped, and driven by need and want, he had been desperate for another kind of life in another place altogether. Every chance he'd been given, he took advantage of, not caring overmuch whether the taking was kind or good or fair. Your chance only came around once, he'd been taught by those who taught him little else, and he believed it.

He undid the buttons on the cuff of his right sleeve and rolled up his shirt well past the elbow. He wanted to see it, run his fingers over it. He needed to reassure himself that it was still there and that it still meant what it meant. He smiled as he looked at the faded minotaur tattoo, then held his eyes in the mirror's reflection. He had won. He wasn't the person he had been all those years ago. He was better, harder. Just as good. He rolled his sleeve down and slipped into his suit jacket. There was no sign of imperfection in the cut of the fabric, not even the tiniest piece of lint dared to light. Lange's shirt was new and neatly pressed, his shoes were Italian and made just for him. His angular face closely shaven, his hair cut short. He was the Man, and at the same time no one.

The field. It had to be Paget. He'd taken a Collier. He wouldn't stop at one. Lange understood the motivation and held no animosity. It was just the way things went . . . this for that, an eye for an eye, an evil for an evil. Now that Brice was gone, the gauntlet thrown down, Paget would go for the next easiest target first, Lange was sure of it. That meant Will Younger. It was the true sign of a real coward.

Lange always chose difficult first, but he was a different kind of man, one who did what he needed to do no matter the obstacle or cost.

Sebastian Collier wanted results, his problem solved. Lange was the man for the job. He was the man who would clear Sebastian Collier's path.

He smiled, declared himself presentable, and then stared into the dead eyes looking back at him.

"Semper anticus."

He turned for the door.

Always forward, Minotaur.

CHAPTER 20

Hailie Kenton sat cross-legged on her bed in her dorm room, rocking back and forth and clutching a tatty teddy bear that looked as though it'd gone through some things. Kenton was nineteen. The bear looked just as old.

Harri and Vera had escorted her out of chemistry class, forgoing the ride back to the office, choosing Kenton's quiet dorm room instead. The room was heavily pink, heavily Taylor Swift, and there was an overwhelming aroma of strawberries. The two lanky cops, like straight andirons at a fireplace, didn't fit.

"Tell us about you and Brice Collier Saturday night," Harri said.

Kenton looked up at them. "What do you mean?"

"We've talked to Shelby," Vera said. "We know you were at the party. We know about the delay in calling 911. We know about the light trick. Let's talk about Brice."

The rocking stopped, but the bear stayed close. "We weren't friends, or anything. I barely knew him. And if you talked to Shelby, you already know everything."

"Did you go to the roof with Brice Saturday night?" Harri asked.

Kenton's eyes widened. "No way."

"What about his bedroom?"

"I had *nothing* to do with Brice."

"So, no you and Brice," Vera asked. "At all."

"He tried to talk to me, but I knew what he was about. Everybody knows about Hardwicke and the Minotaurs. But they still go. You just know you have to be careful."

"You stayed with Shelby the entire night?" Harri asked. "Neither of you peeled off?"

"We stuck together. We already knew what they liked to do with the lights, so we were ready for midnight. When it happened, I elbowed somebody in the face. I heard him yell out. Everybody else was laughing and giggling. Thinking it was all a big joke. When the lights came up, I didn't see anybody holding their nose or anything. Maybe I didn't elbow as hard as I thought I did?"

"And just to make sure we got it," Harri said, "you did *not* meet Brice Collier on the roof or go to his room. You stayed with Shelby."

Kenton watched them. "Why would I go to his room?"

Vera's eyes narrowed. "I can think of a couple reasons."

"What if I told you," Harri said, "someone saw you, *just* you, coming down the stairs at Hardwicke Saturday night?"

Kenton pressed her chin to the top of the bear's head. "Then he's lying. Brice Collier was a letch and an entitled creep. I couldn't stand him. I know you're not supposed to say bad things about dead people, but he wasn't a good person."

Harri stared at Kenton, recalling the last time she'd heard the words *letch* and *entitled creep*. Shelby Ritter had spoken in much the same way about Brice.

"You and Shelby are close?" she asked. "Best friends?"

Kenton shrugged. "I guess."

"Was this your first party at Hardwicke House, or had you both been there before?"

Kenton pulled the bear closer to her and dropped her chin to the top of the stuffed animal's head. "We've been to a couple. We didn't do anything to him. We just found him, and I don't know what else to tell you. We went to a party, that's *all*. And you can't arrest me for that, can you?" She shot each of them a challenging look. Even the teddy bear seemed to glower at them. "Well, can you?"

Kenton was right. They couldn't. Instead, they saw themselves out and enjoyed a lonely trudge back to the car, being gawked at by students who seemed afraid to come within talking distance of either one of them. They were back in the car and belted in before Vera spoke first. "She had us there."

"They're definitely hiding something."

"No love lost for Brice, that's for sure."

"There were a lot of girls at that party," Harri said. "Maybe one who'd been there before and *didn't* get away when the lights went out?"

"And Shelby and Hailie decided to come back and get even?"

Harri turned to Vera. "Why not? They could have had help. Though it doesn't account for the similar case. Paget. Nobody we've talked to was even born thirty years ago."

Vera nodded. "Collier's death an echo of the earlier one? If we can prove a connection."

"That's the challenge."

Vera slid her a look when Harri went quiet. "You want to try the parole officer?"

"I wasn't thinking about that," Harri said.

"Yeah, you were."

Harri checked her watch. "Half the day's gone, and we've got a lead to push. First thing tomorrow?"

Vera put the car in drive. "First thing. But when I get home tonight, I'm going to start teaching my kid how *not* to be a Hardwicke Boy."

Harri sat back. "And the world thanks you."

The remainder of the day proved uneventful, as not a single domino fell into place for them. At end of shift, while Vera headed home to her family, Harri instead drove far south to Beverly, where Noble's sister, Charlene Moran, lived. Beverly, if you asked the chamber of commerce, was diverse. But everybody who knew the neighborhood knew it was diverse in pockets. Parts of it felt like you were driving into a quiet suburb you might find farther away from the city—green and lush and serene—and the parts that directly abutted the border line felt like the city itself, with all the problems the city brought with it, like traffic, gangs, boarded-up gyro shops. Just twelve miles from the Loop, Beverly was good bits and bad. Like everything, like everyone.

Harri turned left on Western at Ninety-Ninth Street, past a struggling strip mall and burger place, and headed south. A lot of cops and firefighters lived in Beverly, a lot of city civilian workers too. The neighborhood was twenty tight blocks from stem to stern of leafy greenery and well-kept single-family homes, and a strong Irish presence represented in well-attended Catholic churches and heavily patronized Irish bars. Clannish. On its surface it all looked nice and homey and safe, and it was if you were careful and mindful of where you went. Only a cop would look at the neat streets, the winter wreaths on the doors, and recall the homicide that had taken place three blocks over. Only they held the repository of trauma and human savagery that a leafy tree or a well-painted fence couldn't mask.

Harri stopped her car in the middle of the street at Noble's last known address. A nice house with a closed-in porch on South Drew. The other houses on the block were much the same. Newish cars parked in front or in driveways. The snow shoveled; the sidewalks salted. Lights shining in the windows. Stable. Hardworking people in homes they loved with people they loved. And down the street, Eddie Noble. Dirty cop, a friend to gang killers and dealers. A cop who made the rest of them look bad.

There was a car parked in front of Noble's old address, and lights on in the front room. Noble had been in prison for almost twenty years. The house belonged to someone else now, but Harri wanted to see it. She wanted to see what Noble had forfeited to greed, and she wondered if he had done the same when he got out.

She knew his whole life story. Parents deceased. A sister and her family nearby, a brother down in Texas. A wife who'd left him when he ruined his name and tarnished the family. Two kids, grown now. Had he reconnected with his kids, or did they want nothing to do with him? Did he have anything else to anchor him?

A single honk of a car horn sounded behind her, which rousted her from her study of the house. She offered a single wave of apology and moved on.

Charlene lived on Wood Street, not far from her brother's old place, and her home was much the same as his. Decent, well maintained, a place you could raise a family in and live a life alongside neighbors doing the same.

Harri parked across the street and sat admiring the many trees planted up and down the block. She could imagine the entire block canopied in greenery in the summer. There would be the constant whir of lawn mowers and kids splashing in plastic backyard pools. Old men would walk their dogs to the park blocks away, and young mothers would stroll their infants before midmorning naps. A neighborhood. Life.

Harri wondered if Noble was inside. Maybe doing something mundane like watching television or reading a book, confident that she had no idea who he was.

Did his sister know what he'd been doing? Did she know what he was? It seemed only fair that she should come to his home when he'd come to hers.

Retaliation. That's what this was about. Noble wanted to strike back at something her father had done, something any good cop would have. He was twisted and dangerous, and he'd gone too far.

She sat idling in the dark, just out of range of the streetlights, her tired eyes glued to Moran's front windows. Maybe he was in there, maybe he wasn't, but watching was what she could do for right now. Noble didn't know her. He didn't know that she could be dangerous, too, when pushed beyond limits.

But she had decided to start with his parole officer and learn all she could about the man. She would be patient, smart. Giving the house one last glance, Harri pulled away and headed home.

CHAPTER 21

Symansky rushed into the office, a stack of blue papers tucked under his arm. "All right. Listen up." He started passing them out to everyone. Flyers. "I got a fundraiser set up for Katie. They got insurance, but that won't cover everythin'. Hospitals charge you for the air you breathe in 'em. Rudy's. Seven o'clock. Sunday. Big barrel set up at the bar for cash and checks. All in. Don't come cheap."

Bigelow read the flyer. "Why Rudy's? That's all the way out near Midway."

"It's a cop bar," Symansky said.

"They got cop bars south," Bigelow countered. "Ace's. The Firing Range."

Symansky glared at him. "Are you walkin'?"

Bigelow's eyes narrowed. "Why would I be walking?"

"I dunno. The way you're carpin', it sounds like distance is a problem for ya. Like your car's in the shop and you need a ride or somethin'."

Bigelow frowned. "Never mind. I'm just saying."

Symansky addressed the group. "Nobody say nothin', just be there with a smile and your wallets open." He cut Bigelow a look. "Got that, *Mr. Mileage*?"

Harri set the flyer on her desk, ignoring the banter, and approached the whiteboard to write down Hailie Kenton's name and underline it. She hadn't slept well, unable to get Noble and cemeteries out of her head. Even with two cups of bad coffee already in, she was finding it difficult to focus and ramp up.

"Kenton's holding back," she said before recounting to the team what she and Vera had learned the day before.

There was more than a little grumbling when she got to the part about the Hardwicke Boys' light trick.

"That settles it," Kelley said. "My kids are *not* going to Belverton."

"You think it's just Belverton?" Vera said. "It's campus culture in general. The drinking. The cliques. The sex. It was the same way when we went, only now it seems even more of a thing."

Bigelow gave Vera a beefy thumbs-up. "All you can do is prepare the kid, cuz you sure as hell aren't going to change any of *that* shit."

"Holdin' back's the same as lyin'," Symansky groused. "Hell, it *is* lyin'. What's to say they're not lyin' about all of it, then?"

He glanced around at the suddenly worried faces. They looked fearful he was about to make a big #metoo faux pas. "Not about the scumbag light show, the gropin', give me some credit. About them not seein' where the Collier kid went. Maybe they did. Maybe *that's* what they're not talkin' about. This could be them not wantin' to go up against the dragons, or whatever they're callin' themselves."

"Minotaurs," Kelley said. "Not dragons."

Symansky glared at him. "Made-up monsters. Same thing."

Harri put a big question mark next to the girls' names.

"Late last night, early this morning, Vera and I did some digging on the Paget case, and we found a connection, maybe even a possible motive." She jotted down Sebastian Collier's name.

"Our billionaire." She pointed at Younger's photo. "And our president. They're both graduates of Belverton. Both lived in Hardwicke House thirty years ago. *Both* knew Paget. And both were thought to have played a part in his death."

Vera got up and handed over copies of old newspaper clippings about the Paget case.

Harri watched as the team read through the articles. "We thought Collier's death could be a case of hazing. It still might be, but Paget's death definitely was, according to reports."

"Paget wasn't rich, but he got into Belverton. From everything we've read, he was a real go-getter with big dreams. Corporate level."

"Like 'wolves of Wall Street,'" Kelley said. "It's a soulless life propelled by greed."

Symansky squinted over at him. "There better not be a speech comin'."

Kelley shrugged. "Just making a point."

"Reading between the lines," Harri said, "Paget gets into the school and goes straight for Hardwicke House because that's where the movers and shakers are. The Minotaur Society. That's what the tattoos are about. We got that from Ritter. Handpicked candidates. Once you're in, you're made. And they only take one or two *regular* kids."

Symansky frowned, folded his arms in front of him. "Poor kids, you mean."

"No fun being king," Bigelow said, "if you got nobody to bow and scrape to you."

Symansky's frown devolved into a full-on grimace. "But you know they're gonna make the scrapers work for it."

Harri broke in. "There's no evidence that Paget was forced. No bruises. And no tattoo, which leans toward some kind of initiation, so he wasn't fully in when he died. I assume the tattoo, the brand, is the last step?"

Bigelow nodded. "You got it right."

Symansky consulted his copies. "The girls left Brice, and the *richies* from Hardwicke left Paget. That's what you call *not* a coincidence. Maybe one of the girls is connected to the family? A cousin or somethin'?"

"Good idea," Harri said. "We can check that."

Kelley lifted a hand. "I'll take it."

Harri nodded her thanks as Vera studied the board. "Paget lay passed out for hours while they pelted him with paper cups, wrapped him in toilet paper. There's more in the witness reports. They took plenty of photos to razz him later, which were used in court. Tragic. They could've saved him."

Bigelow shook his head. "Instead, they decided to save themselves."

"The *they* in this scenario being Sebastian Collier, Will Younger, and another student, Emil Bosch. They carried him out of the house. They're the ones the Pagets held responsible."

Harri drew a circle on the board and jotted the three names down inside it. "The call for help was logged in two hours *after* they dumped him. Not by any of the three, it's important to note. And not by anyone from the house. A passerby. By the time Paget got to the hospital, it was too late."

"So Younger, Bosch, and Collier did the dumping, but Younger, who's now president of the school and won't touch Hardwicke with a ten-foot pole, didn't open his mouth when Brice was found in the exact same field?"

Vera looked over the board at all the notes and bubbles and connecting lines. "In fact, he tried to blame it on city violence."

"So, the three weren't charged, the Pagets lost their suit, then what?" Kelley asked.

Harri capped the marker. "Nothing. Collier, Younger, and Bosch went on to graduate and live their lives. It was David going up against Goliath."

"But David won," Kelley pointed out.

Vera scoffed. "Well, the Pagets didn't. They came away with nothing but lawyers' bills."

Symansky shook his head. "Little guys get screwed again."

"The Pagets couldn't keep fighting forever," Vera added. "Hardworking people. Typical family. Small-business owners on the Northwest Side. Parents, two sons. They send their firstborn off to a good college, and he's dead before Christmas break. College covered their ass, did nothing. So they sued Collier, Younger, and Bosch. Their son was dead, they wanted somebody to take responsibility for it. Fast-forward a few decades and we get Brice."

"If we're thinking it's the Pagets, why wait thirty years?" Kelley asked. "And why Brice and not Sebastian? The kid might have been a sleaze, but he didn't even know Paget."

"His *father* knew him," Vera said. "Maybe Brice heard the name and the story at some point, at least from Sebastian's perspective. This could be a simple settling-the-score type of thing. You take one of ours, we take one of yours."

"Paget's parents have got to be pretty old by now," Kelley said. "What? In their seventies?"

"They're both dead," Harri said. "The mother died a decade ago. The father a decade before that. The court fight wiped them out financially. They lost their business, a family bakery in Bridgeport. Normal deaths, though, no hint of foul play, but likely exacerbated by the stress of losing their kid and the court fight."

"So, who's that leave?" Bigelow asked.

"Extended family, I'd imagine," Harri said, "but specifically a younger brother, Ethan. He was twelve when his brother died. That'd make him, what, forty-two now? He doesn't have a record. He's come back clean. We have a current address, driver's license, and plate number."

Bigelow looked skeptical. "He's going to suddenly bust out and kill a kid? Uh-uh."

"He has a strong motive," Vera said.

"Thirty years, though," Kelley said.

"You know what they say about revenge, Matt. Dish best served cold."

Harri circled Ethan Paget's name. "He's on the board. We talk to him. We also check into Anna Bauer. Something's off there. And see if we can find Freddie and his helper. The three of them had access to the house and access to Brice. Maybe they saw something, heard something. That's a full plate."

She noticed that Griffin had slipped out of her office to watch the rundown. The boss stood with her arms crossed in front of her, listening, looking over the board. They hadn't spoken much since the IA report. Harri hadn't yet found a way to bury the sting of being let down.

It was counterproductive to hold Griffin responsible, she knew, but allowed herself the brief indulgence in the form of a cold shoulder. After a few minutes, Griffin eased back into her office.

"Anybody got any ideas how we get to Sebastian Collier?" Symansky asked.

"We'll have to go through Lange," Harri said. "We can't force Collier back from Geneva, but we can have a conversation."

"He knows what's up." Symansky's eyes narrowed. "And he's covering his ass, stayin' safe in Geneva, even though his kid is dead."

"And what about this Lange?" Bigelow said. "Who is he? Where'd he come from?"

Vera shrugged. "Weird guy. Quiet guy. Creepy guy. Grant called him a hit man. He had her locking up her autopsy suite to keep him out of it. Not many people can spook Grant."

Bigelow smirked. "You got *that* right. She's usually the one doing the spooking."

"Back to Lange," Harri said. "He was Younger's first call when he heard about Brice. They arrived together to talk to us. Younger's connected to Sebastian through Paget. Is Lange connected to Younger, other than by being on Brice's contact list? Right off the bat Lange is . . ." She searched for the right word but couldn't find it.

Vera chimed in. "Hella sus."

The team sat quietly for a moment.

Symansky stood. "I got no idea what Li just said, but I'm too old to waste one more second tryin' to figure it out. Let's get to it. But you all better be at Rudy's Sunday." He turned to Bigelow. "I'll call *you* an Uber."

Bigelow waved him off. "Man, quit playing with me."

Back at their desks, Harri looked over to see Vera pump her fist, the receiver to her desk phone to her ear. She was retrieving her voicemail. Harri waited, desperately in need of a good news break.

"What?" she asked when Vera finally hung up, smiling.

"That was a message from Anna Bauer." She picked up a legal pad from her desk, where she'd transcribed the call. "She said, and I quote, *This is . . . Anna Bauer. I need to talk to you. There are things you need to know. I didn't tell the truth. Not all of it. Call me, please. Before I lose my nerve.*" Vera tossed the pad down. "Crap. This call came in at eleven last night." She checked her watch. "It's almost ten now." She dialed Bauer's number fast but got no answer. "I should have checked for messages first thing, damn it."

Harri was already in her coat, holding her bag, ready to go when Vera hung up.

CHAPTER 22

They made good time getting to Bauer's, but when they knocked at her door, they got no answer; instead Mrs. MacCallum's door opened. This time it opened wide, and they got a full view of the one-woman neighborhood watch.

"Well, it sure took you people long enough," MacCallum said. "I called at twelve oh six this morning. Heard strange noises over there, didn't I? Sounded like wailing. I knocked just like you're doing now, but she didn't answer the door. I knocked a lot. You have to check on people who live alone, don't you? Strange one, she is. Never has visitors. Work and back, that's all. Now, look, here you are, *The View*'s half over. Practically noon."

MacCallum stood in her doorway, dressed in a purple sweatshirt with a Persian cat reading a book appliquéd on the front. Her matching sweatpants gapped at the ankles, and her feet were encased in a formidable-looking pair of walking shoes. In her arms she held a very old and very nervous-looking tabby with a pearl necklace around its neck.

"Excuse me?" Vera said. "Who did you call?"

"I couldn't find that card you slipped under my door. Cheeky, if you ask me. Maybe Monique absconded with it. She's a hoarder." MacCallum ran an affectionate hand down the cat's back. "I didn't think it was an emergency, just odd, so I called 311, not 911. I told them clearly that I heard her key in the lock a little before eleven. I can hear a pin drop, and I *don't* have hearing aids. Quiet building, mostly. Nothing going on. Then the wailing. Then she didn't answer. Then nothing. I didn't hear her go out this morning, so I assume she's still in there."

"You were up at midnight?" Vera asked.

The old woman appeared to take offense. "I stay up as late as I please, young lady. Monique and I watch the Turner Classic Movies. Last night was *Mildred Pierce*."

"And the strange noise?" Harri asked.

"A bumping? Something like that."

"And nobody went in or out?" Vera asked.

MacCallum pet the top of Monique's head. "That's what I said. Not a soul. I would have seen them."

Vera's squinted. "How?"

MacCallum sighed heavily. "Through the peephole, of course."

For a second Harri and Vera stood mesmerized by the woman and the cat, the real one and the one on the sweatshirt, and then the spell broke.

Harri knocked at the door again. "Ms. Bauer, this is the police. We'd like to talk to you."

MacCallum watched from her doorway, as though she had a front-row seat to a command performance. Monique didn't appear moved.

Vera turned to face the old woman. "Ma'am, would you mind going back inside your apartment, please? We'll take care of it from here."

"I can't stand at my own door?"

Vera turned completely around, eyed the cat. "Okay, but we'll have to confiscate Monique."

MacCallum gasped, pedaled back, and slammed the door. Vera craned to hear the locks engage.

Harri shook her head. "Really?"

Vera shrugged. "Got it done, didn't it?" She slipped her phone out of her pocket. "I'm dialing her number. Maybe she'll pick up."

They listened while the phone inside rang without Bauer answering it. Harri knocked again, but there was still no answer.

"She comes in right before she calls you at eleven. The neighbor hears noise at midnight. A bumping. And the wailing. Doesn't hear her go out, or anyone else go in, and I believe she would have." She pressed her ear to the door. "I hear tapping too. Not sure what it is."

She knocked again, more forcefully this time. "Ms. Bauer. Chicago Police."

A couple of doors opened down the hall. Curious neighbors, like MacCallum, wanting to know what was going on.

"Back inside," Vera ordered.

The doors closed again.

"Could be a medical emergency," Vera said.

"Reasonable assumption. Wellness check?"

"She did look kind of depressed when we talked to her."

Harri knocked again, announced again, there was nothing again. "Right. We need a key." She jiggled the knob, put a shoulder to the door but found it solid and unyielding. "Find a super or somebody?"

Vera took off down the hall, headed for the elevators and the manager's office on the ground floor.

Harri rammed the door again, but her shoulder and weight weren't nearly enough to get the job done.

"Ms. Bauer? This is Chicago Police. Are you all right? Can you open the door?"

The door across the hall opened again. MacCallum was back.

"I just googled," she said. "You have no authority to confiscate Monique."

Harri gave Bauer's door another hit, but it was no use. She glared over at MacCallum, done with the cat, full cop face.

170

"Go back inside your apartment and *stay* there."

MacCallum shrank back and slammed her door shut.

"This is police brutality," she yelled from inside her apartment, her voice muffled. "I want your badge number!"

Harri rammed the door again, biting back the impulse to tell the old woman to come and get it. She heard running feet coming her way and turned to see Vera racing back with a round white man in a tie and argyle sweater holding a ring of keys.

"Mr. Longwood," she said. "Manager."

Harri stepped away from the door to give him access to the lock.

"I don't feel comfortable about this," Longwood said. "Shouldn't there be a warrant or something? I mean, our residents are entitled to their privacy."

"What do you know about Anna Bauer?" Harri asked.

Longwood shrugged. "Quiet. Nice, I guess. Never says much. Lives alone. We watch out for the solo residents of a certain age. Don't want any surprises, you know what I mean?"

"When's the last time you saw Bauer?" Vera asked.

Longwood said, "Not sure. Couple days. Coming in from the grocery store. Carrying a bag."

Harri held her hand out, wiggled her fingers. "Give me the key."

Longwood dropped the ring into her hand, his eyes wide.

"Now back up," she ordered. "Over to the side."

He moved back, sliding down the wall a few feet, a frightened look on his face.

Harri eased the door open, and she and Vera stepped inside, their hands on their guns, watchful.

It was freezing inside the apartment. Almost as cold inside as it was outside.

"Ms. Bauer?" Harri called out. "Chicago Police. Detectives Foster and Li."

The short hall ended at the open space that served as both dining and living room. Everything was as neat and tidy as it had been the first time they'd been there. Nothing out of place.

Harri quickly found the source of the tapping and the cold. All the windows were open at least six inches, the curtains pulled back. The tapping was coming from plastic pull rods flapping against a brass bookcase.

They moved toward the back without discussion, the move coordinated only by a look between them. The kitchen was clear and clean, no dishes in the sink, the counters wiped down. The bedroom was next. Bed made. Surfaces dusted. No clothes left strewn about.

Down the hall they moved, slowly, in tandem, eyes scanning right to left and back, for movement, for threat, as they had been trained to do. Harri left, Vera right.

The door to the bathroom stood ajar, the light on inside. They stopped at the door, pressed their backs to the wall on opposite sides of it.

"Ms. Bauer?" Harri called again. "Chicago Police."

Still no answer, and there was a definitive empty feeling in the apartment. Like they were the only ones breathing in it.

Then Harri smelled it. She knew Vera did too. You couldn't be a cop as long as they had been and not instantly recognize the smell of blood. Old blood. Fresh blood. It didn't matter. When it was your job to wade through it in alleys and basements and ditches. In the dark, at sunrise, in all kinds of weather and conditions, you knew blood when you smelled it.

They shared a look, resignation in the exchange. Harri moved to push the door open with the toe of her boot, knowing Vera was ready on her side.

Anna Bauer lay naked in her bathtub, her head lolled back, her eyes half-open. The water in the tub was deep red. Blood. On the floor, lined up on the bath mat like little soldiers, sat half a dozen brown medicine bottles with their white caps missing. The metallic reek of Bauer's exsanguination snaked up their nostrils and filled their mouths with the taste of dirty pennies. Again, not a new experience. There was no threat here. They were too late.

Bauer looked very thin and small in death, Harri noted, almost birdlike. As pale as chalk, the woman lay still and gone, her short, cropped hair, black, wet, and tinged with gray. No makeup. No attempts had been made, it appeared, to pretty up to check out.

Harri eased in to take a closer look. All the bottles were empty. There was more blood smeared on the sides of the tub, and droplets of it on the walls at body level.

Vera gingerly eased toward the tub, mindful of where she stepped while Harri moved around the periphery to take a 360-degree look at the room. Sun yellow walls, plastic bathroom curtains at the small window, colorful daisies adorning them. Then she looked up to find a few drops of blood on the ceiling too.

"The knife's in the tub," Vera said. "Left side. Her wrists have been cut."

"No clothes." With one finger, Harri lifted up the lid to the hamper. It was empty. "She walked in here naked."

They scanned the room. Vera's eyes found the note first.

"Heads up," she said, drawing Harri's attention to the single sheet of stationery propped on an open shelf next to Bauer's shampoos and conditioners.

They approached it. Harri read it aloud.

I'm sorry. I pray I will be received into Heaven. I pray we all will be. It wasn't hate, not for me, but sorrow. Still, it wasn't for us to judge or take. We were wrong about that. That poor boy. Please, God, be merciful. Save him. I couldn't.

Harri looked over at Vera. "We."

"Him," Harri muttered.

Vera walked out of the room and headed for the living room. "I'll call it in."

Harri leaned against the wall outside the bathroom, looking in at the tub, at the woman tied to Hardwicke House, who had had things to tell them, but who was now beyond their reach. Bauer was sorry and had prayed to be forgiven. She wished the same for someone else. Who? Were they looking at one of Brice's killers? How? Why?

She closed her eyes. Just for a moment before she had to do the next thing, and the next after that. Then she went looking for Vera.

CHAPTER 23

Hours later, sitting for a moment in the car, away from the techs and the vans and the neighbors from the building milling around firing questions they didn't have answers to, Harri and Vera didn't speak for a time. Harri knew why Vera was quiet.

"This is not on you," Harri said.

"She called me. I didn't pick up. We've lost whatever she was going to tell us. Not to mention, she's dead. That note sure read like she had something to do with all this. If I'd gotten that message sooner . . ."

Silence.

"Nothing?" Vera asked.

"All that's true. But you're not that powerful, are you? Nobody living is the axis the world turns on. You could have picked up, rushed over, and she'd still be dead. She had time to write that note and an opportunity to put all the answers to our questions in it. She didn't. She told us all she was ever going to."

"She's protecting someone," Vera said. "Someone she obviously cared about."

Harri's phone vibrated in the center console. Symansky. She put it on speaker.

"Goddamn it. Younger's dead," he said.

"What?" Vera pulled at her hair. *"No."*

"When?" Harri asked. "How?"

"We went to his office to talk to him, and his secretary said he had been out a couple days. Sick, or somethin'. So, me and Kelley go boppin' over to his place. Got nothin' when we knocked and announced, so now we're thinkin' he might have had a heart attack or somethin', so we go in and found him hangin'. A jerry-rigged belt over the bedroom door. Looks like he's been there at least a day."

"What the *hell's* going on?" Vera asked.

"Good question," Symansky said, his voice sounding gruff and put-out.

They told him about finding Bauer in the tub. For a moment, Symansky didn't say anything.

"Yeah, got it. We'll finish this up and head back," he said. "This one's gettin' rottener by the second. And not for nothin'. We weren't here two seconds before the vultures showed up, includin' that baby shitface from the *Coronet*. They're buzzing around here now like flies on roadkill. I might have to go bad cop again."

"Was Younger dressed or undressed?" Harri asked.

"You're thinkin' he sexed himself to death? Doesn't look like it. Everythin's on, except for the belt. Even his shoes. It doesn't look like anyone's been in the house, though. No sign of forced entry. Nothing out of place. Guy didn't even have a dog. They're still photographin' and haven't moved him yet. Rosales is back. He dusted the belt quick and in a hurry, but it doesn't look like he got much. Kelley's hoverin' over there now, waitin' to see if he's got one of them minotaur tattoos. Looks like we're swimmin' in a tight little pool here."

"We're on our way in," Harri said. "Meet you there when you're done?"

"Yeah, we'll head in right after, unless somebody else decides to check out."

Symansky hung up.

"Grant's going to give us so much shit," Vera said.

Harri heard, but her mind was on tattoos and a bloody bathtub, and circling around the edges, like a hungry predator, a bad cop holding a grudge. Thinking of Fast Eddie, she had the sickening feeling of being moved around like a game piece on a giant board, and she didn't like it. She couldn't be helpless. She couldn't allow herself to fear what Eddie Noble might do. And now she and the team had two new bodies. That was double the pressure, double the work, double the urgency.

"Earth to Harri," Vera said. "You look a million miles away. You okay?"

Harri wasn't sure, not really, but said, "I'm here. I'm all right." They made good time back and were through the lobby and almost at their desks when Griffin bolted out of her office.

"You two. In here."

Harri gave the whiteboard a quick look. Three of the people on it were now dead. They didn't have time for a departmental goosing.

They walked in to find Griffin behind her desk, her hands folded in her lap. Even all the Irish knickknacks sitting around—the shillelaghs, the green bowlers, the glittery boas, the leprechaun bow ties—couldn't put a glimmer of festivity on Griffin's face. They had three deaths in less than a week, all seemingly connected, and all somehow having to do with Sebastian Collier, the billionaire with the big stick. Bauer's death and Younger's didn't appear to be going down too well.

"Two suicides?" Griffin asked.

"Maybe," Harri said.

"We don't know for sure, of course," Vera added hastily.

Griffin held her arms out, a gesture of frustration. "Well? What's a college president and a housekeeper have to do with each other?"

"The college, the house, seem to be the connection point," Harri said. "Bauer's barely to the ME's. Younger hasn't even made it *that* far. There are no conclusions to be made at this point."

Griffin caught the edge in Harri's voice and knew what was fueling it.

"But we're on it," Vera said, hoping to cut some of the tension. "We'll coordinate with Al and Matt when they get back. Maybe there'll be some connectors discovered in the autopsies?"

"Investigations need time," Harri offered pointedly.

Griffin didn't miss the meaning and took a moment, more than one, to sit with what faced her. Finally, she leaned forward and picked up a pen to get back to work.

"Back to work. Don't take forever. Billionaires turn the wheel fast. And now we have Belverton *parents* demanding results." She shot Harri a look. "We might not like how this all works, but it's how it all works . . . and we all know it."

They walked out into the hall.

"So, that last bit was definitely for you," Vera said.

Harri moved past her. "I got that. Still don't like it." Vera trudged back to her desk. Harri veered off toward the board, snatched up the marker, and focused on the tangled threads that threatened to strangle them alive. She started jotting down the new information they'd gotten from Bauer. She'd mentioned she was divorced and lived alone, that she worked independently of an agency. And her note.

She turned to Vera. "Her note. It read like a confession. I'm sorry. Praying for forgiveness?"

"It did sort of," Vera said. "But you're not thinking she killed Collier?"

"Why not?"

"Well, for one thing, nothing about her says she's capable of 'force.'"

"She said *us*, and *him*." Harri turned back to the board. "She wasn't working alone."

"Younger and Bauer both dead on the same day, both apparent suicides. Younger connects to Collier and Paget and Hardwicke House. Bauer connects to Hardwicke and Brice. She has to connect somewhere else for this to make sense. Who is she? Where'd she come from? Sorrow, she said. We find that, we might find the answer."

Vera walked her chair over to the board. "We deep dive on Bauer. She was in the perfect position to know what was going on in that house and to get close to Brice, if that's what she was about. And, if we believe her, she brought in Freddie and the other guy. Who's to say the three of them didn't kill him?"

"If we're thinking Brice was killed for Paget, and that Anna had some part in that, she'd have to connect to Paget somewhere, or why else did she care? That would connect her to Ethan. Maybe *he's* the he."

"That's a lot of maybes," Vera said.

"Collier, Younger, and Bosch started this whole thing," Harri said. "The first two are accounted for. Where's Bosch? We could be looking at our next victim."

Vera sighed. "Another deep dive. I'm guessing they were all in the same class? Buddies. Lived together. Drank together. Left a boy to die together." Vera rolled back to her desk. "Let's see what we get."

Harri walked to her desk to get started, too, but the moment she sat down, her phone rang in her pocket and she tensed, relaxing only a little when she saw the call was from Sly.

There was a moment's hesitation. She couldn't take another setback today, and it was Sly. Her thumb hovered over the green button longer than it should have before she punched it.

"Hey."

"Bad time?"

Harri looked around the office at all the busy, overworked detectives. "Not sure I would know what a good one would look like."

"I won't keep you. Those photos you left with me? They're bogus. They were mocked up. Good enough to fool most people but not my guy. Thompson was photoshopped in, and so was the guy. Question now is, What the hell's your guy playing at?"

Harri could feel something release inside her, like a knot unwinding, like a pressure valve slowly being turned to let the built-up steam ease out. She shot a look at Griffin's door.

"Sly. Hold on."

She gestured to Vera, pointed toward the women's bathroom down the hall, and they both got up and headed there. Closing the door behind them, Harri checked under the stall for feet before locking the door for privacy.

"Sly, my partner's here with me, Vera Li. I'm putting you on speaker. I have a little more information than I had when I saw you. I think I have a name, and a reason."

She told him what she'd learned up to that point.

"I wouldn't play around with this," Sly said. "He's obviously looking to make some kind of play. Shut him down."

She flicked a look at Vera.

"Don't look at me," Vera said. "I'm with him."

"When I know what he knows, I will," Harri said. "He wants to play first."

"Oh, *hell* no," Sly said. "We're not doing that."

Harri went on as if he hadn't spoken. "There might still be security footage from . . . that day. It's been months, but it could be archived somewhere? If Noble's on it or if there's a car, a plate, or *something*. I'm sure somebody looked at it then, but if they were looking at G and not at anybody else . . ."

"He's crazy," Sly said. "Talking smack. All those years inside? And he was bad going in? He's getting off on twisting you in knots."

Harri didn't think Noble was unhinged. She'd heard his voice. He had sounded solid, locked in, vengeful, not crazy. That's what worried her.

"I didn't think about the tape. I should have long before now," she said. "Some things I can't ever forget. Others are just a blur. It's hard to know what's true and what's nightmare. If there's any chance at the tape—"

"I'll meet you there," Sly said. "Give me a time."

Harri hesitated. "I didn't mean for you to go, Sly. You've done enough, really."

"Is Li in?"

She looked over at Vera and saw her staring back at her, a determined look on her face. "Looks like it," Harri said.

"Then I'll meet you *both* there. When do you want to do this?"

Harri let a moment go. "Whenever we get a break. The case we're on just got messier. I'll have to call you."

"That's losing us time," Sly said. "I've got a better idea. I'll go and ask about the tape. I've got a buddy over there. I'll let you know."

"Sly, I can't—"

"You didn't. I'm offering. For G."

"Thanks."

She ended the call, feeling a little guilty for drawing Sly into her problems. She looked over at Vera. "The bastard's setting G up. I knew it."

"All this to get to you," Vera said. "He's sick. Sly's right. We don't play along. We shut him down. That means getting him violated. It means going official. It means locking him down."

"I agree. We're on the same page."

For a moment neither of them spoke.

Vera smiled. "Seems like a nice guy. *Sly.*"

Harri dropped her phone into her back pocket and turned to wash her hands in the ancient sink.

"He is."

"That was a lot of hesitation, though. How long were you two together?"

Harri's brows lifted. She saw Vera smile in the mirror.

"Not long. We parted friends."

"*You* parted. He's still in it."

"There's no way you got any of that from *one* one-sided phone conversation."

"Says you. I can't wait to meet him. For now, though, let's go try and figure this shit-can case out before creepy cop calls you again. You can fill me in on what happened with *Sly* while we're doing it."

Harri shook her head. "Never going to happen."

"Yeah, it will."

"Never. Going. To. Happen."

Vera chuckled. "It's already begun."

CHAPTER 24

Ethan Paget stood outside Younger's house with all the other onlookers and reporters watching police cars and tech vans finally pull away. He was doing it. Brice. Younger. The big man was next. Years and years and now it was almost done.

He wanted to stay until they carried the body out. He wanted to see Younger lifted into the back of the ME's van, knowing he put him there.

"The son of a bitch," he muttered under his breath. "For my *brother*."

He'd considered fire. Considered bolting all Younger's doors and lighting the entire house up, but the belt was slower, more torturous, more satisfying to watch as his brother's killer got down to his last desperate gasp. He had something more spectacular planned for Sebastian. Something befitting the big man's stature. Something for the front pages, the same ones that had dismissed his parents as money-hungry opportunists for suing the great Colliers for nothing more than a college prank gone wrong.

For now, though, with two down, Ethan stood quietly off to the side of the huddle of curious students and news people, his face obscured by the hood of his jacket, murderous eyes peering out from underneath at the house, the orchestrated chaos, waiting for the body.

Only he had the true conviction to carry on. He wasn't sure what he would do about Hannah. She was the last family he had, his mother's only sister. How could she leave it for him to do alone? And in her frame of mind, what would keep her from betraying them all to the police? How could he trust her? He didn't worry about Freddie and Jesse. They were loyal, up to a point, thanks to the money he'd promised. If that ever changed, he'd know what to do. But family was a sacred thing. You protected it because once it was lost, you could never get it back.

The stretcher appeared in the doorway, carried by two techs, who gently maneuvered it down the stairs and out to the curb. Some in the crowd gasped at the sight but not Ethan. He'd been there when he forced Younger to wrap the belt around his neck and step up on the chair. He'd been there in his robe, his eyes blazing, when he kicked the chair away and Younger dropped. Wiping the belt clean took only seconds.

Younger hadn't even begged for his life. It was almost as though he'd expected him to come for him. Maybe it was guilt that had made him complacent and accepting of his fate. It made no difference to Ethan. One to go. Brice was for the hurt, but also to take the place of Bosch, who got off lucky by dying on him. He took consolation in knowing, though, that dead was dead. He'd settled for pissing on Bosch's grave.

The van door slammed shut, Younger stiff and gone inside in a bag.

"For Mikey," he muttered. "For my sainted mother and father." He slid his hands into his pockets, prepared to go now that Younger was out. "And for *me*. For *vengeance*."

———

The team crowded around the board, well past shift, cartons of half-eaten Chinese food littering their desks. They had been at it ever since Symansky and Kelley returned from the Younger scene, where Rosales had confirmed the presence of a minotaur tattoo on Younger's arm.

He'd been a Hardwicke Boy. Their motive felt solid. But they had been unable to track down Ethan Paget.

Harri asked, "Why can't we find him?"

Bigelow straightened up. "We know where he should be, but nobody in his building has seen him in days. We've got a squad sitting on his place for as long as we can have it, but we're going to have to get real lucky with that. We're hoping one of his neighbors rats him out. But, again, luck."

"Like MacCallum," Vera said, smiling. "And her cat."

"What do we know about him?" Harri asked.

Kelley said, "Forty-three. White. Doesn't owe the IRS. No tickets. Nobody's suing him. His neighbors say he works from home. Some kind of computer stuff. They don't know. Not married. Nobody's seen any kids. He doesn't walk a dog. A loner, it looks like. But I dug deep and found a little trouble. He was arrested about fifteen years ago for setting garbage carts on fire. No jail time, just a fine and probation. Mischief or something deeper, we've got no way of knowing. And, one more thing with the neighbors. Ethan's been getting an awful lot of packages delivered over the last couple months. A couple people complained about him clogging up the small mail room, taking the issue to management."

Harri turned. "What kind of boxes?"

"I asked that. A lot of Amazon stuff, and some they couldn't ID, some of it heavy, like equipment. They assumed since he worked in tech from home, it was computer stuff. Nobody got too into it, only enough to say they noticed, and it's not sitting well with them."

Symansky groaned. "Loner computer nerds. They're the ones you got to worry about."

"And now he's avoiding us," Harri said. "Which means—"

"Which means, he's out there killin' people and he don't want us stoppin' him," Symansky said.

Vera frowned. "*Or* he just hasn't been home in a couple days. Neighbors don't know everything. Maybe he's got a girlfriend or boyfriend. Maybe he's on a business trip."

Bigelow rolled his eyes. "Yeah, and maybe pigs fly south for the winter."

Symansky also didn't look convinced. "What about Bauer, then?"

"We found a lot of Anna Bauers. Not one of them is the woman we found in the tub."

"Fake name?" Kelley said.

Bigelow leaned forward. "How'd she get hired at the house, then, if she had some shady shit like that going on? Don't they do background checks and ask for references?"

"I'm hoping her prints tell us something," Harri said.

"She could be undocumented," Bigelow said. "Working off the books. Prints wouldn't tell us anything in that case."

Symansky narrowed his eyes. "Undocumented?"

"You don't have to be brown to be undocumented," Bigelow said.

Harri underlined Bauer's name. "We find out how she fits with all the rest of this, it'll get us someplace."

She shifted her gaze to Renfro's party photos. There were a dozen shots of kids crowded around Hardwicke House with red cups in their hands and smiles on their faces.

"Back to these," she said.

"Sheesh," Symansky said. "It looks like they had a million kids there."

Harri turned. "Kids. You're right. So, if we're going with Ethan Paget, and right now that's the only thing that makes even a little sense, how'd he get into the house without anyone seeing him or snapping his picture? These kids are eighteen, nineteen, twenty. Paget's our age." She pointed at Paget's driver's license photo on the board. "Old enough to be their father."

Symansky squinted. "Don't see him in any of those photos."

"Somebody would have taken his picture if he was that out of place," Bigelow said.

Vera stood to get a closer look at the photos, though she and Harri had studied them before. "We've got them in order." She put an index finger to the first photo. "Starting here, you can see a progression for the night from this first one to the ones on the end. The eyes get glassier. The cups on the table get more plentiful. We know the party started around nine. Collier was dead around ten, and Ritter, Kenton, they say they left at two."

"Lights out at midnight," Bigelow chimed in. "But it doesn't look like Renfro took photos of that. Wonder why?"

"Middle photo," Kelley said. "That's Ritter and Kenton. Tight little duo, like they said."

Harri walked over to one of the photos toward the end. "But here we have a wide shot of the room, and the girls aren't in it." She turned to the team. "Could be they were on a bathroom run, but they don't show up on any of the photos after this point. At least on Renfro's phone. So, where'd they go?"

Bigelow sighed. "Lying-ass kids."

"Two girls. Very few cups on the tables. That would suggest this was early in the evening. Closer to nine than ten or midnight. Maybe around the time Collier was seen breezing through the kitchen with two beers heading up to the roof."

"We *think* he was going there," Kelley said. "The roof was clean. He could just as easily have been going to his bedroom up the back stairs. The living room was a mosh pit. Secret rendezvous and all that. He's gone. The girls are missing from the photos."

Bigelow stared at the board. "Collier's in only about half of those photos. If he's dead by ten or around then, of course he'd be missing after that."

Harri moved to her desk, deep in thought, and absently picked up a fortune cookie and cracked it open, her eyes narrowed, on the board.

"Another unanswered question," she said. "Bauer worries me. Who is she? Why'd she kill herself almost at the same time Will Younger kills *himself*? Are *they* connected somehow? What had she lied to us about? And why is Sebastian Collier *still* not here?"

"Because he don't give a shit," Bigelow said. "Stop trying to make it make sense. He's over there in Switzerland, moving his money around. We're not looking at father of the year, obviously. They probably didn't even speak. And, if you think about it, all that wild campus living he was doing up there, the parties and the big man on campus rep, could be him acting out, trying to get the old man's attention."

"And not getting it," Kelley added. "From everything we've learned, looks like Brice was on his own for the most part, except for the occasional check-in from this Lange guy. None of that says close to me."

"And outside of all *that*," Symansky said, "if Collier has an idea all this is about what he did back in the day, he's made up *his* mind to stay out of Paget's line of sight. It's called coverin' your ass."

"So, he sends Lange to deal with the details and the fallout, if there is any," Vera said.

"Well, if he sent him to protect his kid, he screwed that up," Bigelow muttered.

"So where was Lange when Brice died? When Younger or Bauer died? We need to talk to him too."

"I could see that cold bastard killin' somebody," Symansky said. "But why'd he kill his boss's kid? And a cleaning lady? *And* the president of the school? What's any of that to him? He's hired help."

"Well, there's at least one thing up there we can cross off and that's Emil Bosch," Kelley said. "He barely made it out of Belverton. He was killed in a car crash in '97. A year after graduation. He's buried in Uptown. Lakegrove Memorial Park."

"Any Bosches left standin' who might have a problem with the Colliers?" Symansky asked.

"Bosch wasn't local. He was from Virginia. So far, I haven't found any family who could be involved in this."

"So, why's he buried *here*?" Vera asked.

Kelley shrugged. "Unknown."

"So, back to Ethan Paget," Bigelow said. "He waited until he got some maturity in him and then decided to get even. We find Ethan, we wrap this whole thing up, in my opinion."

"Meanwhile, we talk to Lange again," Harri said. "Get his timeline. Find out how familiar he was with Younger, and ultimately, we need to talk to Sebastian Collier."

Vera stood, stretched. Harri checked her watch. It was after 7:00 p.m. A long day. A frustrating day. Time to pack it in for the night.

"Paget. Lange. The girls. Autopsy results," Harri said, putting a capper on the session. "Tomorrow's another day. Hopefully, a better one than this one."

"Pray we don't get another body between now and then," Bigelow said. "We're running out of space on that board."

Harri gave the board a look. He was right. She read her fortune. A series of numbers followed by a cryptic message: *Your life will be happy and peaceful.* She threw the sliver of paper into the trash.

Her phone buzzed. Sly. She eyed Griffin's door, found it closed, then put the call on speaker with the volume low.

"They have the tape, but it's locked down," he said. "Nobody's getting a look at it. It's archived in case . . ."

Harri finished what he didn't want to. "In case Mike sues the city."

"Yeah. What else you got?"

"All I have is Noble. I get him pulled, he goes back in, and I get nothing. I was thinking, he's probably trying to find a way to ease back into his old life. What else has he got? He's going to want to make some moves. Get out of his sister's house. Catching him at it could give me some leverage. Meanwhile, I talk to his parole officer tomorrow and get everything on the record." She ran a hand through her hair. "The tape would have told me if he was telling the truth about being there. Anyway, tomorrow, first thing, parole officer."

"Li going with you?"

"I don't think . . ." Harri turned to find Vera standing there with her coat on, bag slung over her shoulder, hanging on every word. Vera nodded.

"Yes," Harri said.

"Good. Safety in numbers. Keep me posted. I'm going to poke around a little more on my end. See what I can come up with. I'll be in touch."

"Thanks, Sly. I seem to be saying that a lot lately."

He let a beat pass. "Stay steady."

He ended the call. Harri put her phone away and turned to Vera.

"So, court building, first thing tomorrow?" Vera asked.

"Yep," Harri said.

Vera swept past her, smiling. "Good night."

Harri watched her go, then turned to stare at Griffin's door. She wanted to go in. She wanted to show her the proof that G was clean, but she needed more. She needed all of it. She needed Noble wrapped up good and tight.

She eyed the trash can with the lying fortune balled up inside it. "*Happy and peaceful.* Right."

CHAPTER 25

Harri idled outside the house of Noble's sister, Charlene. She'd done her digging in between all the other things she had on her plate, at least as much as she could do without raising an alert and getting Griffin and the bosses above her on her case.

Moran, she had learned, was fifty-two, a dental hygienist, the youngest of three kids in the Noble family. Fast Eddie was the middle child, and significantly older. She was divorced and the mother of two sons, one away at college, the other a sophomore in high school. That likely meant Charlene had an empty room available for Eddie.

Charlene's ex worked for the water department and appeared law abiding. The police had never been called to the Moran house. Charlene owned a 2016 Subaru Outback that wasn't currently parked in her driveway. No one was suing her, and she'd promptly paid for the parking ticket she got three months ago—with a personal check. What a contrast, she thought—Fast Eddie on one end of the Noble family tree and hardworking Charlene on the other. Was Charlene the only one who would take him in, she wondered, or were all the Nobles okay with Eddie's bloody hands, Charlene just being the one with the spare room?

Only the outside lights were on—the one over the door, the one on the lawn. Timers, Harri surmised. It had gotten dark almost two hours ago.

Sedate block. Shoveled walks. Lights on inside. Normal. Fast Eddie Noble was the abnormal element.

Harri had no idea how long she would wait. Working on little sleep and a case that still had no real through line, she was beat and keyed up and at her wit's end, but she wanted to see him. You couldn't tell a lot from a photograph or a disembodied voice. His CPD photo only told her part of the story. She had stared into his brown eyes for hours, it seemed, looking for the kink, the tell, anything she could point to and say, *Ah, yeah, there it is. The filth, the taint.* But there'd been nothing. Just the tough, blank expression, the pose. The same one she and every cop offered for their official headshot. The one they plastered on the news if you fell in the line of duty; the one they hung on the honorary wall, along with your star, in memoriam, in honor of your sacrifice. End of watch. But she wanted to see *him.*

Headlights flooded her rearview suddenly, and she watched as a blue Outback rolled past her and turned into the drive at the Moran house. The plate matched the number she had for Moran. After a few seconds, a sturdy-looking woman got out of the driver's seat and opened the back door, retrieving a bag of groceries. Out of the passenger side came an older man with bushy graying hair. Out of the back, a gangly boy of fifteen or so, holding a basketball, an athletic bag slung over his shoulder.

Eddie Noble was seventy now but still walked like a cop, assuredly, squarely, slightly favoring his gun side, after years of having the weight of a weapon there. He wasn't tall. He wasn't short. Under his jacket, it looked like he was still fit, likely attributable to him spending a lot of time with the weights in the prison yard. She squinted but couldn't see his face close enough to 100 percent confirm it was Noble, but chances were good it was. This was the address he put down as the place that would accept him upon his release. Who else could it be, unless Charlene was dating an old cop?

This visit wasn't meant to be a confrontation, only reconnaissance. Information was what she was after. It's what Noble had done with her when he'd turned up at her house, though he'd added to the intimidation factor.

Charlene and Noble made their way to the front door, and Noble took the bag while his sister fumbled with the keys in the lock. Harri stared at the three figures standing under the porch light, imagining what would come next. Moran getting out of her work clothes. Dinner. Noble watching a game on TV.

He was the same age as her father would have been if he were still alive. An old man. That would have made him eighteen when Charlene was born. But twisted didn't have a sell-by date. Hate and anger never got too old to soil the world and wreak havoc.

She had an idea. A way to be sure. She grabbed her phone and scrolled back to the last number Noble had called her from. He was using burners, but maybe he'd tired of switching out so frequently. It was worth a try. She found it, punched in the number, then watched the old man across the street. She couldn't hear his phone ring from where she sat, but she saw his reaction to it right before he handed the bag over to his sister and lifted the phone out of his pocket. Harri could see that he recognized the number, and he scanned the block, on high alert, as if she might be there. She was.

The phone rang again, and Noble held up a finger and watched as his sister and nephew went inside. He turned his back to the house and put distance between him and it.

"This is new," he said. "You calling me."

Harri didn't respond, just watched. She knew now that Noble was the one she wanted. The old man with a chip on his shoulder. The bad cop who'd come up against a good one and lost. Fast Eddie.

"So now you know. Doesn't change anything."

But it did, she thought. Knowing changed everything for her. She knew who and she knew why. She just didn't know how far he'd gone to get back at her father and get closer to her. That meant G.

Harri watched as Noble turned 360 degrees, nervous, cautious, as if she might spring from behind a bush or car. She ended the call and sat for a time, waiting for Noble to satisfy himself that she wasn't there. Maybe three minutes passed. Even when he stepped inside the house, she waited fifteen minutes longer, seeing what lights came on inside, hoping to catch Noble peeking out from behind the curtains.

Finally, Harri started the car, relieved to have heat streaming out of the vents. She gave the normal house one last look, then pulled into the driveway of one of Moran's neighbors, backed up, and drove off without passing the Moran house. For now, she would let him be, which was far more than he'd ever done for her.

"I don't have enough information."

It was an echo of the words Noble had said to her weeks ago, when for a split second she had thought about shooting him in the dark. *Not enough information.*

"Soon, though."

She pointed her car toward home.

"Soon."

CHAPTER 26

It always amazed Lange what and who money could buy. How the promise of even a little of it could twist the mind and blur the lines between right and wrong. Humans were funny things. Imperfect. Changeable. Undefined clay to be shaped and fashioned into whatever you wanted as long as you had enough of what they coveted to make it worth their while.

Lange had Collier money. Collier could buy anyone or anything he wished. With the death of his son, his progeny, what Sebastian Collier wanted was payback, and Lange had been charged with making the transaction.

He stood outside the building where the family bakery used to be. It had been years since the Pagets had lost the business, yet nothing had replaced it. The shop stood locked and abandoned, decomposing by infinitesimal degrees, paint chip by paint chip, rusted pipe by rusted pipe. Of course, it was the economy and the struggling neighborhood, but Lange wondered if the Pagets weren't somehow haunting the place, scaring off prospective tenants, refusing to leave the bakery even in death. It was silly, he knew, but the thought made him smile.

Truthfully, Lange hadn't thought about the Pagets in years. There'd been no need. The Colliers had ruined them and ground them into the dirt. Despite their feeble suit, there had never really been any fear that Sebastian and the others would be charged with Paget's death, but the legal entanglement had been very public, and old man Collier hadn't appreciated the spotlight, the hit to the family name, or the impact it had on his ability to do business. He hammered the Pagets with high-priced lawyers. He bankrupted them, then walked away, figuratively dragging Sebastian along by the ear. Boys will be boys. But now it looked like a Paget had risen from the ashes to strike the Colliers again. Ethan. Lange had read the detectives' last report again after his call with his boss. There'd been nothing in it that raised a single red flag. Ethan Paget was ordinary, unspectacular, normal. There'd been no social media threats, no new suits, no public pronouncements of wrongdoing attributed to the Collier family. There'd been nothing of any concern. And yet Brice Collier lay in the ME's office. But it was not only the who that put Ethan Paget on their radar now, but the how and the where.

One Paget left to stand for all the other Pagets, he mused. The keeper of the flame. He understood the impulse. In theory.

Lange could imagine the loss of their cherished business had hit the family hard. That loss heaped on top of the loss of their son he knew had taken a toll and hurtled the parents to early graves. He also knew he should probably feel a certain way about that, but he didn't.

Feelings were difficult; he knew they existed—he had felt them in the past—but now he could only simulate them. Nothing penetrated beyond the mask; nothing went deep. That was okay, he reasoned. People were different. Some felt deeply, some not at all. It was nothing to fret over in the end.

Lange had learned long ago that things, people, circumstances, agonies, triumphs, all of it, came and went. Everything but death was fleeting, temporary. This thinking was how he'd survived the beatings and the abuse, the depravation, the neglect, as a child. He had learned to shut down, to close off, to endure, to survive, and then to rise. It could just as easily have gone the other way for him, but he had been strong and determined, spiteful. He'd refused to die or be overtaken.

Lange walked back to his car, checked the clock on the leather dash. Almost 10:00 p.m. He watched the street as traffic whizzed by. Nothing spectacular about the neighborhood. It wasn't Paris or Milan. How quickly he'd grown appreciative of the finer things.

Younger was dead. Taken by the vengeful Paget, or so he assumed. His death, following so closely after Brice's, was breaking news, and every reporter in town was salivating. Lange liked the frenzy. It was amusing to watch. He knew any one of them would kill to know that the great billionaire Sebastian Collier had deemed the meek Younger expendable. That he'd offered him up to Paget in hopes of keeping the sickle of death away from his own neck. If Collier had asked, Lange would have told him hate didn't work that way, but Collier had spent a lifetime sacrificing inconvenient people to save himself. It wasn't Lange's job to care, he had decided.

Collier held no great loyalty toward Younger, or anyone, Lange knew. Younger was just another rich man's kid, the one who helped hoist Paget into the field, and then kept quiet about it. But he hadn't been built to deal with hard things and had always been bothered by it. Conscience. As a concept, Lange got that too.

Younger had been a payment. As good as a check. Collier rarely offered anyone anything, and if he did, never more than once.

But that didn't negate the fact that someone would have to pay for taking a Collier. Sebastian was adamant that there should be a price paid. One for one. An evening of a score. Only fair.

Lange chuckled to himself at the very idea that a rich man would have any concept of fairness.

But no one touched a Collier. No one threatened to topple the king. And it was Lange's job to make sure the last Paget never got close enough to try.

He scanned the street, finding it wanting. It was bleak and pedestrian, a dead end that led nowhere. It was a street that reminded him of the streets he'd fled another lifetime ago.

He started the car and listened to the elegant purr of the engine. It was like music to his ears. Lange would find the last Paget and deal with the situation. He would do his job, and not have a single feeling about it.

He straightened his tie in the rearview mirror, clicked his seat belt, and ran his smooth hands over the leather steering wheel cover. The car had cost more than the house of horrors he had grown up in. An alcoholic mother, a brutal father. He'd endured. Outlasted. When the lifeline was thrown, he'd caught it, and he'd pulled himself out of the muck.

And now he was the king's man. The one who guarded the gate. The one for whom the lines between right and wrong had been blurred so long ago. When you got an opportunity, you took it, he'd learned back when he was still covered in dirt and welts. When you saw an open door, you ran for it. You squeezed every ounce of possibility out of the least little thing. That's how you stayed alive. Right or wrong? Meaningless. All that mattered was survival.

Lange breathed in the luxury around him, and then adjusted the mirror, catching a glimpse of himself in the reflection. An impeccable shave. Quite a different man now.

CHAPTER 27

Rita Gomez, Noble's parole officer, walked into the small meeting room where Harri and Vera were waiting at 9:00 a.m. Punctual, Harri noted on first impression—no time to waste, efficient.

Gomez looked fiftyish, graying, and was dressed in slacks and a warm sweater, purple cat-eye glasses hanging from a chain around her neck. Though the day had just begun, Harri could not say that Gomez looked well rested and unharassed. Quite the contrary. Gomez looked like a woman who had spent a lifetime dodging flying knives.

Gomez came in with her cell phone, a legal pad, a pen, and a file folder. Moving quickly, like time was short and she had a million and one other things to do next, Gomez joined them at the table. Harri turned her radio down to mute the crackle of the police calls.

The parole officer slipped her glasses on and peered at them over the rim. "Good morning, Detectives. Foster? Li?"

Harri held her hand up at her name, Vera at hers. Gomez nodded, gave a slight smile. "I didn't want to assume. All right, then. Detective Foster, this is about Edward Noble?" She flipped the file open, her eyes scanning over the sheet inside. "Paroled last June." She looked over at them. "Eight months ago. You mentioned some trouble you've been having with him?" She picked up her pen. "What is that?"

Harri stood and walked over to the window, suddenly in need of a lot of air. One deep breath, though, and she told Gomez about Noble's calls, his visits to the graves, the coins, the connection to her father, and Noble's intent to hold her responsible for his years in prison. She left out her visit to Moran's the night before and the call she'd made to him. That was between Noble and her. She hadn't even told Vera that part.

"I'm not running to mother here," Harri said when she turned to face Gomez. "I'm after information. He's reporting regularly?"

"Like clockwork. He even arrives early. But reporting's only part of what he's obligated to do, as you know. Threatening a police officer?" Gomez stared at Harri. "That's serious and could be cause for violation of his parole. What evidence can you show me?"

"My word and star aren't enough?" Harri knew it wasn't, but she tried anyway.

Gomez's eyes met hers, not an ounce of humor on her face. "Noble had a star once."

"There's a world of difference between me and Eddie Noble."

Harri glanced over at Vera to find her sitting quietly, observantly. She knew she wasn't going to miss a single word that was said, but she also knew she wouldn't miss what *wasn't* said either. After months of working together, she was still unnerved by that. That was the part that had her reaching into her pocket now for the quarter from G's grave.

Harri gripped it in her palm, then rubbed it between her thumb and index finger. Unlike the paper clips and small things she secreted away to ground and soothe her, the quarter had a different effect. It made her think of Noble and of violation. It made her angry, different. He had invaded her world. He'd stood at her son's grave, and at G's. She squeezed the quarter hard, as though her grip could break it, feeling the tiny ridges around the edges, the raised etchings on its face.

Harri came back to the table and sat. "All I have is random numbers from a burner phone. And doctored-up photographs meant to tarnish my former partner's good name. Not enough. So, information. Who he associates with, where he goes, who he sees. His family, besides the sister he's living with. What does he eat for breakfast? Who *is* he?"

Gomez sat back and thought for a moment, choosing her words carefully. "He's a man who ruined his life but can't bring himself to admit it even when he sits in my office. He's a former cop who's now a convicted felon. He's of a certain age without any real job prospects. No business wants to hire a man his age, especially not with his background. He's convinced he was wronged. That he was made the scapegoat. He's a prime candidate for recidivism."

Harri bristled because Noble's interpretation of how it all went down would make her father a liar. And because she had done the research and knew the truth was something wholly different.

"A girl died because of what Noble did," Harri said. "I don't think her parents would agree that he was scapegoated."

Gomez shrugged. "That's how he *feels*. I have no problem believing *Fast* Eddie did exactly what he was sent to prison for. He's not a nice man. He's not a good man. I don't think anything I do here, or the state does ultimately, will change that. He's got a twisted concept of what right and wrong are, I've noticed. If he wants it and gets it, that's right. If he doesn't, if somebody else gets it instead, that's wrong. He's transactional, distrustful, paranoid. I can't overstate how much."

Vera frowned. "Who's he angry at, *exactly?*"

Gomez turned to her. "Everyone who isn't him."

Vera shook her head. "Explains why he ended up where he did."

"You'd be surprised how many of those who walk through these doors feel exactly the same way. But my job is not to fix them, it's only to make them comply with the rules until they're released from their obligation to the state. You see Noble as a bad cop? He doesn't see himself that way. He's broken, warped, but if you asked him, he'd tell you he was a good cop brought down by a corrupt system. He would tell you *he's* the victim."

Harri watched Gomez as she spoke, getting a feel for the man she knew she would have to face.

"How does he spend his days?" Harri asked.

"He's supposed to spend them looking for a job and staying out of trouble. We're working through a list of places that he might be a good fit for. He's prohibited from associating with his old friends, obviously, and he says he hasn't been. I've no way of confirming that. He's barred from owning, possessing, or handling guns. He's drug tested when he reports. There's no problem there. On paper, Eddie Noble is a star pupil. He's required to go to therapy. He has been going. His therapist reports progress is . . . slow."

"The name of the therapist?"

"She won't be able to tell you anything. Doctor-patient confidentiality. She can't even share details with me."

"I know, but for *my* records. In case I need it."

Gomez considered for a moment, before scribbling the name on a piece of paper and then sliding it over to Harri.

"So, what's Noble doing now? With you?" Vera asked.

"Like I said, we're working on getting him a job and a permanent place to live. A support system he can rely on."

"Any other family involved, besides his sister?" Harri asked.

Gomez shook her head. "It's just Charlene, though they're years apart in age. She stood by him while he was in prison. He reports there being tension with his other family members. His downfall was very public. As you can imagine, there was some fallout. Hurt feelings, shame, guilt by association. Hopefully, it's something they can all work out."

"Has he been in contact with any of his friends from the department?" Harri asked. "Cops tend to stick together."

Gomez closed the file. "Not that I'm aware. His social circle is all but nonexistent at this point, I think."

"What about the sister?" Vera asked. "What's her deal?"

"I've spoken to her. She loves her brother and wants to help him," Gomez said.

"By putting her children in potential danger?" Harri asked.

Gomez's eyes held hers for a moment. "She doesn't see it that way."

"If you have to assess his threat level," Harri said, "where would you put it?"

Gomez hesitated. "I don't know how to answer that. Right now, he's stably housed. He's reporting. He's in therapy. Unless he—"

Vera broke in. "Kills someone?"

Gomez let another moment go. "I've sat in a room with Eddie Noble; you haven't. He's hard to take on a personal level. He's filled with misplaced grievance. He even resents coming here, thinking I'm out to trip him up in some way and send him back inside. I've heard it all. I hear it all again every time he reports." Gomez looked from Vera to Harri. "In terms of his threat level, I'd be careful. I'll take those numbers now. I'll call him in. We'll have a talk."

"No," Harri said. "I don't want you to tell him about this visit. I'll give you the numbers, though. For your files. Documentation. In case he escalates."

"Escalation is what I'm here to prevent, Detective," Gomez said, clearly annoyed. "If he's violated the conditions of his parole, then there are steps that need to be taken."

"You said yourself the numbers weren't enough to violate him."

"But they *are* enough for a warning and next steps."

"I'm asking you to hold off on that."

"And if he strikes," Gomez said, "and they ask me why I didn't pull him in, what then?"

Harri considered her next words carefully. "I won't let that happen."

Gomez's brows lifted. "*You* won't?"

"That's right, *I* won't."

"And *I'm* back to threat level," Vera said. "High or low, one to ten. Humor me."

Gomez studied them, her dark, serious eyes finally landing on Harri. "He's capable of ten." Her eyes held Harri's. "I will document this, but I won't call him in . . . yet. I will monitor his activities more closely. One actionable offense and I'll have him in front of the parole board so fast his head swims."

Gomez saw them out, leaving them at the elevator doors, before fast walking away to another case, another file, another problem.

"Ten," Vera said when the doors closed and the car headed for the lobby. "She said *ten*. I *hate* this guy."

Harri glanced over at her. "Watch your back, Vera. He doesn't care who he hurts."

When the door opened, they wove through lawyers, defendants, cops, civilians milling around the lobby, some waiting for their turn through the metal detectors. Outside the building, they made their way down the slushy steps, headed for the parking garage across the street. It was too cold to talk. Conversation would have to wait until they hit the car and slid inside. When they did, Vera started the car, cranked up the defroster, and sat while the ice on the windshield got a blast of cold air.

"Keeping an eye out for the crazy guy, then." She slid Harri a look. "You're pretty calm."

Harri stared out the passenger window at the city bus rattling past down California, then flicked a look at the high fence and razor wire ringing the jail next to the courthouse. "Calm's better."

"We don't have to wait for Gomez, you know," Vera said. "We can bring him in. Have a nice long chat."

Harri knew that wouldn't do it. Noble was working off twenty years of rage. Besides, she knew it would take more than good cop–bad cop to get to Noble.

"Let's set up a call with Sebastian Collier," she said.

Vera blinked. "So, we're done talking about Noble, are we?"

"There's nothing we can do about him right now, is there? Right now, it's Collier. I'll call Lange. We keep looking for Paget. Then we get Kenton and Ritter in a room together and find out what the hell they're hiding. We get *this* done."

"And Noble? Out there lurking?"

Harri thought back to the night before, when she'd watched Noble under the porch light look for her in the dark.

"Vigilance. Caution. Head in the game."

Vera shook her head, dropping it. "Your call." She took a moment. "Well, it's too early for autopsies."

"I don't think Bauer's is going to tell us anything we don't already know. Maybe Younger's will be more promising? But I think we'll get something interesting from Ritter, Kenton."

"The stick-together gals," Vera said. "The keepers of secrets."

Harri nodded. "Meanwhile, I'll call Lange."

"Either way, Paget or the girls, we've got a payback theme going," Vera said. "Unless . . ."

"Unless?"

"Either Younger or Bauer killed Brice. Or both?"

"Motive?"

"Not sure. Just an idea. But then a suicide pact out of remorse or guilt."

"We haven't proven they even knew each other," Harri said.

"She works at Hardwicke," Vera said. "Younger lives across the street."

Harri frowned. "You know *your* neighbor's housekeeper?"

"Just spitballing," Vera said.

"I see that."

"Thinking outside the box."

Harri clicked her seat belt, then sat back and closed her eyes. "Way outside."

Vera put the car in gear. "We got this, and when we're done, we'll go fry Noble's ass."

"And she's back," Harri muttered.

CHAPTER 28

Harri held Lange's ritzy business card in her hand as she and Vera sat across from him in an office at Hardwicke House. Sebastian Collier's office, to be exact, which had been locked, and was only unlocked by Lange. It wasn't what Harri had expected. She'd been in the offices of wealthy people before, and there had been the usual trappings—expensive curtains, displayed antiques, walls of honors and awards—but Collier's office was almost bare. There was a big desk, an executive chair, lamps, rugs, that sort of thing, but nothing personal. No photos, no awards, no degree hung on the wall. The room was dark, wood paneled, masculine looking, and lifeless, unlived in, which fit with Collier's globe-trotting lifestyle. This was an office, his office, but apparently not *the* office.

While the quiet Lange set up the call with his boss, Harri looked around the underutilized space in no position to judge.

"Mr. Collier is based in New York," Vera said. "Doesn't look like he comes here often."

"No," Lange said. "He travels extensively. He can work anywhere."

"And it stays locked whenever he's not here?" Harri asked Lange as he was busy with the laptop.

"Mr. Collier has asked that no one have access. It's his private space."

"That include Brice?"

"That applies to everyone."

It intrigued her that while Lange readied the call, he did so *standing* behind Collier's desk, not sitting in the big man's chair. She wondered if he wasn't allowed. Or perhaps it was Lange's choice not to sit, in deference to his employer, feeling unworthy of the privilege. Either way, she found it interesting.

Vera ran a finger along a bookshelf. No dust. "Someone cleans up in here, obviously. I would have thought that'd be Anna Bauer, but she told us the door was always locked."

The question came just a millisecond before Harri was about to ask the same thing.

Lange looked up. "It was. But if Mr. Collier was coming in, Master Brice would arrange for her to prepare the room. It didn't happen often."

Harri wondered if Bauer had come across something in Collier's office or in the house she wasn't supposed to see. Harri thought of blackmail. Was that what Bauer said she'd lied about? She looked over to find Lange watching.

"She was *always* supervised," he said simply, as if he'd read her mind. "By Master Brice, as he was instructed."

"Did Master Brice always do what he was told?" Vera asked.

Lange's flat eyes slid her way. "Of course."

"How did Mr. Collier feel about the parties thrown here?" Harri said. "Everyone knows about them. The school doesn't intervene. Younger took a hands-off approach, apparently. And an invitation to one of them is a must-go for a lot of students."

"Mr. Collier doesn't concern himself with college parties. Master Brice ran the house. He was responsible for what happened here and was expected to handle it."

"A boy of *twenty*?" Vera asked, a hint of incredulity in her voice.

Lange leaned his head slightly. "He was a Collier."

Lange turned the laptop around to face them as they took seats in the leather chairs in front of Collier's empty desk of power. Lange stepped back, at ease, his arms behind him. Like Sebastian Collier's personal palace guard.

Harri didn't know how this was hitting Vera, but she found the man's behavior oddly unnatural, as though Lange was made not of sinew and bone but bolts and circuits. As to his appearance, he looked much the same as he had the last time she'd encountered him—unruffled, watchful, unreadable. This time only the color of his suit was different, dark gray with the tie matching, instead of devil black.

When Harri had relayed the news of Anna Bauer's and Younger's deaths to him, she had gotten no reaction, not even a spark of curiosity.

Harri glanced down at her watch. Three minutes until their meet time with Collier. With the icy Lange staring at her from behind the desk, waiting until he was needed, that three minutes already felt interminable. Maybe it wouldn't have if they could use the time to get information, but Harri knew already that asking questions of Collier's proxy would only end in frustration.

"Where were you Saturday night, Lange?" Harri watched him closely. "I don't think we ever established that."

His brows lifted a fraction of an inch. "That's a question you ask of suspects. You consider *me* a suspect?"

"It's a question we ask of everyone. It doesn't mean you're a suspect."

"I was in New York. When I got the call about Master Brice, I came immediately."

"Got here pretty fast," Vera said. "Which airline?"

"I flew by private plane."

Vera nodded. "Ah. Forgot for a second. Billionaire."

"Working for the Colliers has its perks."

"That would explain why it took you and Younger till after eleven to make an appearance. Travel time," Harri said. "And an update from Younger on what he knew."

Lange offered a single nod of confirmation. "A delicate situation."

"How long has Mr. Collier been in Geneva?" Harri asked.

"Six weeks, to date. He returns to New York next week. He will expect Master Brice's body to be released to him by then. For the memorial he's having planned."

There was a hint of pressure in what Lange said, which Harri ignored. Their case. Their timeline. Billionaire or no billionaire.

Vera crossed her legs, leaned forward, intrigued. "Are you from New York, Lange? I get that vibe."

"I live there. Not native."

Harri knew what Vera was doing and knew the breezy conversational tone in her voice was a tactic. She also knew that the smiling Li, the engaged Li, the twinkly eyed Li was not the *real* Li. The *real* Li was the circumspect cop behind the smile, the laser-focused investigator behind the twinkle, the one assessing the untalkative majordomo without it looking like she was doing it. Vera, she knew, was reading Lange's body language as she had, noting how he was breathing, whether he fiddled with his hands, shifted from one foot to the other, or blinked too much or not enough. All of it while smiling and shooting the breeze about things unrelated to death and murder.

"Same with me," Vera said. "My family moved here from Bakersfield, California, when I was two and my sister was four. I don't remember a thing about it. But as far as I'm concerned, I'm as native as Foster here. Any idea how Anna Bauer and William Younger might be connected?"

"The maid?" He asked it in a way that sounded as though it were the most ridiculous thing he'd ever heard.

Vera's smile lost a bit of wattage, and her eyes got less friendly. "The *housekeeper*. Yes. The person who cleaned this room. The woman we found dead in her bathtub."

Lange ignored the questions and instead, without consulting a watch or a clock, said, "It's time."

Sebastian Collier's face appeared on the screen, and the moment Harri saw his face, the scowl, the impatience in his expression, the shrewd little eyes, the hardness in them, she disliked him.

"Where's my son's body," Collier asked. "Lange?"

Lange stepped forward and around so Collier could see him. "Not yet released."

Collier stared at them. "Well?"

Harri spoke. "He's right." She briefly told him about Younger and Bauer, though she knew Lange had already fully informed him. "So, you can see, things have become more complicated."

"What have Younger and this Bauer woman got to do with my son? I will not have him lying in a coroner's drawer like a hunk of meat. His service is in the planning. I've scheduled it for next week. The mayor and governor will be in attendance."

"We have a few questions, Mr. Collier," Harri said.

Collier's thin lips twisted into a disagreeable grimace. "You have ten minutes."

"When's the last time you spoke to your son?"

Collier appeared to be sitting in an office much like the one they were sitting in, even down to the chair behind the desk he sat at. Begrudgingly, he picked up his cell phone and scrolled through it. "He was here for Christmas. December 23 through December 27." He tossed the phone back on the desk. "Our last weekly business call was a week ago."

"Business?" Vera asked.

"The family business. The running of the house you're sitting in. Our plans for his future. Where I'd place him in the company for maximum effect. All meaningless now, isn't it?" Collier glowered out of the screen. "What progress have you made?"

"Let's save time, since we have so little of it," Harri said. "You know what happened. I think you also have an idea who did it and why. This death is almost a carbon copy of Michael Paget's. Why didn't you tell us that when we notified you of your son's death? Personally, or through Lange? It would have saved us a lot of time."

"I won't be chastised. Lange."

Lange took a step forward. Harri met his steely gaze, challenging the step, confused by why he was making it. Vera's friendly cop disappeared in a flash.

"Back it up," Vera ordered.

"*Now*," Harri added.

After a moment of hesitation, Lange stepped back, then smiled politely.

"Look, I don't know how you two are used to doing things," Harri said, "but this is not going that way today." She glared at Lange, then Collier through the screen. "This is murder. Murder compounded by two suspicious deaths that appear related. Your son didn't just stagger out of the house and die; we believe he was forced out. Lange here, I'm sure, told you what the ME's report found. This was planned. This was intentional. Either by one of your enemies, Mr. Collier, or one of your son's. We know about Michael Paget. We know what happened in that field. I want to know why you failed to mention the similarity when you were informed of your son's death. We are also aware of Ethan Paget, the victim's brother. He could very well be involved. What do you know of him? Has he made any contact?"

"I'm accustomed to solving my own problems, Detective."

"What's that supposed to mean?"

Harri flicked a look at the stoic Lange, still standing like a stick. Collier didn't answer.

She was tired of the games. They didn't have time for them. Three bodies. Three lives. No real leads.

"Enemies, Mr. Collier. Ethan Paget being a good pick."

There was an edge to her voice, one she hadn't intended but couldn't do anything about.

"He's someone who'd want to hurt you, get back at you. But I'm sure there are others in your circle, business or otherwise, who might also want to take a swing. Give us some names."

"Have there been threats?" Vera asked. "Attempts at blackmail? Lawsuits pending?"

"There are always enemies and lawsuits at my level," he said. "Always threats." He looked directly at Vera. "And do I look like a man who would give in to blackmail?"

Harri ignored the posturing. Again, no time for it.

"So, no threats, and Brice never mentioned receiving any?"

Collier chuckled. "Why would *Brice* receive threats? He's still wet behind the ears . . . or was."

Harri recalled at that moment the light trick the Hardwicke Boys liked to play. The midnight grope fest. Girls huddled together for safety. How funny and harmless Brice and his friends thought it all was. And the photos, she thought of them. Two girls missing from half of them. Motive. She scribbled herself a note, suddenly anxious to be done with the pompous Collier.

"Sexual assault," Harri said.

She told him about the parties at Hardwicke and the flicking of the lights, watching him for a reaction, but not getting one.

"Harmless," he said. "A party trick."

"Since when is assault harmless?" Vera asked.

213

"It *isn't* assault. No one's complained, have they? No one's called the police. Campus high jinks. Besides, that, too, is irrelevant now, isn't it?"

"The Pagets," Harri said. "Let's get back to them."

"One Paget. Also irrelevant. They tried a money grab, and it failed. They tried having me labeled a murderer, and that failed. I barely even knew Michael Paget. He was just some scruffy kid who wanted to run with the big boys. Only he couldn't, could he? He didn't have the right stuff. I've had no contact with the Pagets since we crushed them in court. I assumed that was the end of them."

"Why didn't you, Younger, and Bosch try to save him?" Vera asked. "All you had to do was pick up the phone and call for an ambulance."

"I'm not a doctor. How was I to know he'd die? I figured he'd sleep it off."

"In the field?" Harri asked. "Unmonitored?"

"I didn't want him puking all over the furniture. It's vintage. And we didn't dump him. We just carried him out so he could sleep it off. We didn't kill him. That wasn't a crime. The judge's ruling said so."

"But the Pagets still came after you," Harri said.

"They wanted millions for wrongful death. They lost. We won. The end."

"Maybe not the end," Vera said.

Collier glowered back at her. "I'm done discussing it."

"Tell us about the Minotaur Society. Brice had a minotaur tattoo, Renfro has one, Younger had one. I assume everyone living here has one," Harri said. "We've heard stories. But why don't you explain it to us."

Collier's face turned to stone. "Lange. Ten."

Lange stepped forward and ended the Zoom call. Harri glanced down at her watch. It had been exactly ten minutes from start to finish.

Lange extended his arm toward the door. "Detectives? This way, please."

They stood and were ushered out of Collier's office. Standing on the steps of Hardwicke House, the door locked behind them, the chill setting in quick and bone deep, Harri turned to Vera.

"Nobody wants to talk about the tattoo."

Vera wrapped her scarf tighter around her neck. "I saw that."

"I had an idea while Collier was blowing smoke. We've been asking who might have wanted to get back at Sebastian Collier, but what if all this has to do with Brice? Someone wanting to get back at *him*?"

"The party lights," Vera said.

"That could be a motive for Ritter and Kenton. One drunk kid, two of them working together. That could be enough force."

Harri stared down the street at Younger's old place, the president's house, standing vacant and dark. No media trucks now. The reporters gone. No one seemed to hang around long for suicide. It was almost as though people thought it contagious and insidious, a living thing with the ability to worm itself into their own lives and houses. As if it were an evil spirit, and not pain.

"Collier knew about Ethan Paget," Harri said.

"Which means Lange knows."

Harri sighed. "Which means they can connect the dots just like we can."

A gust of freezing wind blew through them. It took a half second for Harri's brain to get over the frigid assault to her system.

"Bauer," she finally said.

Vera grabbed her phone. "I'll check in with Matt."

"And we still have Grant, but while we're up here, you want to take another look at her place?"

"You think we missed something?"

They reached the car. Harri slid into the driver's seat. "I think we might have." When Vera got in across from her, she asked, "I didn't know you were from Bakersfield."

"Never been. I was born here. Grew up in Lincoln Park. Graduated from Francis Parker."

"College?"

"Michigan."

Harri smiled. "Sister?"

Vera grinned. "Nope."

"Remind me never to play poker with you."

CHAPTER 29

Bauer's apartment was warmer with the window closed, but still felt icy and lonely to Harri as she and Vera walked through it again, hoping to find something that explained why the woman had taken her life.

"She traveled light, that's for sure," Vera said, peeking into drawers and cabinets. "There's hardly anything here, and Longwood says she's been a tenant for over a year."

"Bedroom next," Harri said, already making her way back.

But they got the same nothing in there. Just the necessities—bed, lamp, table, closet. It became evident fairly quickly that they hadn't missed anything their first time through and that this was all there was or ever would be to explain Bauer.

"Two things," Harri said as she stood in the center of the almost nothing. "Either she lived like this, or she planned her death down to the last detail and dumped everything she owned that might have helped us ID her."

"Maybe she was a fugitive," Vera said. "Broke out of prison years ago, lived under the radar, but just couldn't take it anymore. Or."

Harri waited for the rest of it but ran out of patience after a few seconds.

"What?"

"She's Brice's mother."

"His *dead* mother?"

"We only got that from Lange," Vera said. "We glossed right over it. So, think about estrangement. Sebastian Collier's a tool who forbids her access to his heir apparent. Brice and Bauer work up this housekeeper thing because they know Sebastian wouldn't approve. This way they can be in each other's lives, even if it's under wraps. Brice is killed. She can't handle it. Decides to . . ."

"Wouldn't Lange have recognized her? He'd be in and out all the time. He could have lied to us about knowing her, but I don't think he'd keep it from his boss that she was in contact with his son."

Vera shrugged. "He wouldn't have had to cross paths with her if they worked it right. He's anchored in New York. He only comes here when there's something to come here for. It wouldn't have been hard for them to tap-dance around the visits. She did say she was divorced."

"She also said she had no kids."

"She *also* said she lied to us and wanted to come clean."

Harri wasn't convinced the fantastical subterfuge added up, but it gave her an idea, a way they might check. She grabbed her phone and started searching.

"Not sure the age works out," she said. "Bauer's late fifties, Sebastian Collier's, what? Fifty? Fifty-one? A techno wunderkind with a billion dollars in his pockets?"

"Age is just a number, Harri."

"The great Sebastian Collier, from what we've learned, likes them younger—arm candy. Brice was twenty. That would have put Bauer in her midthirties when he was born? Not saying it *couldn't* have happened, it just doesn't feel like it did. She has to connect some other way. And how does Younger fit? Two suicides, one on top of the other, both tied to one house."

"What are you searching for?"

"Billionaires don't get married and nobody takes pictures of the . . . ugh. Not her."

She held her phone up to show Vera a happy wedding photo of a grim-looking Sebastian Collier in a gray morning suit and a beaming blonde in a white mermaid wedding dress taken in 2002.

"Lillith Victor," Harri said, reading the caption. "An artist. Divorced in 2012. Died in 2014. Cancer."

"Only the one marriage?"

Harri consulted Google. "Only one on record. Numerous relationships, naturally. Most with celebrities. None I recognize."

"Any one of them could be Brice's mother, then."

Harri put her phone away, unsatisfied. "But none of them are Anna Bauer." Harri scanned the room one more time. "No sense in standing here wasting time we don't have. We'll have to find out who she was some other way."

Vera gave the room one last look. "She connects. To Brice, for sure, maybe even to Paget." She turned to Harri. "And Kenton and Ritter lied to us. To our faces. We didn't push it. I blame that sad-looking teddy bear. Hard to go bad cop in front of *that* guy."

Harri put on her gloves, preparing to hit the cold again. "Full experience next time. Lawyers. Cop faces. We don't look at the bear. Agreed?"

Vera slid her beanie on. "Can't unsee the bear. But agreed. Let's do this."

———

Vera reached into the greasy bag filled with corned beef sandwiches from Manny's, courtesy of Symansky, who'd stopped by for a sandwich for himself and had picked up some for the rest of them. The smell of rye bread, mustard, corned beef, and dill pickles even drew Griffin out of her office with an uncustomary smile on her face. Symansky had brought a sandwich for her too. No small talk, though, for the boss. Just a hand dip into the bag, a corned beef retrieval, then a nodded thank-you, and she was back in her office to take heat from the mayor's office and the superintendent.

Kenton and Ritter were in interview rooms with lawyers their parents had arranged for. Harri and Vera were letting them settle before approaching them again. Kenton had come in without her bear.

"No parents," Vera said as she peeled back the deli paper from her sandwich. "I can't get over all this hands-off business. Sebastian Collier. No-show. Now the Kentons and the Ritters hire lawyers, but that's it? If my kid was in a police station being questioned, I'd be sitting in the same chair with him whether he was eighteen or forty-five."

Harri smiled, bit into her pickle spear. "I'd pay good money to see that."

Vera shrugged, took a bite of corned beef. "I'd let you in for free."

Harri took the first bite of her sandwich, the spicy mustard tickling her nose. She hadn't realized how hungry she was until then. "It's been a half hour. Long enough for them to confer."

Vera tossed a potato chip into her mouth. "Let's give them another fifteen. There are cookies in that bag too."

———

They took them separately. Vera took Shelby Ritter and her lawyer in one room; Harri took Hailie Kenton and hers in another. In the interest of time, the game plan was the same—straightforward cop heat, get it done.

Kenton sat next to her lawyer and stared across the table at Harri. No one spoke for a time. The last question asked was still unanswered. What had she been doing upstairs at Hardwicke House Saturday night? The lawyer, a young woman, maybe midthirties, with short, cropped hair and severe horn-rimmed glasses, sat tight lipped and humorless next to her client. Harri flicked a look down at the woman's business card she'd slid across the table toward her. Frances Bonetti of Garner, Sung, and Wade. A State Street address, too, but not North State, where it used to be great and where they could likely charge more per billable hour, but at the south end, close to where the now-defunct Warshawsky auto parts place had once operated for decades. Fueled by corned beef and chips, Harri was well past the gentle, coaxing stage. This time, Kenton had the bad luck of facing a full, energized, busy cop whose time she had wasted.

"I wasn't," Kenton answered finally, but there didn't appear to be too much conviction behind the repeated lie.

Harri turned to Bonetti. "Class B misdemeanor. Obstructing a police investigation. Up to six months in jail."

Kenton's eyes widened. "What?" She reeled to face Bonetti. "What'd she say? Jail? I didn't do anything. All we—" Hailie broke off, slid back in her chair. "This is *crazy*."

Harri's eyes stayed on Bonetti, the only other adult in the room. "I'll wait two minutes, then I will get up from this table and put your client under arrest. My partner is having a similar conversation with Ms. Ritter. Depending on how things go, either both young women will leave here today free, or they will be detained."

"That Class B is a stretch," Bonetti said, but she appeared slightly unsure. "We're dealing with kids here."

Harri slid a cold glance over at Kenton. "In here, she's an adult, and she's playing a dangerous game that's going to end in handcuffs and a sad bologna sandwich over in the lockup." Harri glanced down at her watch, then back at the lawyer. "Clock's ticking, Ms. Bonetti."

"You're threatening my client."

Harri eased her handcuffs off the clip on her belt and plopped them on the table, where they landed with a thuddy clunk that could have made a murderer cry for his mommy. "One minute. Then I walk her out in these."

Kenton's eyes widened. She began to nervously chew at her lower lip. "She can't do that, can she? She can't, right?"

Bonetti leaned over to consult with Kenton, keeping her voice low and her lips shielded behind her hand. Harri waited patiently, knowing the same scenario was playing out next door. She liked her and Vera's chances. Either Kenton would talk first, or Ritter would, but somebody was going to crack today.

While Bonetti whispered to her client, Kenton's wide eyes held Harri's, who could tell the second reality sank in, as the young woman's face paled and her mouth hung agape. When Bonetti finished explaining the situation to her client, she leaned away and tapped Kenton on the shoulder.

"All right," Kenton said, dropping the bravado, her eyes on the cuffs. "We went to Brice's room. We were going to trash it. Send a message. All the sketch stuff he's done. Treating us like things? Laying claim to me like I'd be so *honored* he was even talking to me? And getting away with it just because his father owns half the school? There was supposed to be more of us, but everybody else chickened out, so just Shelby and I went.

"It was her idea to spray-paint the walls in his room, really plaster them. We were going to write things like *pig* and *loser* and *rapist*. We waited till the party got going, then slipped upstairs. Nobody saw us, or we didn't think so. Everybody was already a lot of beers in. We got up there, got the cans out, and we were about to do it when we heard someone coming up the stairs. We didn't have time to do anything. We just froze, hoping whoever it was wasn't coming in, but then we heard the doorknob turn, and we ran and hid in the closet. I dropped my can. I saw it roll under the bed, but I didn't have time to get it. The door opened. It was Brice. I could see through the crack in the closet door. I just knew we were busted."

"What happened next?" Harri asked.

"He was already buzzed; I could see that. I kept looking at the can under the bed, sure he'd see it. I was shaking all over. Brice took a note off his desk and read it out loud. He didn't know we were there. It was supposedly from me, but *I for sure* didn't write it. He put the note in his pocket, checked his hair in the mirror, and then left. We waited a few more minutes just to be sure he was really gone, and then we got out of there fast. I was so scared I forgot all about the can until we got back downstairs, but there was no way I was going back to get it. Then after what happened, I got really scared. My fingerprints were all over that can, right? If the police found out I was in his room, they could think *I* killed him. Me up against the Colliers? No way anyone would believe me."

Harri thought back to the photos of the girls taken at the party—each had been holding a purse. "And you never saw Brice after that?"

Kenton shook her head.

"He read the note aloud. What did it say?"

"It was all fake," she said. "Somebody playing a joke, or something."

"What'd it *say*?" Harri asked again, more persistently.

Hailie squeezed her eyes shut to recall. *"I'm into you too. Meet me up top. We'll have some fun. Bring the note. Our little secret. Hailie.'*

"He smiled when he read it, then he left. We were so scared but figured we'd dodged some trouble, so we went back to the party and pretended nothing happened. That's the truth. All of it. We just wanted to get back at him."

"That wasn't enough to get you in trouble with us," Harri said. "A dropped paint can? There's more."

Kenton looked over at Bonetti and got a nod in return.

"I swiped his school ID. You're dead on campus without it, and it's a hassle to get a new one. I figured taking it would make him suffer a little bit." She dropped her head. "Stupid now."

"What'd you do with it?"

Kenton looked up at her. "I threw it into the lake. We lied about all of it. We ran because we committed a crime. Trespassing, I guess. And then taking the ID. If you guys turned it into something bigger? We'd get kicked out of school; our parents would go nuts. If we went to *jail*, we'd never get a decent job *anywhere*. So we decided to keep our mouths shut. That's all of it. That's all we did."

"We needed to know about that note days ago," Harri said, her tone tense. "*Days.* You do realize that?"

Kenton nodded, her chin to her chest. Bonetti spoke. "Well?" Harri stood, grabbed up her cuffs, and glared for a moment at the contrite Kenton. "She's free to go, if she's sure that's all of it now?"

Kenton nodded again.

Harri picked up her notepad. "Then she can go."

Minutes later Harri and Vera watched Kenton and Ritter and their lawyers walk out of the building free as birds.

"Spray paint," Vera groused. "And they thought that was a good idea."

Harri headed back to her desk to take a look at the tech report and the photos of Brice's room. "Yeah, there it is." She handed the photo to Vera. "Can under the bed." She skimmed through the report. "It wasn't dusted for prints."

Vera handed the photo back. "They had no reason to suspect the can didn't belong to Brice. Wouldn't have helped us anyway. Neither Kenton nor Ritter are in the system. Dumb kids' prank. Dodgy kid thinking. Instead of going to the college or us."

"Younger told us himself it was hands off where Hardwicke and the Colliers were concerned. He was pals with Sebastian, in on the Paget death, and a Minotaur."

"Turned a blind eye," Vera said. "Trash move. Not enough to kill yourself over, though, is it?"

Harri thought for a moment. "We're assuming he did."

"And you're assuming Ethan Paget came calling."

"Well, one thing we do know? Somebody lured Brice to the roof. His death was planned. So, we concentrate on who had access to the house, to him. Anybody who had it in for Brice or his father. That's Ethan, who's got one hell of a motive for wanting Brice and Younger dead."

"And then there's Anna Bauer," Vera said. "The one thing that's not like the others."

"Access works," Harri said. "Motive we don't have, or any idea how she connects with Younger, or even if she does."

Vera smiled. "Yet. We don't have motive *yet*."

Harri rubbed her tired eyes. "A lot of work to do."

"You okay?" Vera asked.

"I'm fine." Harri checked her watch. "It's past six. Doesn't look like we're getting a call from Grant tonight."

"We *are* keeping her busy." Vera looked down at the morning's paper still sitting on her desk, the glaring headline reading *Collier Scion Slain. CPD Stumped.* "Reporters really bug me. We are not *stumped*. If they think this is so easy, let them get out there and do it. Painting us as a bunch of Keystone Cops." Her eyes cut to the board with all the lines and loops and arrows on it. Ethan Paget still a giant question mark. "We're almost there. I can feel it."

Harri nodded. "Right. See you tomorrow."

Vera stared a moment longer. "I'm worried about you with Noble out there running loose."

"Protect yourself and your family, Vera. No, I mean it. Noble's not right. It might not be me he comes after."

"Head on the swivel, then. For both of us." Vera slipped into her coat, grabbed her phone and bag. "Night. Go home. Get some rest. You look like one of those zombies from *Walking Dead*."

Harri frowned. "Thanks."

"If I don't tell you, who's going to?"

She watched Vera leave but stayed put in her chair, taking a moment to sit and breathe. She had no reason to rush home. No one was waiting for her there. She slid the quarter from G's headstone from her pocket and laid it on her desk, staring at it while she rubbed the face of her watch, something she did out of habit now. It wasn't a fancy watch; it was a beat-up old Timex that had seen better days. It didn't glow in the dark or track her steps. It didn't even tell her the date or day of the week. The leather strap was worn and cracked, watch face scratched; the only thing it did was tell time. And it had belonged to her son. She wished she understood why she fixated on *things*. The watch, the quarter, paper clips, the marbles she dropped into the vase at home. Why, when they were all clearly anchors instead of wings?

She eyed the phone on her desk. Maybe she should call Mike, G's husband, to tell him about Noble, or should she wait until she had it all? When she knew for sure that Noble had done what he'd claimed he had. He needed to know the photos were fake, that Glynnis was clean. She needed to tell him that she was gone because of her, because of what her father had done, because of a grudge held by a spiteful old cop out of his mind, and not anything he or she had missed. If not for her, G would be alive, mothering her kids, and there was nothing Harri could do to change it.

Not ready to call Mike, she picked up her cell phone to call Sly instead but didn't get too far with that either. She was a mess. An absolute mess and she knew it. Mad at herself, she grabbed her coat, her things, and logged out. There wasn't a single thread she could pull tonight that she and Vera hadn't already pulled at twice during their shift. Maybe Vera's feeling was right. Tomorrow would be a better day, the day they solved this whole thing, the day all the questions got answered. Hope, though Harri didn't trust it as a concept anymore. After pushing out of the building, she crossed the lot to her car, her warm breath sending up puffs of air she could watch disperse into nothing. She had time to start the car, her foot on the brake, but only that before she felt the muzzle of a gun pressed to the back of her head where her skull met her spinal column. There was no mistaking the feel of it. The hard metal. The small cylindrical shape. Perfectly round. She could even feel the front sight dig into her soft flesh.

She'd committed a fatal error, and she knew it in that instant. She was so tired that she had failed to check the back seat before she got in. It's advice she gave women all the time. Check before you get in. Run, don't engage. Save your life, let the phone and bag go. But she hadn't done it, and now there was a gun to her head. Her gun and ID were in her bag. End of shift. Quitting time. No good to her.

Slowly, her eyes lifted to the rearview mirror as she waited for the round; she felt surprisingly calm, considering the last seconds of her life were ticking away. She wanted to see her killer.

"I thought it was time to stop dicking around, Harri." He grinned. He pressed the gun in harder. "Go on. Beg me not to kill you."

She searched for words but not to beg for her life. Even in this situation, dire as it seemed, she couldn't bring herself to beg. Harri wanted profound words to be her last, but none came to her. It was the feel of the muzzle against her head that prevented her from coming up with a dying declaration.

It was all about the gun. The press. The muzzle was slightly tilted upward so that when the round fired, it would bore a hole in her skull, obliterate her brain stem, and lodge in the middle of her head. A kill shot. She'd be dead even before the sound of the bullet firing died away . . . that was something, at least.

Last words then, she thought, her mind racing. Something deep, meaningful. Words to see her off. The last ones she'd ever utter. She opened her mouth to speak.

"Go to hell, Eddie Noble."

CHAPTER 30

"That's not nice. Not nice at all," Noble said. "Hands on the wheel."

Harri lifted her hands, placed them slowly on the steering wheel.

Through the defrosting windshield, she surreptitiously scanned the parking lot. Any other time there'd be cops coming and going, on and off shift. Yet, now, there wasn't a blue shirt in sight. And she knew for a fact she was parked in a blind spot because the spots closer to the building and the door had all been taken when she'd gotten to work that morning. Fatal error number two. She'd have done better parking along Eighteenth Street, where the city cameras were closer, but that was a moot point now, she figured.

"Cards on the table," Noble said. "I got nothing against you personally, but somebody's got to pay your old man's bill. I haven't killed you yet because I'm still thinking it over. I like playing this out, to tell the truth. All those years inside with nothing to do, listening to dumb shits talk shit, dreaming of the day I could blow your old man's head off. Thinking up ways to do it. Then he up and dies on me. He and his two lying buddies. Whatever happened to loyalty, huh? Cops are supposed to stand with cops."

The gun pressed in harder. Harri flinched, swallowed hard, then squeezed her eyes shut, preparing herself for death. Though Noble just told her he wasn't in a hurry to kill her, she didn't trust a word he said.

"Cat got your tongue, *Detective* Harriet Foster?" He chuckled. "You sure went a lot farther up than your old man did. *Homicide.* Must be real smart, huh? Probably got a close rate through the roof too."

Harri heard his voice, every utterance, but her mind was on other things. She'd be gone once Noble fired, lights out. It was her mother she worried about, knowing the hurt she'd feel. And for Felix having to be the one to tell her, and then help her through it. For a split second, there was even a thought of escaping her own grief, believing she would soon see Reg again. Noble didn't know what a dilemma he'd given her. Play along and maybe stay, or do something stupid and go.

Still, no one in the lot. Even if there were, she thought, her windows were slightly tinted. It was dark out. All a passing cop would see was her car idling in the spot. Not unusual. No cause for alarm. What could happen in a cop lot? She flashed to G. For a moment it felt like her heart had stopped beating one round too soon. And she knew for sure. In that instant, she knew. The timing. The hate. The pain he wanted to spread around, the hurt. *His* game twenty years in the planning.

"This is how you did it. You snuck up behind her like the piece of garbage you are. You shot her with her own gun."

Noble said nothing. The gun held steady. Harri's brain fired, thoughts, details, flooding through. It'd been raining that day, murky, gray. G had been running late, she remembered now.

"A different lot, a different day," Noble said.

"You're a coward," she hissed. "If you wanted *me*, you should have come for *me*."

"And miss all this fear? You, anticipating the bullet? Knowing it could come at any second? Or not. Nah. I did it right. I wanted you to feel it, and you did. You still do. *That's* why. And I've just started. There's more to come."

There it was. Not suicide. Not something G did, not something Harri had missed. It had been Noble. But still her fault. He wouldn't have come near G if not for her. Her hands, slick with sweat, tightened on the wheel. She could feel a pressure, a rage, building in her chest.

"But your knowing doesn't change anything, does it? We're still going to do this between the two of us. I'll make you suffer a little more. I'm an old man now. I need my entertainment. This visit is just to prove I can get to you anywhere I want, whenever I want. You came to where I live. I know where *you* live . . . I even know where your mother lives. Nice-looking woman, by the way. And your partner, with that cute little kid and the old lady living in the house."

Harri shifted, not physically—her hands were still on the wheel, her eyes on the rearview, her back straight. The shift was internal, subtle. Not seismic, volcanic, but smoldering, a baleful stir. She could almost swear she'd heard a click as if a switch had been flipped.

Noble had just changed the game. Her for her father was a deal she could die with. Her mother for her, or Vera and her family for her, was not one she could make. Could he tell, she wondered? Had he heard the click?

"We're done, you and me," she said. "Shoot or get out."

"I don't take orders anymore, *Detective*. From *anybody*."

Her eyes burned with fury. "I said, shoot or get out."

She saw Noble smile in the mirror, but he hesitated too. Suddenly, he pulled the gun away from her head.

"Not the time," he said. "I've got twenty years to work off. I'll let you worry about when. How's that?" Her back door opened. Noble left it ajar for a second as icy air swept in.

"Remember to keep your doors locked," he said. "Otherwise, anybody could just push their way in. See you next time, Harri."

He got out, slammed the door behind him. Gone. Harri released a breath, the one she'd held as if it were a treasure, thinking it would be her last. She stared at her stricken expression in the mirror, saw the fear in her eyes, but she saw the other thing too.

A cop walked out of the building and hurried to his car, his chin burrowed into his collar, oblivious to her close call. Now, she thought. *Now?*

She shoved the driver's door open and bolted from the car, doubling over once she was out, her shaking hands resting on trembling knees, gulping in frigid air as though she couldn't get enough of it, thankful to be able to breathe at all. Fire from her belly threatened to scorch her throat, but instead of tamping it down, she allowed herself to feel it; she let it do what it was going to do.

There was no use looking for Noble, she reasoned. The night had swallowed him up. It was more important to breathe, to steady herself, to feel.

After a few minutes, Harri pulled herself up, transferring steadier hands from knees to hips. She tilted her face toward the sky, her chest still heaving. Noble. *Noble.* The fire escaped. She couldn't contain it a second longer. Harri beat her fists against the hood of her car, over and over and over again. Half-crazed, out of control. It was rage unleashed after months and years. After countless paper clips and tacks, and marbles and numbness. After death and grief and nothing. *Rage.* Over and over her fists hit the hood. All the while she wished the hood was Noble.

"Hey, you okay over there?"

She stopped, winded, a spell broken, and turned to see a passing PO, her keys in her hand, a concerned look on her face. Harri waved an okay but couldn't manage words.

The cop smiled, waved back, and continued on. All clear. All fine. All good.

See you next time.

Harri got back in the car, buckled in, and started up, cold air from the vents adding to the car's frigid interior. She felt different, like she was in another country or was another person living another life. Changed by the gun. She gripped the wheel, her fists sore and bruised, and drove away.

CHAPTER 31

She sat in the car outside G's house, needing to go in but not wanting to. It had always been an inviting place. G and Mike, the kids, had made it a chaotic, messy, noisy, lived-in nest . . . safe, protected, loving. It had taken Noble to destroy all that. G had been cop of the block here, and Harri had always teased her about it. She recalled a story G told her of a neighbor ringing her doorbell at 5:00 a.m. on a Sunday to report a suspicious car parked on the block. Instead of giving the neighbor an earful, G got dressed and went out to check. For the block, it had always been G first, 311 and 911 second.

G was dead because of her, because of something her father had done, because of a bad cop who kept getting worse. If G had been partnered with someone else, someone without the baggage, a vendetta tailing them, she'd still be alive and home with her kids. It hadn't been suicide. She hadn't chosen to go; she'd been taken. Harri took time to sit with that, to feel the guilt, to take responsibility for the loss.

Out of the car and making her way up the walk, Harri thought of what she'd say, how she'd say it. All the way up to the door, she wrestled with the words, knowing whatever she said, however it came out, the words were going to hurt. G didn't have to die. She shouldn't have. The door opened. Mike stood there in an old U of Wisconsin sweatshirt and jeans, a bewildered look on his angular face. When their eyes met, the bewildered look went away, his eyes widened, and she could see him brace himself. He'd lost his wife. His kids had lost their mother. Harri's loss in no way compared to theirs. But now she had the answer, the truth, and it was going to tear her apart to tell it and for Mike and the kids to hear it.

"Mike," she said. "I should have called. It's late. But I . . ."

She could still feel the gun at her head, the clock ticking. *Noble.* She hated him. She hated everything he was, every breath he took, every grin, every word he uttered. She hated the ground he walked on. She loathed him for taking G instead of her.

"You know something," he said. She could see the dread creeping into his expression, the fear. "There's news."

"The kids here, Mike?"

"They're in their rooms doing homework." He stepped aside, held the door open. "Get out of the cold, Harri."

She didn't want to say the words with the kids in the house. She kicked herself now for not planning this better, for not waiting to talk to Mike alone, but she had no idea what Noble would do. Her feet stayed planted to the stoop, the door open in front of her.

"Or we can talk in your car," Mike said. "I'll grab a coat. Let the kids know."

She exhaled, relieved. "Thanks."

It took five minutes for him to come out, a few more minutes for her to say what she'd come to say. Then she waited.

"He killed her," Mike said. "Everything was a fake? All because of what your father did? He made us think . . . our kids. Oh my God."

"I'm sorry, Mike."

Mike looked over at her, angry, gutted. "Don't you *dare* be sorry. This is him, not you. *He's* the one. I want him arrested. I want him to *pay*." He grabbed his hair and pulled at it, wrecked, beyond consolation. "Oh my God, Glynnie. What are we doing? What happens next? I want him gone, Harri."

She'd kept out the part about Noble's gun to her head but told it now. "The admission isn't enough. It'll take more." Her eyes held his. "I'll get it."

"He could have killed you tonight."

"I need you to watch out. To be careful and smart. Keep the kids close. I'll fix it. I promise."

"Fix it," he muttered. "There's no fixing what he did. She's gone. But I want him to pay for it. I want him in a box."

"Then that's what I'll do."

He reached over and grabbed her hand and squeezed it. "Glynnie would be doing the same thing you're doing if he'd come after you straight on, you know that, right? This is not on you. It's *him*. Say it."

She shook her head, not trusting herself to say a single word more. She couldn't say it because she didn't believe it. She never would.

"You need to get back inside, Mike."

He opened the door, slid a leg out. "Go home, Harri. Get some sleep. Then we get him."

She nodded, then watched as he slowly walked inside his house, the home he'd built with G, the one Noble had wrecked.

Tears stung her eyes. She couldn't stop them. Sleep. She might never sleep again.

CHAPTER 32

"Are you all right?" Vera asked the next morning when they pulled into the ME's lot at nine. "You've barely said one word. And you look off."

Harri parked, got her stuff together. "I didn't sleep well. And off how?"

Li studied her, eyes narrowed. "Can't put my finger on it. Different."

"I'm good. Ready to go?"

"Anything happen last night? With Noble? Another call?"

She couldn't talk about it. Too fresh, too raw. "No calls. All fine."

Li didn't look convinced but didn't pick at it. "Good."

The ME's building was quiet when they walked in. One look and the uninitiated might think that meant all was right with the city and that there were no homicides to process. Harri knew differently.

There was even a hypothesis among the learned that the city's homicide rate fluctuated with the weather. That in the spring and summer, when temperatures rose, tempers flared, the wrong people were out and about, and the number of killings increased. And that conversely in winter, when temps dropped close to zero or below, the numbers fell because even the wrong people prone to the worst impulses valued their extremities, feared frostbite, and stayed indoors. But cops had a street-eye view of the whole thing and knew that nothing stopped killing. Not weather. Not economics. Not prison. Not laws. Not religion. People killed outside in summer and inside in winter, whether they were hot or cold, with guns and knives and chains, with shoes and pillows and just about anything else that came to hand. She remembered a case—not that she could ever forget it—where a schizophrenic off his meds bludgeoned his mother with a meat-tenderizer mallet, dismembered her body, and then barbecued the remains on a Weber grill in the backyard. In the dead of winter.

No, she thought as she breathed in the still air of the ME's building. Weather didn't do a thing to stop killing.

The quiet was a sham, a lie. Harri knew Grant's autopsy tables and mortuary cabinets were full, and that at least one of those cabinets and two of those tables held bodies attached to their case.

They found Symansky waiting outside Grant's autopsy room. Tybo Sawyer was with him. Neither looked happy.

"What's wrong?" Harri asked when she and Vera reached them.

Symansky threw his hands up. "Tybo here says we gotta take a number like we're at the deli counter orderin' up Genoa salami."

Tybo turned to Harri and Vera, not the least bit flustered by Symansky's dramatics. "Two cases. One by one. That's how it's done. The prelims were sent to your emails already. But if you want to confirm visually, it's one by one." She flicked a look at Symansky. "No numbers. Dr. Grant decides who goes first. And it's the Bauer case."

"Why *that* one?" Symansky groused. "I was here first."

Vera's eyes widened. "Seriously? You're fighting to get *into* an autopsy room?"

"It's the principle of the thing. I got dibs."

Tybo looked up at him, stern of face, unmovable and incorruptible at a feisty four foot eleven. She pointed to the bench a couple of yards down the hall. "You can wait there. You're next."

Symansky huffed. "So, I'll just cool my heels out in the hallway like a schlump, is that it? Take your time. I got all day, don't I?"

Symansky trudged to the bench, plopped down onto it, crossing his arms to his chest. His display didn't faze Tybo. She opened the door and held it for Harri and Vera.

"Vera, you want to start?" Harri said. "Give me a minute."

Vera stared at Symansky for a second. "Yeah, okay. Good luck with *that*."

Vera followed Tybo inside, and Harri sat down on the bench with Symansky. Neither said anything for a minute.

"Katie?" Harri finally said.

"Sick as a dog from the chemo. Almost seems like the cure's worse than the cancer. Sorry about that deli crack. You know how it is when you know you're bein' a prick, but you can't stop yourself from bein' one?"

Harri smiled. "Never had the experience."

Symansky took a deep breath and eased it out. "I'm good. You better get in there before Grant tosses Li out by the seat of her pants. Never in a million years thought you two'd get along like a house a'fire. But you're like firin' on all cylinders."

Harri slid a look toward the doors to the autopsy room. "It's not hard to work with good cops. You worked closely with Lonergan for a long time. He'll be back."

"Yeah. Maybe." He flicked a look her way. "We weren't datin', or nothin'. And he's a pain in the ass."

She chuckled. She wanted to ask him about Eddie Noble. Symansky had been with the department decades longer than she had; he must have heard about his case and his conviction. But she couldn't bring herself to open the door. The fewer people involved in her mess, the better.

"You good?" she asked.

"Better than good." He turned to look at her. "*You* good? You look a little rocky."

Harri stood to ward off a conversation. "One of those nights. I think I need a new mattress."

She then filled him in on their call with Sebastian Collier to get the focus off her.

"Asshole," he said when she'd finished.

"We'll exchange notes when we're done."

He waved her on. "Yeah, go. Do it. Get a new mattress too. You don't wanna mess your back up sleepin' on springs. And don't go cheap. Cheap'll kill ya faster than a poisoned dart."

Vera was waiting at the slanted table, a grim-looking Grant across from her, Anna Bauer's body between them covered up to her clavicles in a sheet. The chalky pallor to her skin, the emptiness of the body, devoid of its spirit, was something Harri would never get used to.

"It's been five minutes," Grant said dryly. "Detective Li here has asked five thousand questions. Some of them a little personal."

Vera rocked on her heels. "Hoping to get underneath that tough exterior. Get a feel for the real you."

Grant's eyes narrowed. "You couldn't handle the real me."

"Do I smell a challenge?"

"You smell ammonia."

Harri looked from Vera to Grant, then back. "What are we doing?"

Grant reached for a clipboard. "Li's pissin' in the wind. I'm working. Time is short. I'll only do top of the charts. Symansky's waiting, and I hear he's feeling a certain way about it. You have the prelim report already, but I've got an interesting ripple for you. A match you're going to love."

"Fingerprints?" Harri asked, hopeful at the prospect.

"No."

"Dental records?" Vera asked. "Pacemaker?"

Grant lowered the clipboard. "We going to do this all day?"

Harri was impatient. "What then?"

"DNA." She watched their shocked faces, pleased with herself. "That's right. The mother lode. We did a real rush job, but your Anna Bauer shares DNA with—"

"It's Brice Collier, isn't it?" Vera said.

Grant sighed, shot Li a look that hinted at a desire to commit *copicide*. "*With* Michael James Paget. About twenty-five percent, in fact, which would make her his aunt."

Harri and Vera exchanged a look; Vera's mouth hung agape.

"She didn't have a pacemaker, or any significant dental work, and her prints came back without a hit," Grant reported. "So, the DNA match was an out-of-the-park home run for you two. You can read the report for the rest, but wrapping it up tight and putting a bow on it, nothing spectacular about cause of death. Exsanguination due to the wounds on her wrists. Tox is still running, but the med bottles found near the tub take the suspense out of that for the most part. Slight hardening of the arteries due to age. Heart fine. Lungs fine. Everything fine. No brain abnormalities. Normal weight and size." She tossed the clipboard on the counter behind her. "Now get out. Send Symansky in. I don't have anything quite so dramatic for him, but at least he can get it firsthand like you two did."

"Is Younger a Paget too?" Vera asked.

"Now that would be something, wouldn't it?" Grant said. "The answer's no. But weirdly, he ties in with Collier by way of the tattoo. Bauer to Paget. Younger to Collier. Tight little circle." Grant looked pleased with herself. "Tybo?"

The little woman, who must have been standing right outside, stuck her head in the door, the signal that Harri and Vera were being cycled out of the room so Symansky could be cycled in.

"Wow," Vera said when they were in the hall again and Symansky had brushed past them. "She was a Paget."

"That gives us motive and opportunity," Harri said.

"And a likely accomplice," Vera added. "Her nephew."

"Now all we need to figure out is means. How'd they do it?" Harri was already moving. "Let's go."

Vera double-timed it to keep up. "What about Al?"

"We'll text him from the car."

CHAPTER 33

Ethan hoped she wasn't mad at him. She was the only family he had left. Without her he was alone in the world, the last of the Pagets. He hoped he could make her see that he was right. She always had before. What had changed, he wondered? She had wanted to avenge Mikey's murder just as much as he had. She blamed Collier just as much as he did for the death of his mother, her sister.

A bouquet of pink flowers in his hand, he knocked at her door, a little nervous about what she might say when she opened it and saw him there. She had to know this was the only way to honor the family.

There was no answer. He knocked again. The door across the hall opened, and an old woman stood in the doorway with a cat.

"No one's there," she said. "You a friend of hers?"

Ethan didn't see how that was the old woman's business, but he answered. "Something like that."

"Pretty flowers. But sorry to have to tell you, your friend passed away the day before yesterday. Took her own life is what I heard. The police found her in her tub. Slit wrists. Such a tragedy for someone that young."

Ethan heard the woman, but the words sounded far away, as though they were coming from the bottom of a deep well.

"That can't be right," he heard himself say. "I just saw her. Talked to her. She was all right."

The woman looked sad, truly affected. "That's how it can happen sometimes, son. All right one minute, next minute not. And none of us can judge." The woman petted her cat. "I didn't hear where they were taking her, but I'm sure if you called the police, they'd tell you."

Ethan was alone. Truly, completely, finally alone. It was something he had said. It was the thing he couldn't do for her. He'd let her walk away and hadn't even tried to stop her, he was so consumed by malice. Gone. Alone.

He stared down at the flowers. No longer needed as a peace offering. He looked again at the old woman and her contented cat and held the bouquet out to her.

"You like flowers?"

The old woman smiled sweetly; it was likely decades since she'd been gifted with a bouquet.

"Pretty ones like that? Yes."

She took them, smelled them. "Such beautiful flowers. Your friend would have loved them, I'm sure. I'm always so sad when people die. Whether you knew them or not, it always feels like the world is a little emptier, a little less happy when anyone leaves it. She seemed like a good person, though always so sad."

Ethan nodded. "She was both things. Thank you."

She smelled the bouquet again. "I've got the names of the detectives who found her, if you want to contact them?"

Ethan turned and walked away. "That won't be necessary."

He stood at the elevator. He knew now he could never stop, not until Collier was dead. He'd hated too long to let it all go. But if he couldn't take the one he wanted now, he'd take who he could get, and he'd keep on taking until someone took him.

It was as good an end as he could imagine.

CHAPTER 34

"We gotta find Ethan Paget," Symansky said.

They were circled around the board, this time with more of the gaps filled in; this time the arrow of suspicion squarely pointed at Paget.

"Everybody's looking," Vera said. "He can't stay hidden forever."

"Meanwhile, we have to worry about where the next shoe's going to drop."

"He might be crazy enough to go for Hardwicke House or half that campus up there," Symansky said. "Every other building's got Collier's name on it."

Kelley read from his legal pad. "I did some digging once we got that DNA match. Michael's father was an only child, so no aunt on that side. But his mother had two sisters, Hannah and Audrey. Audrey died in her teens, long before Michael was thought of. Hannah . . ." Kelley stood and walked a photo over to the board. The photo was of a happy family standing in front of a bakery window. Harri recognized Michael Paget, a few years younger than he had been when he died, standing next to a smaller boy she assumed was Ethan. Kelley pointed to the dark-haired woman on the right, her arm around a beaming woman who bore a strong resemblance to her. Sisters.

"That's Hannah. Two years older than her sister. Married at the time to Henry Bauer, not in the picture, but also now deceased. *Hannah* Bauer, *Anna* Bauer. She didn't change much, did she?"

"So, it's Ethan," Vera said.

"Looks like it."

Harri got closer to the photo and stared into the eyes of the little boy, who had no idea at the time the photo was taken how wildly his life would change in a few short years.

"Nothing to lose," she muttered. "Everybody he's ever cared about or who cared for him is dead." She turned around. "The relationship explains Bauer's note. She felt she had failed him. Her note said *It wasn't for us to judge or take.*"

"Sounds like a confession to me," Bigelow said.

"But why make it and then kill yourself?" Kelley asked. "Follow a rational act with an irrational one?"

"Maybe it wasn't about her," Vera said. "She'd accepted what she'd done and made up her mind to answer for it. I think she was trying to save Ethan."

The team agreed with shrugs and nods. Harri turned back to the board, to the underlines, the question marks, the cross throughs, the arrows that led to Ethan, the little boy who'd lost it all.

"This has legs," she said. "It makes sense."

Her eyes moved over the name of the fix-it guy, Freddie. "Anybody find anything on him and his buddy? Bauer brought them in for Hardwicke. It's a good bet she did that for Ethan. If so, that makes four takers, three of them with confirmed access to the house. It wouldn't have been hard for her to leave a door open, find a key and copy it, come up with a way for the four of them to slip in and up to the roof to wait for Brice. She could have been the one to put that note in Brice's room. It wouldn't have been impossible for her to overhear him talk about Hailie and then to use her as the bait. Brice wouldn't have noticed the help, would he? To some people, they're like pieces of furniture. They say all kinds of things in front of them. *Oh, don't mind Jeeves.* But Jeeves knows everything."

"Nothing on either one of them," Bigelow said. "Nobody at the house had last names. Nobody we've talked to knows anything about them. They're like smoke."

"We keep trying," Harri said. "Ethan, Bauer, these two . . . looks like a hit squad."

"We'll need confessions," Symansky said. "Because if it's them, who did Younger? They didn't leave a speck of dust behind 'em. No prints on the belt kinda says somebody helped him onto that chair, but we can't link nothin' to somethin', can we?"

Harri put the marker down and turned from the board. "We have a lot to do. Ethan, Freddie, his buddy. We may not know where they are, but we know where they'll likely be, don't we? Hardwicke House. Sebastian Collier is still alive. The house is still standing. They might want to take another swipe. Anything to get Collier's attention and force him back so they can get at him."

Bigelow snorted. "That doesn't look like it's going to happen. If he didn't show up when his own kid was killed, I can't see him swooping in now."

"Twisted priorities," Kelley muttered. "Lousy father."

"Maybe," Vera said, "but I don't think that matters anymore. Brice is dead for something his father did. Sebastian's going to have to live with that."

There was silence for a moment, and then the team broke up, their priorities clearly set. Harri had a feeling they didn't have a lot of time either. There was a good chance Bauer's death sped the clock up. Ethan would hold Collier responsible for yet another loss. His desire to seek vengeance would be even more pronounced.

Back at her desk, Harri picked up her cell phone to find a text from Sly. Got something you have to see. When can you meet?

She looked up. Vera was watching.

"Noble?" she asked.

She shook her head. "Sly's got something. He wants to meet. We're heading out now anyway. Let's—"

Vera was already grabbing her coat and bag. "Meet you in the car."

"Make a stop first." Harri completed the sentence, but Vera was already gone.

———

"Hot cocoa."

Vera took a slow sip from her mug as they sat in Sly's warm kitchen, her curious eyes peering out over the rim. "Yum."

Harri knew Vera hadn't missed a single thing since the moment they walked into Sly's house, including the nervousness Harri felt about being here again with company.

Sly smiled, impressed by the eagle-eyed Li. "So, what do you think, Vera?"

She put her mug down. "Nice place." She glanced over at Harri sitting beside her with a mug of her own, noting how uncomfortable her partner looked. "Interesting vibe. Beautiful home. And you're . . . a great cocoa maker."

Harri could feel herself blush and was desperate to move things along. They still had a case, which she knew Vera knew full well, though she seemed hell bent on getting as much out of Sly as she could manage.

"You said you had something?"

"Yep. Hold on."

He left the room. Vera smiled and opened her mouth to say something.

"Don't," Harri said. "Just do not."

She shrugged and went back to her cocoa. "I'll save it."

Sly was back quickly with a manila envelope that he slid across the table to Harri. She opened it and pulled out black-and-white photographs. It took all of two seconds to identify the cop lot where G died and only a second more to notice the time stamp that pinned the images to *that* day. The revelation nearly stole her breath, and she recoiled.

"Where? How? You said the tapes were locked down."

"The tapes are. But I know a guy who knows a guy, who knows *the* guy. And two of those guys owed me. I couldn't get you the tapes, but I got you stills *from* the tapes."

Harri laid the photos out on the table. There were a half dozen that she lined up one after the other. Her hands were sweating.

"There are none of the car," she said, unable to look at Sly for fear of showing him too much.

He paused. "Just the lot and who was in it."

Vera squinted at the grainy images, then her eyes slowly widened. She set her mug aside, then reached out and picked up one photo to examine it closely. "Wow."

Sly pointed at one of the photos. "*That's* Noble. And you. This is proof he was there. We don't have him near G's car, but you can see how he did it. How he wouldn't have raised a single red flag."

She studied the photographs. There was an officer in uniform holding her back from getting to G's car. Graying hair. The same face. He'd aged, of course, since the last time he'd worn a uniform. Nineteen years in prison will do that to you, but it was Noble clear as day. He'd have been paroled a couple of months by then, but his old uniform still fit.

What had he said on the phone? *I could have let you see, but I didn't. I spared you.* She homed in on his face, on his grip on her as she struggled to get free and get to G. And he'd known the entire time that he'd caused the carnage to begin with.

"These get him locked up again," Sly said. "They end it. You don't have to do anything else beyond this point."

Harri didn't respond. She was somewhere else. Back in that lot, being held back by the cop she didn't know from Adam. She'd blocked the whole thing out over the ensuing months, remembering only bits and pieces, pushing away the images and feelings that hurt the most. Until now. Now she saw it in black and white. Now she remembered someone had held her back. She recalled struggling to break the hold and get to the car, sure she could save G, render aid. Desperate to get there. She had fought the cop who'd grabbed her, cursed him. He had said something then. That she couldn't at the moment call up. What was it?

"Right," she offered.

Vera picked up each photo and examined them. "He could have kept the uniform, but he wouldn't have been able to keep his star."

Harri focused on the badge pinned to Noble's uniform blouse. She'd done her research. She'd gone back through Noble's entire police record, up to and including his trial and conviction.

"It's a fake. That's not his star number." She picked up the photo and zeroed in on his holster. "He's carrying. A Glock. Can't see if it's regulation, but who would have checked that closely? Impersonating an officer *and* he's on parole. That's enough."

"You're right. He fits right in," Vera said. "Nobody would have given him a second look."

"I didn't. He'd been inside so long, anybody he had worked with would have likely been long retired. The uniform gets him in. He mills around. Who'd question him if he kept his head down?"

Harri sat staring at the photos, unable to look away, pestered by not being able to recall what he'd said to her. He'd said it calmly, too, close to her ear. That she knew. *That* she could recall. How calm he'd been, how steady his voice was.

She pointed to a clear shot of her and Noble. Her mouth was open, her eyes crazed and trained on G's car; she was screaming and fighting.

There had been a glimmer of hope; she remembered feeling it, that she wasn't too late.

"He said something. Whispered it almost."

"Noble? What?" Vera said.

She racked her brain but still couldn't come up with it. "I don't know. I can almost . . . but it keeps slipping away."

"He planned it perfectly, that's for sure," Sly said. "Waltzed right in and acted like he belonged there."

"Nobody knows cops better than another cop," Vera offered.

"He slid into her back seat," Harri said.

"How do you know that?" Vera asked.

Harri avoided eye contact. "We need to talk."

Harri gathered up the photos, stuffed them in her bag. She'd send copies to Gomez, present a set to Griffin. "I need to call Gomez. Noble's little game is over."

She stood, reached for her jacket slung over the back of her chair. "I appreciate this, Sly. We've got to get going, though. This case we're on. We're close."

Vera and Sly watched her, their brows knit together, neither sure of what they were witnessing.

"Harri? Maybe you want to take a minute?" Sly said.

"I would if I had a minute, but I don't. I'm clean out of minutes, Sly. He's out there plotting, enjoying himself. It stops here. I'll be in touch. Tell you how it turns out."

Sly rose to show them out.

"Don't get up," Harri said. "We'll show ourselves out." She paused, aware she'd been harsh, short. "I'm sorry. It's a lot."

Sly stared at her. "No problem. I understand."

He and Vera exchanged a worried look, but neither said a word. There was no conversation in the car, only the crackle of radio transmissions. Vera left it there, not sure what to say. Yet.

———

Harri tailed Noble to an Irish bar on Western and sat outside watching the sweaty windows, the name Boyle's lit up in green neon. She thought of Griffin and wondered if she knew the place. It seemed right up her alley.

The envelope of photos sat in her passenger seat like an unwanted guest. There had been no movement on Ethan Paget all day. He'd had decades to plot his revenge, as Noble had, and it appeared he'd planned for every contingency.

It wasn't a good feeling, having a murderer lead you around your own city by the nose, but they couldn't check every hole. CPD simply didn't have enough bodies with badges.

She hoped Vera was cuddled up at home with her family as she should be. She would need to tell her about Noble in the back seat of her car. First thing tomorrow, she decided. Meanwhile, she was here. Watching windows. Waiting.

Waiting for what? Even she wasn't sure. She wanted to confront him with the photos. She needed to remember what he'd said to her. She wanted to know how he could have done such a thing and still live with himself. She glared down at the envelope. Noble was a killer. He was sick, twisted. What had he said?

A parolee, he couldn't legally own a gun or carry one. He wasn't even allowed inside the bar she was watching unless he had Gomez's permission, and Harri would bet the bank that he didn't have it. Yet here he was at Boyle's.

It looked like Noble was going right back to what he'd always been doing—the wrong thing. But he'd made a big mistake. He'd killed her partner, and he'd come after her. If she took him in herself now, he'd walk, plus she couldn't control the situation outside a bar with an armed felon looking at spending the rest of his life in prison. What would Noble have to lose?

Harri waited three hours, watching the neon sign and the door to Boyle's. Then Noble came out with another man. White, stocky, about the same age as him.

From across the street, Harri saw the two stand on the sidewalk long enough for the other man to light a cigarette and toss the match away before heading to a black Ford Escape. They got in, the car started up, and after a couple of minutes of warm-up, the car pulled away from the curb and headed south down Western.

Harri flicked a look at the clock on her dash. Just after 10:00 p.m. She put the car in gear, made a U-turn, and followed the Escape.

Her eyes on the back left taillight, she was careful to keep three car lengths behind with two cars between them. She'd already gotten the license plate to run later. The Escape wasn't going to Moran's. Wrong way. Staying with it, Harri followed as the streets went from commercial to residential to industrial, before the SUV pulled up in front of a building at Ninety-Sixth and Ewing. Traffic on Ewing was sparse, so Harri pulled over behind a parked Chevy Tahoe half a block down under a busted-out streetlight and then cut her engine.

The building looked like it might be some kind of warehouse, but it was painted mustard yellow with brown trim like it had been something else in a previous life. There was a car parked out front when the Escape arrived. A gray Dodge Charger covered in street salt and grime. Harri got its plate number too.

A Latino man in his twenties came out of the warehouse when the driver of the Escape sounded the horn. Two short beeps. Noble and his friend got out to greet him, and the three exchanged handshakes and bro hugs. Harri grabbed her cell phone, zoomed in, and took a few photos.

Then she sat, waiting. She didn't dare get out of the car or risk getting closer. She had no way of knowing who or what was inside the building, but she was off book. The plates and the photos were likely all she could get tonight, but still she stayed, unwilling to let it go, remembering Noble's gun, his threat. Fast Eddie Noble wasn't going to take another thing from her.

He didn't stay long. Just fifteen minutes or so by the dash clock. Noble and his pal got back into the Escape and drove away, and their friend got into his Charger, made a U-turn in the middle of the street, and headed the opposite direction. Meeting over. Plans made? Deal struck?

Harri waited for the Charger to pass, watched in the rearview as its taillights disappeared around the corner, and then started up and followed the Escape, but it became evident quickly that it was headed back to Moran's to drop Eddie off at home. When it got there, when Noble stepped inside his sister's house, she called it a night and headed home.

What was Noble up to besides riding her? Who was his friend from the bar? The one in the Charger? The questions worried her all the way home, and even as she stood in front of the whiteboard in her living room, a twin of the one at work, she had no answers.

She'd added the plate numbers and the address of the warehouse to the map of details in front of her. It was a start.

At the other end of the board, there was all the information she and the team had on the Collier case. The same arrows, circles, question marks, strike-throughs. The questions. Ethan Paget. Her eyes stopped on the name Emil Bosch. Dead in the grave, and the only one who'd played a part in Michael Paget's death that Ethan couldn't get at.

But what about family? Ethan couldn't get to Emil, but maybe he could get to someone in his family. Like Noble had gotten to her. Maybe that's where Paget was, killing someone Bosch had left behind.

Harri stepped back from the board to survey the length of it, her eyes sweeping from right to left and back. Twin troubles. Ethan. Noble. Murder. Suicides. She could admit it to herself, she was not at her best. There was too much at stake, too many people to look out for.

Ethan. Her mind ping-ponged from one problem to the other. *Where* would he be if he couldn't go home? An answer popped into her head. Her eyes slid down the board to Noble's side, again. What had been in that warehouse? Back and forth. Noble. Ethan. Her brain working overtime on fumes and frustration, trying to keep them both straight, knowing both things had to be solved at once and there weren't enough hours in the day.

It was well after midnight, but she opened her laptop and started looking for anything she could find on Emil Bosch's family . . . and the warehouse on Ewing.

CHAPTER 35

Armed with the plate numbers she'd gotten the night before, Harri slid into her office chair early the next morning before shift to run them. It didn't take long for her to come up with what she already knew. Noble was still dirty. There'd been no great rehabilitation in prison. He was what he likely always had been, only now he was bitter and more dangerous.

Noble's friend from Boyle's was a thief by the name of Brendan Moore who'd been arrested more than a dozen times. His last imprisonment, unsurprisingly, was in the same facility Noble had just been released from. She checked his driver's license photo against the ones she'd taken on her phone. They were a match. The Charger was owned by Mateo Flores, a banger with a record a mile long. Drug offenses mostly, but also numerous assaults and an attempted murder charge that didn't stick. His photos also matched.

Harri sat back, staring at the screen, her mind busy with what it all meant for her. She had enough for Gomez, but the situation was fraught with risks. Noble had dangerous friends. Getting him locked up wouldn't necessarily solve her problem. There would be nothing to stop him from hiring someone from inside to keep up his game of revenge. She couldn't protect her mother or Felix around the clock. Vera couldn't do the same for her family either.

"Now what?" she muttered.

Harri was still sitting there when the room filled up with the team and the coffee got brewing and the noise level rose, and the cop carping began. She glanced at her watch. A little after eight. She'd been lost in thought for nearly an hour. When she looked up, the entire team was standing over her.

"Somethin's up," Symansky said. "What?"

Her tired eyes narrowed. "Our *case*?"

"Nope. Something else," Bigelow said, "and it's been up for a while. A lot of hush-hush between you and Li. A lot of time in the girlie john whispering."

"Come clean," Kelley added. "Or else."

Her brows lifted at the *or else*, but she didn't respond; instead Harri, a little claustrophobic with the closeness, rolled her squeaky chair back to give herself some breathing room.

"There's a lot of snow on your car," Vera said. "How long have you been here?"

Harri stood, not comfortable with the hovering. "What's happening right now?"

Symansky adjusted his belt, stuck his chest out. "Somethin's eatin' ya, and we want to know what. Five heads are better than one, even if one of 'em belongs to Kelley here."

Kelley slid Symansky a look. "You're a real piece of work, you know that, Al?"

Symansky waved him off. "Yeah, stow it. It's Foster we're workin' on right now."

"No, you're *not*," Harri said, finding her voice. "We are *not working* on me. We are working this case, and all of you need to be about the business of getting on it. Leave me *alone*."

Nobody moved. Harri stood watching nobody move, then slowly glanced over at Griffin's door. Not in yet, but the office had other cops milling around in it. Not a place to share her secrets, at least the ones that involved her immediate problem.

She could tell from the determined looks she wasn't going to get out of this. They weren't going to let her off the hook.

"I don't go prying into your personal business, do I?"

Symansky bristled. "First off, I got nothin' worth pryin' into, but if you wanna pry, pry. Second, Kelley's personal business ain't worth knowin' about, so good luck there."

Kelley held up a hand with his thumb and index finger pinched close together. "You're this close, old man."

"I have two ex-wives," Bigelow said.

Vera shrugged. "You know my situation. Busy husband. Small child. Mother in residence. It's enough to curl your hair."

"I'm handling it," Harri said.

Bigelow's eyes narrowed. "Handling *what*?"

She looked over at Vera. Vera looked back. No help there. She had no out. Resigned, Harri said simply, "Bathroom."

As they crowded around the sinks and stalls, she told them about Fast Eddie. The why and how and when. After one final hesitation, she relayed what happened in her car, the gun to her head, the fear she might die. She needed them to be safe and aware of the threat. She braced for the blowback, especially from Vera, at having been left in the dark, but none came.

"That son of a bitch," Bigelow said. "Okay. Let's suit up. Posse time. Who's riding shotgun?"

Harri shook her head. "No."

Kelley clutched the handcuffs on his belt, a vein in his neck pulsing in a way that worried her.

"*No*," Harri repeated. "I've handed it all over to Gomez. I'll let her handle it."

Symansky was uncharacteristically quiet, staring off into the distance.

Vera waved her hand in front of his face. "Al?"

"I'm old enough to remember that case," he said. "Noble was bad police any way you cut it. A lot of cops knew what he was doin' but turned a blind eye. I can't remember the partner's name, but he was in on it too. Both of them got pinched."

"Leonard Krieg," Harri said. "He's a ghost."

Bigelow snorted. "I would be, too, shit."

Symansky looked Harri up and down, seemingly impressed. "That was your dad who blew the whistle, huh? Explains a lot."

"You're saying Noble's a *cop* killer?" Kelley asked.

"He admitted doing the same to Glynnis that he did to me, only he shot her with her own gun."

"All day yesterday," Vera said, "you never said anything. I *knew* something was up. How could you not say *anything*? A gun to your head? *Harri!*"

"I couldn't talk about it," Harri said. "Knowing G was in the same situation. Knowing all he had to do was pull the trigger. I'm still processing it."

"That son of a bitch," Bigelow repeated. "Okay, let's crunch it. What do we have?"

"All of it. The video, the faked photos, the taunting, even the back seat visit. It's weak," Harri said. "He knows it. It might just be enough to jam him up with Gomez, but it's no slam dunk. There are enough holes in what I have that he could drive a Mack truck through it."

"The boss know about this?" Kelley asked.

"I haven't given her an update, if that's what you mean. Her knowing or not knowing doesn't change anything, does it? I know what he did, and I know what G *didn't* do. And CPD's not interested in any of it." She told them about the IAD report.

Symansky's eyes narrowed. "*That's* what's going on between you and Griffin."

"It's not her, it's me. I'll get over it."

"So, this handlin' you're doin' is all you?" Symansky asked.

"I'm building a case," Harri said. "First, I get him off the streets, then I get him for killing G."

The group stood without speaking for a moment. "Five of us, one of him," Bigelow finally said.

"*No*," Harri said. "There's none of you. This is something I have to do."

"An ass-kickin' before he goes back inside might do him some good," Symansky said. "How we did it back in the day. That rubber-hose business wasn't some made-up fairy tale."

Harri met each face with a warning. "Absolutely *not*."

For a moment there wasn't a sound in the room.

"So, that's what's been eating me," she said, breaking the silence, "and now you know, and we can all get back to what we need to do and let me handle this."

"Nah," Symansky said, "lone wolf ain't gonna cut it. Get your head around it."

Everyone appeared to be in agreement, except for Harri.

Kelley cleared his throat. "Now that's settled, and since we're sharing and in here under the cone of confidences, as a team, I'd like to know more about Bigelow's two ex-wives."

Bigelow frowned. "None of your damned business."

"I wouldn't mind knowing what Al does on his days off," Vera said. "He's like a ghost."

Symansky glowered at them, then jabbed a pudgy thumb in Bigelow's direction. "Same answer he just gave ya." He headed for the door, yanked it open. "And ghost my *ass*."

———

By midmorning, Harri had to admit she felt lighter having unburdened herself, but she couldn't let that make her complacent. It was good the team knew. Now Noble couldn't sneak up on them. But right now, she focused on Emil Bosch. Vera approached as she was putting his details on the board.

"Why are you putting stuff up for a dead guy?" she asked.

Kelley scooted his swivel chair over. "Yeah, didn't I find him in the cemetery?"

"We looking for spirits now?" Bigelow asked, a FOP mug of steaming coffee in his hand. "Because if we are, I'm out. I don't fool with that shit. You're dead, you need to stay the fuck dead."

Symansky crossed his arms, huffed. "I'm not trudgin' through any boneyards. Below my pay grade and bad for the ticker."

"You think Ethan will go after Emil's people," Vera said.

Harri turned from the board. "It would fit his pattern. It might even explain why we can't put eyes on him."

She crossed over to her desk, picked up the notes she'd taken. "There wasn't much information on Bosch's obituary, so I put in a call to the cemetery and got a couple things. What the obit did say is that Emil was survived by a father, Aaron, and that his mother, Katherine, preceded him in death. No mention of siblings. No extended family either."

"So, what'd the cemetery say?" Symansky asked.

"I asked who paid for Bosch's plot and headstone, and who's paying for upkeep, hoping that gave us a contact name. Maybe an address for the father."

Kelley leaned forward. "And?"

"And all they would say is that everything was paid in full on day one. In cash. And that the father's name was nowhere on the paperwork."

"So, who buried Emil?" Vera asked.

"And who pays for a plot in cash?" Bigelow said.

Kelley nodded, then rolled back to his desk. "I'm on it."

"Do you know where the father is now?" Vera asked.

"I couldn't find anything after about fifteen years ago. No death record. Also, no renewed driver's license. No offenses. He'd be about eighty now. Nursing home, maybe? There are a ton of them."

"Well, one good thing," Bigelow said. "If we can't find him, chances are good Ethan can't either."

"Let's hope that's true," Harri said. "For now, let's see who buried Emil and see where that leads us."

CHAPTER 36

"This is a long shot," Vera groused as she stared out of the passenger window of the moving car.

They were headed toward the Pagets' bakery, now out of business, the sleet hitting the windshield like a barrage of birdseed.

"I know. But we never actually checked it. He's not at his place. He hasn't got any more family that we know of. All he had, all he has ever had a connection to, is that old business."

"So, you think he's squatting inside."

"We go. We check. If I'm wrong, we cross it off and go after something else. He's gotta be somewhere. We didn't find him on any flights. No trains. Buses."

"Easy to slip through," Vera offered. "We know he's not on his way to Switzerland. He's never applied for a passport. Doesn't rule out black market, but these days with the updated security protocols? That'd be a real trick."

"He's in a hole somewhere," Harri said. "The bakery *could* be it."

Vera took a sip from her Starbucks cup, then dug into a thin bag to pinch off a piece of croissant to pop into her mouth. A breakfast of champions.

"I'm surprised you told everybody."

"I didn't have much choice, did I?"

"You wouldn't have a couple months ago. It shows you trust us. Those photos, though. I can't imagine being there. Or what you're feeling now. I know you don't want to talk about it. Because, well, you don't. But both my ears work, if you need them."

Harri thought about it. "Seeing it. Going back. Knowing it's all tied to me."

"Not you. You didn't even know Noble existed."

"She's still dead. He's still walking around the streets."

Vera closed up the bag, set it in the console. "He won't be for long. He's done and done."

Harri nodded. "Right."

"Figures Noble would come out and start right up again. The scumbag. You didn't ask, but I checked on some of his known *associates*. Most of them are dead, but there are enough still in action for Noble to get back in the game, including the two you clocked."

"What value would he be to them, though?" Harri asked. "He's not on the job anymore."

"He might not have the access he once did, but he's got the knowledge, the background. He knows how we operate. He might have been able to talk himself into a role."

Harri pulled up in front of the building that once housed the Paget bakery.

"Let's take a look," she said, getting out of the car.

The front door was locked tight; the windows facing the street were gritty, dusty, and topped with frost. No one had been in the building, it appeared, for years, maybe not since the Pagets had been forced to relinquish it.

They peered inside past the grit to see a gloomy inside. A couple of abandoned café tables, empty shelves, wires hanging from the ceiling where light fixtures had been ripped out.

"Their pride and joy," Vera said sadly. "Snatched away from them."

"Let's check around the back."

They returned to the car and drove around to the alley, but the back door was also locked, a metal gate pulled closed in front of it, but not secured. Harri pushed it back, the squeal and groan of the rusted works an affront to the ears.

Vera tried the doorknob. No give. She rammed a shoulder against the door.

"Not very heavy," she announced. "Guess they counted on the gate keeping thieves out." She stepped back. "Ethan'd probably still have a key to this. It doesn't look like the bank's done a thing to protect the property. We wouldn't necessarily notice a breach."

"Abandoned," Harri said. "A killer at large."

They weighed their options.

"Last time we were in this predicament, you got knifed," Vera said.

"And you fell down the stairs and busted your ass," Harri said.

Vera scowled. "I was *pushed*."

They stood deliberating for a moment.

Harri walked over to the car, popped the trunk, and drew a crowbar out. Back to the door, it took just two hits before the lock gave way, the flimsy door swung free, and they slipped inside. People were dying, she reasoned; they needed to find Ethan.

Flashlights on, they stood for a second waiting for their eyes to adjust to the gloom, watching as particles of old bakery dust flitted across their beams. The smell of dirt and damp and something fetid and dead wafted up their nostrils.

"Chicago Police!" Harri called out to the rats.

"What she said," Vera added.

The place felt desolate, Harri thought. Sad too. As they crossed the room, their feet crunching across frozen tile, she could almost see how nice it would have been with the family babying the business and putting all their hard work into it. To see it now, left to rot, knowing all but one of the Pagets had met tragic ends, was depressing.

The shelves were empty, the display counter too. They searched the entire place, the kitchen in back, the freezer, the storage room, but there were no signs that Ethan had been there. Maybe he couldn't bring himself to see the bakery again.

"Hey."

Harri turned to find Vera staring at a framed photograph on the wall. It wasn't a professional shot; instead it appeared to be cut out of a neighborhood newspaper and included the entire Paget staff posed in front of the shop. All smiles, happy, together, much like the photo Kelley had come across, but this one looked like everyone was present, not just the family.

Li pointed her beam at it. "The Pagets. There's Bauer. And Ethan. Michael." Her beam dropped to the caption below and stopped at a name. "There it is. Fred Nowak." The beam shifted right. "And his brother, Jesse."

"They worked for the Pagets," Harri said. "One big happy family. Michael dies, they lose the business, then the parents die. They've got nothing left. So, if Ethan says they go after Collier . . ."

Vera finished the sentence. "They go after Collier."

"That's the four. Ethan, Bauer, Freddie, Jesse. Four to hold down a kid and drown him in booze. Four to take revenge."

"More than enough to leave bruises behind," Vera said, reaching for the photo and lifting it off its hook. "The four horsemen of the apocalypse. The executioners."

Harri stared at the spot where the photo had been. "That hasn't always been there." She shone her light on the spot. "No dust formed around the frame. It's been years since the bakery's been open. There should be loads of dust. We should be seeing a perfect outline under that photograph."

She looked around the room, the walls, her light moving along, stopping at a spot on the other side of the counter where a cash register might have stood. Over it there was an area the size of the frame Vera now held, where the photograph had certainly hung.

They crossed the room. Vera lifted the frame up against the spot. A perfect fit.

"They took it with them when they cleared out," Vera said. "And Ethan brought it back. But why not put it back where it was?"

Harri scanned the room. Nothing there but debris, cold tile, and dirt accumulated over the years. On the floor across the room from where the photo had been rehung, there was a pallet of old newspapers, yellowed with age, spread out on the floor, a can of Coke beside it. Harri squatted down and ran the light over them.

"These papers have been here since the bakery shuttered. Dates match. He didn't move a thing except that picture because he could see it better sitting here with it hanging *there*."

"That Coke can doesn't look that old," Vera said. "Not a lot of dust. It's not rusted, but I don't think he's coming back for it."

Harri looked around, felt the loneliness of the place. "You're probably right. I think he's let it all go. Except for the end." She ran the light along the floor, stopping at a word scrawled in the dusty buildup. *Justice*. "My guess? This is his why."

Vera walked over to take a look. "As far as he sees it. Wrong end of the stick, though. None of this is justice."

Harri shrugged. "Open to interpretation."

"Not where we work." Vera tucked the photo under her arm. "All we have to do now is catch him."

Harri crossed the room, took one last look, then they headed for the back door. "Before *justice* prevails. But where the hell is he?"

CHAPTER 37

Ethan stood at the door of Hardwicke House not the man he had been just a week ago. He had changed. He was a monster now.

He could feel the darkness lying like molten coal in his belly. It felt like everything inside him had turned as black as pitch. Sebastian Collier had taken everything from him, and now it was his turn to take everything.

Brice had been easy, too easy, really, to satisfy him. He had wanted the boy to suffer more and to have his father care that he had suffered, but neither thing had happened. Sebastian Collier hadn't come back to Hardwicke, and Ethan had no way of getting to him. He wanted Sebastian Collier to burn and linger, to feel the pain of death. His wish had been denied.

So, he would take the house and anyone in it. There were no innocents here. The world as he saw it hadn't a single innocent in it anymore. Why should they live when his family hadn't? Why should he be the only one alone? The fire he'd considered for Younger before changing his mind wouldn't do for Hardwicke. That needed bigger. He wanted to blow up what the Colliers had built. He wanted bricks to fly and windows to shatter. He wanted all Collier's fancy things to burn. Ethan wanted destruction. It was good Hannah wasn't here to see what she had forced him to do alone. She wouldn't have had the stomach for it.

He held the heavy toolbox in his hand, careful not to bump it or unsettle it too much.

There was no sympathy, no remorse for what he was about to do. He was well past that now.

He gripped the metal handle, committed to his plan. He was here to take what Collier owned, what he coveted, what he'd stolen. Step by step, patiently.

"And damn him to hell."

———

Lange answered the door to find Ethan Paget standing there dressed like a workman. He'd even gone so far as to have the name Bob stenciled on a breast-pocket patch on his dark-green work shirt. Lange appreciated the commitment to detail.

He looked a lot like his brother. Same dark hair. Same dark eyes. The family resemblance was unmistakable.

After Younger, Lange had expected Ethan to make his play here, but the middle of the day on a Saturday was a bold move. Personally, he would have gone for the cover of darkness, the middle of the night, to exact the maximum impact.

Lange wondered as he stared at him what he had in mind. His eyes slid down to the toolbox in Ethan's hands. It looked heavy, and Ethan switched the box from one hand to the other. Likely not tools, Lange thought. Something else.

Ethan glanced behind him as though he was watching out for the police. He had to know the police were on to him, Lange thought. He wanted to ask Ethan how he'd evaded them thus far but didn't. It didn't really matter, not now that he was here.

He waited patiently in his black suit and tie for Ethan Paget to say his lines. He didn't want to deprive him of his moment, given the work he'd obviously put in with the shirt. It was the least he could give the man.

"Yes?" Lange finally said. "May I help you?"

Ethan came up with a fake smile as bright as the sun. "Good morning. Bob Simms." He pretended to consult the clipboard. "I got a call from a Brice Collier last week? Trouble with the water heater? I'm here to fix it." He tapped a finger against the pocket patch. "Simms Plumbing."

Ethan held up the battered clipboard with a work order attached. Lange knew the order was bogus, though it looked legitimate, right down to the Simms Plumbing logo that Ethan had likely run off on a laser printer. Glancing past him, Lange noticed the same logo attached to a peel-off decal on the side of a compact car parked at the curb. Stolen, if he had to guess. Paget wouldn't be dumb enough to drive his own car up to Hardwicke's door.

"I wasn't aware there was a problem with the water heater."

Ethan shrugged. "I don't know. He called for the service. I'm here to check it out."

"Simms?" Lange's piercing eyes held his.

Ethan switched the toolbox from his right hand to his left. "That's right. Bob Simms."

Lange let a moment go.

"Mr. Simms, unfortunately, the house has suffered a devastating loss. Mr. Collier passed away suddenly. As you can imagine, things are *chaotic* here at the moment."

Ethan feigned surprise. Lange found it amusing but didn't show it.

"Oh, jeez, that's too bad. Never met him personally. We only talked over the phone. Was it an accident, or something?"

Lange considered the question before answering it. "It was an unfortunate mistake."

The toolbox shifted from left to right.

"That's too bad. I guess you don't want me to look at that heater, then? Only it's wicked cold. The pipes could freeze. A house this size? That could really cost you."

"But *you* can fix it," Lange said.

"I can be in and out in no time."

Lange opened the door to let Ethan in. "Well, we wouldn't want the pipes to freeze."

Ethan stepped inside, and Lange locked the door behind him. He wondered how Ethan felt stepping into the lion's den, since he couldn't quite gauge his feelings by his nonreaction. He was in the home of the man he held responsible for his brother's death, yet his expression gave nothing away.

"You work here in the house?" Ethan asked. "Mr. ah . . ."

Lange reached into his pocket for his card, which he handed to Paget. "My name is Lange. I'm overseeing things until permanent arrangements for the house can be made."

"Got it." Ethan craned to see inside the great room. "Nice place. If there's anybody else in here, they won't be able to use the water while I'm working on the heater."

"That won't be a problem. I'm the only one here at the moment." Lange gestured toward the back. "The students are all on campus. The basement's this way."

"Great. Let's do this, then, huh?"

Lange smiled. "That's what you came for."

Lange ushered Ethan down to the heater and stood watching as he set the toolbox down and then fiddled with the drain valve, pretending to know what he was doing. In Lange's other life, his father had been a man who worked with his hands and could build and fix anything, and he'd been forced to watch and learn or get beaten. He knew water heaters. He knew with just one look that this one was working as it should and that Ethan Paget didn't know that. Lange also knew that Paget had a plan in his toolbox.

With the slightest of smiles, he gave the box a final look.

"I'll leave you to it, then," he said.

"Yeah, yeah. I've got this. Won't take me long."

"No rush. Take your time. You've waited a long time."

"What's that?"

"You said you were contacted over a week ago?"

"Oh, yeah. Yes. A long time. I get it now."

Lange left Ethan with the heater. He hadn't thought it would be so easy, so effortless, and he smiled, genuinely, as he climbed the stairs.

Hate and anger clouded the mind, he thought as he closed the basement door behind him and then stood for a time with his hand pressed against the wood. It causes a person to do irrational things in stupid ways.

"Bob Simms." Lange shook his head, then locked the door, and pulled up a chair to face it, waiting. He spent a great deal of his time waiting for things. Waiting for orders. Waiting for the right time to act. Waiting for people to die. Like now.

He thought about the toolbox, certain that Ethan had chosen to destroy Collier's property either by bomb or fire. Lange didn't care a wit about the loss of Hardwicke House, and he knew neither would Sebastian Collier. With his son gone, the house was nothing but brick and mortar. It was full of things that had no meaning. Collier had other things, many things, all around the world. He was sure he would even soon have another son to carry on the family name. There would be plenty of women eager to carry his heir. That's how it worked for the very rich and the very powerful. Nothing was difficult or impossible to attain.

Lange checked his nails, pristine as always. Then he heard Ethan's boots hit the bottom step as he started up. Quickly, Lange could hear, as though he was in a hurry. Lange had no idea how much time he had. Maybe Ethan would tell him.

He heard the knob rattle as Ethan tried to turn it.

"Hello?"

The knob rattled again, this time more insistently.

"Mr. Lange?"

Unhurried, Lange rose, slid the chair away, not that it mattered where he positioned it. He had a good feeling that the house would be gone in a few minutes.

"Mr. Lange?"

Rattle, rattle. And something new, a kick from the boot. "Hey! The door's locked."

Lange adjusted the cuffs on his blazer. "Mr. Simms?"

"Hey, yeah. There you are. I thought you left. Eh, the door's locked?"

"You're done with the heater, then?"

"Yeah, everything's just fine. You're good to go."

Ethan tried the knob again. Still locked.

"Door seems to be jammed, or something."

"It's locked."

"What? What for?"

Lange approached the door. He didn't smell smoke on his side, and Ethan wasn't coughing on his. Bomb, not fire, then.

"How much time did you put on the timer, Ethan?"

The rattle stopped. "What?" His tone had changed. Bob Simms disappeared; a different man replaced him.

"The timer on the bomb from your toolbox. The one meant to destroy this house."

"Are you insane? I don't have a bomb. I'm a *plumber*."

"Ethan Paget *not* Bob Simms, although it was fun watching you pretend. We all play parts, though, don't we? I'm playing one right now."

"Let me out of here."

Lange looked around the kitchen, wondering how much of it would be gone soon. It would depend on the size of the explosive, of course, and on Ethan's expertise. Both unknown factors.

"I knew your brother, Michael. Mike. Not well. Maybe if he'd been smarter, we would have become friends. Both of us from humble beginnings; both trying to get ahead. He at least had a loving family, a brother. I had nothing like that. Do you want to know what he said the night he died? His last coherent words?"

He listened for Ethan, but there was nothing from the other side of the door. Lange smiled, knowing he had his full attention.

"Of course you do. His last clear words were *Let me sleep*." Lange tapped the door with his knuckles. "We did. How were we to know? It was Sebastian's idea to carry him outside. He didn't want his father's precious carpets ruined by vomit or shit."

"Who *are* you?" Ethan's voice came through the door as hard as rock.

Lange went on as if he hadn't heard the question. "Mike let himself get pushed too far. It's important that a man know his limits. We wanted to become Hardwicke Boys, *Minotaurs*. The Minotaur *Society* is a cut above any fraternity or club here. Mike almost made it.

"But you know what I learned that he didn't? There's no becoming one of them. They'll always make a distinction between them and everyone else. What you have to do is use membership to your advantage, forget about making friends. That's what I did. If it's any consolation, *Ethan*, there really was nothing we could have done to save him." He glowered at the door. "Unlike what you did with Brice and Will Younger? *That* was murder."

Ethan slammed against the door again in a frantic attempt to break it down. "Open it. Who the fuck are you?"

"I recognized you the moment I opened the door, of course. Your family's bakery failed. Your parents lost the house. All because they couldn't let it go. Sebastian always knew you'd come after him. You killed his son instead. And Younger, I assume? Well, you have his attention, Ethan. And you've made my job easier by coming here. It saves me the trouble of coming to you."

Lange thought about time and the ticking clock, slightly amused by Ethan's predicament. He hadn't thought about a bomb, but it made a certain amount of sense now. You couldn't destroy a king's throne with a bullet or a rope.

"Open the door. *Now.*"

"How much time?" Lange asked.

Ethan slammed again and again, like a captured animal fighting to escape from a cage.

"Not long, then."

"You're a liar. There was nobody named Lange at Hardwicke when Mikey died. Who the hell are you?"

"I told you. My name's Lange. I work for Sebastian Collier. The rest doesn't matter." Lange drew in a breath and let it ease out. "At least not to you anymore. I'll leave you to it, then."

"I'll kill you!" Ethan screamed over the rattle and the ramming. "Let me out."

"I never understood, Ethan, why your family couldn't accept that your brother's death was a tragic mistake. Why they *insisted* on ruining innocent lives? The lawsuits, the publicity, the constant pressure. They had to know it would ruin them in the end. Didn't they know that?"

"They killed him!" Ethan screamed. "The bastards killed him. Collier, Younger, Bosch. I'll *never* let it go."

"Hmm. I see that now. Then it's good that you've chosen to rejoin your family, Ethan. We'll breathe easier when you're gone, and then what happened in the past will fade away." The banging stopped. Lange cocked his head. "Ethan? Still there?"

"*We?* But that's not possible. How can—"

Lange smiled, but Ethan couldn't see it. "Magic."

Ethan gave the door one last kick. "You and Collier can go to *hell*."

"Maybe we will. But not today. Today, you go first."

The sound of Ethan's body hitting the door that would not break was the last thing Lange heard as he strolled out of the house. No one would die today except for Ethan. He'd made sure of that. He'd cleared the house out the day before, anticipating a visit from Paget. The boys had moved their things and found temporary accommodations with friends. The family's wishes, Lange had told them, at this difficult time.

He saw no reason any of the boys should die for something done so long ago. This courtesy, this act of humanity, feigned though it was, at least was something in his favor.

A bomb, Lange thought, as he walked toward the field. "I had something simpler planned for him."

He gave Hardwicke one last glance, wishing he could stay to see it go, but knowing it was better to be somewhere else when it did.

Without a single feeling, he walked away.

"Tick, tick . . . boom."

CHAPTER 38

"What the fuck am I lookin' at?" Symansky stared wide eyed at the smoldering remains of Hardwicke House.

The team stood beside him, equally shocked by the sight of the great house with most of its windows blown out and acrid smoke billowing out of the gaps, though the structure itself had mostly held. They watched as firefighters raced in and out, extinguishing the flames and doubling down on their search for victims. Those in blue stood outside, keeping everyone a safe distance away, while all around them reporters, camera crews, and onlookers crowded the street, murmuring and gasping every time heat from the fire exploded expensive things inside.

"That's a real shame," Bigelow said. "All that money up in smoke."

"At least the boys are out," Vera said. "Unless somebody slipped back in?"

Symansky frowned. "Well, if they did, that's the worst mistake they ever made."

"They say they're all accounted for," Harri said as she glanced over at the boys huddled in a bunch near a news van. "Lange told them to pack their things and go yesterday. Collier's orders."

"Yeah, and that's not weird at all," Vera said. "You think he knew something like this was coming?"

"He'd be stupid if he didn't," Symansky said. "Paget already killed his kid. He's not gonna be up for torchin' his place?"

Harri scanned the crowd, the street. She had a feeling someone was watching her. Though she couldn't pick him out in the crowd of onlookers and media people, she knew Eddie Noble was there because her skin was crawling.

"He wouldn't dare," Vera said.

Harri didn't need to say who she'd been looking for, and Vera, apparently, didn't need to hear her say the name.

"He who? What're we on now?" Bigelow said a half second before he got it. "Oh, hell no. Eddie Noble better not be here." He turned 360 degrees, scanning the crowd, itching for a fight. "I'll whip his old convict ass right here in these streets."

Symansky glared at the crowd, too, reading faces, ready to charge in right after Bigelow. "If he's here, he's gettin' locked up. I don't care what we ain't got on him."

"Gomez is on it," Harri said. "They just haven't been able to put hands on him yet. He left his sister's. Nobody's seen him since. He hasn't reported in. There's a warrant out."

"He's gone under," Symansky said. "That didn't take long."

Bigelow clocked every face in the crowd. "I don't see him."

"Neither do I," Harri said. "But I can feel him."

Symansky's eyes held hers. "They'll get him. He's not gettin' away with what he's been doin'. Count on it."

Harri nodded. "I know."

"Cops like that," Bigelow said, "make us all look like criminals. People look at us, and we're the enemy right from jump street. Can't blame half of them. How the hell can they tell the good guys from the bad ones when we're all wearing the same badge?"

For a time, they all stood around in silence, watching firefighters pass them with hoses and axes and apparatus, the smoke from the house going from black to gray, the hiss of steam sounding like a hundred slithering snakes.

"So, we're all thinking Paget?" Vera said.

Bigelow pulled his cap down over his ears. "It'd make sense. He's who this has always been about."

"He's still a ghost, though," Symansky said.

Vera looked over the crowd. "I don't see him watching. You'd think he'd want to see the damage he caused."

"And I don't see Lurch," Symansky said.

Vera squinted. *"Lange?"*

"Whatever. Anybody lay eyes on that creepy coffin nail?"

Harri looked across the way to see Lange strolling toward them. "Speak of the devil."

Bigelow scoffed. "You got *that* right."

"Detectives," Lange said when he reached them. "What happened?" He stared at the wrecked house. "This is devastating."

"Who called *you?*" Symansky asked.

"One of the boys. They had my number. Was it a gas leak?"

"We got nothin' yet. Place is still burnin', as you can see with your own eyes."

Lange studied the house. Harri studied him.

"That's a lot of history lost. I've informed Mr. Collier, of course. He'll be looking for updates."

"Where were you around ten this morning?" Harri asked him.

Lange seemed surprised by the question. *"Me?* You don't think *I'd* burn the place down."

Harri held steady. "Somewhere we could check and verify?"

Lange smiled, but his eyes didn't get the memo. "My job is to put out fires, not start them, Detective Foster."

"Simple question," Vera said. "There should be a simple answer."

Lange straightened his tie. "I was on my way to a meeting downtown. I got a call from Renfro saying this terrible thing had happened, and I rushed right over."

Harri's brows rose. "It took you almost an hour?"

"There was a backup on the Drive. My driver tried a detour, but it was worse."

Symansky scowled. "Driver, huh?"

"Uber or private?" Harri asked.

"Private. I can give you the company Mr. Collier uses. The driver's name is Joseph."

"Where downtown?" Bigelow said.

Lange looked around. "Four detectives to one man. Hardly seems fair."

"I like the numbers from where I'm standin'," Symansky said. "So, where was your meetin'?"

"Collier Corp. has offices on Randolph."

"And your first thought's gas leak," Bigelow said, "not the guy whose brother your boss and his friends dumped and left for dead?"

Symansky nodded. "The guy we've been lookin' for and can't run to ground?"

Harri kept her eyes on Lange, but the man seemed calm and unrattled.

"I don't know anything about that. My job now is to make sure the boys are taken care of and properly housed. They're traumatized."

Harri glanced over at the boys from Hardwicke, who were taking selfies with the house in the background and joking around with the blond reporter from Channel 7.

"I can see that. So, they called, you turned around and came back. Can I see your call log? For the *exact* time."

"Is that really necessary?"

"We'd appreciate your cooperation," she said.

Lange pulled his phone from his pocket, tapped the screen, then turned the device around so they all could see it.

"Ten sixteen a.m.," Harri said. "Thanks." She jotted down the time in her notebook before snapping the cover shut. "They told us you cleared the house out. Told them to pack up."

"Mr. Collier wanted the house empty and locked up. In honor of his son. He hasn't decided what to do with the old place, but for right now, he doesn't want anyone in it. I made sure everyone found a temporary place. They're all fine."

"Was he plannin' on sellin' it?" Symansky asked.

"He didn't say. I didn't ask. I guess it doesn't matter now, does it?" Lange took the house in. "I hope you find this Paget. If you don't, there's no telling what he might do next."

Harri pointed to a car in front of the house, its right side singed and the tires blown. On the passenger side door there was a decal for a plumbing service.

"Simms Plumbing. You know anything about that? Was there work being done in the house?"

"I have no idea. I didn't arrange for a plumber. Maybe someone in one of the other houses?"

"It's parked in front of Hardwicke," Vera said.

Lange shrugged. "No plumber. Sorry."

"Where are you staying, Lange?" Vera asked.

"In a Collier executive apartment." He slipped one of his cards out of his suit pocket and an expensive pen from the pocket of his shirt and wrote something on the back. He handed the card to Vera. "That's the address, and, again, my cell number."

"Have you ever heard the name Emil Bosch?" Harri asked. "He was an old friend of your boss's."

Lange pursed his lips. "I don't think so. Old friend? Why? Is Paget after him too?"

"He's dead," Symansky said.

Lange looked confused. "Then I don't understand . . ."

Harri slid her notepad into her pocket. She didn't think she'd get any more from Lange. "Right. We'll be in touch."

"This Paget is wasting his time, if he thinks these petty little swipes are going to hurt Sebastian Collier."

"You consider the murder of his son a petty little swipe?" Harri asked.

"I meant the fire, of course."

Symansky squinted. "Did ya? Because it was hard to tell just then. You bein' you."

Lange gave them a slight courtly bow, then walked back to the Hardwicke Boys. Harri watched for a moment to see how he interacted with them. Formally, detached, she decided, as he had with them, as she suspected he acted with everyone. The odd thing was how *they* interacted with *him*. With something resembling deference and familiarity. She was missing something.

"Smooth operator, that one," Symansky muttered. "Like he's got ice in his veins."

"I wonder how much he gets paid for kissing billionaire butt," Bigelow said.

Symansky watched Lange across the way. "Private cars and such. That suit he's wearin'? Probably a month's pay."

Harri continued watching Lange as he talked to the boys. "We check with the driver. We hit a brick wall when we dug into Lange," she said. "We need to try again." She looked over at the burned car. "And let's find that plumber."

Kelley was back at the office looking into Bosch's next of kin. Harri sent him a text with the plate number to the burned car.

"Well, no sense standing around," she said when she'd sent the text off. "Let's spread out. Talk to people. See if anyone saw anyone get out of that car."

Nobody moved.

"Everybody but Harri's thinkin' it," Symansky said, "but nobody's sayin' it."

"I'll say it," Vera said. "The plumber's inside the house."

"We don't know that until we know it for sure," Harri replied.

"But sometimes you get a feelin'," Symansky said, "before you know, and I got one. But let's do it your way. Let's spread out, see what we get."

The canvass proved fruitless, and as they had walked the block, it had gotten colder and begun to snow.

Nobody had seen the car pull up, and no one admitted to calling a plumber. Bigelow had looked up Simms Plumbing. The business was legit, but *that* Simms had not taken a job at Hardwicke House.

Harri worried that Symansky's feeling might be right. Still, they waited for the firefighters to finish up and sound the all clear, Harri a little nervous that someone would be found inside.

The news crews had thinned out, most of the onlookers, too, and the boys, but Lange was still there, standing stoically near the street, his eyes transfixed on the house, his hands in the pockets of his cashmere overcoat. Like a sentinel, Harri thought, waiting for his call to action.

The CFD battalion chief found them for an update. Introductions weren't necessary. The report would be short and factual; everybody was busy and tired and knew how it needed to go. The chief's name, Hennessy, was on his helmet.

"Fire's out. Looks like the whole thing started in the basement. Blew out the windows. The door off its hinges."

"Gas?" Harri asked.

Hennessy looked grim. "Bomb."

They stood stunned.

"What'd you just say?" Bigelow said.

Symansky stood with his mouth open like a carp out of water. "Yeah, what was that?"

"Not a sophisticated one," Hennessy said. "Looked like something homemade. But, yeah, my guys found metal remnants and scorched wires attached to the furnace. The device wouldn't win any awards for sophistication, but it got the job done. It's a wonder the place is still standing. If he'd made it any bigger, placed it in a different spot, and the place wasn't made like a Sherman tank, it wouldn't be. We went all through the place, but there was nothing else. We're good. We're taking one last sweep just to make sure we didn't miss anybody. It shouldn't be—"

Three firefighters came out the front door looking smoky and haggard in their heavy coats and equipment. One of them threw Hennessy a thumbs-up.

Hennessey turned to them. "Lucky day. Nobody's dead. We'll be wrapping up in a few."

"What about the *bomb*?" Bigelow said.

Hennessy pedaled backward, his radio out, ready to get to the next thing. "It's blown. Nothing but wasted parts now. Investigators will come out once everything stops smoking. Who put it there? That's all you guys."

Harri's shoulders relaxed as the tension released. No one was dead inside the house. She watched Hennessy trudge away and the firefighters go back to their trucks.

"A bomb?"

"Paget *really* wants to get this guy," Vera said.

"He could have killed those kids," Bigelow said. "And if he'd made it big enough, he could have flattened this whole block."

"He's not thinkin' about anybody else right now," Symansky said. "He's gone scorched earth."

"Which means our clock just started ticking faster," Harri said.

She glanced over at Lange and noticed that his usually unreadable expression had changed. He looked shocked and upset. He'd heard the all clear, seen the thumbs-up. Was it that, she wondered? Had he expected something different?

Lange caught her watching him and turned to leave. She raced after him.

"Lange. *Lange.*"

He stopped. "Detective Foster. I don't have a lot of time. I need to update Mr. Collier."

"No casualties," she said. "You heard."

"Yes. Good news."

"You seemed surprised by the news. Who'd you think they were going to find?"

"Excuse me?"

"The *all clear* shocked you." She stepped closer, her eyes on his. "Who did you expect to be inside?"

Something flickered in his eyes. Harri saw it, but it was there and gone in an instant.

"What's your real name?" she asked. "The one you were given at birth. It isn't Lange."

He said nothing.

"People who hide their identities usually have good reason. Who are you? What do you *really* do for Sebastian Collier? How long have you known him? What's your connection to this house and *those* boys? To Younger? To Ethan Paget?"

Lange tugged at his coat cuffs. "I'm not sure where you're going with all that."

"Truthfully, neither am I, but there's something there. A through line from thirty years ago to Brice . . . and you're in there somewhere, aren't you?"

He turned to leave without answering. Harri watched him go. Vera and the others eased in beside her.

"That guy is frosty as fuck," Bigelow said.

"He ain't right, that's for sure," Symansky said.

"We *have* to find out who he is," Harri said. "That could be the piece we're missing."

"Not like we haven't been trying," Vera said. "All roads lead nowhere. A DNA swab or prints would help."

Symansky snorted. "*That* guy ain't givin' up none of that."

"He's somewhere," Harri said. "Connected to Collier, to this place, maybe even to Paget. We *find* him."

Bigelow frowned. "Working off a fake name?"

Harri turned toward the campus, then slid a look at Hardwicke, then glanced over at the president's house, where Younger had been found. A neat little triangle, she thought.

"We never looked for him here," she said. "Collier went here. Younger. Who says this isn't where Lange met them both?"

"That house is for rich brats with more money than sense," Symansky said. "I don't get that from the ice king. If he was one of them, why's he doin' Collier's grunt work?"

"Paget wasn't a rich brat," Vera said. "He was a scholarship kid."

"Age fits," Bigelow said. "And he looks pretty comfortable walking around here."

"Maybe a class photo would help," Harri said. "We're here. Vera and I can check on that."

"The name Lange ain't gonna get you far with school records," Symansky said. "We all know it's fake."

"He can change his name," Vera said. "He can't change his dead eyes."

The last of the news crews were packing up, the fire department, too, leaving the grounds of Hardwicke muddy and slushy and trampled upon. When the slush froze, the entire area would be a skating rink.

"We find the face," Harri said, confident they were on the right track, "we find the man."

CHAPTER 39

Ethan searched through the boxes of family things, memories burning his heart as he saw again the precious treasures that reminded him of his parents. An old billfold with his father's last driver's license still inside. His mother's holiday apron. He held it up to his face. It still smelled of cinnamon.

He looked around the storage unit stacked with old furniture from his childhood home, the last place he felt safe and whole. For a moment he held the apron and pictured his mother's face. He didn't care what the doctors said; he knew she died of a broken heart. She died because she wanted to be with Mikey.

Ethan gently placed the apron back in the box. He was looking for something specific and needed to find it; his determined hand began digging through the boxes as he maneuvered around the tight space crammed with living room chairs, lamps, and tables. He avoided looking at the flocked Christmas tree propped up against the back wall. His mother went absolutely giddy when they'd hauled it up from the basement every year. She had loved Christmas so much. Why did he keep it? Why did he keep any of it? He couldn't bring himself to look at the tree, but he knew he would never be able to get rid of it.

He spotted the trunk he wanted. Mikey's things. He lifted it up, carried it to a clear spot on the floor, and dusted off the top, for a moment afraid to open it. He didn't want the memories, and yet he couldn't let them go.

The things here were useless to anyone else, but every chair, every rug, every apron, every pair of old shoes were all the family he had left. These things were all that kept him from being nameless.

On a deep breath, Ethan opened the trunk, and his brother, Mikey, flooded out of it. His scent. His essence. He could feel him. *Let me sleep.* His last words if he believed Lange. What his mother would have given to know his last words.

He was a grown man. Forty-three. Yet his eyes stung with a little boy's tears. Mikey had wanted to sleep; he never asked to die. One mistake. One decision. One loss, then two, then three, then . . . nothing but things in storage, a flocked tree, an apron, a billfold. Ghosts.

"He knew Mikey. He *knew* him. I think I know who he is."

Ethan sat cross-legged in front of the trunk and began going through it, setting aside Mikey's old college essays and Belverton T-shirts, his tennis racket, and a beat-up old pair of running shoes. He was looking for photos he knew were there. The ones they'd taken down from Mikey's room at Hardwicke after he died. How his mother suffered that day. It had only been a few months since they'd all moved Mikey in. He had been so excited, so ready to make a success of himself. He'd wanted the world on a string, and Ethan was sure he would have gotten it.

Hardwicke didn't take just anybody; that's what he'd said. *These are the top guys.* The smile on his face was a mile wide. *And I'm almost in, baby.*

His hands grazed the stack of photographs, and he pulled it out to get a better look, pushing the trunk aside.

I'm one of them. That's what Mikey had told him, though Ethan hadn't believed it then, and especially not now. There was always a line you couldn't cross, a level you couldn't reach. That soulless-eyed monster. And why did Ethan have the feeling now that Lange had been expecting him? He knew right off he wasn't the plumber. He thought he knew who he could be, but he didn't believe in magic.

Ethan's hands gripped the photos, a wave of anger rushing in again. He'd planned to take the whole house down with everyone in it. There was no way Lange could have known that, so why did it feel now that he had walked into a trap of his own making? Why did he have a sense that Lange had been expecting him? Not the bomb, *him*.

Lange would have been just fine if Ethan had died in that basement, he decided, recalling the lack of feeling in the man's voice as it came through the door. He'd been playful, even taunting. Ethan had barely made it through that narrow window after smashing out the glass and breaking the latch before the bomb blew. He was lucky to be alive, and had fought to live, not wanting to die in the house of the man who'd killed his brother. Why had he fought so hard? He looked around the unit crammed with pieces of past lives and saw none of the joy, none of the love, only emptiness and heartache. Theft. That's what it was. His family had been stolen. Maybe it would have been easier not to have escaped the basement? He could have just closed his eyes and waited for death. Why didn't he? Why not follow everyone he'd loved to the grave? He wasn't so sure why when he broke through that window and limped away from the house. Now he was.

He fanned the photos out on the floor in front of him, looking for the ones he needed, the ones he'd helped remove from the walls and placed in a box when his mother's hands shook too much to do it. One by one, Ethan set aside photographs of Mikey with pretty girls, Mikey on the tennis court, and Mikey running track, until he came to two that mattered. He picked them up, one in each hand, and examined them. The photos showed Mikey beaming, his hair tousled, standing with a group of young men in front of the house. There was the smug Sebastian Collier, the golden boy. How many times had he stared at his face in court, wishing him dead? He picked out the bespectacled Will Younger, too, before his eyes landed on a thin, intense-looking young man on the right who stood slightly apart from the others, with them but somehow not fully.

The boy's cold eyes and wry half smile gave him the look of a predatory animal biding its time. It was the eyes Ethan recognized. He'd just seen them. They were the eyes that had looked right through him down in that basement.

"There you are, you son of a bitch."

Ethan turned the photo over. He knew Mikey had been meticulous in all things, so he was not surprised to see each of the boys' names written there. The one with the eyes, the one with them but apart, was Emil Bosch.

Ethan slipped the photos into his pocket and locked up the unit, feeling an energy the ghosts of his past helped fuel. He and Bosch had business to finish. His only concern now: How to kill a man who's already supposed to be dead?

CHAPTER 40

He was supposed to be dead, and in a way, he was, Lange mused as he buttoned his suit jacket, brushed a speck of lint off the sleeve, and inspected himself in the mirror. There was freedom in death. The old was buried, the new reborn. It's not that anyone had cared that much, had they? So, why wait? Why not start another life at twenty-two?

He stared at his reflection, critical of the suit, the lint, the error he'd made. Paget had come directly to him. He'd had the perfect chance to end his threat to Collier. Instead, he'd left his fate to a homemade bomb. He had felt it fitting at the time. He assumed Paget would die by his own hand, but he hadn't. Now he was out there somewhere, and he *knew*.

Lange didn't like making mistakes. They were a sign of weakness. Mistakes meant he had been unprepared, flat footed. Though he'd been cryptic in teasing Paget, now he worried he'd given too much away.

He hadn't informed Collier, of course, when he'd called to report the explosion. Ethan set the bomb. The house was heavily damaged. Collier, even with all his billions and levels of security, would never be completely safe with Paget on the loose. He had kept it at that.

With a determined assailant, he knew, it only took one chance encounter, one moment of distraction, one lapse in protocol. He couldn't blame Collier for not wanting to look over his shoulder the rest of his life. Neither did he. And he had no intention of doing it.

He straightened his tie, thinking it through. He would wait for Ethan to reach out to him. That hadn't been the expectation when he'd handed him his card. Truthfully, after eyeing the toolbox, Lange had expected it to burn when Ethan burned and liked the idea of his name following the last Paget to hell. But now Lange was going to have to earn his pay. When they met again, he would have to finish it.

He winked at himself in the mirror. "End of the line, Ethan."

He armed himself, grabbed his keys, and left the apartment. The afternoon was young. Maybe he'd go for lunch in a nice restaurant and wait for Ethan's call. He stopped short, smiled to himself. No. Not a restaurant . . . he had a better idea. They would meet where Bosch ended and Lange began.

CHAPTER 41

Harri hung up her phone and put her head down on the desk, then closed her eyes. She'd had a lead on Leonard Krieg, and it had just died in her hands. No one she had tapped knew where he could be.

Vera walked over from the kitchen, a bottle of water in her hand. "Do not tell me we have another body?"

Harri lifted up. "I thought I could get something from Krieg, but he's nowhere."

"When'd he get out?"

"Eight years after he went in. Noble got nineteen years; Krieg got ten, served eight. Then . . . poof." She picked up her notebook, flipped it open. "There's nothing out there past his release. His wife divorced him while he was inside, just like Noble's. Nothing on her either."

"Bet you Krieg went completely under. New place, new name, new life. Dirty cop's a lot to try and wash off, even in this town. No known associates?"

Harri frowned. "Noble. The ex-wife."

"Ouch. I'd get out of town, too, then," Vera said. "Fresh start. Moving on. Noble's gangbanger friends can't be too happy *he's* out. Old man, old news. And if he's trying to insert himself into whatever they've got going these days, that's not going to sit well."

Harri thought of the warehouse and Noble's meeting with some of his old associates. "Unless he has something they need or want."

"I can't see it," Vera said. "The man's older than Symansky. If they're going to own a cop, they're going to want one who can do something for them. Noble's washed up. What's he offering?"

"He'd be willing to do anything, I think," Harri said. "What else has he got?"

Vera's eyes held hers. "He's counting on you."

Harri stiffened. "Then he's got nothing."

Harri got up and went to the board, her hands on her hips, her mind in a million places. Her eyes glided over the names and photos, lines and arrows. Younger dead. Brice dead. Bauer dead. Hardwicke bombed. And at the center of it, a thirty-year-old accidental death and a surviving brother seemingly bent on dishing out payback.

"He can't get to Collier," she mused as Vera came up behind her. "So, he takes Brice. There's nobody left but him to take revenge on, so what the heck is he doing?"

"Scorched earth?" Vera asked.

Harri's phone pinged. An email from Younger's admin with the class photo they'd requested attached. She pulled it up, expanded it, scanning the faces, excited eyes landing on a somber-looking boy standing in the second row near the end. There was a list of names to identify each class member and their position in the photograph; she didn't need it. She recognized the eyes. "Bosch."

Harri turned to Vera; then, scanning the office, she held her phone up. Just then Kelley shot up from his desk, his arms raised like two goalposts, and yelled, "Bosch!"

Kelley raced over. Symansky and Bigelow walked their chairs to the board. Even Griffin, in answer to Kelley's victory scream, came out of her office.

"You first," Harri told Kelley.

Kelley stepped up to the board. "I finally tracked down a former manager from the Lakegrove Memorial Park, where Bosch is buried.

Gary Stewart. He's almost eighty now, but still sharp as a tack." Kelley picked up the marker, found an empty space on the board. "The plot, the arrangements, everything was paid for by Seaborne Industries. He knows for a fact a check showed up every month for upkeep.

"Stewart also remembers there was no service, no family present at interment. Everything was low, *low* key. They got the casket in, they put it in the ground, and plopped some flowers on top." Kelley wrote down the name Seaborne. "Three guesses who owns Seaborne?"

Bigelow looked around at the team. "If anybody here needs three guesses, I don't want to know you anymore."

"Why the hell would Collier, or his father, more likely, pay for Bosch's funeral?" Symansky asked.

Kelley shook his head. "Not his father. Seaborne is completely Sebastian's. It is today. It was even then. Daddy's starter project, it looks like. Show the boy how to run a company by giving him a company to run."

"If he was already rich and already running a company, why was he at Belverton in the first place?" Bigelow asked.

"Family tradition would be my guess," Kelley said. "Great-grandfather helped start the place, grandfather graduated there, father, too, so I guess Sebastian was expected to follow right behind. And then, of course, Brice."

Griffin moved in closer; the worry lines on her face had grown worry lines of their own in the few short days Sebastian Collier had been CPD's headache, and therefore hers.

"So? Collier paid for Bosch's funeral," Griffin said. "He's still dead. He's not our killer. To be as clear as crystal here, we have bodies and an *explosion*. Explain to me how a boy who's been dead thirty years relates to *any* of that."

Harri stepped forward, her phone in her hand. "Bosch isn't dead. Lange is Bosch."

She passed her phone around.

"Younger's admin just sent us this. That's Bosch near the end. A row in front of Sebastian Collier. Younger's in the back. Same class. Same accident. Same Hardwicke House."

Symansky put on his glasses and leaned in for a better look. "Yep. That's him. Those eyes are as evil as ever. But why all the sneaky crap? Makin' up an accident, buryin' an empty casket, payin' good money all these years for a hole with nothin' in it?"

"We don't know there's nothing in it," Vera said. "Nobody's seen Bosch's father in, what? How long?"

Symansky turned. "You're sayin' he killed his father and buried him in a grave marked for him?"

Vera shrugged. "It's possible."

"Whoa, dial it way back," Griffin said. "Our immediate concern, *today*, is that friggin' bomb that just went off in my city and the trail of bodies somebody on that board is leaving us to follow. I don't like being led around by the nose, and I know none of you do, either, because if you did, none of you would be working here."

"Wow. Little harsh," Kelley muttered under his breath.

"Zip it, Kelley. So, Paget came looking for Bosch, or Bosch went looking for Paget?" Griffin asked.

"I think it's Ethan driving the train," Vera said. "What reason would Lange have for wanting Brice dead?"

Kelley thought about it for a moment. "So, Ethan set the bomb to kill Lange, who's really Bosch."

"Not so fast," Harri said. "It's possible Ethan doesn't even know Lange is Bosch. We didn't until just now."

Vera got closer. "But Lange's paid to know, right? And he's got a stake in making sure Ethan goes away and stays away." She glanced over at the class photo. "Hardwicke House. That means they're both

Minotaurs. Ethan's not. Who do you think's going to come out of this with the short end of the stick?"

"We need to find Ethan before Lange does," Harri said.

Symansky rolled his eyes. "Well, that's the understatement of the year."

Griffin crossed the room to the television the squad had anchored to the wall and flicked it on. "Understatement or no. Get on it because *this* is what we're up against."

Channel 7's 4:00 p.m. newscast popped on; they were leading with the Hardwicke-bomb story, a reporter standing outside a damaged Hardwicke giving her dour update. Demonstrators milled about in the background with handmade posters and banners, cell phones held up recording the action. The signs were varied: Who's Next? . . . Burn, Baby, Burn . . . Endangered Species . . . Billionaires Kill . . . Down with Anarchists.

At the bottom of the screen, the news crawl reported *Belverton protests following arsonist's fire.*

"How'd anarchists get into this?" Vera asked. "And what *exactly* are they protesting?"

Symansky frowned. "Like they need a reason."

Bigelow cut Symansky a look. "A bomb almost on their doorsteps is good enough."

"They don't know it was a bomb. The reports are just sayin' fire, and CFD's not correctin' 'em, and neither are we."

Griffin stood with her hands on her hips. "The mayor knows it's a bomb. The superintendent sure knows. Fire or bomb, it's giving off the same heat."

Bigelow nodded. "With that heat on top of everything else? We're lucky they aren't marching over here to burn *this* place down."

"Well, I had an idea," Kelley said. "About Ethan. The bakery's a bust. You guys checked that. He's abandoned his apartment. I started checking hotels, motels, even SROs. But there'd be people everywhere. Every cop in the city's looking for him. He'd want somewhere out of the way. Someplace he could come and go without anyone clocking him."

"A lot of places like that," Harri said. "Too many."

"I started checking rental spaces—Airbnbs, near Belverton—figuring he wouldn't want to get too far."

"I don't see an Airbnb working for him," Vera said. "That's the opposite of getting off the grid. Even worse than a hotel."

"You need a hole," Symansky said. "One way in, one way out. No eyes."

"His parents died, then the house he grew up in was lost to foreclosure," Kelley said. "I started thinking their stuff had to go somewhere, unless Ethan tossed it, and I can't see him doing that."

Vera clapped her hands together. "Storage!"

Kelley grinned. "There's a storage facility not far from the bakery. Just a couple blocks, actually. The guy in the office was pretty cagey over the phone. I figure a couple of us go over there and have a little talk with him."

Everyone turned to Griffin.

"Kelley stays on Bosch," Griffin said. "Li and Foster take storage."

Symansky held his arms out. "What about me and Bigelow over here?"

"Am I dealing with children? Find something to do that's useful. Pull a string. Hit the streets. I've been called to the superintendent's office to explain to him why a bomb went off on a quiet block with rich people on it." She glared at each of them. "And I've got bubkes. So, get out of here, all of you, except Kelley, and get me something." She pointed at the television. "Before the villagers bring out the pitchforks and storm my castle."

As she grabbed her coat and bag, Harri noticed Griffin fiddling with a red rubber band around her right wrist.

"What's that for?"

Griffin glowered back at her. "A gift from my husband. Some new way of relieving stress and centering yourself."

Griffin popped the rubber band again, and again. Her wrist at this point was nearly the color of the band. Vera watched the assault on Griffin's wrist as she wiggled into her jacket.

"Doesn't look like it's working," she said. "Maybe he should have given you *two* bands."

Griffin let the band go; she glared at Vera. "You have someplace to be, don't you? A priority to attend to?"

Vera gave her a salute. "Yes, boss. On it."

Griffin stormed back to her office and slammed the door.

"Why do I feel sorry for that band?" Vera said. "And her husband."

CHAPTER 42

"I tell ya, I don't see 'em come or go, all right? I man the desk. Right here. All day. Half the night, depending on my hours."

"And you don't have any unit out there rented to an Ethan Paget?" Vera asked for the second time.

"Told you. Nobody by that name, and I was doing you a favor by checking. I'm not supposed to give out *any* information. Company policy."

Harri stared at the grungy-looking stick figure behind the counter at ZDec Storage, dressed in a faded AC/DC T-shirt ripped at the pits. The one with the yellowed teeth and unkempt soul patch and scraggly mustache that didn't match his badly dyed black hair, which hung limp and greasy to kiss his narrow shoulders. The one with the ferret-like eyes and the incongruous name—Neville.

Harri held up Paget's photo again. "And he isn't familiar to you?"

Neville's eyes barely skimmed the photo. "Nope. He looks like a lot of guys. What'd he do, steal something?"

Harri put her phone away, met Neville at the eyeballs. "He sets fires in storage-facility offices. Actually, the fire is secondary. The bomb comes first."

Neville blanched. "Are you serious?"

"He's dangerous," Vera said. "And a little off."

"What'd *we* do to him?"

"Who knows? He strikes in the late afternoon," Harri said. "And he likes to watch."

Neville looked from Harri to Vera, scared. "Watch what?"

Vera's eyes widened. "People burn."

Neville paled; his mouth hung open. "What the *fuck*?"

Vera leaned over the counter. "Yeah, he's burned two guys alive already. We're on to him, but he manages to stay just one step ahead of us. By the time the fire department arrives, and we do, it's too late. But if you haven't seen him, you haven't seen him; maybe he's targeting some other place." She rapped the counter with her knuckles. "Thanks for your time. Stay safe."

Harri slid her card toward Neville. "Here's our number if you *do* see him. I wouldn't engage. Just call and let us handle it."

"I'll be dead by then."

Neville literally pounced on the computer on the counter and began tapping the keyboard, his eyes lasered in on the screen.

"They don't pay me enough to burn." The tapping stopped. "Unit 7F, but he didn't give Paget as the name. He's Ed Harris."

"Like the actor?" Vera asked.

Neville stared blankly at them. "*What* actor?"

"He give an address and phone number?" Harri asked.

Neville swiveled the monitor around for them to see for themselves.

The address wasn't to Paget's apartment or the bakery, probably fake, but Harri jotted the information down anyway on the off chance it wasn't.

"Thanks."

Neville swung the monitor back around to his side, then dug into a top drawer and pulled out a single gold key with 7F stenciled on it. He handed it to Harri.

"Unit 7F. Walk out, turn left, row seven's in the back. He keeps to himself. I think he's even slept in there a couple times."

"What makes you think that?" Vera asked.

"I see him coming out real early and coming in real late. Nobody's got that much business in a storage unit, do they? Unless he's keeping somebody hostage in there."

"You never thought to call the police?" Harri asked, unamused. "Report suspicious activity?"

Neville's hands flew up in a sign of defense. "Hey, I mind my business, okay? What goes on in the units has nothing to do with me."

Harri and Vera stared at him for a moment, neither able to hide the disdain they felt.

"When's the last time you saw Mr. Harris?" Harri asked, the coldness in the tone impossible to miss.

"Couple of hours ago? Didn't stay long. When he left, he was moving, like he had someplace to be. Cameras on the gate caught him plain as day."

Harri asked, "Was he driving?"

Neville shook his head. "Walked out. More like stormed out. Carrying a backpack. Big. Black. Carrying it like he had something valuable in it. He went up the street. I had no idea he was a pyro. What're you going to do? We should shut this whole place down. He could come back anytime." He reached for the phone. "I'm calling my manager."

"Why don't you hold off on that for a sec. Let us take a look at his unit."

"What if he walks in here and sets me on fire?"

"Call 911 *immediately*."

Neville was sweating. "That's *it*? He could fry my ass long before anybody gets here. She just said—"

"Relax," Vera said. "We've got this. You're probably safe."

"Probably?"

Harri gripped the key tight in her hand. "You're welcome to come with us. Be there when we open it."

Neville backed away from the counter like it had teeth and might bite. "Like hell I will. There's no telling what he's got stashed back there."

"You sure?" Vera held a straight face. "Because we have no problem with you joining us."

Neville took another step back. "Go, will you? *Check it.* Then find his ass and lock him up. God, this city is the worst. Cops doing nothing. Us out here like baby lambs with tigers roaming around. I been robbed twice already and it's just *February*? What are you all doing about it, huh?"

"Thanks for your cooperation," Harri said. "We'll bring the key back shortly."

"If I die, I'm suing this whole city, starting with the cops."

They left the office, upsetting the tinkling bell over the door, listening to Neville rail against Chicago and CPD. She and Vera did as Neville directed and turned left at the door, striding through an inch of new snow. Just after 6:00 p.m., it would be full-on dark soon, and the temperature, now in the high thirties, would drop like a stone.

The units were set up in long identical rows organized in numerical and then alpha order. The property was well lit, Harri observed, clean, and the security fence that surrounded them looked decently effective against all but the most determined of thieves.

"He could have been here the whole time we've been looking for him," she said.

"It's sad," Vera said.

"He killed people."

"I know, but he had a whole life—family—and one bad thing wiped it all out. Like somebody knocking over a house of cards. And he ends up here? Bauer, too, in that tiny apartment. They both let hate ruin them. My mother loves her Chinese proverbs. One she recited all the time when we were growing up is *To die is to stop living but to stop living is something entirely different than dying*. Ethan and Anna stopped living years ago."

Harri knew Li's words applied to her as well, and she took them in to process later when she was alone in her own little hole. She glanced at Li out of the corner of her eye. If she'd learned anything about Detective Vera Li, she knew she was purposeful in all things. The proverb applied to Ethan, but she'd also meant it for Harri. Smart Li. Subtle Li.

"That's no justification for murder."

"No, but it takes the why out of it. It's cause and effect. The road not taken."

"Anymore Chinese proverbs?"

Vera chuckled. "Are you kidding? Tons. Chinese civilization is five *thousand* years old."

"So, there'll be more proverbs, is what you're saying?"

"Maybe. I don't like to overuse."

For a time, the only sound between them was the crunch of their footsteps on the quarter inch of snow beneath their feet. Harri was trying to work it through, Ethan and Lange. The cause and effect, as Vera had mentioned. She knew her partner was doing the same.

"He *walked* out," Vera said as they moved past row two. "That'd mean he either has a car stowed somewhere close, or he plans to steal one. I can't see him getting a cab in this neighborhood, and Uber or Lyft aren't an option if he's gone dark."

Harri dug her gloves out of her pocket, put them on. "Makes sense. When we turn the key back in, let's see if we can get a look at Neville's security tape."

They walked on. Row four.

"If Bosch was a Hardwicke Boy and graduated with Collier from Belverton, how'd he end up working for him instead of running a corporation?" Vera said. "I mean, that's the point of the whole thing. Elite college, elite club, the leg up."

"There's obviously something we're not getting," Harri said. "Lange doesn't act like just an employee to me."

They walked farther on, counting off rows until getting to seven.

Vera turned around to look back in the direction of the office.

"A hike from the front."

Harri kept walking to unit F. "The way he planned it."

They stopped at 7F and the locked roll door securing it.

"There're just a couple more rows past this one," Vera noted. "He *really* didn't want anybody in his business."

Harri slid the key in the lock, heard the click, then stopped before lifting the door up.

"What if he booby-trapped this thing?"

"Burning his own things up?"

"Scorched earth. Why not?"

"It would take forever to get bomb squad here," Vera said.

Harri gripped the door handle. "Stand back and away. No sense in both of us getting blown up."

"Not comforting," Vera muttered before giving Harri a nod. "Do it."

Harri slowly lifted the door, her eyes squeezed shut. Thankfully, nothing exploded as must and the stink of packed-away things escaped into the crisp air. Vera flipped the light switch, and a confused jumble of furniture and household items shoved together and boxes stacked upon boxes came into view.

Harri pulled out her mini flashlight and trained the beam along the piles and stacks.

"All his stuff," Vera said, her eyes moving over the plastic bins of clothes and shoes and hats.

"His whole family's, it looks like. There's enough in here to fill a house."

She scanned the ten-by-thirty-foot space, knowing this was all that remained of the Pagets.

She watched as Vera boldly ventured farther in, navigating one of the narrow channels Ethan had created amid all the cluttered left behinds.

Harri spotted a few folding chairs leaning against the side and grabbed a couple, extended them, and set them under the roll door before following Vera in.

"Fear of confined spaces," Vera called back. "Check."

"I'm not afraid of confined spaces. I just don't want to get locked in a metal box with *Neville* in the front office being our only shot at getting out."

Vera smiled. "Cautious. I knew that already, though. This stuff must have been here for *years.*"

Harri chose another channel, peeking into moving boxes, breathing in dust and likely mold.

"There's a cot back here," Vera called from her side. "He's been sleeping here, all right. Solves one mystery. Must have been miserable. It's freezing in here. How does this happen to a person?"

Harri lifted the lid on a box of old books, then looked around at all the things Ethan Paget couldn't bear to let go of. She understood how.

"Got something," Vera said.

Harri hurried over, and the two of them stared at an old open dorm trunk that had been pulled away from the rest of the mess. On the top, resting on the contents of the trunk—clothes, shoes, books—sat photos fanned out for display; the last one in the line had a kitchen knife sticking out of it.

"I'm thinking that knife isn't a good sign," Vera said.

"It's pinning the photo to a Belverton T-shirt. This has to be his brother's stuff." Harri squatted down to get a closer look. "Hardwicke Boys. There's Will Younger. That's Sebastian Collier. Michael Paget."

Her eyes moved down the line of photos until she got to the one with the knife in it. "And—"

Vera blew out a breath, a puff of warm air testifying to how cold it was in the unit. "That knife goes right through Emil Bosch's chest."

Harri looked up at her partner. "Another mystery solved. He knows who Lange is."

"And Lange knows he knows," Vera said.

She ran her light along the walls of the unit, stopping the beam on a map about eleven by fourteen, with little boxes in circular patterns all over it. She stood and moved toward it for a better look. "It's a cemetery map." She moved the beam up to the top. "Lakegrove Memorial Park. Where Bosch is supposed to be."

"There's an X on it. Want to bet what it marks?"

Harri snatched the map off the wall, stuffed it into her pocket. "Ethan knows Bosch is alive. He knows he's Lange. They're on a collision course. And they know we're close."

Vera's eyes landed on a table pushed against the back wall. "Uh-oh. What's that?"

The two stared down at a metal folding table with bits of wire, tools, and metal remnants strewn all over it. Vera picked up a slender wire splicer. "He made two."

Harri was already moving. "Ethan left here with a backpack. I don't think he was carrying books. Back to the office. We have to see that tape."

They raced back, double-timing it through the snow, only to arrive out of breath at the office door to find it locked and the lights inside out. They stared at the **CLOSED** sign on the door.

Vera slammed a frustrated fist against the plate glass. "That little candy-ass."

Harri thought it through for a moment. "All right. We deal with it. It's got to be the cemetery, right? He made the bomb. He checked the map. There had to be some way they connected. Lange's good at his job, and Ethan's determined to kill everybody involved in his brother's death. That means he's gunning for Lange."

"Tonight?"

"Would he want to walk around for days with a bomb strapped to his back?"

"Good point. Then we go check," Vera said. "If we're wrong, we're wrong."

Harri remembered Lange's card and dug it out of her notepad. "I'm calling Lange."

Vera pulled her phone out too. "I'll try calling the number Kelley found for Ethan."

They both dialed, hanging on every ring. Seconds passed. Nothing happened. Vera ended her call.

"Nothing. You?"

Harri shook her head. "No pickup either."

She and Li exchanged a worried look.

"We go check," Vera repeated.

Harri nodded. "We can call Griffin on the way."

CHAPTER 43

Lange switched off his phone and slipped it back into his pocket. He recognized Detective Foster's number from her business card, but now was not the time for conversation or for the police.

He'd gotten the go-ahead from Sebastian to *finish it*. That meant Ethan Paget. That meant tonight. That meant once and for all, or else he and his boss would always have to look over their shoulders, always worry that Paget would be there to wreak havoc. Better to deal with it, him, here and now. With Ethan gone, that left only Lange to hold the knife to Collier's throat, but he doubted Sebastian even thought about that, even considered that Lange would not be loyal and totally committed to *his* needs over his own. But Lange was a Minotaur. Minotaurs ruled the world. Lange hadn't reinvented himself and found his niche only to serve and not benefit.

He'd waited patiently for Ethan to call. His text, as Lange had expected, had been venomous, the message clear. Ethan wanted him and Sebastian dead, like Younger and Brice.

The field outside of Hardwicke House. One hour is how Ethan's text had ended.

After a laugh, Lange's text had been just as succinct. **Dream on.**

Then he remembered he was duty bound to finish it. Ethan was *his* responsibility, and Sebastian expected resolution. A standoff he knew was unwise, irrational, but required—but not on Ethan's terms, *his*.

Lange liked the better odds. I'll be where you thought I was, he'd texted back, resigned to the inevitable conclusion. I'll wait.

Now Lange stood staring down at his own grave, wondering who had placed the fresh bouquet of flowers in the weathered holder next to his headstone. He'd left no one behind to mourn him. He'd made sure. The flowers were . . . odd.

He looked over the grounds in front of him, which were as quiet as, well, a tomb, he thought, the little joke amusing him far more than it should have. There were other flowers on other graves. Were they a service the cemetery provided? A light snow mixed with cold rain landed on the frozen lawn as softly as cat paws on beach sand. The air smelled clean, though he knew it wasn't. Half a graveyard away, beyond the front gate, he could hear the muffled grind of rubber tires against city road salt as cars inched their way east and west along Irving Park Road. Going places, he thought, as opposed to those who rested beneath his feet, having reached their final destination.

Lange cast a jaundiced eye toward the night sky. The universe was vast, and he only a tiny speck of renaissance, but he was free. He could go anywhere, do anything. He was no longer a Bosch and anchored to ignorance and privation. He had taken what he needed. There was no man who was his better, not even Sebastian Collier. This was how it should be and would be, after tonight.

Tonight. He knew after all these years Ethan Paget couldn't let another day go by without making a move now that he knew the truth. But Lange wanted it to be here, and he wanted to be the first to arrive. Only fitting since it was his grave.

Lange closed his eyes for a moment, listening to the snow and the tires; then suddenly he felt the air shift. He was no longer alone. He opened his eyes but didn't bother turning around. He knew.

"Hello, Ethan."

There was no answer.

Lange stared at his headstone. Gray. Simple. A lie. "I'm not one for small talk either."

He turned around expecting to face Ethan, finding instead three robed and hooded figures all in black. His eyes dropped to the hunting knife in one figure's right hand, and then they shifted to the heavy rope in the hand of another.

"We are Vengeance," they said in unison.

Lange laughed. He couldn't help it. It was a big, booming, gut-roiling laugh. "A knife, a rope. No candlestick? Ethan, you insult me." He slid a hand into his pocket, pulled a gun out. "Vengeance brought a knife to a gunfight."

Ethan slid his hood back to reveal his face and the contemptuous sneer on it. "The knife's not for you. It's to cut the rope."

Jesse pulled his hood down, then tossed the rope to the ground in front of him.

"And you intend to tie me up with that?" Lange asked. "Then what? Ply me with alcohol until I die? I'm not a boy, Ethan. I came prepared. A rope and knife won't do it. But three does pose a problem. I had only planned for you."

Freddie lowered his hood, his robe parted. "That's what the Taser's for."

There was little time for Lange to react, or even aim. There was only enough time as he fell, and the gun flew out of his hand, to register that he was in serious trouble. Lange hadn't anticipated *Vengeance*. An error. Hopefully, he thought, not a fatal one?

Lange couldn't speak; his limbs were not under his control. He felt himself being dragged along the frozen ground toward his headstone, with no idea where his gun was. He was at Ethan's mercy, and that enraged him.

"I'll . . . kill . . . you," he hissed. He'd lost control for a moment and fought to get it back. Control was power. He couldn't cede it to Ethan Paget.

Ethan leaned down, his face just inches from Lange's. "Not if I kill you first."

Ethan's fist came like a hammer blow. It was the last thing Lange saw before the world faded to black.

CHAPTER 44

Vera scanned the circular drive outside the main office at Lakegrove Memorial Park as Harri screeched to a stop. "The manager, Tomey, is supposed to be out here waiting for us."

They'd called ahead to put the park on alert that they were coming and that there might be trouble brewing at Bosch's grave.

"I don't see . . . ah, there he is. Just coming out."

They bolted out of the car to greet him. The others were headed their way—Symansky, Kelley, Bigelow. And they'd asked for squad cars along all the exit gates. If they were wrong about Lange and Ethan facing off here tonight, Griffin was going to rake them both over the coals.

They presented their badges, though the flashing blue light on the car spoke volumes.

On the phone earlier, Tomey reported that he hadn't seen any suspicious activity in or out all day and looked genuinely out of his depth now, obviously not used to this much life and movement at his graveyard.

"*Still* nothing?" Vera asked.

"There never is," he said. "Look where we are?"

Harri presented the map. "We have this. Where are we going? Which direction?"

Tomey squinted at the page. "Serenity Vale." He pointed up a small hill west of the office. "Down that way, slight left after a bit. It'll be tricky in the dark. You'll have to leave the car on the path. The grave you're looking for is going to be a ways in and toward the back. If you come to an oak tree, you've gone too far south. I can show you. It'd be quicker."

"No," Harri said. "We'll find it."

The last thing they needed was to add a jittery civilian to the long list of things they had to worry about.

She folded the map and slipped it back in her pocket. "Stay here. Direct the officers who'll be coming after us. There should be nobody else in here, right?"

"At night?" He shook his head. "And we closed to visiting at six. Open at ten a.m. No one ever comes after dark."

Vera shot Harri a knowing look but said nothing.

"How many entrances?"

Tomey took a second to count them up in his head. "The main gate and then an access gate. It's south. The maintenance trucks, the lawn service, they use that one."

"All right. Good."

"We've never had a problem before," Tomey said.

"All right. Stay here. Show the others the way," Vera instructed.

Harri and Vera got back in the car and drove off.

"No one all day," Vera said.

"That *he* saw. It's not too hard to slip into a cemetery. Look at these gates."

Vera checked the tautness on her bulletproof vest, thinking three steps ahead. "There won't be much cover as we walk up."

Harri scanned the cemetery fences, seeing a few squads already taking up positions beyond the wrought iron. "No lights or sirens. Good. I'm counting on the element of surprise."

Harri crept the car along, peering through the snow-splattered windshield—the worn cop wipers working at intervals—searching for the cutoff to Serenity Vale where X marked the spot.

CHAPTER 45

Lange wouldn't give Vengeance the satisfaction of fear, not a single sign of desperation. He sat calmly tied to his own headstone, the rope around his chest, his hands bound behind his back with zip ties pulled from one of the robed men's pockets. He'd never been tased before. It hadn't been a pleasant experience. He found it interesting to be sitting on his grave when he should have been lying in it six feet under. About dying he had no feeling. Maybe that was something he needed to worry about, he thought. He stared at Ethan Paget. When he got free, he would kill him and his friends.

"It's taken all this time, you bastard," Ethan said, fury in his voice, a fury that trembled and hissed and appeared to claw up from some devilish inferno. "I hated you were dead. It meant I couldn't *kill* you. But here you are. I get my chance." He smiled. "You'll be the man who dies *twice*, ending up in the same place."

Lange stared at his gun in Ethan's hand. The rope was tightly secured around him. There was no chance of escape. He would have to convince one of the three to let him go, but as he stared into their stern faces, he could tell his chances of that were slim.

"Who are the other two monks?" he asked. "Friends? Can't be family. You haven't got any left."

Neither man spoke.

"Then I'd guess hired hands," Lange said. "Bought cheap, since you have nothing."

Another fist came flying, this time from one of the cronies.

"So, this is how you killed Brice, is it? The robes. The rope."

"You thought you could hide from me," Ethan said.

"I never gave you a moment's thought, actually. I did it for me. Like shedding off an old skin and taking on a new one. It's called renaissance."

"You killed him, and you locked me in that basement to die."

Lange angled his head, confused by the anger, the blame. "Didn't you bring the bomb, Ethan? What did *you* intend to do with it? Kill boys? We gave you Younger, hoping he satisfied you. But it was clear we weren't dealing with a rational person. You're the one who should be tied to this stone, not me."

Ethan stepped forward. "Shut your mouth."

"Or what? You'll kill me? You've overstepped. Once you get here, there's only one place else you can go, isn't there? You've chosen to spend the rest of your life in a cage you built for yourself. Why?"

Ethan took another step forward, the knife turning in his hand. "Justice."

Lange laughed. He watched as the three took it badly, but he didn't hold back. What did he have to lose, he thought. He was tied to a grave, and it was three against one. "I thought you were Vengeance? Can't make up your mind? The two are not the same." Lange's eyes fixed on Ethan's. "You can kill me and Collier. Hell, you can kill the whole world, and you gain nothing. And the robes? Just embarrassing. Halloween dress-up. You think like a child and act like a child."

Ethan lunged forward, put the knife to Lange's throat. "I could end you right now."

Lange didn't flinch. "You won't. Too close. You'd rather ditch and run."

"Beg, like Younger did."

Lange smiled. "Will Younger. I didn't know him all that well, but what I knew of him, I didn't respect. He was soft, undefined. He never questioned anything that night. He just went along. I'm not surprised he begged. I won't, though."

Ethan looked over at the bouquet of flowers.

"Ah. That's it, then? I wondered where the flowers came from. Another one of your little gifts hidden inside? Too scared to slit my throat face to face?"

Ethan stood. "I want you to think about dying before you do."

"I think about dying every day, Paget. Don't we all? So what? What do you get when I'm gone? Tell me. You obviously didn't get whatever you were after with Brice or Younger, or else we wouldn't be here. What do you hope killing *me* will give you? I hope you don't say closure because there really isn't such a thing."

"I want you dead. Collier's next."

Lange shook his head. "You'll never get Sebastian. I don't think you'll ever get out of this cemetery." He turned to the other two. "Them either. It's over, except for this final part. You chose wrong, Ethan. You could have had a life, and you chose *this* instead. I go boom. I explode into a million pieces. And you know what you get, Ethan? *Zip.* You'll be just as empty then as you are now. I'm curious. Why bombs? A bit unusual. Takes a special kind of freak, if you don't mind my saying."

"A bullet to the head's too quick," Ethan said. "I want you both in pieces. Destroyed. Obliterated."

Lange nodded. "I suppose that makes sense . . . to you."

Ethan drew a small kitchen timer out of his pocket and set it on the ground in front of Lange. He checked his watch. Then set the timer for fifteen minutes.

"That's how long you have," he said. "I don't have to see it. I'll just watch for the fireball. Knowing you're gone, *really* gone this time, will be enough."

"It'll never be enough," Lange said, his head resting on the cold stone.

Lange didn't feel anything about dying. Death was just a thing that was. You breathed one day, he thought, and then one day you didn't. It stung a little that Ethan Paget got to decide when, but even that wasn't enough to upset him. He gave Ethan a pitying smile.

"Die." Ethan spit out the word with force, like it was a command or an order from on high. "This time for good."

"As I said. Like a child."

Ethan lurched forward and plunged the knife into Lange's right thigh, twisted it deep, then pulled it out, watching his face contort in pain.

Lange held the scream, though his leg sent waves of white-hot agony through his entire body. He glared at Ethan. Ethan glared back. Their faces just inches from one another.

"Beg me."

Lange glared at him, then smiled. "Doesn't matter," Ethan said. "You dead is still good."

Ethan slid a look at the quietly ticking timer and backed away. He took one last look at Lange, and at the trap he'd set, then he turned and walked away, taking his accomplices with him. "See you in hell, Emil."

Lange stared at the blood oozing out of his pant leg. Not an insignificant wound. He glowered at the backs of the three men as they retreated down the rise. They called themselves Vengeance, he thought. Vengeance was nothing. It was powerless. Vengeance was an empty calorie. A popped bubble. A spent dream. It wasn't a thing you could hold. It wasn't a thing that could sustain you. It was just hurt activated, a primal scream with iron fists. He knew this firsthand. And he knew this would be his last true thought.

Lange looked out over the graveyard. The headstones in front of him. Rows and rows of the dead. People once. Bones now.

"Everyone ends in a place like this." He checked the timer. "Me, in just nine minutes."

CHAPTER 46

Coats off, vests on, and their radios silenced, Harri and Vera slowly made their way up a small rise toward Bosch's plot. They'd only taken a few steps when Harri stopped suddenly, hearing someone coming toward them.

"Someone's coming this way," she whispered.

"More than one," Vera said.

They drew their weapons, held them to their sides, then braced and waited. The footsteps grew louder on the frozen grass. Definitely more than one person. The light wasn't good. The grounds were murky, full of tricky shadows, the only illumination coming from the moon overhead and a few lights along the path.

Three figures appeared in front of them a few yards away. Men in dark robes, their hoods down, moving quickly toward the service gate. Harri recognized them—Ethan Paget and the Nowak brothers.

"Police!" she yelled as her gun came up. "Hands up! Down on the ground!"

All three froze, startled by their presence. For a moment, no one moved, and then the Nowaks took off running.

Ethan didn't look bothered by the abandonment. Harri noticed he didn't look bothered at all. He appeared happy, content.

Vera repeated the orders. "Hands up. *Down.*"

Slowly, Ethan raised his hands, clasping his fingers behind his head, and got down. "You got me."

"Spread eagle. Belly first," Harri ordered.

She was singularly focused on Ethan. She knew Vera was too. Things could quickly turn during arrests. Every move they made was purposeful until Ethan was down and cuffed. Vera watched for the Nowaks in case they doubled back while Harri stood Ethan up and searched him. Not ideal, she thought; a male officer should have done it, but there was just her and Vera here, and if Ethan had anything on him that could kill them, they needed to know about it. She started at the shins.

"I can save you the trouble," Ethan said. "I have a knife."

Harri stopped patting him down, stood up. "Where?"

"Right pocket."

Harri glowered at him. "Anything else that's going to poke or stick me . . . or blow up in my face?"

Ethan grinned. "Blow up. That's funny. No, I have nothing against *you*."

Harri pulled a hunting knife out of Ethan's pocket. There was blood on it. She held it up by the guard with her thumb and index finger.

"What'd you do?" she asked.

"I gave him something to think about before he dies."

There was the sound of a commotion a distance away, the disturbance of running feet and bodies hitting the ground, the clink of handcuffs, the gruff voices of cops. All of it carried like the wind in a quiet cemetery.

"Looks like your friends didn't get far," Vera said with a smirk. "It's hard to haul ass dressed like a Capuchin monk. You and the Nowaks are done."

"They knew the risks. We all did."

"Only it didn't work out so well for your aunt Hannah," Vera said.

"Now I'm the last," he said. "The keeper of the flame." He looked over the rise, then grinned. "Speaking of flames."

Harri gently put the knife down and moved Ethan away from it. "Where's Lange?"

"Bosch," he corrected, "and you're too late. He'll be dead soon. I guess I *will* get to see it."

"You left him at the grave," Vera said.

Ethan shrugged. "Where he belonged the whole time. It's what he deserves."

"Another bomb?" Harri asked, a queasy feeling in her stomach. "Another fire. How long do we have?"

"*We?* There's no we. *Him!*"

Vera's voice rose. "How *long?*"

Ethan smiled, easy, like he had all the time in the world. "How long would you say we've been standing here?"

"Five minutes, a little less."

He grinned. "Not long, then."

Vera grew more insistent. "*How* long?"

"Long enough for him to be afraid and hurt and know he's going. Like Mikey did." His smile widened. "Tick. Tick. Tick."

Harri got on the radio. "Yeah, we need the bomb squad. And Fire. He's set a device on the grave. Lange's there, and he's injured. We'll need paramedics too. I don't think we have a lot of time before it blows if he's telling the truth."

"I am," Ethan said.

The cemetery burst with activity, cops everywhere, flashlight beams bouncing off the gravestones, heavy cop feet crunching across the grass. They'd keep a good distance back until the bomb techs got there, but they were present and ready for what happened next.

They rushed Ethan back to the path and handed him off to a PO, who placed him in the back of a car, the first in a long line of squads that had slid in behind theirs. They finally had Ethan, but it didn't appear that he was in any way bothered by it. He had gotten what he wanted, mostly, Harri thought; the last bit was Bosch, and after thirty years, Ethan seemed confident it would all be over in a few short minutes.

"Just so we're clear. You killed Brice Collier and Will Younger," Harri said. "You, the two that just ran . . . and Bauer."

"Judge, jury, and executioners," Ethan beamed. *"Justice."*

Vera called Symansky.

"We're at the friggin' gate headin' in," he said. "You said bomb, didn't ya? What the double fuck are you two still doin' up there, then?"

"Lange's still alive," Vera said.

"The grave's just a few yards up," Harri added. "We'll take a look. See if we can get him."

"Negatory. Bomb guys are rollin' already. Leave it to them."

"How far out?" Harri asked.

"They're tellin' us fifteen to twenty."

She shook her head. "Yeah, I don't think we have that much time."

There was some kerfuffle on Symansky's end, and then Griffin's voice popped on, mottled by static, but unmistakably lethal.

"You two clear out," she ordered. "Do *not* approach."

"He's alive," Harri said. "If there's a chance—"

"It's too dangerous. Stand. *Down.*"

"Griffin, with all due respect—"

"Foster, do *not* 'with all due respect' me, goddamn it. Get your asses out of there."

Vera grimaced. Harri looked out over the graveyard. The Bosch plot was just up a slight rise. It was them or no one. If they left, Lange would die. If they stayed, they might die with him.

"I don't hear you two walking." Griffin's voice blasted out of the radio. "Get back to the gate."

A moment of silence passed between them.

"That's it," Griffin said. "I'm heading up there, and if I find either one of you anywhere *near* that grave, I will take off my boots and beat you with them."

Vera clicked the radio off. The click was offense number one. They stood together in the dark yards from the bomb and Lange, a quick decision to make.

"Go or stay?" Harri asked. "This affects both of us."

"I don't particularly care for Lange," Vera said. "Just wanted to say that."

"Duly noted."

They each took a deep breath. Neither moved.

"It's either the bomb or Griffin," Harri said.

Vera groaned, aggrieved, already moving up the rise. "I'll take my chances with the bomb. How fast can you run?"

Harri kept up, her eyes scanning the grounds. There were cop lights flashing outside the fence and toward the front gate and pockets of uniformed cops and those in soft clothes standing like pickets in a fence a safe distance away.

"From a bomb? Flo-Jo fast."

They moved in silence for a bit, quickly, their eyes on the area where they expected to find Bosch's plot.

"What kind of boots does Griffin have?" Vera asked. "Fashion or down and dirty Chicago-ugly?"

"Never paid attention."

"If we don't die, we're going to be in so much trouble."

"Hate to tell you this, Vera, but we passed *so much trouble* when you clicked that radio off."

CHAPTER 47

They saw the grave. Lange was sitting on it, his head slumped, his back to the stone, tied there by rope.

"Oboy," Vera muttered.

They approached slowly, keeping back, taking in the scene, though there wasn't much left to the imagination. A grave. A man. A rope. A bouquet of fresh flowers.

"Where's the bomb?" Vera whispered.

Harri's eyes swept over the plot, over Lange, then slid to the bouquet. "It has to be in the flowers." She took another careful step. "Lange?"

She trained her flashlight beam at him, and his head slowly lifted. He was pale, his lips off color. Harri moved the light over his body, looking for where the blood on the knife had come from. She stopped at Lange's right thigh, which was covered in blood, a puddle of deep red soaking the snow underneath him. At his feet sat a small timer, the kind used in a home kitchen. Bright yellow. Ticking. Despite the cold, the light snow, she began to sweat. They were too close. None of them would survive the bomb.

"If you were thinking about getting any closer," he said, "I wouldn't. He put a bomb in the flowers. I should have expected it." His voice was weak, his tone resigned. Blood loss, Harri figured. "Not much time left.

Ethan Paget killed Brice and Younger . . . and me." He leaned his head back against the stone. "The irony of this situation is not lost on me."

Harri moved gingerly around to sneak a look at the timer. Five minutes left. She held her hand up to Vera, flashing five fingers. Vera mouthed the word *fuck*. Before they could even think of running, they had to first free Lange from the rope.

Harri moved around to the back of the stone to see how the rope was tied. While she did that, Vera studied Lange and the timer and then trained her light on the bouquet to see if she could get a peek at the device.

"You're losing valuable time," Lange said. "There are three of them. All in robes. Like fools."

"We know," Vera said. "We caught Paget and his buddies."

Lange squirmed against the rope, grimaced in pain. "He's a coward and a killer."

Harri ignored him. There wasn't time. She turned instead to Vera. "Options?"

"Two," Vera said. "Run or die."

"We have five minutes," Harri said.

"Less. You've been here at least sixty seconds," Lange said, "and that's if he got it right. He might not have. He's not a stable person."

"Is that rope tied to anything besides him and the stone?" Vera asked.

Harri shook her head. She could see the oak tree Tomey had mentioned maybe ten yards in front of them. A weathered stone bench sat beside it, overlooking a grave with an ornate angel on top.

"No cover," Harri said, "except that tree and bench. Ten yards? We get the rope off, drag him away, run like hell." She flicked a nervous look at the timer. "Four minutes."

"*If* he got it right," Vera said, repeating Lange's words.

Echo

Harri tested the rope. It was good and secure, no give. "We can't shoot it off."

Vera bent down, lifted her right pant leg to reveal a sheath with a small tactical knife in it. "Get ready. On three. Cut. Drag left, lift, run. Got it?"

Lange shook his head. "It won't work. I can't run on this leg."

"Would you rather run on it," Vera said, "or have cops pick it up off the snow down the hill?"

"Too much talk," Harri said. "Two minutes. *Now* is when we have to do this."

They counted off, braced themselves, and then after a nod, Vera unfolded the knife, slashed the rope, and grabbed Lange by the left arm and pulled while Harri did the same on the right, dragging him off the plot.

"Move!" Harri yelled as they yanked him up and took off running, Lange hobbling on one leg between them.

"Faster!" Vera prodded.

Lange was heavy. It was a struggle to keep him upright and moving. It was more of a dead man's carry than light support, and every second that ticked away, Harri prepared herself for the big boom that would knock them off their feet and scatter them to the four winds.

Her eyes focused on the bench, lasered in on it. The bench was everything. But the ten yards felt more like a hundred miles. Every step felt like three steps back.

She wasn't particularly fond of Lange, either, she thought. He hadn't made their jobs any easier. He could have helped them solve it all a lot sooner, but she knew fondness didn't factor into the job she and Vera, or any cop, had to do.

"Almost there," Vera said.

"Almost doesn't count," Harri hissed back through clenched teeth.

Harri bore down, Lange's heavy arm thrown over her neck. "Go. Go. Go."

On spent legs, huffing like freight trains, they dove behind the bench and flattened out, low to the ground, hands over their heads, bracing for the blast. Harri could feel her heart practically beating out of her chest. If pressed, she would swear she could hear Vera's and Lange's doing the same.

"Homemade bomb," she said, her breaths ragged. "Limited range?"

"His first one blew a hole in Hardwicke's basement, so I wouldn't count on *limited*," Vera said.

Harri lifted her head up a little and noticed there were winged cherubs carved out of stone perched on each armrest of the bench. They were not a comforting sight. They were potential projectiles.

Vera turned her head to look at her, as though she'd read her mind. "Bench is solid enough, but we might want to move away from the baby angels."

"Lange? Okay?" Harri asked, squinting over at him.

"I will *never* be buried in this cemetery again," he said.

"When did he find out who you were?" Vera asked.

Lange didn't answer.

Harri looked over at him. "It was when he came to Hardwicke with that bomb. You expected us to find his body in that basement, didn't you?"

Lange closed his eyes. "I'm in no condition to answer."

Harri peeked around the bench at Bosch's plot, at the bouquet. Nothing. She turned back to Vera.

"You still carry a duty knife?"

Vera smiled. "For tight spots. Like ropes around headstones in a cemetery with a bomb in a flower bouquet."

Harri let a beat pass. "Good to know."

Lange groaned. "The timer's off."

Li lifted up on her elbows. "You're right. That's the longest two min—"

The boom and fireball that followed lit up the graveyard, throwing dirt and ice and bits of Bosch's headstone up in a violent plume of debris that forced Li's head back to the ground. Rubble and pieces of cherub rained down on their backs, but the bench held.

Harri didn't move for a time, the sound of the blast still reverberating in her ears, the thunder of the bomb loud enough to wake the dead.

The profound quiet that followed was eerie. Harri popped up, Li, too, hesitating a second before getting to their feet. They had to run. There was nothing that said Paget hadn't made three bombs. They confirmed the plan with a quick nod, then they each grabbed Lange by the shoulder of his coat and took off running south toward the back access gate, dragging Lange along with them.

Lights lit up around the cemetery fence, sirens wailed. The cavalry. Still running, Harri slid her radio out.

"We're headed toward the south gate," she announced to the dispatcher. "We need paramedics. One victim. Stab wound to the leg. Substantial blood loss."

The dispatcher's voice relayed the details, dispatching units, calling Fire for an ambulance, moving units in. All coordinated. High alert. All business. A sense of relief swept over her as she ran and pulled, her eyes on the prize—the back gate. Her legs felt like rubber, and her arm strained from exertion. Lange wasn't talking, which worried her. Were they dragging a dead man to safety?

Vera looked back; the plot was quiet again, though Bosch's headstone was gone, scattered over the nearby graves.

"I can't believe we're alive," she said.

Harri focused on the gate ahead of them, almost there. She used the flashing blue lights on the cop cars as guiding beacons. She was able to pick out Symansky, Bigelow, and Kelley standing on the other side of the gate. Then she saw Griffin glowering beside them.

"Vera."

"I see her. Too late to turn around and hit the other gate?"

"Yep."

"Well, it's been nice knowing you, Harri."

"Same here."

CHAPTER 48

Ethan's fists beat down on the interview table. "You *saved* him? Why? *Why would you do that?* He killed my brother. My parents are dead, hounded into early graves. Now, Hannah. I have *nothing.*"

Vera and Harri stood watching Ethan's meltdown. A PO stood off to the side, ready to escort the killer to a holding cell.

It was nearly ten o'clock, and they'd been at it with Ethan for more than an hour. He was obsessed not with the lives he'd taken but with the one he'd tried to take, and couldn't. Emil Bosch. Paget was a killer, but Harri could see how he had gotten there. Wasn't Eddie Noble her Emil Bosch? What would it take for her to become Paget? What more would she have to lose? What more would Noble have to threaten to take? He was a killer two times over, she had to remind herself again, but that didn't stop her from seeing that he was broken too.

"You, Hannah, the Nowaks, you planned to kill Brice," Harri said, "but you needed access to Hardwicke."

Ethan glowered up at her. "That was easy. You know those privileged assholes weren't going to clean up after themselves. They get people like us to do it for them. Hannah got in no problem as their housekeeper. They jumped at it, actually."

"And she brought in the Nowaks, the guys from your family's bakery?" Vera asked.

Ethan shook his head. "They lost what we lost. The Colliers *had* to pay. Hannah believed that, till she didn't. She just didn't have the stomach for it. I do." He glared at Harri. "I could have had Bosch. I almost had him. He underestimated me. He thought I was *nothing*." He looked hopeful for a moment and smiled. "He could still die. I poked him pretty good."

"Not good enough," Harri said. "Lange—Bosch—is in surgery, but they say he'll be okay."

Ethan yelled out in anguish. "He killed *me*, and *he* gets to live?"

The PO perked up, ready to subdue Paget if he had to, but the scream apparently was all Paget had left in the tank.

"Hannah regretted what she'd done," Vera said, thinking of Bauer's suicide note. "She tried to get you to stop."

"I'll never stop," Ethan said. *"Never."*

Ethan Paget in custody was the end to their case, Harri knew, but it wasn't a victory. Ethan's was another life lost. He had let the worst human things twist him into a killer, and there was no coming back from that.

Harri knew Griffin was watching through the two-way glass from the next room. She could feel her boss's glare scorching the back of her neck. Griffin hadn't said a single word to her or Vera since the cemetery, but she knew that wouldn't last. Maybe they'd have a job in the morning, maybe they wouldn't. Maybe she would be okay with that. Meanwhile, the suspense was like waiting for another of Paget's bombs to blow.

They'd read him his rights. He'd declined a lawyer. Ethan had confessed to Younger and Brice and the bomb at Hardwicke and the one in the cemetery. Anna Bauer—*Hannah*—had been an even sadder result of it all. Just as lost as Ethan, she'd also made the wrong choice. It was only later that she discovered she couldn't live with it. Maybe that was a lesson for Harri, too, she thought. Maybe there could be no justification for killing the thing that broke you.

The adrenaline rush that had gotten her and Vera through the dead man's pull at the graveyard had dissipated and left her wrung out and exhausted. All she wanted to do now was sleep for a thousand years. But first, Ethan and his companions. There were reports to write, statements to give, processing, and still Noble, the gun to her head.

He killed me. The words echoed in Harri's brain. She shifted uncomfortably as she stood over Ethan Paget. She saw parts of herself in the man. Justice. Retribution. Living with parts of you gone. It was all too close. Her job was here in this room, but she didn't want to be here.

Vera reached over and picked up Ethan's signed confession from the table. It was done; so was he.

"You didn't have to do this," Vera said gently. "There was help out there. You could have had a life."

Ethan stared at her through narrowed, spiteful eyes. "What do you know about it?" He fixed Harri with the same angry eyes. "Or you?"

"I think we're done here," Harri said. "Again, you're under arrest for the murders of Will Younger and Brice Collier and for the attempted murder of Emil Bosch. Again, you have the right to an attorney. Any questions?"

It didn't appear that Ethan heard her. He was somewhere else.

Vera angled her head. "Ethan? Do you hear?"

He nodded. "What does it matter?"

Harri signaled to the PO, and he stood Paget up and walked him out.

Vera shook her head. "There's a lot he could have done to help himself before he got to the bombs." She looked over at Harri. "You okay?"

"Sure."

Harri's phone buzzed in her pocket just as the door opened and an angry Griffin walked in.

"We need to talk," Griffin said.

Harri stared down at a text from an unknown number, an image attached. Her heart stopped. It was a selfie of Eddie Noble standing outside her mother's house. The message accompanying the photo was short and sweet. **Game on.**

Vera took one look at Harri's stricken expression. "What is it? What's happened?"

"It's Noble." Harri held the photo up so Vera and Griffin could see it. "He's at my mother's house." She looked at Griffin. "I can't talk now. Family emergency. I have to go."

Harri could barely breathe. Her mind was blank. Nothing made sense. Noble was going after her family. He wasn't going to stop.

She rushed out of the room, Griffin and Vera behind her.

"I'm coming with you," Vera said.

Harri was already running to grab her coat and bag.

"What's the address?" Griffin asked. "I'll send a car. It'll get there faster than you will."

Harri gave it to her, and Griffin peeled off to make the call.

Fear and near panic gripped Harri. She dialed her mother's number, anxious. Had Noble made it inside the house? What had he done? Moments ago, she had been tired and ready to sleep; now there was no chance of sleep tonight, and maybe not for a long time.

Her mother answered. "Hello?"

"Ma, you okay?"

She could tell she'd woken her mother from a sound sleep. She hadn't thought about the time but checked it now. It was just after eleven.

"I'm fine," her mother said. "What's wrong? What's happened?"

She explained about the text, the photo.

"We're sending a car," Harri said. "And I'm on my way. Protect yourself."

Harri was referring to her father's gun, which she knew her mother kept in a lockbox in her nightstand drawer. He had taught all of them how to load, aim, and shoot in self-defense. She realized now why.

"He'd be crazy to try anything," her mother said. "You're the police."

"He used to be the police, too, Ma. And he *is* crazy. I'm on my way. Felix still there?"

"I sent him home. I don't need babysitting, Harriet."

Harri bit back the expletive. "I'll call him and have him come back. On my way." She ended the call.

"What's up?" Symansky asked.

The others gathered around, concerned.

"Noble," Vera said. "He's at Harri's mother's place."

"He's *what*?" Bigelow said.

They all reached for their coats and hats.

"Let's go," Symansky said. "Address?"

Harri had opened her mouth to tell them all not to come, but it was her mother. Noble had put a gun to Harri's head, and she was the police. She didn't even want to think about how far he would go with her family. She would take all the help she could get. Harri gave them the address.

Griffin hurried out of her office with her coat on. "Car's rolling. Let's hit it. I'll ride with Li and Foster."

"You're going, too, boss?" Kelley asked.

Griffin brushed past him. "Is my coat on, Matt? Nobody fucks with family. Move."

Vera grabbed her coat. "Toss me your keys. I'll drive."

CHAPTER 49

It was well after office hours, Harri knew, but as Vera sped to her mother's, she emailed the photo Noble had sent her to Rita Gomez. More evidence. Stronger case. When she'd finished typing, she sat coiled in the passenger seat, oddly calm, focused on what she needed to do.

She could hear Griffin breathing from the back. The boss hadn't said much since getting in; neither had she. The ride along said something, though, Harri decided.

"We've got cars moving," Griffin said. "He's got to be the dumbest idiot alive."

All Harri could think about, worry about, was getting to her mother's.

"Vera?"

Her partner sped up. "Hear ya."

When they pulled up in front of the house, there were two squad cars, lights flashing, idling at the curb, and every light in her mother's house was on. Harri spotted Felix's Audi parked across the street. Pulling in right behind them were Symansky, Bigelow, and Kelley.

Harri bounded out of the car and ran for the house, taking the front steps two at a time to lay on the doorbell, resorting to knocking when the bell didn't get a quick enough response.

Finally, Felix opened the door, took one look at her face, and said, "She's okay. Nothing's happened."

He held the storm door open, and she brushed past him, rushing into the living room to find her mother sitting on the couch in her pajamas and robe, looking a little put-out by all the commotion. Her mother stood when she saw her and drew her robe around her.

"Harriet, do you really think one photo deserves all this activity? Police cars in front of my house, lights flashing. I have neighbors."

She noticed then that Harriet had been followed in by Vera, Griffin, Symansky, Bigelow, and Kelley, chatter on their radios, faces worried, completely locked in—all there to make sure she was safe.

"What's Noble think he's playing at?" her mother asked.

Felix fumed. "And why's he still walking around?"

Harriet showed her mother the photo Noble had sent her. "This is too close. We have people checking around outside. I'll check too. He's messed up. He's going back to jail."

"You have to catch him first," Felix snapped. "You haven't, have you?"

"I'll take care of it, Felix."

Her mother sat down on the couch. "Can I get anyone something to drink?"

The cops standing around declined.

Felix didn't look convinced. "What's our plan. I mean, this can't be it. Ma lives here alone. Who's to say what he's planning to do."

Harri felt small here, powerless, not like a cop but like a kid in the house she grew up in, around the things and people that had formed her. Felix was right. This couldn't be it. She'd let Noble go too long. Why had she? Even after the gun to her head??

Glancing around the front room, including the mantel lined with family photos that spanned her and Felix's childhoods and had captured their accomplishments, she felt as though she were a stranger here. Another life, another person. There were more photos on the end tables, some of Reg, some of her father and mother together—ghosts of ghosts amid candy dishes filled with tiny peppermints, which had been her father's favorite.

Harri felt exposed and uncomfortable, yet there was nothing she could do.

"I'll fix it," Harri told her brother.

"I want him *arrested*."

"I *said* I'll fix it."

"You're doing great so far," he shot back.

"Felix. Harriet." Their mother rarely raised her voice, and she didn't now.

Their names called out in just that way was enough to stop them. Harri needed air. She turned for the front door.

"I'm going to check outside."

"Like he's going to be hiding in the bushes?" Felix needled.

She knew he was scared; she was, too, so she let the swipe go. Everyone but Griffin followed her out. The boss would stand with her family, offer support, protection, and Harri's thankfulness melted her frosty demeanor almost instantly.

Symansky, Bigelow, and Kelley took the front of the house; she and Vera made their way around back, their flashlights out, looking for anything Noble might have left behind.

They rattled every first floor window in the bungalow, making sure each was locked up tight. They did the same for the side and back doors, the likeliest entry points.

Harriet and Felix had put a top-of-the-line alarm system in the house when their father died, which offered some peace of mind, and there was the added benefit of her mother being on good, close terms with her neighbors. A watchful eye was helpful.

"Doesn't look like he touched the house," Vera said as they stood in the middle of the backyard under floodlights with motion sensors Felix had insisted on.

"He wasn't here for that," Harri said. "He just wanted me to know he could."

Vera flicked off her flashlight. "Well, he's long gone now, and he's punched his ticket."

Harri nodded. Noble was gone, but she could feel him slithering around in the shadows, ever present, ever dangerous.

"You okay?" Vera asked.

Harri could hear cop feet walking the alley, see the beams of their lights bouncing off garages and trash cans as they went. They weren't going to find anything.

She flicked her light out, dropped it into her coat pocket, then opened her mouth to tell Vera that she was fine. It was the answer she always gave to insulate herself, push people away, hide. But tonight, she couldn't even pretend to be fine, thanks to Noble. He'd threatened her mother. She was in a different place now. Suddenly, fine had become too heavy a thing to carry.

She stood for a time in a state of silent dread in an emotional space that felt dangerous and uncharted.

Harri shook her head, exhaled. Finally, after years, after losses, after this, exhausted, she was laid bare. "No. I'm not."

Vera paused for a moment, then nodded, seemingly pleased. "*Finally.* That's progress." She motioned for the others to make their way back to the house. "Now let's go ruin Noble's frickin' life."

CHAPTER 50

Harri sat fully dressed on the guest bed in her old bedroom, staring at the clock on the dresser. Two a.m. She'd also watched the clock turn from midnight to one, and then one to two. Her mother was sleeping. Her brother, Felix, was in his old room down the hall. When the house cleared out of cops and the squads out front pulled away, both of them had refused to leave their mother in the house alone until Noble had been picked up. Her mother hadn't been happy with their decision but was ultimately forced to accept it.

Harri rose to pace the floor, scanning the small room that her mother had turned into a spare room when she left for college. Gone were the pink walls and the white princess bed, the posters of Prince.

There'd been no word that Noble had been spotted and taken in. He hadn't been at his sister's when officers were sent to look for him. He wasn't at Boyle's.

She couldn't settle. It was fear. Could she survive another loss? A look at the clock. Only two minutes had passed. Why, she wondered, did it feel like the clock was mocking her? Why wouldn't the night end? She needed it to end.

Noble. She paced the floor. She almost had it, the words he'd said to her as he held her back the day he shot G. Almost. It niggled at the back of her brain, pulsing like a heartbeat, getting closer. It was something short. Something he'd whispered close to her ear. But she'd been too frantic to retain it. She was desperate to get to the car. *Look*, something. It had gone in one ear, and out the other. Her memory of the day spotty, she couldn't recall what she'd worn or what kind of day it had been, or even what case she and G had been working on. What she remembered clearly was the car, blood spattered on the driver's side window, G's body slumped inside. And she remembered screaming. *Look, he'd* said. She stopped suddenly, afraid to move a single muscle for fear of dislodging the thought. It was there, finally. *Look behind you.* That's what he'd said. She could feel herself knot up, draw in. "Look behind you."

He was telling her then what he'd done, what he intended to do. Noble had nineteen years to scheme and plan, the entire rest of his life to execute, to dangle the sword over her head and the heads of her family. Pacing wasn't working. The room was too small, too confining.

Her lungs felt tight. She could no longer breathe here, so she eased out and tiptoed down the stairs, and after grabbing her coat off the back of the couch, she fled. Action was better than inaction, she decided, as she disengaged the alarm, gently opened the door, and set the alarm again so she could run from her mother's house. Where she was going, she had no plan, just out, away. Out into the dark to breathe, to think, to *do* something. She'd take a drive, and then come back. She'd clear her head, come up with a plan of her own. Eddie Noble had forfeited his right to breathe free, she decided. In the car, she sent a simple text to Felix. **Back soon. Alarm's on.** She knew he would protect their mother at all costs. There was nothing new on her phone from Noble, no new taunts. He was a coward. Cowards shot you in the back or crept up behind you, hidden by shadows. Cowards were more dangerous. She started the car and drove off, giving the house a final glance in the rearview mirror as she turned the corner.

Not fine, she thought as she drove away, her eyes focused on the ice-slick street. Vera had declared it progress, but was it? Her thoughts felt too chaotic, too alien, for that.

Fast Eddie Noble. Her father. Paget and his desire for vengeance. All of it swirled around in her brain, a drumbeat, a ticking clock playing in the background. Like Ethan's timer, like his lethal bomb ticking down to zero.

"Breathe," she told herself.

She hadn't planned it, but she found herself parked in front of the warehouse on Ewing. The lights were off inside, steel gates pulled across the door and secured by a padlock. The only cars parked on the street were hers and a couple of dark SUVs covered in a fresh dusting of snow a half block away, one on the north side of the street, the other on the south. No sign of Charlene Moran's Outback. A part of her felt relieved because she couldn't say for sure, even to herself, what she would have done if Noble had been inside. Hopefully, she would have decided to call it in and step aside, but she didn't know now. Noble had hit her where she lived, where she was the most vulnerable, down beneath, where instinct trumped reason.

It took her a moment to give it up, to accept that Noble wasn't here. She drove away but couldn't go back to the small room at her mother's. She found herself instead at Sly's front door. It wasn't fair, she knew it, but her reaching out felt like a break in the ice, a return from a faraway place. So why couldn't she bring herself to ring the bell? Turning to leave, having talked herself out of it, she heard the door open behind her, and there he stood. Words would have been nice, but she didn't have them. Only a moment went by before he held the door open for her. Without words, she stepped inside.

CHAPTER 51

A dog barked down the street, ushering in the devil's hour, 3:00 a.m. Fast Eddie Noble was up to his old tricks. Brendan Moore was bad news, a spinner of crooked deals, a user; the Floreses, son, Mateo, and the father, Reynaldo, were opportunists who dabbled in everything from flesh to fentanyl. There was no telling what was in the warehouse, but the fact that Noble was there, and Moore, guaranteed that it was illegal and lucrative and bad for the city.

After a time, the door opened, and Moore and Noble stepped out into the night air, looking pleased with themselves. Negotiations, whatever they were, must have gone well. The driver watched as Moore slapped Noble on the back and then got in his car and drove off. Noble stood in front of the building long enough to light a cigarette, blow out the first stream of poison, before walking across the street to the Subaru Outback he'd driven up in a half hour earlier.

The driver got out quietly, barely moving the air. Hidden by the dark, keeping close to the parked cars, eyes on the prize. This was a meeting a long time coming. A reckoning. Noble, who must have sensed he wasn't alone, reeled around, his right hand flying off the car's door handle toward his jacket pocket. Their eyes met. Recognition dawned for Noble, the driver could tell.

"Uh-uh. Hands up."

Noble raised his hands slowly but began to laugh.

"No way. You have *got* to be kidding me? *This* is your play?"

There was no need for a conversation. They both knew what this was about. Noble dropped the cigarette, and it landed at his feet. The driver's eyes never left Noble's. He tried lowering his arms.

"Keep them up," the driver commanded.

Noble raised them again.

"Didn't think you had it in you. Squeaky clean. By the book. Too straight to bend."

Noble seemed calm, unbothered by the gun pointed at him, but that was a lie. The truth was in his eyes. He was a cornered rat, and it showed. The driver held the gun in a two-handed grip and aimed it straight for Noble. It would end here for him. Tonight. There would be no more deals, no more games, no more anything for the ruined cop who'd wrecked his life and the lives of so many others and hadn't had the decency to care.

Noble smirked. "Took you long enough. So, what happens now? You shoot me? Then what? . . . or we could talk this out. Come to some arrangement." He cocked his head toward the warehouse. "There's enough to go around for everybody. Give me a number. It's yours."

He meant money, as though any amount would pay for what he'd done. The driver approached, out of striking range but close enough to finish the job. Noble stood confident in his power, cocky, despite having no cards to play.

"You shoot me, that whole warehouse empties, and you're dead. You know the Floreses? You know what they're about. I'm their *guy*." Noble scanned the street. No one on it but the two of them. "You alone? You don't stand a chance. But I'm willing to forget this. Let's say it's water under the bridge, and let it go at that, huh? What's living in the past going to do for either of us?"

Noble's hands started to drop again. The driver flicked the gun up. Noble's arms rose again. Even in the dark, Noble's evil eyes appeared piercing. He was dangerous even like this, even with his hands raised, even with the distance between them. Any sudden movement, even a twitch, could prove fatal. There was no trusting Eddie Noble. His word was no good.

Noble nodded, a sneering smirk on his face. "You're not going to do anything, are you? You can't. It isn't in you. That's your weakness. The reason you—"

The round hit Noble right between the eyes. The driver watched as the hole it made filled with blood that slowly trickled down the center of Noble's face. His stunned eyes that moments ago held fire and swagger, dulled, then became fixed in death. Like a marionette whose strings had been cut, Noble dropped lifeless to the dirty snow. No more words. No more lies. No more Noble.

He landed on his back with his eyes open, his arms flung out like he'd been crucified, which in a sense he had been. The driver leaned over the hood of Noble's car, the gun aimed at the warehouse door, prepared for whoever came running out to see about the shot, but seconds went by, then minutes, and no one did. Wrong kind of neighborhood, wrong time of night for much concern over the sound of gunfire.

The driver lifted off the hood, gave Noble one last look, then slipped the gun into a pocket. Out of the other came a dime—Noble's fare for safe passage across the River Styx. For a moment, the driver worked it between steady fingers, then threw it onto Noble's body, where it landed on the dead man's chest. One last look, then a turn, and the driver walked away. It was done. Fast Eddie Noble was already where he should have been sent a long time ago—hell.

CHAPTER 52

There were enough cops crowding Rudy's bar at 7:00 p.m. to seriously deplete the number of bodies on the street to cover the crime. All stripes, all persuasions, all units represented, the space inadequate for the volume, but there were no complaints lodged.

Symansky stood at the front door, directing those who entered to a big tub of money sitting on the bar.

"Drop whatcha got in the bucket," he said. "Empty those wallets."

A cop dropped a twenty in, and Symansky went sinister. "What am I lookin' at? A *twenty*? Are you serious?" He turned to the crowd. "Hey, anybody know this cheap bastard?"

"That's Gant. From sixteen," a voice called back. "C'mon, man. You're embarrassing us."

Symansky glared at Gant, who was now holding up the line. "Gant. From sixteen." He waited for Gant's wallet to open again and its contents to get emptied into the bucket before he let him through. He then turned to those still standing at the door to get in.

"All right, general announcement. Do not *think* you're goin' to walk in here with chump change. We got a sick kid we're tryin' to save, so I want that friggin' bucket filled up!"

Bigelow, Kelley, and Vera watched the public fleecing take place at the door, beers in their hands, mouths agape, a little proud of Symansky, but a little frightened too.

"Oh my God," Vera said, "Al's lost it."

"Good cause," Kelley said. "Some cheapskates need motivation."

Bigelow sipped his beer. "That's what you call it?"

"Harri's coming, right?" Kelley asked. "Or is she out there dancing on Noble's grave?"

The news of Eddie Noble's killing had gotten around, but there were no sad faces among the team, and they knew the department wasn't about to hang funeral bunting or lower any flags to half staff.

Vera shot him a warning look. "She's not like that, and we all know it."

Bigelow scoffed. "Hell, *I'm* like that. He was a sick fuck, and somebody out there did us a solid."

"Well, if he'd come after *my* mother—" Kelley said.

Vera cut him off, her eyes hard. "Don't even *think* it."

Kelley sipped his beer. "Well, *whoever* did it saved us from having to take out the trash."

They were quiet for a bit.

"Anybody else feel a certain way about showing up for a fundraiser for a guy who'd vote to keep us from moving into his neighborhood?" Bigelow slid a look to Kelley. "Except for Matt, of course."

"It's for the kid," Kelley said.

Vera shook her head. "I still remember that 'girl cop' crack, but Matt's right. It's for Katie. In the interest of solidarity."

Bigelow took another sip of beer. "Whatever. Symansky owes me gas money. And Harri ain't showing up. Lonergan rode her pretty hard when she transferred in. He's lucky she didn't knock his teeth out. It's one thing to have to work with the old dinosaur. Doesn't mean we have to socialize."

"We're not socializing," Vera said, eyeing the door with Symansky at the bucket. "We're helping a kid. And Harri'll be here. She just had something to do first."

Eddie Noble was dead. That's the news she had brought to Mike. She'd sat with the news all day, and her feelings were complicated, but now she could talk about it. It was satisfying finally knowing what happened to G. It felt good knowing Noble was no longer breathing, and she didn't feel at all bad about it. Mike waited for Harri to come before he told the kids. There were bound to be a million questions, questions he couldn't answer. Harri answered every last one, holding nothing back. When she was done, staring down at stunned, shattered faces, she waited for the kids, mostly, to come to terms with what she'd said. "*He* shot her?" Todd asked. "She didn't? Like they said?"

He was ten. G had missed his double-digit birthday.

Harri shook her head emphatically. "She did *not*. She was killed." She drew in a breath, then let it out very slowly. "Your mother died doing her job protecting this city and all of you. She's a hero."

Jamie, fourteen, sat sullenly next to his brother, quiet, insulated, but Harri knew he was just as hurt as the rest of them. "And he's dead now, so he doesn't have to pay for what he did."

Harri looked over at Mike; she didn't want to say the wrong thing, a damaging thing, but he was gone someplace else, a faraway look in his eyes.

"Not here," Harri said. "He'll pay somewhere else. I believe that."

"She was brave," Todd said, his eyes filling. "I *know* she was."

Jamie looked up at her. "Did *you* kill him?"

Mike came alive. "Jamie, for God's sake!"

"Well, *did* you?" he repeated defiantly, his eyes narrowed. "Because you should have."

Mike stood up. "Okay. We've all got a lot to process, guys. Why don't we each take some time. We can talk about this later after we've all had a good think, and a good cry." He hugged Harri. "Thanks, Harri, for seeing this through. You did Glynnie proud." He looked into her eyes. "And you gave us peace. Now you find yourself some. Promise?"

Peace, she thought, as she eased into her car and sat there for a moment looking out at the gray and cold. February *was* an ugly month in Chicago, but it was what it was.

Because you should have.

She dug Noble's quarter out of her pocket. He'd left it behind to hurt her, and it had. But he was gone now, and she didn't want or need it in her pocket. She wasn't glad Noble was dead. What kind of person would feel gleeful about that? But she didn't mourn his loss either. It *was* good he was dead. Why should he live when G couldn't? No more taunts. No more threats. Her family was safe. That was the end of it.

Harri slid the driver's window down and threw the quarter out. Maybe she didn't have to look behind her anymore. Maybe it was all right for her to live.

She started the car. She was expected at Rudy's for Lonergan's Katie. "Progress."

ACKNOWLEDGMENTS

Every writer has a village. We didn't get to books on shelves without countless mentors, teachers, family, friends, advisers, and even a few detractors who spurred us on. I would like to thank my wonderful agent, Evan Marshall, for his professionalism and advocacy on my behalf. Thanks also to the fantastic folks at Thomas & Mercer, especially my editor, Liz Goyette Pearsons, a rock star, who champions my work at every turn, and editor Clarence Haynes, that eagle-eyed word wrangler, who takes my messy manuscript and literally hacks a book out of it. Every writer should have a Clarence. Thanks also to my proofreader pros at T&M, Miranda G. and Alicia L. Awesome! Thank you to my publicity pros at Kaye Publicity in Chicago, who know more about getting my work out there than I could ever learn. Each and every one of them is a treasure. My undying appreciation to Dana Kaye, Julia Borcherts, Eleanor Imbody, Jordan Brown, Hailey Dezort, and Nicole Leimbach. And thank you to my police heroes, who I bug for technical information far more frequently than they have time for, yet they never turn me away. Thank you, Chief Keith Calloway, Chicago Police Department (retired); Officer Marco Johnson, Chicago Police Department (retired); Officer Leah Thomas (Gray), Chicago Police Department (retired); and Detective Gregory Auguste, Chicago Police Department. Greg's still on the job, fighting the good fight. Thank you for your service, all. And, of course, thanks to my writing community, my fellow scribblers who are on the same journey and battling the same words, for offering occasional commiseration, expert advice, undying support, and priceless fraternity, right back atcha! A special shout-out to my fams—Crime Writers of Color, Mystery Writers of America, Rogue Women Writers, and Sisters in Crime. Worth their weight in gold.

ABOUT THE AUTHOR

Tracy Clark is the author of the acclaimed Cass Raines Chicago Mystery series featuring Cassandra Raines, a hard-driving African American PI who works the mean streets of the Windy City, dodging cops, cons, and killers. Clark received Anthony Award and Lefty Award nominations for series debut *Broken Places*, which was short-listed for the American Library Association's RUSA Reading List and named a CrimeReads Best New PI Book of 2018, a Midwest Connections Pick, and a *Library Journal* Best Book of the Year. *Broken Places* has since been optioned by Sony Pictures Television.

A Chicago native, Clark roots for all Chicago sports teams equally. Tracy is a member of Crime Writers of Color, Mystery Writers of America, and Sisters in Crime, and she sits on the boards of Bouchercon National and the Midwest Mystery Conference. You can find the author on Facebook (https://facebook.com/tclarkbooks), X (@tracypc6161), Instagram (@tpclark2000), and her website (https://tracyclarkbooks.com).